"Gilean, the Book! Gray Voyager! Sage of Truth, Gate of Souls! By this fire, open my eyes and allow me to read from the book of all-truth!" The cleric's voice was strong, resonating through the empty hall. "Open the *Tobril*! Find for Speaker Sithel the fates of his two sons, born this day!"

Vedvedsica laid the dry leaves on the coals. They caught fire immediately, flames curling around them with a loud crackle. Smoke snaked up from the brazier, thick, gray smoke that condensed as it rose. Sithel gripped the arms of his throne and watched the smoke coil and writhe. Vedvedsica held up his hands as if to embrace it.

Gradually the smoke formed into the wavering shape of an open scroll. The back of the scroll faced Sithel. The front was for Vedvedsica only. The cleric's lips moved as he read from the book that contained all the knowledge of the gods.

In less than half a minute the leaves were totally consumed. The fire flared three feet above the golden brazier, instantly dispelling the smoke. In the flash of flame, the priest cried out in pain and reeled away. Sithel leaped up from his throne as Vedvedsica collapsed in a heap.

After descending the steps from the throne platform, Sithel knelt beside the cleric and carefully turned him over. "What did you see?" he asked urgently. "Tell me—I command you!"

Vedvedsica took his hands from his face. His eyebrows were singed, his face blackened. "Five words . . . I saw only five words, Highness," he said falteringly.

"What were they?" Sithel nearly shook the fellow in his haste to know.

"The *Tobril* said, 'They both shall wear crowns . . .' "

FROM THE CREATORS OF THE **DRAGONLANCE**® SAGA

The Art of the DRAGONLANCE Saga
Edited by Mary Kirchoff

The Atlas of the DRAGONLANCE Saga
By Karen Wynn Fonstad

DRAGONLANCE Tales:
Volume 1—The Magic of Krynn
Volume 2—Kender, Gully Dwarves, and Gnomes
Volume 3—Love and War

Edited by
Margaret Weis and Tracy Hickman

DRAGONLANCE Heroes
The Legend of Huma
Stormblade
Weasel's Luck

DRAGONLANCE Preludes
Darkness and Light
Kendermore
Brothers Majere

DRAGONLANCE Heroes II
Kaz, the Minotaur
The Gates of Thorbardin
Galen Beknighted

DRAGONLANCE Preludes II
Riverwind, the Plainsman
Flint, the King
Tanis, the Shadow Years

Elven Nations Trilogy
Volume One

DragonLance® Saga

Firstborn

Paul B. Thompson
& Tonya R. Carter

Cover Art
Brom

Interior Illustrations
Robin Raab

TSR, Inc.

DRAGONLANCE® Saga
Elven Nations

Volume One

Firstborn

Copyright ©1991 TSR, Inc.
All Rights Reserved.

Distributed to the book trade in the United States by Random House, Inc., and in Canada by Random House of Canada, Ltd.

Distributed to the toy and hobby trade by regional distributors.

First Printing: February 1991
Printed in the United States of America.
Library of Congress Catalog Card Number: 90-71491

9 8 7 6 5 4 3 2 1

ISBN: 1-56076-051-6

TSR, Inc.
P.O. Box 756
Lake Geneva, WI
53147 U.S.A.

TSR Ltd.
120 Church End, Cherry Hinton
Cambridge CB1 3LB
United Kingdom

For Marty and Renee

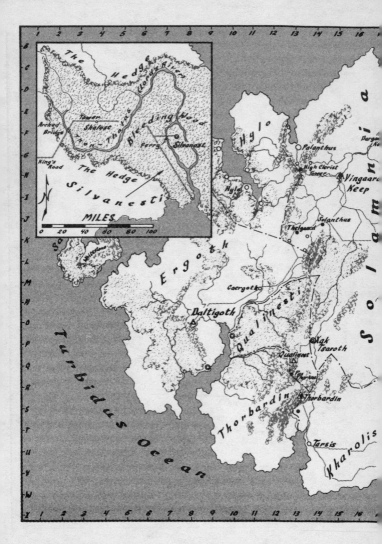

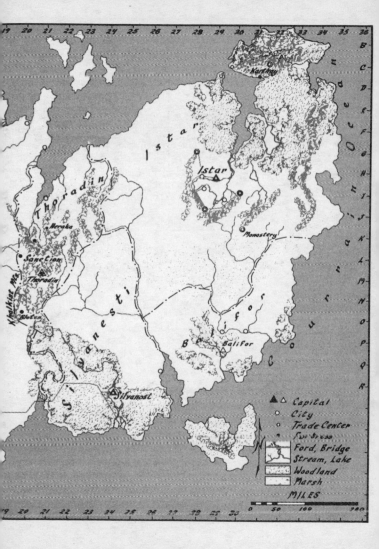

✒ PRELUDE ✒

YEAR OF THE DOLPHIN (2308 PC)

THE GREAT RIVER Thon-Thalas flowed southward through the forests of Silvanesti. Three-quarters of the way down its length, the broad waterway branched and twin streams flowed around an island called Fallan. On this island was the capital city of the elven nation, Silvanost.

Silvanost was a city of towers. Gleaming white, they soared skyward, some dwarfing even the massive oak trees on the mainland. Unlike the mainland, Fallan Island had few trees. Most had been removed to make way for the city. The island's naturally occurring marble and quartz formations had then been spell-shaped by the Silvanesti, transforming them into houses and towers. Approaching the island from the west on the King's Road, a traveler could see the marble city gleaming with pearly light through the trees. At night, the city absorbed the starlight and moonlight and radiated it softly back to the heavens.

On this particular night, scudding clouds covered the sky and a chill rain fell. A brisk breeze swirled over the island. The streets of Silvanost, however, were full. In spite of the damp cold, every elf in the city stood outside, shouting, clapping, and singing joyfully. Many carried candles, hooded against the rain, and the dancing lights added to the strange yet festive air.

A wonderful thing had happened that evening in the capital. Sithel, Speaker of the Stars, ruler of all Silvanesti, had become a father. Indeed the great fortune of Speaker Sithel was that he had *two* sons. He was the father of twins, an event rare among elves. The Silvanesti began to call Sithel "Twice Blest." And they celebrated in the cool, damp night.

The Speaker of the Stars was not receiving well-wishers, however. He was not even in the Palace of Quinari, where his wife, Nirakina, still lay in her birthing bed with her new sons. Sithel had left his attendants and walked alone across the plaza between the palace and the Tower of the Stars, the ceremonial seat of the speaker's power. Though common folk were not allowed in the plaza by night, the speaker could hear the echoes of their celebrations. He strode through the dark outlines of the garden surrounding the tower. Wending his way along the paths, he entered the structure through a door reserved for the royal family.

Circling to the front of the great emerald throne, Sithel could see the vast audience hall. It was not completely dark. Six hundred feet above him was a shaft in the roof of the tower, open to the sky. Moonlight, broken by clouds, filtered down the shaft. The walls of the tower were pierced by spiraling rows of window slits and encrusted with precious jewels of every description. These split the moonlight into iridescent beams, and the beams bathed the walls and floor in a thousand myriad colors. Yet Sithel had no mind for this beauty now. Seating himself on the throne he had occupied for two centuries, he rested his hands on the emerald arms, allowing the coolness of the stone to penetrate and soothe his heavy heart.

A figure appeared in the monumental main doorway. "Enter," said the speaker. He hardly spoke above a whisper, but the perfect acoustics of the hall carried the single word clearly to the visitor.

The figure approached. He halted at the bottom of the steps leading up to the throne platform and set a small brazier on the marble floor. Finally the visitor bowed low and said, "You summoned me, great Speaker." His voice was light, with the lilt of the north country in it.

"Vedvedsica, servant of Gilean," Sithel said. "Rise."

Vedvedsica stood. Unlike the clerics of Silvanost, who wore white robes and a sash in the color of their patron deity, Vedvedsica wore a belted tabard of solid gray. His god had no temple in the city, because the gods of Neutrality were not officially tolerated by the priests who served the gods of Good.

Vedvedsica said, "May I congratulate Your Highness on the birth of his sons?"

Sithel nodded curtly. "It is because of them that I have called you here," he replied. "Does your god allow you to see the future?"

"My master Gilean holds in his hands the *Tobril*, the *Book of Truth*. Sometimes he grants me glimpses of this book." From the priest's expression it appeared this was not a practice he enjoyed.

"I will give you one hundred gold pieces," said the speaker. "Ask your god, and tell me the fate of my sons."

Vedvedsica bowed again. He dipped a hand into the voluminous pockets of his tabard, and brought out two dried leaves, still shiny green, but stiff and brittle. Removing the conical cover from the brazier, he exposed hot coals and held the leaves by their stems over the dully glowing fire.

"Gilean, the Book! Gray Voyager! Sage of Truth, Gate of Souls! By this fire, open my eyes and allow me to read from the book of all-truth!" The cleric's voice was stronger now, resonating through the empty hall. "Open the *Tobril*! Find for Speaker Sithel the fates of his two sons, born this day!"

Vedvedsica laid the dry leaves on the coals. They caught fire immediately, flames curling around them with a loud crackle. Smoke snaked up from the brazier, thick, gray smoke that condensed as it rose. Sithel gripped the arms of his throne and watched the smoke coil and writhe. Vedvedsica held up his hands as if to embrace it.

Gradually the smoke formed into the wavering shape of an open scroll. The back of the scroll faced Sithel. The front was for Vedvedsica only. The cleric's lips moved as he read from the book that contained all the knowledge of the gods.

In less than half a minute the leaves were totally consumed. The fire flared three feet above the golden brazier, instantly dispelling the smoke. In the flash of flame, the priest cried out in pain and reeled away. Sithel leaped up from his throne as Vedvedsica collapsed in a heap.

After descending the steps from the throne platform, Sithel knelt beside the cleric and carefully turned him over. "What did you see?" he asked urgently. "Tell me—I command you!"

Vedvedsica took his hands from his face. His eyebrows were singed, his face blackened. "Five words . . . I saw only five words, Highness," he said falteringly.

"What were they?" Sithel nearly shook the fellow in his haste to know.

"The *Tobril* said, 'They both shall wear crowns . . .' "

Sithel frowned, his pale, arching brows knotting together. "What does it mean? Two crowns?" he demanded angrily. "How can they both wear crowns?"

"It means what it means, Twice-Blest."

The speaker looked at the brazier, its coals still glowing. A few seconds' glimpse into the great book had nearly cost Vedvedsica his sight. What would the knowledge of Gilean's prophecy cost Sithel himself? What would it cost Silvanesti?

✤ 1 ✤

Spring, Year of the Hawk
(2216 PC)

Clouds scattered before the wind, bright white in the bril-
liant sunshine. In the gaps of blue that showed between the
clouds, a dark, winged form darted and wheeled. Far larger
than a bird, the creature climbed with powerful strokes of its
broad wings. It reached a height above the lowest clouds and
hovered there, wings beating fast and hard.

The beast was a griffon, a creature part lion, part eagle. Its
magnificent eagle's head and neck gave way to the torso and
hindquarters of a lion. A plumed lion's tail whipped in the
wind. Behind the beast's fiercely beaked head and unblinking
golden eyes, the leather straps of a halter led back to a saddle,
strapped to the griffon's shoulders. In the saddle sat a helmeted
figure clad in green and gold armor. An elven face with brown

eyes and snow-colored hair peered out from under the bronze helmet.

Spread out below them, elf and griffon, was the whole country of Silvanesti. Where wind had driven the clouds away, the griffon rider could see the green carpet of forests and fields. To his right, the wandering silver ribbon of the Thon-Thalas, the Lord's River, flowed around the verdant Fallan Island. On this island was Silvanost, city of a thousand white towers.

"Are you ready, Arcuballis?" whispered the rider to his mount. He wound the leather reins tightly around his strong, slender hand. "Now!" he cried, drawing the reins sharply down.

The griffon put its head down and folded its wings. Down they plummeted, like a thunderbolt dropped from a clear sky. The young elf bent close to the griffon's neck, burying his fingers in the dense, copper-hued feathers. The massive muscles under his fingers were taut, waiting. Arcuballis was well trained and loyal to its master; it would not open its wings again until told to do so. If its master so desired, the griffon would plunge straight into the fertile soil of Silvanesti.

They were below the clouds, and the land leaped into clear view. The rich green canopy of trees was more obvious now. The griffon rider could see the pines and the mighty oaks reaching up, connecting soil to sky. It was a view of the land few were ever granted.

He had dropped many thousands of feet, and only a few hundred remained. The wind tore at his eyes, bringing tears. He blinked them away. Arcuballis flexed its folded wings nervously, and a low growl sounded in its throat. They were very low. The rider could see individual branches in the trees, see birds fleeing from the griffon's rapidly growing shadow.

"Now!" The rider hauled back sharply on the reins. The broad wings opened slowly. The beast's hindquarters dropped as its head rose. The rider felt himself slide backward, bumping against the rear lip of the tall saddle. The griffon soared up in a high arc, wings flailing. He let the reins out, and the beast leveled off. He whistled a command, and the griffon held its wings out motionless. They started down again in a steep glide. The lower air was rough, full of eddies and currents, and the griffon bobbed and pitched. The rider threw back his head and laughed.

They skimmed over the trees. Abruptly the woods gave way to orderly rows of trees, orchards of cherry, plum, and fima nuts. Elves working in the orchards saw only a large object hurtle over their heads, and they panicked. Many tumbled down ladders, spilling baskets of fruit. The rider put a brass horn to his lips, sounding a shrill note. The griffon added its own eerie call, a deep, trilling growl that was also part lion, part eagle.

The rider urged the beast up. The wings beat lazily, gaining a few dozen feet of height. They banked right, swooping over the slow-flowing waters of the Thon-Thalas. There were many watercraft plying the river: flat log rafts poled by sturdy, sun-browned elves, piled high with pots and cloth to be traded in the wild south; the slender dugouts of the fishers, the bottoms of which were silvered with the morning's catch. The griffon swept over them in a flurry of wings. The rafters and fishers looked up idly from their work. As travelers up and down the great waterway, they were not easily impressed, not even by the sight of a royal griffon in flight.

On they flew, across the river to Fallan Island. The rider wove his flying steed among the many white towers so skillfully that the griffon never once scraped a wingtip. Their shadow chased them down the streets.

The rider approached the center point of the city, and the center point of every elf's life and loyalty, the Tower of the Stars. At six hundred feet, it was the tallest spire in Silvanost and the seat of power of the Speaker of the Stars.

He steered the griffon in a quick circle around the white marble tower. The horn was at his lips again, and he blew a rude, flat warning. It was a lark, a bit of aerial fun, but halfway around the tower the rider spied a lone figure on the high balcony, looking out over the city. He reined back and sideslipped Arcuballis toward the tower. The white-haired, white-robed figure was no one less than Sithel, Speaker of the Stars.

Startled, the rider clumsily turned the griffon away. His eyes met those of the elven monarch for a moment, then Sithel turned and re-entered the tower. The griffon rider shook his head and made for home. He was in trouble.

North of the tower, across the ornate Gardens of Astarin, stood the Palace of Quinari. Here the descendants of Silvanos, the House Royal, lived. The palace stood clear of the trees and consisted of three, three-story wings radiating from a rose-colored marble tower. The tower soared three hundred feet from base to pinnacle. The three wings of the palace were faced with beautiful colonnades of green-streaked marble. The columns spiraled gracefully upward from their bases, each in imitation of a unicorn's horn.

The rider's heart raced as the palace came into view. He'd been away four days, hunting, flying, and now he had an appointment to keep. He knew there would be trouble with the speaker for his insolent behavior at the Tower of the Stars, but for now thoughts of his upcoming rendezvous made him smile.

He brought the griffon in with firm tugs on the reins. He steered toward the eastern wing of the palace. Lion's claws behind and eagle's talons in front touched down on the cool slate roof. With a tired shudder, Arcuballis drew in its wings.

Servants in sleeveless tunics and short kilts ran out to take the beast's bridle. Another elf set a wooden step ladder against the animal's side. The rider ignored it, threw a leg over the griffon's neck, and nimbly dropped to the rooftop. More servants rushed forward, one with a bowl of clean water, the other with a neatly folded linen towel.

"Highness," said the bowl bearer, "would you care to refresh yourself?"

"A moment." The rider pried off his helmet and shook his sweat-damp hair. "How goes everything here?" he asked, dipping his hands and arms in the clean water, once, twice, three times. The water quickly turned dingy with dirt.

"It goes well, my prince," the bowl bearer replied. He snapped his head at his companion, and the second servant proffered the towel.

"Any word from my brother, Prince Sithas?"

"In fact, yes, Highness. Your brother was recalled yesterday by your father. He returned from the Temple of Matheri this morning."

Puzzlement knit the rider's pale brows. "Recalled? But why?"

"I do not know, my prince. Even now, the speaker is closeted with Prince Sithas in the Tower of the Stars."

The rider tossed the towel back to the servant who'd brought it. "Send word to my mother that I have returned. Tell her I shall see her presently. And should my father and brother return from the tower before sunset, tell them the same."

The servants bowed. "It shall be done, my prince."

The elf prince went briskly to the stair that led from the roof top into the palace. The servants hastened after him, sloshing dirty water from the bowl as they went.

"Prince Kith-Kanan! Will you not take some food?" called the bowl bearer.

"No. See to it Arcuballis is fed, watered, and brushed down."

"Of course—"

"And stop following me!"

The servants halted as if arrow-shot. Prince Kith-Kanan rattled down the stone steps into the palace. As it was early summer, all the window shutters were open, flooding the interior corridors with light. He strode along, scarcely acknowledging the bows and greetings of the servants and courtiers he met. The length of the shadows on the floor told him he was late. She would be angry, being kept waiting.

Kith-Kanan breezed out the main entrance of the palace. Guards in burnished armor snapped to attention as he passed. His mood lightened with every step he took toward the Gardens of Astarin. So what if his father dressed him down later?—it wouldn't be the first time, by any means. Any amount of lecturing was worth his hurried flight home to be on time for his rendezvous with Hermathya.

The gardens bulked around the base of the great tower. Not long after Silvanos, founder of the elven nation, had completed the Tower of the Stars, priests of the god Astarin asked for permission to create a garden around the structure. Silvanos gladly granted their request. The clerics laid out a garden in the plan of a four-pointed star, each point aligned with one of the cardinal directions. They wove spells granted to them by Astarin, the Bard King, spells that formed the trees and flowers in wonderful ways. Thornless red and white roses grew in delicate spirals around the trunks of evergreen oaks. Wisteria dripped purple blossoms into still, clear pools of water. Lilacs and camellias drenched the air with their perfume. Broad leaves of ivy spread over the garden paths, shading them and protecting strollers from all but the harshest rains. And most remarkably, laurels and cedars grew in circular groves, their tops coming

together to form perfect shelters, where elves could meditate.
Silvanos himself had favored a grove of laurels on the west side
of the garden. When the august founder of the elven nation had
died, the leaves on the laurels there changed from green to
gold, and they remained that way ever after.

Kith-Kanan did not enter the Gardens of Astarin by one of
the paths. In his deerskin boots, he crept silently beside the
shoulder-high wall of spell-shaped mulberry. He hoisted himself over the wall and dropped down on the other side, still
without a sound. Crouching low, he moved toward the grove.

The prince could hear the impatient rustle of footsteps inside
the golden grove. In his mind he saw Hermathya pacing to and
fro, arms folded, her red-gold hair like a flame in the center of
the gilded trees. He slipped around to the entrance to the grove.
Hermathya had her back to him, her arms folded tight with
vexation. Kith-Kanan called her name.

Hermathya whirled. "Kith! You startled me. Where have you
been?"

"Hurrying to you," he replied.

Her angry expression lasted only a moment longer, then she
ran to him, her bright blue gown flying. They embraced in the
arched entry of Silvanos's retreat. The embrace became a kiss.
After a moment, Kith-Kanan drew back a bit and whispered,
"We'd best be wary. My father is in the tower. He might see us."

In answer, Hermathya pulled the prince's face down to hers
and kissed him again. Finally, she said breathlessly, "Now, let
us hide." They entered the shelter of the laurel grove.

Under the elaborate rules of courtly manners, a prince and a
well-born elf maiden could not consort freely, as Kith-Kanan
and Hermathya had for the past half-year. Escorts had to accompany both of them, if they ever saw each other at all. Protocol demanded that they not be alone together.

"I missed you terribly," Hermathya said, taking Kith-Kanan's
hand and leading him to the gray granite bench. "Silvanost is
like a tomb when you're not here."

"I'm sorry I was late. Arcuballis had headwinds to fight all
the way home." This was not strictly true, but why anger her
further? Actually Kith-Kanan had broken camp late because he
had stayed to listen to two Kagonesti elves tell tall tales of adventures in the West, in the land of the humans.

"Next time," Hermathya said, tracing the line of Kith-Kanan's jaw with one slender finger, "take me with you."

"On a hunting trip?"

She nipped at his ear. Her hair smelled of sunshine and spice. "Why not?"

He hugged her close, burying his face in her hair and inhaling deeply. "You could probably handle yourself right enough, but what respectable maiden would travel in the forest with a male not her father, brother, or husband?"

"I don't want to be respectable."

Kith-Kanan studied her face. Hermathya had the dark blue eyes of the Oakleaf Clan and the high cheekbones of her mother's family, the Sunberry Clan. In her slender, beautiful face he saw passion, wit, courage—

"Love," he murmured.

"Yes," Hermathya replied. "I love you too."

The prince looked deep into her eyes and said softly, "Marry me, Hermathya." Her eyes widened, and she pulled away from him, chuckling. "What is funny?" he demanded.

"Why talk of marriage? Giving me a starjewel will not make me love you more. I like things the way they are."

Kith-Kanan waved to the surrounding golden laurels. "You like meeting in secret? Whispering and flinching at every sound, lest we be discovered?"

She leaned close again. "Of course. That makes it all the more stimulating."

He had to admit his life had been anything but boring lately. Kith-Kanan caressed his lover's cheek. Wind stirred through the gilded leaves as they drew closer. She entwined her fingers in his white hair. The prince thought no more of marriage as Hermathya filled his senses.

* * * * *

They parted with smiles and quiet touches on each other's faces. Hermathya disappeared down the garden path with a toss of bronze-red hair and a swish of clinging silk. Kith-Kanan stood in the entrance of the golden grove and watched her until she was lost from sight. Then, with a sigh, he made for the palace.

The sun had set and, as he crossed the plaza, the prince saw that the servants were setting lamps in the windows of the palace. All Silvanost glimmered with light by night, but the Palace of Quinari, with its massive tower and numerous tall windows, was like a constellation in the heavens. Kith-Kanan felt very satisfied as he jauntily ascended the steps by the main doors.

The guards clacked their spears against their shoulder armor. The one on Kith-Kanan's right said, "Highness, the speaker bids you go to the Hall of Balif."

"Well, I'd best not keep the speaker waiting," he replied. The guards snapped to, and he passed on into the deep, arched opening. Even the prospect of a tongue-lashing by his father did little to lower Kith-Kanan's spirits. He still breathed the clean, spicy scent of Hermathya, and he still gazed into the bottomless blue depths of her eyes.

The Hall of Balif, named for the kender general who had once fought so well on behalf of the great Silvanos, took up an entire floor of the central tower. Kith-Kanan swung up the broad stone stairs, clapping servants on the back and hailing courtiers heartily. Smiles followed in the elf prince's wake.

Oddly, two guards stood outside the high bronze doors of the Hall of Balif. The doors were not usually guarded. As Kith-Kanan approached, one guard rapped on the bronze panel behind him with the butt of his spear. Silently Kith-Kanan stood by as the two soldiers pushed the heavy portals apart for him.

The hall was indifferently lit by a rack of candles on the oval feasting table. The first face Kith-Kanan saw did not belong to his father, Sithel.

"Sithas!"

The tall, white-haired young elf stood up from behind the table. Kith-Kanan circled the table and embraced his twin brother heartily. Though they lived in the same city, they saw each other only at intervals. Sithas spent most of his time in the Temple of Matheri, where the priests had been educating him since he was a child. Kith-Kanan was frequently away, flying, riding, hunting. Ninety years they'd lived, and by the standards of their race they were barely adults. Time and habit had altered the twins, so much so that they were no longer exact copies of each other. Sithas, elder by scant minutes, was slim and pale, the consequence of his scholarly life. His face was lit by large hazel eyes, the eyes of his father and grandfather. On his white robe he wore a narrow red stripe, a tribute to Matheri, whose color it was.

Kith-Kanan, because of his outdoor life, had skin almost as brown as his eyes. The life of a ranger had toughened him, broadened his shoulders and hardened his muscles.

"I'm in trouble," he said ruefully.

"What have you done this time?" Sithas asked, loosening his grip on his twin.

"I was out flying on Arcuballis—"

"Have you been scaring the farmers again?"

"No, it's not that. I was over the city, so I circled the Tower of the Stars—"

"Blowing your horn, no doubt."

Kith-Kanan sighed. "Will you let me finish? I went 'round the tower, very gently, but who should be there on the high balcony but Father! He saw me and gave me that *look*."

Sithas folded his arms. "I was there too, inside. He wasn't pleased."

His twin lowered his voice to a conspiratorial whisper. "What's this all about? He didn't call me here to chastise me, did he? You wouldn't be here for that."

"No. Father called me back from the temple before you came home. He's gone upstairs to fetch Mother. He's got something to tell you."

Kith-Kanan relaxed, realizing he wasn't going to get dressed down. "What is it, Sith?"

"I'm getting married," said Sithas.

Kith-Kanan, wide-eyed, leaned back on the table. "By E'li! Is that all you have to say? 'I'm getting married?' "

Sithas shrugged. "What else is there to say? Father decided that it's time, so married I get."

Kith-Kanan grinned. "Has he picked a girl?"

"I think that's why he sent for you and Mother. We'll all find out at the same time."

"You mean, you don't know who it is yet?"

"No. There are fourteen suitable clans within House Cleric, so there are many prospective brides. Father has chosen one based on the dowry offered—and according to which family he wants to link with House Royal."

13

His brother's eyes danced with merriment. "She will probably be ugly and a shrew, as well."

"That doesn't matter. All that matters is that she be healthy, well-born, and properly worship the gods," Sithas said calmly.

"I don't know. I think wit and beauty ought to count for something," Kith-Kanan replied. "And love. What about love, Sith? How do you feel about marrying a stranger?"

"It is the way things are done."

That was so like him. The quickest way to insure Sithas's cooperation was to invoke tradition. Kith-Kanan clucked his tongue and walked in a slow circle around his motionless twin. His words rang off the polished stone walls. "But is it fair?" he said, mildly mocking. "I mean, any scribe or smith in the city can choose his mate himself, because he loves her and she loves him. The wild elves of the woods, the green sea elves, do they marry for duty, or do they take as mate a loving companion who'll bear them children and be a strength to them in their ancient age?"

"I'm not any smith or scribe, much less a wild elf," Sithas said. He spoke quietly, but his words carried as clearly as Kith-Kanan's loud pronouncements. "I am firstborn to the Speaker of the Stars, and my duty is my duty."

Kith-Kanan stopped circling and slumped against the table. "It's the old story, isn't it? Wise Sithas and rash Kith-Kanan," he said. "Don't pay me any heed. I'm really glad for you. And I'm glad for me, too. At least I can choose my own wife when the time comes."

Sithas smiled. "Do you have someone in mind?"

Why not tell Sithas? he thought. His twin would never give him away.

"Actually," Kith-Kanan began, "there is—"

The rear door of the hall opened, and Sithel entered, with Nirakina at his side.

"Hail, Father," the brothers said in unison.

The speaker waved for his sons to sit. He held a chair out for his wife, then sat himself. The crown of Silvanesti, a circlet of gold and silver stars, weighed heavily on his brow. He had come to the time in his life when age was beginning to show. Sithel's hair had always been white, but now its silky blondness had become brittle and gray. Tiny lines were etched around his

14

eyes and mouth, and his hazel eyes, the sign of the heritage of Silvanos, betrayed the slightest hint of cloudiness. All these were small, outward signs of the great burden of time Sithel carried in his lean, erect body. He was one thousand, five hundred years old.

Though past a thousand herself, Lady Nirakina was still lithe and graceful. She was small by elven standards, almost doll-like. Her hair was honey brown, as were her eyes. These were traits of her family, Clan Silver Moon. A sense of gentleness radiated from her, a gentleness that soothed her often irritable husband. It was said about the palace that Sithas had his father's looks and his mother's temperament. Kith-Kanan had inherited his mother's eyes and his father's energy.

"You look well," Nirakina said to Kith-Kanan. "Was your trip rewarding?"

"Yes, Lady. I do love to fly," he said, after kissing her cheek.

Sithel gave his son a sharp glance. Kith-Kanan cleared his throat and bid his father a polite greeting.

"I'm glad you returned when you did," Sithel said. "Has Sithas told you of his upcoming marriage?" Kith-Kanan admitted he had. "You will have an important part to play as well, Kith. As the brother of the groom, it will be your job to escort the bride to the Tower of the Stars—"

"Yes, I will, but tell us who it is!" insisted the impatient prince.

"She is a maiden of exceptional spirit and beauty, I'm told," Sithel said. "Well-educated, well-born—"

"Father!" Kith-Kanan pleaded. Sithas himself sat quietly, hands folded on his lap. Years of training in the Temple of Matheri had given him formidable patience.

"My son," Sithel said to Sithas, "your wife's name is Hermathya, daughter of Lord Shenbarrus of the Oakleaf Clan."

Sithas raised an eyebrow approvingly. Even he had noticed Hermathya. He said nothing, but nodded his acceptance.

"Are you all right, Kith?" Nirakina asked. "You look quite pale."

To her surprise, Kith-Kanan looked as if his father had struck him across the face. The prince swallowed hard and nodded, unable to speak. Of all the eligible daughters, Hermathya was to marry Sithas. It was incomprehensible. It could not happen!

None of his family knew of his love for her. If they knew, if his father knew, he'd choose someone else.

"Ah," Kith-Kanan managed to say, "who—who else knows of this?"

"Only the bride's family," said Sithel. "I sent Shenbarrus acceptance of the dowry this morning."

A sinking feeling gripped Kith-Kanan. He felt like he was melting into the floor. Hermathya's family already knew. There was no going back now. The speaker had given his word. He could not, in honor, rescind his decision without gravely offending Clan Oakleaf.

His parents and brother began to discuss details of the wedding. A tremor passed through Kith-Kanan. He resolved to stand up and declare his love for Hermathya, declare that she was his and no one else's. Sithas was his brother, his twin, but he didn't know her. He didn't love her. He could find another wife. Kith-Kanan could not find another love.

He rose unsteadily to his feet. "I—" he began. All eyes turned to him.

Think, for once in your life! he admonished himself. What will they say to you?

"What?" said his father. "Are you ill, boy? You don't look well."

"I don't feel too well," Kith-Kanan said hoarsely. He wanted to shout, to run, to smash and break things, but the massive calm of his mother, father, and brother held him down like a thick blanket. He cleared his throat and added, "I think all that flying has caught up with me."

Nirakina stood and put a hand to his face. "You do feel warm. Perhaps you should rest."

"Yes. Yes," he said. "That's just what I need. Rest." He held the table edge for support.

"I make the formal announcement when the white moon rises tonight. The priests and nobles will gather in the tower," Sithel said. "You must be there, Kith."

"I—I'll be there, Father," Kith-Kanan said. "I just need to rest."

Sithas walked with his brother to the door. Before they went out, Sithel remarked, "Oh, and leave your horn at the palace, Kith. One act of impudence a day is enough." The speaker smiled, and Kith-Kanan managed a weak grin in reply.

"Shall I send a healer to you?" asked Nirakina.

"No. I'll be fine, Mother," Kith-Kanan said.

In the corridor outside, Sithas braced his brother's shoulders and said, "Looks as if I'm to be lucky; both brains and beauty in my wife."

"You are lucky," Kith-Kanan said. Sithas looked at him in concern. Kith-Kanan was moved to say, "Whatever happens, Sith, don't think too badly of me."

Sithas frowned. "What do you mean?"

Kith-Kanan inhaled deeply and turned to climb up the stairs to his room. "Just remember that nothing will ever separate us. We're two halves of the same coin."

"Two branches of the same tree," Sithas said, completing the ritual the twins had invented as children. His concern deepened as he watched Kith-Kanan climb slowly up the stairs.

Kith-Kanan didn't let his brother see his face contort with pain. He had only a scant two hours before Solinari, the white moon, rose above the trees. Whatever he was going to do, he had to think of it before then.

* * * * *

The great and noble of Silvanesti filed into the open hall of the Tower of the Stars. Rumors flew through the air like sparrows, between courtier and cleric, noble clan father and humble acolyte. Such assemblies in the tower were rare and usually involved a matter of state.

A pair of young heralds, draped in bright green tabards and wearing circlets of oak and laurel, marched into the hall in perfect step. They turned and stood on each side of the great door. Slender trumpets went to their lips, and a stirring fanfare blared forth. When the horns ceased, a third herald entered.

"Free Elves and True! Give heed to His Highness, Sithel, Speaker of the Stars!"

Everyone bowed silently as Sithel appeared and walked to his emerald throne. There was a spontaneous cry of "All hail the speaker!" from the ranks of the nobles; the hall rang with elven voices. The speaker mounted the steps, turned, and faced the assembly. He sat down, and the hails died.

The herald spoke again. "Sithas, son of Sithel, prince heir!"

Sithas passed through the doorway, bowed to his father, and approached the throne. As his son mounted the seven steps to the platform, Sithel held out his hand, indicating his son should stand to the left of the throne. Sithas took his place, facing the audience.

The trumpets blared again. "Lady Nirakina, wife, and Prince Kith-Kanan, son of Sithel!"

Kith-Kanan entered with his mother on his arm. He had changed to his courtly robes of sky-blue linen, clothing he rarely wore. He moved stiffly down the center aisle, his mother's hand resting lightly on his left arm.

"Smile," she whispered to him.

"I don't know four-fifths of them," Kith-Kanan muttered.

"Smile anyway. They know you."

When he reached the steps, the pommel of Kith-Kanan's sword poked out from under his ceremonial sash. Nirakina glanced down at the weapon, which was largely concealed by the voluminous folds of his robe.

"Why did you bring that?" she whispered.

"It's part of my costume," he replied. "I have a right to wear it."

"Don't be impertinent," his mother said primly. "You know this is a peaceful occasion."

A large wooden chair, cushioned with red velvet, was set in place for the speaker's wife on the left of Prince Sithas. Kith-Kanan, like his twin, was expected to stand in the presence of his father, the monarch.

Once the royal family was in place, the assembled notables lined up to pay their respects to the speaker. The time-honored ritual called for priests first, the clan fathers of House Cleric next, and the masters of the city guilds last. Kith-Kanan, far to the left of Sithel, searched for Hermathya in the press of people. The crowd numbered some three hundred, and though they were quiet, the shuffling of feet and the rustle of silk and linen filled the tower. The heralds advanced to the foot of the speaker's throne and announced each group as they formed up before Sithel.

The priests and priestesses, in their white robes and golden headbands, each wore a sash in the color of their patron deity—silver for E'li, red for Matheri, brown for Kiri Jolith, sky blue for Quenesti Pah, and so on. By ancient law, they went barefoot as well, so they would be closer to the sacred soil of Silvanesti.

The clan fathers shepherded their families past the speaker. Kith-Kanan caught his breath as Lord Shenbarrus of Clan Oakleaf reached the head of the line. He was a widower, so his eldest daughter stood beside him.

Hermathya.

Sithel spoke for the first time since entering the Tower of the Stars. "Lady," he said to Hermathya, "will you remain?"

Hermathya, clad in an embroidered gown the color of summer sunlight, her striking face framed by two maidenly braids—which Kith-Kanan knew she hated—bowed to the speaker and stood aside from her family at the foot of the throne platform. The hiss of three hundred whispering tongues filled the hall.

Sithel stood and offered a hand to Hermathya. She went up the stairs without hesitation and stood beside him. Sithel nodded to the heralds. A single note split the air.

"Silence in the hall! His Highness will speak!" cried the herald.

A hush descended. Sithel surveyed the crowd, ending his sweep by looking at his wife and sons. "Holy clerics, elders, subjects, be at ease in your hearts," he said, his rich voice echoing in the vast open tower. "I have called you here to receive joyous news. My son, Sithas, who shall be speaker after me, has reached the age and inclination to take a wife. After due consultation with the gods, and with the chiefs of all the clans of House Cleric, I have found a maiden suitable to be my son's bride."

Kith-Kanan's left hand strayed to his sword hilt. A calm had descended over him. He had thought long and hard about this. He knew what he had to do.

"I have chosen this maiden knowing full well the disappointment that will arise in the other clans," Sithel was saying. "I deeply regret it. If this were a barbarian land, where husbands may have more than one wife, I daresay I could make more of you happy." Polite laughter rippled through the ranks of the nobles. "But the speaker may have only one wife, so one is all I have chosen. It is my great hope that she and my son will be as happy together as I have been with my Nirakina."

He looked at Sithas, who advanced to his father's side. Holding Hermathya's left hand, the speaker reached for Sithas's right. The crowd held its breath, waiting for him to make the official announcement.

"Stop!"

The couple's fingers were only a hairsbreadth apart when Kith-Kanan's voice rang out. Sithel turned in surprise to his younger son. Every eye in the hall looked with shock at the prince.

"Hermathya cannot marry Sithas!" Kith-Kanan declared.

"Be silent," Sithel said harshly. "Have you gone mad?"

"No, Father," Kith-Kanan said calmly. "Hermathya loves me!"

Sithas withdrew his hand from his father's slack fingers. In his hand he held a starjewel, the traditional betrothal gift among elves. Sithas knew something had been brewing. Kith-Kanan had been too obviously troubled by the announcement of his bride-to-be. But he had not guessed at the reason.

"What does this mean?" demanded Lord Shenbarrus, moving to his daughter's side.

Kith-Kanan advanced to the edge of the raised floor. "Tell him, Hermathya. Tell them all!"

Sithas looked to his father. Sithel's gaze was on Hermathya. Her cheeks were faintly pink, but her expression was calm, her eyes cast down.

When Hermathya said nothing, Sithel commanded, "Speak, girl. Speak the truth."

Hermathya lifted her gaze and looked directly at Sithas. "I want to marry the speaker's heir," she said. Her voice was not loud, but in the tense silence, every sound, every word was like a thunderclap.

"No!" Kith-Kanan exclaimed. What was she saying? "Don't be afraid, Thya. Don't let our fathers sway you. Tell them the truth. Tell them who you love."

Still Hermathya's eyes were on Sithas. "I choose the speaker's heir—"

"Thya!" Kith-Kanan would have rushed to her, but Nirakina interposed herself, pleading with her son to be still. He gently but firmly pushed her aside. Only Sithas stood between him and Hermathya now.

"Stand aside, Brother," he said.

"Be silent!" his father roared. "You dishonor us all!"

Kith-Kanan drew his sword. Gasps and shrieks filled the Tower of the Stars. Baring a weapon in the hall was a serious offense, a sacrilegious act. But Kith-Kanan wavered. He looked at the sword in his hand, at his brother's and father's faces, and at the woman he loved. Hermathya stood unmoving, her eyes still fixed on his twin. What hold did they have on her?

Sithas was unarmed. In fact no one in the hall was armed, except for the flimsy ceremonial maces some of the clan fathers carried. No one could stop him if he chose to fight. Kith-Kanan's sword arm trembled.

With a cry of utter anguish, the prince threw the short, slim blade away. It skittered across the polished floor toward the assembled clerics, who moved hastily out of its way. It was ritually unclean for them to touch an edged weapon.

Kith-Kanan ran from the tower, blazing with frustration and anger. The crowd parted for him. Every eye in the hall watched him go.

Sithas descended to the main floor and went to where Kith-Kanan's sword lay. He picked it up. It felt heavy and awkward in his unpracticed hand. He stared at the keen cutting edge, then at the doorway through which Kith-Kanan had departed. His heart bled for his twin. This time Kith had not merely been impudent or impetuous. This time, his deeds were an affront to the throne and to the gods.

Sithas saw only one proper thing to do. He went back to his father and bride-to-be. Laying the naked blade at Sithel's feet, he took Hermathya's hand. It was warm. He could feel her pulse throbbing against his own cool palm. And as Sithas took the blue starjewel from the folds of his robe, it seemed almost alive. It lay in his hand, throwing off scintillas of rainbow light.

"If you will have me, I will have you," he said, holding the jewel out to Hermathya.

"I will," she replied loudly. She took the starjewel and held it to her breast.

The Tower of the Stars shook with the cheers of the assembled elves.

2

later that Night
___

Sithel strode with furious energy down the corridors of the Palace of Quinari. Servants and courtiers backed away from him as he went, so fierce was the anger on his face. The assembly had ended on a triumphant note, but the Speaker of the Stars could not forget the outrage his own son had committed.

The corridor ended at the palace's great central tower. Sithel approached the huge bronze doors that closed off the private rooms of his family from the rest of the palace. The doors were eighteen feet high, inlaid with silver runes that kept a protective spell on them. No one not of the blood of Silvanos could open the doors. Sithel hit one door with each palm. The immense portals, delicately balanced, swung inward.

"Where is he? Where is Kith-Kanan?" he demanded, setting

his feet wide apart and planting his fists on his hips. "I'll teach that boy to shame us in front of a public assembly!"

Within the chamber, Nirakina sat on a low, gilded couch. Sithas bent over her, proffering a goblet of sweet nectar. The prince straightened when his father entered, but neither he nor his mother spoke.

"Well?" demanded Sithel.

Nirakina looked up from her goblet. Her large amber eyes were full of sadness. "He is not in the palace," she said softly. "The servants looked for him, but they did not find him."

Sithel advanced into the room. His hard footsteps were lost in the deep carpets that covered the center of the floor, and his harsh words were muffled by the rich tapestries covering the cold stone walls.

"Servants, bah, they know nothing. Kith-Kanan has more hiding places than I've had years of life."

"He is gone," Sithas said at last.

"How do you know that?" asked his father, transferring his glare to his eldest son.

"I do not feel his presence within the palace," Sithas said evenly. The twins' parents knew of the close bond that existed between their sons.

Sithel poured a goblet of nectar, using this simple task to give himself time to master his anger. He took a long drink.

"There is something else," Sithas said. His voice was very low. "The griffon, Arcuballis, is missing from the royal stable."

Sithel drained his cup. "So, he's run away, has he? Well, he'll be back. He's a clever boy, Kith is, but he's never been out in the world on his own. He won't last a week without servants, attendants, and guides."

"I'm frightened," said Nirakina. "I've never seen him so upset. Why didn't we know about this girl and Kith?" She took Sithas's hand. "How do we know she will be a good wife for you, after the way she's behaved?"

"Perhaps she is unsuitable," Sithas offered, looking at his father. If she were, perhaps the marriage could be called off. Then she and Kith-Kanan—"

"I'll not go back on my word to Shenbarrus merely because his daughter is indiscreet," Sithel snapped, interrupting his son's thoughts. "Think of Hermathya, too; shall we blacken her reputation to salve Kith's wounded ego? They'll both forget this nonsense."

Tears ran down Nirakina's cheeks. "Will you forgive him? Will you let him come back?"

"It's outside my hands," Sithel said. His own anger was failing under fatherly concern. "But mark my words, he'll be back." He looked to Sithas for support, but Sithas said nothing. He wasn't as sure of Kith-Kanan's return as his father was.

* * * * *

The griffon glided in soundlessly, its mismatched feet touching down on the palace roof with only a faint clatter. Kith-Kanan slid off Arcuballis's back. He stroked his mount's neck and whispered encouragement in its ear.

"Be good now. Stay." Obediently the griffon folded its legs and lay down.

Kith-Kanan stole silently along the roof. The vast black shadow of the tower fell over him and buried the stairwell in darkness. In his dark quilted tunic and heavy leggings, the prince was well hidden in the shadows. He avoided the stairs for, even at this late hour, there might be servants stirring about in the lower corridors. He did not want to be seen.

Kith-Kanan flattened himself against the base of the tower. Above his head, narrow windows shone with the soft yellow light of oil lanterns. He uncoiled a thin silk rope from around his waist. Hanging from his belt was an iron hook. He tied the rope to the eye of the hook, stepped out from the tower wall, and began to whirl the hook in an ever-widening circle. Then, with practiced ease, he let it fly. The hook sailed up to the third level of windows and caught on the jutting stonework beneath them. After giving the rope an experimental tug, Kith-Kanan started climbing up the wall, hand over hand, his feet braced against the thick stone of the tower.

The third level of windows—actually the sixth floor above ground level—was where his private room was located. Once he'd gained the narrow ledge where his hook had wedged, Kith-Kanan stood with his back flat against the wall, pausing to catch his breath. Around him, the city of Silvanost slept. The white temple towers, the palaces of the nobles, the monumental crystal tomb of Silvanos on its hill overlooking the city, all stood out in the light of Krynn's two visible moons. The lighted windows were like jewels, yellow topaz and white diamonds.

Kith-Kanan forced the window of his room open with the blade of his dagger. He stepped down from the sill onto his bed. The chill moonlight made his room seem pale and unfamiliar. Like all the rooms on this floor of the tower, Kith-Kanan's was wedge-shaped, like a slice of pie. All the miscellaneous treasures of his boyhood were in this room: hunting trophies, a collection of shiny but worthless stones, scrolls describing the heroic deeds of Silvanos and Balif. All to be left behind, perhaps never to be seen or handled again.

He went first to the oaken wardrobe, standing by an inside wall. From under his breastplate he pulled a limp cloth sack, which he'd just bought from a fisher on the river. It smelled rather strongly of fish, but he had no time to be delicate. From the wardrobe he took only a few things—a padded leather tunic, a pair of heavy horse-riding boots, and his warmest set of leggings. Next he went to the chest at the foot of his bed.

With no concern for neatness, he stuffed spare clothing into the sack. Then, at the bottom of the chest, he found something he hadn't wanted to find. Wrapped in a scrap of linen was the starjewel he'd bought for Hermathya. Once exposed, it glittered in the dim light.

Slowly he picked it up. His first reaction was to grind the delicate gem under his heel, but Kith-Kanan couldn't bring himself to destroy the beautiful scarlet gem. Without knowing exactly why, he slipped it into the fisher's bag.

From the rack by the door he took three items: a short but powerful recurve bow, a full quiver of arrows, and his favorite boar spear. Kith-Kanan's scabbard hung empty at his side. His sword, forged by the priests of Kiri Jolith, he'd left in the Tower of the Stars.

The prince put the arrows and the unstrung bow in the sack and tied it to the boar spear. The whole bundle he slung from his shoulder. Now for the door.

The latch whispered backward in its slot. Kith-Kanan pulled the door open. Directly across from his room was Sithas's sleeping chamber. A strip of light showed under his brother's door. Kith-Kanan lowered his bundle to the floor and reached out for the door handle.

Sithas's door opened silently. Inside, his white-robed twin was kneeling before a small table, on which a single cut rose lay. A candle burned on the fireplace mantle.

Sithas looked up. "Come in, Kith," he said gently, "I was expecting you." He stood, looking hollow-eyed and gaunt in the candlelight. "I felt your presence when you returned. Please, sit down."

"I'm not staying," Kith-Kanan replied bitterly.

"You need not leave, Kith. Beg Father for forgiveness. He will grant it."

Kith-Kanan spread his hands. "I can't, Sith. It wouldn't matter if he did forgive me, I can't stay here any longer."

"Because of Hermathya?" asked Sithas. His twin nodded. "I don't love her, Kith, but she was chosen. I must marry her."

"But what about me? Do you care at all how I feel?"

Sithas's face showed that he did. "But what would you have me do?"

"Tell them you won't have her. Refuse to marry Hermathya!"

Sithas sighed. "It would be a grave insult to Clan Oakleaf, to our father, and to Hermathya herself. She was chosen because she will be the best wife for the future speaker."

Kith-Kanan passed a hand over his fevered eyes. "This is like a terrible dream. I can't believe Thya consented to all this."

"Then you can go upstairs and ask her. She is sleeping in the room just above yours," Sithas said evenly. Kith-Kanan turned to go. "Wait!" Sithas said. "Where will you go from here?"

"I will go far," Kith-Kanan replied defiantly.

Sithas leaped to his feet. "How far will you get on your own? You are throwing away your heritage, Kith! Throwing it away like a gnawed apple core!"

Kith-Kanan stood still in the open doorway. "I'm doing the only honorable thing I can. Do you think I could continue to live here with you, knowing Hermathya was your wife? Do you think I could stand to see her each day and have to call her 'Sister?' I know I have shamed Father and myself. I can live with shame, but I cannot live in sight of Hermathya and not love her!"

He went out in the hall and stooped to get his bundle. Sithas raised the lid of a plain, dark oak chest sitting at the foot of his bed.

"Kith, wait." Sithas turned around and held out his brother's sword. "Father was going to have it broken, he was so angry with you, but I persuaded him to let me keep it."

Kith-Kanan took the slim, graceful blade from his brother's hands. It slid home in his scabbard like a hand into a glove. Kith-Kanan instantly felt stronger. He had a part of himself back.

"Thank you, Sith."

On a simultaneous impulse, they came together and clasped their hands on each other's shoulders. "May the gods go with you, Brother," said Sithas warmly.

"They will if you ask them," Kith-Kanan replied wryly. "They listen to you."

He crossed the hall to his old room and prepared to go out the window. Sithas came to his door and said, "Will I ever see you again?"

Kith-Kanan looked out at the two bright moons. "As long as Solinari and Lunitari remain in the same sky, I will see you again, my brother." Without another word, Kith-Kanan stepped out of the window and was gone. Sithas returned to his sparsely furnished room and shut the door.

As he knelt again at his small shrine to Matheri, he said softly, "Two halves of the same coin; two branches of the same tree." He closed his eyes. "Matheri, keep him safe."

On the ledge, Kith-Kanan gathered up his rope. The room just above his, Sithas had said. Very well then. His first cast fell short, and the hook came scraping down the stone right at his face. Kith-Kanan flinched aside, successfully dodging the hook, but he almost lost his balance on the narrow ledge. The falling hook clattered against the wall below. Kith-Kanan cursed soundlessly and hauled the rope back up.

The Tower of Quinari, like most elven spires, grew steadily narrower as it grew taller. The ledges at each level were thus correspondingly shallower. It took Kith-Kanan four tries to catch his hook on the seventh floor ledge. When he did, he swung out into the cool night air, wobbling under the burden of his sack and spear. Doggedly he climbed. The window of the room above his was dark. He carefully set the bundle against the outside wall and went to work on the window latch with his dagger.

The soft lead of the window frame yielded quickly to his blade. He pushed the crystal panes in.

Already he knew she was in the room. The spicy scent she always wore filled the room with a subtle perfume. He listened and heard short sighs of breathing. Hermathya was asleep.

He went unerringly to her bedside. Kith-Kanan put out a hand and felt the soft fire of her hair. He spoke her name once, quietly. "It is I, my love."

"Kith! Please, don't hurt me!"

He was taken aback. He rose off his knees. "I would never, ever hurt you, Thya."

"But I thought—you were so angry—I thought you came here to kill me!"

"No!" he said gently. "I've come to take you with me."

She sat up. Solinari peeked in the window just enough to throw a silver beam on her face and neck. From his place in the shadows, Kith-Kanan felt again the deep wound he'd suffered on her account.

"Go with you?" Hermathya said in genuine confusion. "Go where?"

"Does it matter?"

She pushed her long hair away from her face. "And what of Sithas?"

"He doesn't love you," Kith-Kanan said.

"Nor do I love him, but he is my betrothed now."

Kith-Kanan couldn't believe what he was hearing. "You mean, you *want* to marry him?"

"Yes, I do."

Kith-Kanan blundered backward to the window. He sat down hard on the sill. It seemed as though his legs would not work right. The cool night air washed over him, and he breathed deeply.

"You cannot mean it! What about us? I thought you loved me!"

Hermathya walked into the edge of the shaft of moonlight. "I do, Kith. But the gods have decided that I shall be the wife of the next Speaker of the Stars." A note of pride crept into her voice.

"This is madness!" Kith-Kanan burst out. "It was my father who decided this marriage, not the gods!"

"We are all only instruments of the gods," she said coolly. "I love you, Kith, but the time has come to lay aside pranks and secret garden passions. I have spoken with my father, with your father. You and I had an exciting time together, we dreamed beautiful dreams. But that's all they were—dreams. It's time to wake up now and think of the future. Of the future of *all* Silvanesti."

All Kith-Kanan could think of at this moment was his own future. "I can't live without you, Thya," he said weakly.

"Yes, you can. You may not know it yet, but you can." She came toward him, and the moonlight made her nightdress no more than a cobweb. Kith-Kanan squeezed his eyes shut and balled his hands into tight fists.

"Please," Hermathya said. "Accept what will happen. We can still be close." Her warm hand touched his cold, dry cheek.

Kith-Kanan seized her wrist and shoved her away. "I cannot accept it," he said tersely, stepping up on the window sill. "Farewell, Lady Hermathya. May your life be green and golden."

The irony of his words was not lost on her. "May your life be green and golden" was what elven commoners said when taking leave of their lords.

Kith-Kanan shouldered his sack and slipped over the stone ledge. Hermathya stood for several seconds, gazing at the empty window. When the tears came she did not fight them.

* * * * *

Faithful Arcuballis was his only companion now. Kith-Kanan tied the sack to the saddle pillion and stuck the boar spear into the lance cup by his right stirrup. He mounted Arcuballis, strapped himself to the saddle, and turned the beast's head into the wind.

"Fly!" he cried, touching his heels into the griffon's brawny breast. "Fly!"

Arcuballis unfolded its wings and sprang into the air. Kith-Kanan whistled, and the griffon uttered its shrill cry. The least he could do, Kith-Kanan decided, was to let them know he was going. He whistled again and once more the griffon's trilling growl echoed between the white towers.

Kith-Kanan put the waxing red moon on his right hand and flew southwest, across the Thon-Thalas. The royal road stood out misty gray in the night, angling away north from the city and south to the seacoast. Kith-Kanan urged the griffon higher and faster. The road, the river, and the city that had been his home vanished behind them. Ahead lay only darkness and an endless sea of trees, green-black in the depths of night.

❦ 3 ❦

the next day

kith-kanan had no plans except to get away from Silvanost.
More than anything, he craved solitude right now. He pointed
Arcuballis's beak southwest, and gave the griffon its head.

Kith-Kanan dozed in the saddle, slumped forward over the
griffon's feathered neck. The loyal beast flew on all night,
never straying from the course its master had set. Dawn came,
and Kith-Kanan awoke, stiff and groggy. He sat up in the saddle and surveyed the land below. There was nothing but treetops as far as the eye could see. He saw no clearings, streams,
or meadows, much less signs of habitation.

How far they had flown during the night Kith-Kanan could
not guess. He knew from hunting trips down the Thon-Thalas
that south of Silvanost lay the Courrain Ocean, the boundaries

of which no elf knew. But he was in the East; the rising sun was almost directly ahead of him. He must be in the great forest that lay between the Thon-Thalas on the east and the plains of Kharolis to the west. He'd never ventured this far before.

Looking at the impenetrable canopy of trees, Kith-Kanan licked his dry lips and said aloud, "Well, boy, if things don't change, we can always walk across the trees!"

They flew for hours more, crisscrossing the leafy barrier and finding no openings whatsoever. Poor Arcuballis was laboring, panting in deep, dry grunts. The griffon had been flying all night and half the day. When Kith-Kanan lifted his head to scan the horizon, he spied a thin column of smoke rising from the forest, far off to his left. The prince turned Arcuballis toward the smoke. The gap closed with agonizing slowness.

Finally, he could see that a ragged hole had been torn in the tapestry of the forest. In the center of the hole, the gnarled trunk of a great tree stood, blackened and burning. Lightning had struck it. The burned opening was only ten yards wide, but around the base of the burning tree the ground was clear and level. Arcuballis's feet touched down, its wings trembled, and the beast shuddered. Immediately the exhausted griffon closed its eyes to sleep.

Kith-Kanan untied his sack from the pillion. He crossed the narrow clearing with the sack over one shoulder. Dropping it at his feet, he squatted down and started to unpack. The caw of a crow caught his ear. Looking up at the splintered, smoldering trunk of the shattered tree, he spied a single black bird perched on a charred limb. The crow cocked its head and cawed again. Kith-Kanan went back to his unpacking as the crow lifted off the limb, circled the clearing, and flew off.

He took out his bow and quiver, and braced a new bow-string. Though only three feet long when strung, the powerful recurve bow could put an iron-tipped arrow through a thick tree trunk. Kith-Kanan tied the quiver to his belt. Taking the stout boar spear in both hands, he jammed it as high as he could into the burned tree. He stuffed his belongings back in the sack and hung the sack from the spear shaft. That ought to keep his things safe from prowling animals.

Kith-Kanan squinted into the late afternoon sun. Using it as a guide, he decided to strike out to the north a short distance, to see if he could flush any game. Arcuballis was safe enough, he figured; few predators would dare tangle with a griffon. He put his back to the shattered tree and dove into the deeply shadowed forest.

Though the elf prince was used to the woods, at least the woods around Silvanost, he found this forest strangely different. The trees were widely spaced, but their thick foliage made it nearly as dim as twilight down below. So dense was the roof of leaves, the forest floor was nearly barren. Some ferns and bracken grew between the great trees, but no heavy undergrowth. The soil was thickly carpeted with dead leaves and velvety moss. And even though the high branches stirred in the wind, it was very still where Kith Kanan walked. Very still indeed. Rings of red-gilled mushrooms, a favorite food of deer and wild boar, grew undisturbed around the bases of the trees. The silence soon grew oppressive.

Kith-Kanan paused a hundred paces from the clearing and drew his sword. He cut a hunter's sign, a "blaze," into the gray-brown bark of a hundred-foot-high oak tree. Beneath the bark, the white flesh of the tree was hard and tough. The elven blade chipped away at it, and the sound of iron on wood echoed through the forest. His marker made, Kith-Kanan sheathed his sword and continued on, bow in hand.

The forest seemed devoid of animals. Except for the crow he'd seen, no other creature, furred or winged, showed itself. Every thirty yards or so he made another blaze so as not to lose his way, for the darkness was increasing. It was at least four hours till sunset, yet the shadowed recesses of the forest were dimming to twilight. Kith-Kanan mopped the sweat from his brow and knelt in the fallen leaves. He brushed them aside, looking for signs of grazing by deer or wild pigs. The moss was unbroken.

By the time Kith-Kanan had made his tenth blaze, it was dark as night. He leaned against an ash tree and tried to see through the closely growing branches overhead. At this point he'd just as soon have squirrel for dinner as venison. That was growing more likely, too.

Tiny points of sunlight filtered through the leaves, dancing as the wind stirred the branches. It was almost like seeing the stars, only these points of light moved. The effect was quite hypnotic, which only made Kith-Kanan more tired than he already was. He'd dozed only fitfully in the saddle and had eaten nearly nothing since the day before. Perhaps he'd stop for a moment. Take a bit of rest. Overhead the points of light danced and swayed.

Kith-Kanan's sword, resting in the crook of his arm, slipped from his grasp and fell to the ground, sticking point first in the soft soil.

Points of light. Dancing. How very tired he was! His knees folded, and he slid slowly down the trunk until he was sitting on his haunches, back against the tree. His gaze remained on the canopy of leaves overhead. What an odd forest this was. Not like home. Not like the woods of Silvanost—

As in a dream, the prince saw the airy corridors of the Palace of Quinari. The servants bowed to him, as they always did. He was on his way to a feast in the Hall of Balif. There would be simmered roasts, legs of lamb, fruits dripping with juice, fragrant sauces, and delicious drafts of sweet nectar.

Kith-Kanan came to a door. It was just a door, like any other in the palace. He pushed the door open, and there, in loving embrace, were Sithas and Hermathya. She turned to face him, a smile on her face. A smile for Sithas.

"No!"

He leaped forward, landing on his hands and knees. His legs were completely numb. It was pitch dark around him, and for a few seconds Kith-Kanan didn't know where he was. He breathed deeply. Night must have fallen, he realized. But the dream had seemed so real! The elf's senses told him he'd broken some spell, one that had come over him as he looked at the patterns of light and shadow up in the trees. He must have been dreaming for hours.

After a long minute waiting for the feeling to return to his legs, Kith-Kanan cast about for his sword. He found it sticking in the moss. He freed the weapon and shoved it into its scabbard. A vague sense of urgency turned him back to the blasted clearing. His last blaze was visible in the night, but the second to last was almost gone. New bark was covering the cut he'd made. The next mark was a mere slit, and the one after that he found only because he remembered the oddly forked trunk of the ash tree he'd hacked it into. There were no more to find after that. The cuts had healed.

For a moment the elf prince knew fear. He was lost in the silent forest at night, hungry, thirsty, and alone. Had enough time passed for the cuts to heal naturally, or was the grove enchanted? Even the darkness that surrounded him seemed, well, darker than usual. Not even his elven eyesight could penetrate very far.

Then the training and education of a prince reasserted itself, banishing much of the fear. Kith-Kanan, grandson of the great Silvanos, was not about to be bested on his first night in the wilderness.

He found a dry branch and set about making a torch to light his way back to the clearing. After gathering a pile of dead leaves for tinder, Kith-Kanan pulled out his flint and striker. To his surprise, no sparks flew off the iron bar when he grated the flint against it. He tried and tried, but all the fire seemed to have gone out of the flint.

There was a flutter of black wings overhead. Kith-Kanan leaped to his feet in time to see a flock of crows take up perches on a limb just out of reach. The dozen birds watched him with unnerving intelligence.

"Shoo!" he yelled, flinging a useless branch at them. The crows flapped up and, when the branch had passed, settled again in the same place and posture.

He pocketed his flint and striker. The crows followed his movements with unblinking eyes. Tired and bewildered, he addressed the birds directly. "I don't suppose you can help me find my way back, can you?"

One by one, the black birds took wing and disappeared into the night. Kith-Kanan sighed. I must be getting desperate if I'm talking to birds, he concluded. After drawing his sword, he set off again, cutting new blazes as he hunted for the clearing where he had left Arcuballis. That way, at least he could avoid walking in circles.

He smote the nearest elm twice, chipping out palm-sized bits of bark. He was about to strike a third time when he noticed the shadow of his sword arm against the gray tree trunk. Shadow? In this well of ink? Kith-Kanan turned quickly, sword ready. Floating six feet off the ground, more than a dozen feet away, was a glowing mass the size of a wine barrel. He watched, half-anxious, half-curious, as the glowing light came toward him. It halted two feet from his face, and Kith-Kanan could clearly see what it was.

The cool yellow mass of light was a swarm of fireflies! The insects flew in circles around each other, creating a moving lamp for the lost prince. Kith-Kanan stared at them in shock. The glowing mass moved forward a few yards and halted. Kith-Kanan took a step toward them, and they moved on a bit farther.

"Are you leading me back to the clearing?" the prince asked in wonder. In response, the fireflies moved another yard forward. Kith-Kanan followed warily, but grateful for the soft sphere of light the fireflies cast around him.

In minutes, they had led him back to the clearing. The blasted tree was just as he remembered—but Arcuballis was gone. Kith-Kanan ran to the spot where the griffon had lain to rest. The leaves and moss still carried the impression of the heavy beast, but that was all. Kith-Kanan was astonished. He couldn't believe Arcuballis had flown off without him. Royal griffons were bonded to their riders, and no more loyal creatures existed on Krynn. There were tales of riders dying, and their griffons following them into death out of sheer grief. Someone or something must have taken Arcuballis. But who? Or what? How could such a powerful creature be subdued without sign of a struggle?

Sick in his heart, Kith-Kanan wandered to the lightning-seared tree. More bad news! His boar spear remained stuck in the trunk, but the sack containing his possessions was gone. Angrily, he reached up and wrenched the spear free. He stood in the clearing, gazing at the dark circle of trees. Now he was truly alone. He and Arcuballis had been companions for many years. More than a means of transport, the griffon was a trusted friend.

He sagged to the ground, feeling utterly wretched. What could he do? He couldn't even find his way around the forest in broad daylight. Kith-Kanan's eyes brimmed, but he steadfastly refused to weep like some abandoned child.

The fireflies remained by his head. They darted forward, then back, as if reminding him they were there.

"Get away!" he snarled as they swooped scant inches from

his nose. The swarm instantly dispersed. The fireflies flew off in all directions, their tiny lights flitting here and there, and then were gone.

*　*　*　*　*

"Won't you come in? You'll catch a chill."

Sithel drew a woolen mantle up over his shoulders. "I am warmly dressed," he said. His wife pulled a blanket off their bed, wrapped it around her own shoulders, and stepped out on the balcony with him.

Sithel's long white hair lifted off his neck as a chill wind passed over the palace tower. The private rooms of the speaker and his consort took up the penultimate floor of the palace's tower. Only the Tower of the Stars provided a higher vantage point in Silvanost.

"I felt a faint cry not long ago," Sithel said.

"Kith-Kanan?" The speaker nodded. "Do you think he is in danger?" asked Nirakina, drawing her blanket more closely about herself.

"I think he is unhappy. He must be very far away. The feeling was faint."

Nirakina looked up at her husband. "Call him, Sithel. Call him home."

"I will not. He offended me, and he offended the noble assembly. He broke one of our most sacred laws by drawing a weapon inside the Tower of the Stars."

"These things can be forgiven," she said quietly. "What else is it that makes it so hard for you to forgive him?"

Sithel stroked his wife's soft hair. "I might have done what he did, had my father given the woman I loved to another. But I don't approve of his deed, and I will not call him home. If I did, he wouldn't learn the discipline he must have. Let him stay away awhile. His life here has been too easy, and the outside world will teach him to be strong and patient."

"I'm afraid for him," Nirakina said. "The world beyond Silvanost is a deadly place."

Sithel raised her chin so their eyes met. "He has the blood of Silvanos in his veins. Kith-Kanan will survive, beloved, survive and prosper." Sithel looked away, out at the dark city. He held out his arm. "Come, let us go in."

They lay down together, as they had for more than a thousand years. But while Nirakina soon fell asleep, Sithel lay awake, worrying.

4

three days later

after three sunrises, kith-kanan was in despair. He'd lost his griffon and his spare clothing. When he tried his flint and striker again, he managed to start a small fire. It comforted him somewhat, but he found no food whatsoever to cook. On his third morning in the forest, he ran out of water, too.

There was no point remaining in the clearing, so he shouldered his spear and set out to find food and water. If the maps he remembered were correct, the Kharolis River lay to the west. It might be many miles, but at least it was something to aim for.

The only animals he saw on the way were more crows. The black birds stayed with him, flitting from tree to tree, punctuating their flight with short, sharp caws. The crows were Kith-

Kanan's only company, so he started talking to them. It helped keep his spirits up.

"I don't suppose you know where my griffon is?" he asked. Not surprisingly, the birds didn't answer, but continued to fly from tree to tree, keeping up with him.

The day dragged on and grew hotter. Even down in the eternal shade of the deep forest, Kith-Kanan sweltered, because no breeze stirred the air. The lay of the land grew rougher, too, with hills and gullies running north to south along his line of march. This encouraged him at first, because very often springs and brooks could be found at the bottom of ravines. But as he scrambled up one hill and down another, he found only moss and stones and fallen trees.

After skidding down a hillside into the nineteenth gully, Kith-Kanan paused to rest. He sat on a fallen tree, dropping the spear in front of him. He licked his dry lips again and fought down the rising feeling that he had made a grave mistake by running away. How could he have been so foolish to abandon his life of privilege for this? As soon as he asked himself the question the vision of Hermathya marrying his brother rose up in his mind, horribly vivid. Pain and loss welled up inside. To dispel the image, he stood up abruptly and started off again, shouldering his boar spear. He took two steps across the bottom of the ravine, and his feet sank an inch or so into mud, covered by a thin layer of dead leaves.

Where there's mud, there's water, he realized happily. Kith-Kanan went along the ravine to his right, looking for the water that must be there somewhere. He could see the ravine widen up ahead. Perhaps there was a pool, a pool of clear, sweet water. . . .

The ravine converged on several others, making a steep-sided bowl in the hills. Kith-Kanan slogged through the increasingly wet mud. He could smell water ahead. Then he could see it—a small pool, undisturbed by a ripple. The sight drew him like magic. The mud rose above his knees but he plunged on, right to the center of the pool. Cupping his hands, he filled them with water and raised them to his lips.

Immediately he spit the water out again. It tasted vile, like rotted leaves. Kith-Kanan stared down at his reflection in the water. His face twisted with frustrated rage. It was no use. He would just have to keep going.

His leg wouldn't come up out of the pool. He tried the other. It was also stuck. He strained so hard to pull them up, he nearly lost his balance. Arms flailing, Kith-Kanan twisted his hips from side to side, trying to work himself free. Instead he sank deeper into the mire. He glanced around quickly for a tree branch to grab, or a trailing vine. The nearest trees were ten feet away.

The mud was soon up to his waist. He began to sink even faster. "Help!" he cried desperately. "Is there anyone to hear?"

A flock of crows settled on the hillside facing Kith-Kanan. They watched with unnerving calm as he foundered in the killing mud.

You won't pick my eyes, he vowed silently. When the end comes, I'll duck under the mud before I let you black carrion-eaters pick me over!

"They're not really so bad once you get to know them," said a voice. Kith-Kanan jerked as if struck by lightning.

"Who's there?" he shouted looking around at the still trees. "Help!"

"I can help you. I don't know that I will." It was a high, childish voice, full of smugness.

In replying, the speaker had given himself away. Kith-Kanan spotted him, to his left, in a tree. Sitting comfortably on a thick branch, his back propped against the ancient oak trunk, was a slender young person, clad in mottled green-brown tunic and hose. A hood was drawn up over his head. The tan face that showed under the hood was painted with loops and lines, done in bright red and yellow pigment.

"Help me!" Kith-Kanan shouted. "I can reward you handsomely!"

"Really? What with?"

"Gold. Silver. Jewels." Anything, he vowed to himself. Anything in all of Krynn.

"What is gold?"

The mud was halfway up Kith-Kanan's chest. The pressure against his body made it difficult to draw breath. "You're mocking me," he gasped. "Please! I haven't much time!"

"No, you haven't," noted the hooded figure uninterestedly. "What else would you give me if I help you?"

"My bow! Would you like that?"

"I can pick that out of the mire once you're gone."

Blast the fellow! "I haven't anything else!" The cold muck was nearly at his shoulders. "Please, for the gods' sake, help me!"

The hooded figure rolled nimbly forward onto his feet. "I will help you, for the gods' sake. They often do things for me, so it seems only fair I do something for their sake now and again."

The stranger walked heel to toe along the branch until he was almost directly over Kith-Kanan. The prince's shoulders were in the mud, though he held his arms above his head to keep them free until the last possible second. The fellow in the tree unwrapped a belt from his waist. It had circled his slim body several times and, when unwound, was over ten feet long. Laying flat on the branch, he lowered the leather strap to Kith-Kanan. The prince caught it in his left hand.

"What are you waiting for? Pull me out!" Kith-Kanan ordered.

"If you can't pull yourself out, I cannot do it for you," his rescuer remarked. He looped the belt around the tree limb a few times and secured it with a knot. Then he lay on the branch, his head propped on one hand, awaiting the outcome.

Kith-Kanan grimaced and started to haul himself out by the strap. With much gasping and cursing, Kith-Kanan climbed out of the deadly mire and pulled himself up to the tree branch. He threw a leg over the branch and lay panting.

"Thank you," he finally said, a little sarcastically.

The young fellow had moved several feet back toward the oak tree and sat with his knees drawn up. "You are welcome," he replied. Behind the barbarous face paint, his eyes were brilliant green. He pushed back his hood, revealing himself to be a boy with a shock of bone-white hair. His high cheekbones and tapered ears bespoke his heritage. Kith-Kanan sat up slowly, astride the branch.

"You are Silvanesti," he said, startled.

"No, I am Mackeli."

Kith-Kanan shook his head. "You are of the race of the Silvanesti, as am I."

The elf boy stood on the branch. "I don't know what you mean. I am Mackeli."

The branch was too narrow for Kith-Kanan to stand on, so he inched his way forward to the tree trunk. The deadly mud below was hidden once more under its covering of water. He shuddered as he looked down upon it. "You see we are alike, don't you?"

Mackeli, hopping nimbly along the branch, glanced back at Kith-Kanan and said, "No. I don't see that we are alike." Exasperated and too tired to continue, Kith-Kanan gave up that line of conversation.

They climbed down to solid ground. Kith-Kanan followed the scampering boy slowly. Even so, he lost his grip on the trunk and fell the last few feet. He landed on his rear with a thud and groaned.

"You are clumsy," Mackeli observed.

"And you are rude. Do you know who I am?" the prince said haughtily.

"A clumsy outlander." The elf boy reached around his back and brought around a gourd bottle, laced tightly with deerskin. He poured a trickle of clear water into his open mouth. Kith-Kanan watched intently, his throat moving with imaginary swallows.

"May I—may I have some water?" he pleaded.

Mackeli shrugged and handed him the bottle. Kith-Kanan took the gourd in his muddy hands and drank greedily. He drained the bottle in three gulps.

"May the gods bless you," he said, handing the empty container to the boy.

Mackeli upended the bottle, saw that it was indeed completely dry, and gave Kith-Kanan a disgusted look.

"I haven't had any water in two days," Kith-Kanan explained. "Nor have I eaten. Do you have any food?"

"Not with me. There is some at home."

"Would you take me there?"

Mackeli raised his hood again, hiding his startlingly white hair. With it covered, he was superbly camouflaged, blending into the forest. "I don't know if that would be right. Ny might not like it."

"I appeal to you, friend. I am desperate. I have lost my steed and my way, and I cannot seem to find any game in this accursed forest. If you don't help me, I shall starve in this wilderness."

The elf boy laughed, a pleasant sound in the still air. "Yes, I heard there was an outlander blundering about in these parts. The corvae told me about you."

"Corvae?"

Mackeli pointed to the crows, still watching from the nearby hillside. "They know everything that happens in the forest. Sometimes, when something strange occurs, they tell me and Ny about it."

Kith-Kanan remembered the unnerving attention the crows had paid him. "Do you truly speak with birds?"

"Not only birds." Mackeli held up a hand and made a shrill cawing sound. One of the black birds flew over and alighted on his arm, like a falcon returning to its master.

"What do you think?" the boy asked the bird. "Can I trust him?" The crow cocked its head and uttered a single sharp screech. Mackeli frowned. The whorls above his eyes contracted as he knitted his brow together.

"He says you carry an object of power. He says you cut the trees with it."

Kith-Kanan looked down at his mud-caked scabbard. "My sword is not magical," he said. "It's just an ordinary blade. Here, you can hold it." He reversed his grip and held the pommel out to Mackeli. The elf boy reached out tentatively. The crows chorused as if in warning, but Mackeli ignored them. His small hand closed over the diamond-shaped pommel.

"There *is* power here," he said, snatching his hand back. "It smells like death!"

"Take it in your hands," Kith-Kanan urged. "It won't hurt you."

Mackeli grasped the handle in both hands and lifted it out of the prince's hand. "So heavy! What is it made of?" he grunted.

"Iron and brass." Mackeli's face showed that he did not know iron or brass, gold or silver. "Do you know what metals are, Mackeli?"

"No." He tried to swing Kith-Kanan's sword, but it was too heavy for him to control. The point dropped to the ground.

"I thought as much." Gently the prince took the sword back and slid it into its sheath. "Are you satisfied I'm not dangerous?"

Mackeli sniffed his hands and made a face. "I never said you were dangerous," he said airily. "Except maybe to yourself."

He set off and kept up a brisk pace, slipping in and out of the big trees. Mackeli never walked straight more than a few yards. He pushed off from the massive trunks, hopped over fallen limbs, and scampered like a squirrel. Kith-Kanan trudged along, weighed down by hunger and several pounds of stinking mud. Several times Mackeli had to double back to find the prince and guide him along. Kith-Kanan watched the boy's progress through the forest and felt like a tired old man. He'd thought he was such a fine ranger. This boy, who could be no more than sixty years old, made the foresters of Silvanost look like blundering drunkards.

The trek lasted hours and followed no discernible path. Kith-Kanan got the strong impression Mackeli didn't want him to know where they were going.

There were elves who dwelt entirely in the wilderness, the Kagonesti. They were given to the practice of painting their skin with strange patterns, as Mackeli did. But they were dark-skinned and dark-haired; this boy's features were pure Silvanesti. Kith-Kanan asked himself why a boy of the pure blood should be out here in the deep forest. Runaway? Member of a lost tribe? He finally imagined a secret forest hideaway, inhabited by outlaws driven from Silvanesti by his grandfather Silvanos's wars of unification. Not everyone had followed the great leader into peace and unity.

Suddenly Kith-Kanan realized that he no longer heard Mackeli's light tread in the carpet of fallen leaves. Halting, he looked ahead, then spied the boy a score of yards away, on his right. Mackeli was kneeling, his head bowed low. A hush had fallen over the already quiet forest.

As he observed the boy, wonderingly, a feeling of utter peace flowed over Kith-Kanan, a peace he'd never known before. All the troubles of recent days were washed away. Then Kith-Kanan turned and saw what had brought this tranquility, what had brought Mackeli to his knees.

Framed by ferns and tree trunks wrapped in flowering vines was a magnificent animal with a single white horn spiraling from its head. A unicorn—rarest of the rare, more scarce than the gods themselves. The unicorn was snowy white from her small, cloven hooves to the tips of her foaming mane. She radiated a soft light that seemed the essence of peace. Standing on a slight rise of ground, fifteen yards away, her eyes met Kith-Kanan's and touched his soul.

The elf prince sank to his knees. He knew he was being granted a rare privilege, a glimpse of a creature thought by many to be only legend.

"Rise, noble warrior." Kith-Kanan raised his head. "Rise, son of Sithel." The voice was deep and melodic. Mackeli, still bowed, gave no sign that he had heard.

Kith-Kanan stood slowly. "You know me, great one?"

"I heard of your coming." So enticing was the majestic creature, he wanted very badly to approach her, to see her more closely, to touch her. Before he could put the thought into action, she said sharply, "Stand where you are! It is not permitted for you to come too near." Kith-Kanan involuntarily took a step back. "Son of Sithel, you have been chosen for an important task. I brought you and the boy Mackeli together, so he could be your guide in the forest. He is a good boy, much skilled in the ways of beast and bird. He will serve you well."

"What do you wish me to do?" Kith-Kanan asked with sudden humility.

The unicorn tossed her head, sending pearly waves of mane cascading along her neck. "This deep forest is the oldest in the land. It was here that leaf and limb, animal and bird first lived. The spirits of the land are strong here, but they are vulnerable, too. For five thousand risings of the sun special ones have lived in the forest, protecting it from despoilers. Now a band of interlopers has come to this land, bringing fire and death with them. The spirits of the old forest cry out for help to me, and I have found you as the answer. You are the fated one, the one who carries iron. You must drive the despoilers out, son of Sithel."

At that moment, Kith-Kanan would have fought armies of dragons had the unicorn but asked. "Where will I find these interlopers?" he said, his hand coming to the pommel of his sword.

The unicorn took a step backward. "There is another, who lives with the boy. Together, you three shall cleanse the forest."

The unicorn took another step backward, and the forest itself seemed to close around her. Her alabaster aura shone briefly, and then she was gone, vanished into the secret depths of the greenwood.

After a few seconds Kith-Kanan recovered himself and ran to Mackeli. When he touched the boy's shoulder, Mackeli shook himself as if coming out of a trance.

"Where is the Forestmaster?" he whispered.

"Gone," said Kith-Kanan regretfully. "She spoke to me!"

A look of awe spread over Mackeli's sharp face. "You are greatly favored, outlander! What did the Forestmaster say?"

"You didn't hear?" Mackeli shook his head. Apparently the unicorn's message was for him alone. He wondered how much to tell the boy and finally decided to keep his own counsel.

"You are to take me to your camp," he said firmly. "I will need to learn everything you know about living in the woods."

"That I will gladly teach you," Mackeli said. He shivered with excitement. "In all my life, I have never seen the Forestmaster! There were times I sensed her passing, but never have I been so close!" He grasped Kith-Kanan's hand. "Come! Let's hurry. I can't wait to tell Ny about this!"

Kith-Kanan glanced at the spot where the Forestmaster had stood. Flowers had burst up where her hooves had touched the ground. Before he could react, Mackeli had jerked him into motion. At breakneck speed, the sure-footed boy drew Kith-Kanan deeper into the forest. The undergrowth got thicker, the trees larger and closer together, yet Mackeli never faltered. At times he and Kith-Kanan had to wriggle through gaps in the trees so tight and low they had to go on hands and knees.

Just before sunset, when the crickets had begun to sing, Mackeli reached a large clearing and stopped.

"We are home," said the boy.

Kith-Kanan went to the center of the open space, more than forty paces across, and turned a circle on one heel. "What home?" he asked.

Mackeli grinned, the effect weirdly emphasized by the red lines of paint dabbed on his cheeks. Jauntily he walked forward to the base of a truly massive oak. He grasped at a patch of relatively smooth bark and pulled. A door opened in the trunk of the tree, a door made from a curving section of oak bark. Beyond the open door was a dark space. Mackeli waved to Kith-Kanan.

"Come in. This is home," the boy said as he stepped into the hollow tree.

Kith-Kanan had to duck to clear the low opening. It smelled like wood and spice inside, pleasant but strange to his city-bred nose. It was so black he could barely make out the dim curve of the wooden walls. Of Mackeli he could see nothing.

And then the boy's hand touched his, and Kith-Kanan flinched like a frightened child. "Light a candle or a lamp, will you?" he said, embarrassed.

"Do what?"

"Light a—never mind. Can you make a fire, Mackeli? I can't see a thing in here."

"Only Ny can make fire."

"Is Ny here?"

"No. Gone hunting, I think."

Kith-Kanan groped his way along the wall. "Where does Ny build his fires?" he asked.

"Here." Mackeli led him to the center of the room. Kith-Kanan's foot bumped a low hearth made of rocks plastered together with mud. He squatted down and felt the ashes. Stone cold. No one had used it in quite a while.

"If you get me some kindling, I'll make a fire," he offered.

"Only Ny can make fire," Mackeli repeated doubtfully.

"Well, I may not be the stealthiest tracker or the best forester, but, by Astarin, I can make fire!"

They went back out and gathered armfuls of windblown twigs and small dead branches. A weak bit of light cut into the hollow tree through the open door as Kith-Kanan arranged the dry sticks in a cone over a heap of bark and shavings he had whittled off with his dagger. He took out his flint and striker from the pouch at his waist. Leaning on his knees on the stone hearth, he nicked the flint against the roughened iron striker. Sparks fell on the tinder, and he blew gently on them. In a few minutes he had a weak flicker of flame, and not long after that, a crackling fire.

"Well, boy, what do you think of that?" the prince asked Mackeli.

Instead of being impressed, Mackeli shook his head. "Ny's not going to like this."

Lightened by the fire, the interior of the hollow tree was finally visible to Kith-Kanan. The room was quite large, five paces wide, and a ladder led up through a hole to the upper branches and the outside of the tree. Smoke from the fire also went out through this hole. The walls were decorated with the skulls of animals—rabbit, squirrel, a fierce-looking boar with upthrust tusks, a magnificent eight-point buck, plus a host of bird skulls Kith-Kanan could not identify. Mackeli explained that whenever Ny killed an animal not killed before, the skull was cleaned and mounted on a peg on the wall. That way the spirit of the dead beast was propitiated, and the god of the forest, the Blue Phoenix, would grant success to future hunts.

"Which of these did you kill?" Kith-Kanan asked.

"It is not permitted for me to shed the blood of animals. That's Ny's work." The elf boy slipped back his hood. "I talk to the animals and listen to what they say. I do not shed their blood."

Kith-Kanan sat down on a pallet filled with moss. He was weary and dirty and very hungry. Mackeli fidgeted about, giving the prince frequent looks of displeasure. Eventually, Kith-Kanan asked Mackeli what was wrong.

"That's Ny's place. You must not sit there," the boy said irritatedly.

Kith-Kanan heaved himself off. "This Ny has more privileges than the Speaker of the Stars!" he said, exasperation clear in his voice. "May I sit here?" He indicated the floor of the hollow tree, which was covered with pine needles. Mackeli nodded.

Soon after that exchange, Kith-Kanan asked for something to eat. The elf boy scampered up the ladder and, leaning out to the center of the hollow space, pushed aside various gourds and skin bags that hung by thongs from the ceiling. He found the one he wanted and brought it down. Sitting cross-legged beside Kith-Kanan, Mackeli bade the prince hold out his hands. He did, and the boy filled them with roasted wild chestnuts, neatly peeled.

"Do you have any meat?" Kith-Kanan asked.

"Only Ny eats meat.

The prince was getting tired of the litany of things only Ny could do. Too tired, in fact, to dispute with the boy. Kith-Kanan ate chestnuts in silence; he was grateful for whatever he could get.

"Do you know," he said at last, "you've never asked me my name?"

Mackeli shrugged. "I didn't think you had one."

"Of course I have a name!" The elf boy rubbed his nose, getting yellow paint on his fingers. "My name is Kith," the prince said, since Mackeli obviously wasn't going to ask.

Mackeli shook more chestnuts into his paint-stained palm. "That's a funny name," he noted and popped a chestnut into his mouth.

5

fiVE WEEKS LATER

"Lady Nirakina, wife of the speaker," announced the maid-servant. Hermathya looked up from her mirror and nodded. The servant opened the door.

"Time is short, Lady," Nirakina cautioned as she entered.

"I know." Hermathya stood motionless in the center of a maelstrom of activity. Servants, dressmakers, and perfumers dodged and weaved around her, each trying to make final, finishing touches before the wedding ceremony began.

"You look beautiful," Nirakina said, and she was not merely being polite to her daughter-to-be. The finest creators of beauty in Silvanost had labored for weeks to make Hermathya's wedding gown and to compound the special oils and perfumes that would be hers alone.

The gown was in two parts. The first was an overdress in sheerest linen, too light to be worn alone and maintain modesty. Beneath this, Hermathya was wrapped in a single swath of golden cloth, many yards long. Six members of the Seamstress Guild had begun the winding Hermathya wore at her neck. A huge drum of gold was slowly wound around her, closely over her breasts and torso, more loosely over hips and legs. She had been forced to stand with her arms raised for two hours while the elf women worked.

Her feet were covered by sandals made from a single sheet of gold, beaten so thin it felt and flexed like the most supple leather. Golden laces crisscrossed her legs from ankle to knee, securing the sandals.

The elf's hair and face had been worked over, too. Gone were the maidenly braids framing her face. Her coppery hair was waved, then spread around her shoulders. In the elven custom, it was the husband who gave his new wife the first of the clasps with which she would ever after bind her tresses.

The bride's skin was smoothed of every roughness or blemish with aromatic oils and bone-thin soapstone. Her nails were polished and gilded, and her lips were painted golden. As befitted her noble rank and wealthy family, Hermathya wore sixteen bracelets—ten on her right arm and six on her left. These were all gifts from her parents, her siblings, and her female friends.

"That's enough," Nirakina said to the agitated servants. "Leave us." With much bowing and flourishing, the mob funneled out the doors of the Hall of Balif. "All of you," said the speaker's wife. The regular palace servants withdrew, closing the doors behind them.

"So much work for such a brief ceremony," Hermathya said. She turned ever so slowly, so as not to disturb her hair or gown. "Is this as great as your wedding, Lady?"

"Greater. Sithel and I were married during the Second Dragon War, when there was no time or gold to spare on fancy things. We didn't know then if we'd be alive in a year, much less know if we'd have an heir to see married."

"I have heard stories of those times. It must have been terrible."

"The times make those who live in them," Nirakina said

evenly. Her own dress, as the speaker's wife and mother of the groom, was quite conservative—white silk embroidered in silver and gold with the arms of House Royal. But with her honey-brown hair and liquid eyes she had a serene beauty all her own.

There was a loud, very masculine knock at the door. Nirakina said calmly, "Come in."

A splendidly attired warrior entered the hall. His armor was burnished until it was almost painful to look at. Scarlet plumes rose from his helmet. His scabbard was empty—the ceremony was one of peace, so no weapons were allowed—but his fierce martial splendor was no less imposing.

"My ladies," announced the warrior, "I am Kencathedrus, chosen by Lord Sithas to escort you to the Tower of the Stars."

"I know you, Kencathedrus," replied Nirakina. "You trained Prince Kith-Kanan in the warrior arts, did you not?"

"I did, my lady."

Hermathya was glad she was facing away. Mention of Kith-Kanan brought a rush of color to her powdered face. It wasn't so much that she still loved him, she decided. No, she was over that, if she ever *did* truly love him. But she knew that Kencathedrus, a mere soldier, was performing the duty Kith-Kanan should be doing. To escort the bride was a duty brother owed to brother.

Hermathya composed herself. This was the moment. She turned. "I am ready."

In the corridor outside the Hall of Balif an honor guard of twenty warriors was drawn up, and farther down the hall twenty young elf girls chosen from the families of the guild masters stood ready to precede the honor guard. And beyond them, filling the other end of the corridor, were twenty elf boys dressed in long, trailing white robes and carrying sistrums. The size of the escort took Hermathya back for a moment. She looked out at the sea of expectant faces. It was rather overwhelming. All these people, and thousands more outside, awaited her. She called upon the core of strength that had carried her through troubles before, put on her most serene expression, and held out her hand. Kencathedrus rested her hand on his armored forearm, and the procession to the Tower of the Stars began.

Nirakina walked three steps behind them, and after her the honor guard fell in with the clank and rattle of armor and metal sandals. The boys led the procession in slow step, banging their sistrums against their hands. To this steady rhythm the elf girls followed, strewing flower petals in the path of the bride.

Outside, the sun was high and bright, and every spire in Silvanost boasted a streaming banner. When Hermathya appeared on the steps of the Palace of Quinari, the assembled crowd let out a shout of greeting.

"What do I do?" Hermathya murmured. "Do I wave?"

"No, that would be vulgar. You must be above it all," said Nirakina softly.

A phalanx of pipers, clad in brilliant green, formed in front of the sistrum-bearing boys and played a bright fanfare. The music settled into a march as the procession wound around the Gardens of Astarin, following the circular road. According to ritual, the bride was first taken to the temple of Quenesti Pah, where she underwent a rite of purification. At the same time, the groom was receiving similar rites in the temple of E'li. Then the two came together before the speaker in the Tower of the Stars, where they exchanged golden rings shaped to resemble twining branches and where their joining was finally accomplished.

The sun shone down from a spring sky unsullied by a single cloud, and the marble buildings glowed in the midst of velvety green foliage. The crowd cheered mightily for the spectacle. Perhaps, Hermathya thought idly, in time they will cheer so for me. . . .

"Careful, Lady," warned Kencathedrus. The flower petals were being trodden to mush, and the road was getting a bit treacherous. Hermathya's golden sandals were stained with the crushed pulp. She lifted the hem of her diaphanous white gown out of the debris.

The squat, conical tower of the Temple of E'li appeared ahead on her right. Hermathya could see Sithas's guard of honor—at least a hundred warriors—drawn up on the steps. Just as her own attendants were bedecked in gold and white, so Sithas's attendants wore gold and green. She tried to keep her eyes straight ahead as they passed the temple, but she was drawn irresistibly to look in the open doors. It was dark inside the house of worship, and though she could see torches blazing on the wall, she could see neither Sithas nor anyone else within.

As the bride's entourage rounded the curve, the press of the crowd became greater and the cheering intensified. The shadow cast by the Tower of the Stars fell across the street. It was thought to be good luck to stand in the structure's shadow, so hundreds were crammed into the narrow space.

On a sudden impulse, Hermathya abandoned her distant, serene demeanor and smiled. The cheering increased. She raised her free hand and waved once to the people of Silvanost. A roar went up such as the city had never heard, a roar that excited her.

In the Temple of E'li, Sithas heard the roar. He was kneeling before the high priest, about to be anointed with sacred oils. He raised his head slightly and turned one ear toward the sound. The warrior who knelt behind him whispered, "Shall I see what is the matter, Lord?"

"No," replied Sithas levelly. "I believe the people have just met my bride."

*   *   *   *   *

The Temple of Quenesti Pah, goddess of health and fertility, was a light, airy vault with a roof of transparent tortoiseshell. There was no great central tower, as in most of the other temples. Instead, four thin spires rose from the corners of the roof, solid columns of rock that reached skyward. Though not as imposing as the House of E'li, or as somber as the Temple of Matheri, Hermathya thought the Temple of Quenesti Pah the prettiest building in Silvanost.

The pipers, sistrum players, and flower girls all turned aside and flanked the entrance to the temple. The honor guard halted at the foot of the steps.

Nirakina stepped up beside Hermathya. "If you have finished performing for the crowd, we will go in." In her tone could be detected a sharpness, and Hermathya hid a smile. Without replying, Hermathya gave the crowd one last wave before she entered the temple.

Nirakina watched her ascend the steps. She was really trying to get along with the girl, but every passing moment added to her irritation. For Sithas's sake, she wanted the marriage to be a success, but her overwhelming feeling was that Hermathya was a spoiled child.

Inside, the ritual was brief, consisting of little more than prayers and the washing of Hermathya's hands in scented water. Nirakina hovered over her, her distaste for the younger woman's behavior just barely concealed. But Hermathya had understood Nirakina's annoyance, and she found that she enjoyed it. It added to her sense of excitement.

The ritual done, the bride rose to her feet and thanked Miritelisina, the high priestess. Then, without waiting for Nirakina, she walked swiftly from the temple. The crowd was waiting breathlessly for her reappearance, and Hermathya did not disappoint them. A thunder of approval built from the back of the crowd, where the poorest elves stood. She flashed them a smile, then moved with quick grace down to Kencathedrus. Nirakina hurried after her, looking harassed and undignified.

The procession reformed, and the pipers played "Children of the Stars," the ancient tune that every elf knew from childhood. Even Hermathya was surprised, however, when the people began to sing along with the pipers.

She slowed her pace and gradually stopped. The procession strung out until the pipers in the fore realized that those behind had halted. The music swelled higher and louder until Hermathya felt that she was being lifted by it.

With little prelude, the bride sang. At her side, Kencathedrus looked at her in wonder. He glanced over his armored shoulder to Lady Nirakina, who stood silent and straight, arms held rigidly at her sides. Her voluminous sleeves covered her tightly clenched fists.

Some in the crowd ceased their own singing that they might hear the bride. But as the last verse of the song began, they all joined in; once more the sound threatened to raise the city from its foundations. When the last words of "Children of the Stars" faded in the throats of thousands, silence fell over Silvanost. The silence seemed more intense because of the tumult earlier. Everyone assembled in the street, every elf on rooftops and in tower windows had his or her eyes on Hermathya.

Casually the bride took her hand from Kencathedrus's arm and walked through the procession toward the Tower of the

Stars. The flower girls and sistrum-bearers parted in complete silence. Hermathya walked with calm grace through the ranks of the pipers. They stood aside, their silver flutes stilled. Up the steps of the Tower of the Stars she moved, appearing in the doorway alone.

Sithas stood in the center of the hall, waiting. With much less fanfare, he had come from the Temple of E'li with his retainers. Farther inside, Sithel sat on his throne. The golden mantle that lay on the speaker's shoulders spread out on the floor before him, trailing down the two steps of the dais, across the platform and down the seven steps to where Sithas stood. In front of the throne dais was an ornate and intricately carved golden tray on a silver stand. On the tray rested the golden rings the couple would exchange.

Hermathya came forward. The silence continued as if the entire elven nation was holding its breath. Part of the sensation was awe, and part was amazement. The bride of the speaker's heir had broken several traditions on her way to the tower. The royal family had always maintained an aloofness, an air of unbreachable dignity. Hermathya had flaunted herself before the crowd, yet the people of Silvanost seemed to love her for it.

Sithas wore ceremonial armor over his robe of gold. The skillfully worked breastplate and shoulder pieces were enameled in vibrant green. Though the cuirass bore the arms of Silvanos, Sithas had attached a small red rosebud to his sleeve, a small but potent symbol of his devotion to his patron deity.

When Hermathya drew near, he said teasingly, "Well, my dear, has the celebration ended?"

"No," she said, smiling sweetly. "It has just begun."

Hand in hand, they went before Sithel.

*　*　*　*　*

The feasting that began that evening continued for four days. It grew quite wearing on the newlyweds, and after the second day they retired to the fifth floor of the Quinari tower, which had been redecorated as their living quarters. At night, Hermathya and Sithas stood on their balcony overlooking the heart of the city and watched the revelries below.

"Do you suppose anyone remembers what the celebration is

for?" asked Hermathya.

"They don't tonight. They will tomorrow," Sithas said forcefully.

Yet he found it difficult being alone with her. She was so much a stranger to him—and always, in the back of his mind, he wondered if she compared him to Kith-Kanan. Though they were nearly identical in looks, Sithel's heir knew that he and his brother were worlds apart in temperament. Sithas grasped the balcony rail tightly. For the first time in his life he was at a loss as to what to do or say.

"Are you happy?" Hermathya asked after a long, mutual silence.

"I am content," he said carefully.

"Will you ever be happy?" she asked coyly.

Sithas turned to his wife and said, "I will endeavor to try."

"Do you miss Kith-Kanan?"

The calm golden eyes clouded for a moment. "Yes, I miss him. Do you, Lady?"

Hermathya touched the starjewel she wore pinned to the throat of her gown. Slowly she leaned against the prince and slipped an arm about his waist. "No, I don't miss him," she said a little too strongly.

6

the Same Day, In the Forest

Shorn of his armor and city-made clothes, Kith-Kanan padded through the forest in a close-fitting deerskin tunic and leggings such as Mackeli wore. He was trying to circle Mackeli's house without the boy hearing him.

"You're by the gray elm," Mackeli's voice sang out. And so Kith-Kanan was. Try as he might, he still made too much noise. The boy might keep his eyes closed so he wouldn't see the heat of Kith-Kanan's body, but Mackeli's keen ears were never fooled.

Kith-Kanan doubled back six feet and dropped down on his hands. There was no sound in the woods. Mackeli called, "You can't steal up on anyone by sitting still."

The prince stepped only on the tree roots that humped up

above the level of the fallen leaves. In this way he went ten paces without making a sound. Mackeli said nothing, and the prince grinned to himself. The boy couldn't hear him! At last.

He stepped far out from a root to a flat stone. The stone was tall enough to allow him to reach a low limb on a yew tree. As silently as possible, he pulled himself up into the yew tree, hugging the trunk. His green and brown tunic blended well with the lichen-spotted bark. A hood concealed his fair hair. Immobile, he waited. He'd surprise the boy this time!

Any second now, Mackeli would walk by and then he'd spring down on him. But something firm thumped against his hood. Kith-Kanan raised his eyes and saw Mackeli, clinging to the tree just three feet above him. He nearly fell off the branch, so great was his surprise.

"By the Dragonqueen!" he swore. "How did you get up there?"

"I climbed," said Mackeli smugly.

"But how? I never saw—"

"Walking on the roots was good, Kith, but you spent so much time watching your feet I was able to slip in front of you."

"But this tree! How did you know which one to climb?"

Mackeli shrugged his narrow shoulders. "I made it easy for you. I pushed the stone out far enough for you to step on and climbed up here to wait. You did the rest."

Kith-Kanan swung down to the ground. "I feel like a fool. Why, your average goblin is probably better in the woods than I am."

Mackeli let go of the tree and fell in a graceful arc. He caught the low branch with his fingertips to slow his descent. Knees bent, he landed beside Kith-Kanan.

"You are pretty clumsy," he said without malice. "But you don't smell as bad as a goblin."

"My thanks," said the prince sourly.

"It's really just a matter of breathing."

"Breathing? How?"

"You breathe like this." Mackeli threw back his shoulders and puffed out his thin chest. He inhaled and exhaled like a blacksmith's bellows. The sight was so absurd, Kith-Kanan had to smile. "Then you walk the way you breathe." The boy stomped about exaggeratedly, lifting his feet high and crashing them into the scattered leaves and twigs.

Kith-Kanan's smile flattened into a frown. "How do you breathe?" he asked.

Mackeli rooted about at the base of the tree until he found a cast-off feather. He lay on his back and placed it on his upper lip. So smoothly did the elf boy draw breath, the feather never wavered.

"Am I going to have to learn how to breathe?" Kith-Kanan demanded.

"It would be a good start," said Mackeli. He hopped to his feet. "We go home now."

Several days passed slowly for Kith-Kanan in the forest. Mackeli was a clever and engaging companion, but his diet of nuts, berries, and water did not agree with the elf prince's tastes. His belly, which was hardly ample to start with, shrank under the simple fare. Kith-Kanan longed for meat and nectar. Only Ny could get meat, the boy insisted. Yet there was no sign of the mysterious "Ny."

There was also no sign of the missing Arcuballis. Though Kith-Kanan prayed that somehow they could be reunited, he knew there was little hope for this. With no idea where the griffon had been taken and no way of finding out, the prince tried to accept that Arcuballis was gone forever. The griffon, a tangible link with his old life, was gone, but Kith-Kanan still had his memories.

These same memories returned to torment the prince in his dreams during those days. He heard once more his father announce Hermathya's betrothal to Sithas. He relived the ordeal in the Tower of the Stars, and, most terrible of all, he listened to Hermathya's calm acceptance of Sithas. Kith-Kanan filled his days talking with and learning from Mackeli, determined to build a new life away from Silvanost. Perhaps that life would be here, he decided, in the peace and solitude of the ancient forest.

One time Kith-Kanan asked Mackeli where he'd been born, where he'd come from.

"I have always been from here," Mackeli replied, waving absently at the trees.

"You were born here?"

"I have always *been* here," he replied stubbornly.

61

At that, Kith-Kanan gave up. Questions about the past stymied the boy almost as much as queries about the future. If he stuck to the present—and whatever they were doing at the moment—he could almost have a conversation with Mackeli.

In return for Mackeli's lessons in stealth and survival, Kith-Kanan regaled his young friend with tales of Silvanost, of the great wars against the dragons, and of the ways of city-bred elves.

Mackeli loved these stories, but more than anything metal fascinated him. He would sit cross-legged on the ground and hold some object of Kith-Kanan's—his helmet, a greave, a piece from his armor—and rub his small brown fingers against the cold surface again and again. He could not fathom how such hard material could be shaped so intricately. Kith-Kanan explained what he knew of smithy and foundry work. The idea that metal could be melted and poured absolutely astounded Mackeli.

"You put metal in the fire," he said, "and it doesn't burn? It gets soft and runny, like water?"

"Well, it's thicker than water."

"Then you take away the fire, and the metal gets hard again?" Kith-Kanan nodded. "You made that up!" Mackeli exclaimed. "Things put in the fire get burned."

"I swear by E'li, it is the truth."

Mackeli was too slight to handle the sword, but he was able to draw the bow well enough to shoot. He had an uncanny eye, and Kith-Kanan wished he would use some of that stealth to bring down a deer for dinner. But it was not to be; Mackeli didn't eat meat and he refused to shed blood for Kith-Kanan. Only Ny . . .

On a gray and rainy morning, Mackeli went out to gather nuts and roots. Kith-Kanan remained in the hollow tree, stoking the fire, polishing his sword and dagger. When the rain showed signs of letting up, he left his weapons below and climbed the ladder to the upper part of the oak tree. He stood on a branch thicker around than his waist and surveyed the rain-washed forest. Drops fell from the verdant leaves, and the air had a clean, fertile smell. Deeply the prince inhaled. He had found a small measure of peace here, and the meeting with the Forestmaster had foretold great adventure for his future.

Kith-Kanan went back down and immediately noticed that his sword and dagger were gone. His first thought was that Mackeli had come back and was playing a trick on him, but the prince saw no signs the boy had returned. He turned around and was going back up the tree when something heavy struck him from behind, in the middle of his back.

He crashed against the trunk, spun, and saw nothing. "Mackeli!" he cried. "This isn't funny!" Neither was the blow on the back of his head that followed. A weight bore Kith-Kanan to the ground. He rolled and felt arms and legs around him. Something black and shiny flashed by his nose. He knew the move of a stabbing attack, and he put out both hands to seize the attacker's wrist.

His assailant's face was little more than a whorl of painted lines and a pair of shadowed eyes. The flint knife wavered, and as Kith-Kanan backhanded the knife wielder, the painted face let out a gasp of pain. Kith-Kanan sat up, wrenched the knife out of its owner's grasp, and pinned his attacker to the ground with one knee.

"The kill is yours," said the attacker. His struggles faded, and he lay tense but passive under Kith-Kanan's weight.

Kith-Kanan threw the knife away and stood up. "Who are you?"

"The one who is here. Who are you?" the painted elf said sharply.

"I am Kith, formerly of Silvanost. Why did you attack me?"

"You are in my house."

Understanding quickly dawned. "Are you Ny?"

"The name of my birth was Anaya." There was cool assurance in the voice.

He frowned. "That sounds like a female name—"

Anaya got up and kept a discreet distance from Kith-Kanan. He realized she *was* a female elf of the Kagonesti race. Her black hair was cut close to her head, except in back, where she wore a long braid. Anaya was shorter than Kith-Kanan by a head, and much slimmer. Her green-dyed deerskin tunic ended at her hips, leaving her legs bare. Like her face, her legs were covered with painted lines and decorations.

Her dark, hazel eyes darted left and right. "Where is Mackeli?"

"Out gathering nuts, I think," he said, watching her keenly. "Why did you come here?"

"The Forestmaster sent me," the prince stated flatly.

In less time than it takes to tell, Anaya bolted from the clearing. She ran to an oak tree and, to Kith-Kanan's astonishment, ran right up the broad trunk. She caught an overhead limb and swung into the midst of the leaves. Gaping, he made a few flat-footed steps forward, but the wild elf was completely lost from view.

"Anaya! Come back! I am a friend! The Forestmaster—"

"I will ask the Master if it is so." Her clear, high voice came from somewhere above his line of sight. "If you speak the truth, I will return. If you say the Master's name in vain, I will call down the Black Crawlers on you."

"What?" Kith-Kanan spun around, looking up, trying to locate her. He could see nothing. "Who are the Black Crawlers?" But there was no answer, only the sighing of the wind through the leaves.

* * * * *

Night fell, and neither Mackeli nor Anaya had returned. Kith-Kanan began to fear that something might have happened to the boy. There were interlopers in the forest, the Forestmaster had said. Mackeli was clever, but he was innocent of the ways of ambush and murder. If the boy was in their hands . . . and Anaya. There was a strange creature! If he hadn't actually fought with her, felt the solidness of her flesh, he would have called her a wraith, a forest spirit. But the bruise on his jaw was undeniably real.

Growing tired of the closeness of the hollow tree, the prince cleared a spot in the leaves to build a fire outside. He scraped down to bare soil and laid some stones for a hearth. Soon he had a fine fire blazing. The smoke wafted into the darkness, and sparks floated up, winking off like dying stars.

Though it was summer, Kith-Kanan felt a chill. He held his hands out to the fire, warming them. Crickets whirred in the dark beyond the firelight. Cicadas stirred in the trees, and bats swooped into the clearing to catch them. Suddenly the prince felt as if he was in the center of a seething, crawling pot. His eyes flicked back and forth, following odd rustlings and scrapings in the dry leaves. Things fluttered overhead, slithered behind his back. He grasped the unburned end of a stick of wood and pulled it out of the fire. Dark things seemed to leap back into the shadows when Kith-Kanan brought the burning torch near.

He stood with his back to the fire, breathing hard. With the blazing brand before him like a noble blade, the elf kept the darkness at bay. Gradually the incessant activity lessened. By the time Solinari rose above the trees, all was still.

After throwing the stump of the burned limb back on the dying fire, Kith-Kanan sat down again and faced the red coals. Like a thousand lonely travelers before him, the prince whistled a tune to keep the loneliness away. It was a tune from his childhood—"Children of the Stars."

The chorus died when his lips went dry. He saw something that froze him completely. Between the black columns of two tree trunks were a pair of red staring eyes.

He tried to think what it could be. The possibilities were not good: wolf, bear, a tawny panther. The two eyes blinked and disappeared. Kith-Kanan jumped to his feet and snatched up a stone from the outside edge of his campfire. He hurled it at the spot where he'd last seen the eyes. The rock crashed into the underbrush. There was no other sound. Even the crickets had ceased their singing.

Then Kith-Kanan sensed he was being watched and turned to the right. The red eyes were back, creeping forward a foot or so off the ground, right toward him.

Darkness is the enemy, he suddenly realized. *Whatever I can see, I can fight.* Scooping up a double handful of dead leaves, he threw them on the embers of the fire. Flames blazed up. He immediately saw a long, lean body close to the ground. The advance of the red eyes stopped, and suddenly they rose from the ground.

It was Anaya.

"I have spoken with the Forestmaster," she said a little sulkily, her eyes glowing red in the light from the flames. "You said the truth." Anaya walked sideways a few steps, never taking her eyes off Kith-Kanan. Despite this good news, he felt that she was about to spring on him. She dropped down on her haunches and looked into the fire. The leaves were consumed, and their remains sank onto the heap of dully glowing ashes.

"It is wise you laid a fire," she said. "I called the Black Crawlers to watch over you while I spoke with the Forestmaster."

He straightened his shoulders with studied nonchalance. "Who are the Black Crawlers?"

"I will show you." Anaya picked up a dead dry branch and held it to the coals. It smoked heavily for an instant, then burst into flame. She carried the burning branch to the line of trees defining the clearing. Kith-Kanan lost his hard-won composure when Anaya showed him what was waiting beyond the light.

Every tree trunk, every branch, every square inch of ground was covered with black creeping things. Crickets, millipedes, leaf hoppers, spiders of every sort and size, earwigs, pill bugs, beetles up to the size of his fist, cockroaches, caterpillars, moths, flies of the largest sort, grasshoppers, cicadas with soft, pulpy bodies and gauzy wings . . . stretching as far as he could see, coating every surface. The horde was motionless, waiting.

Anaya returned to the fire. Kith-Kanan was white-faced with revulsion. "What sort of witch are you?" he gasped. "You command all these vermin?"

"I am no witch. This forest is my home, and I guard it closely. The Black Crawlers share the woodland with me. I gave them warning when I left you, and they gathered to keep you under watchful eyes."

"Now that you know who I am, you can send them away," he said.

"They have already departed. Could you not hear them go?" she scoffed.

"No, I couldn't." Kith-Kanan glanced around at the dark forest, blotting sweat from his face with his sleeve. He focussed his attention on the fascinating elf woman and blotted out the memory of the Crawlers. With her painted decorations, grime, and dyed deerskin, Kith-Kanan wasn't sure how old Anaya might be, or even what she really looked like. She perched on her haunches, balancing on her toes. Kith-Kanan fed some twigs to the fire, and the scene slowly lightened.

"The Forestmaster says you are here to drive away the intruders," Anaya said. "I have heard them, smelled them, seen the destruction they have caused. Though I have never doubted the word of the great unicorn, I do not see how you can drive anyone away. You are no ranger; you smell of a place where people are many and trees few."

Kith-Kanan was tired of the Kagonesti's casual rudeness. He excused it in Mackeli, who was only a boy, but it was too much coming from this wild woman.

"I am a prince of House Royal," he said proudly. "I am trained in the arts of the warrior. I don't know who or how many of these intruders there are, but I will do my best to find a way to get rid of them. You need not like me, Anaya, but you had better not insult me too often." He leaned back on his elbows. "After all, who wrestled whom to the ground?"

She poked the dancing bowl of flames. "I let you take my knife away," she said defensively.

Kith-Kanan sat up. "You what?"

"You seemed such a clumsy outlander, I did not think you were dangerous. I let you get the advantage to see what you would do. You could not have cut my throat with that flint blade. It was dull as a cow's tooth."

Despite his annoyance, Kith-Kanan found himself smiling. "You wanted to see if I was merciful, is that it?"

"That was my purpose," she said.

"So I guess I really am a slow, dumb outlander," he said.

"There is power in your limbs," she admitted, "but you fight like a falling stone."

"And I don't breathe properly either." Kith-Kanan was beginning to wonder how he had ever lived to the age of ninety, being so inept.

Mentioning breathing reminded the prince of Mackeli, and he told Anaya the boy still hadn't returned.

"Keli has stayed away longer than this before," she said, waving a hand dismissively.

Though still concerned, Kith-Kanan realized that Anaya knew Mackeli's ways far better than he did. The prince's stomach chose that moment to growl, and he rubbed it, his face coloring with embarrassment.

"You know, I am very hungry," he informed her.

Without a word, Anaya went inside the hollow oak. She returned a moment later with a section of smoked venison ribs wrapped in curled pieces of bark. Kith-Kanan shook his head;

he wondered where those had been hiding all these weeks.

Anaya dropped down by the fire, in her characteristic crouch, and slipped a slender flint blade out of her belt pouch. With deft, easy strokes, she cut the ribs apart and began eating.

"May I have some?" the prince inquired desperately. She promptly flung two ribs at him through the fire. Kith-Kanan knew nicety of manner was lost on the Kagonesti, and the sight of the meat made his mouth water. He picked up a rib from his lap and nibbled it. The meat was hard and tangy, but very good. While he nibbled, Anaya gnawed. She cleaned rib bones faster than anyone he'd ever seen.

"Thank you," he said earnestly.

"You should not thank me. Now that you have eaten my meat, it is for you to do as I say," she replied firmly.

"What are you talking about?" he said, frowning. "A prince of the Silvanesti serves no one but the speaker and the gods."

Anaya dropped the clean bones in the fire. "You are not in the Place of Spires any longer. This is the wildwood, and the first law here is, you eat what you take with your own hands. That makes you free. If you eat what others give you, you are not a free person; you are a mewling child who must be fed."

Kith-Kanan got stiffly to his feet. "I have sworn to help the Forestmaster, but by the blood of E'li, I'll not be anyone's servant! Especially not some dirty, painted savage!"

"Being a prince does not matter. The law will be done. Feed yourself, or obey me. Those are your choices," she said flatly.

Anaya walked to the tree. Kith-Kanan grabbed her by the arm and spun her around. "What have you done with my sword and dagger?" he demanded.

"Metal stinks." Anaya jerked her arm free. "It is not permitted for me to touch it. I wrapped a scrap of hide around your metal and carried it from my house. Do not bring it in again."

He opened his mouth to shout at her, to rail against her unjust treatment of him. But before he could, Anaya went inside the tree. Her voice floated out. "I sleep now. Put out the fire."

When the fire was cold and dead, the prince stood in the door of the tree. "Where do I sleep?" he asked sarcastically.

"Where you can fit," was Anaya's laconic reply. She was curled up by the wall, so Kith-Kanan lay down as far from her as he could, yet still be in the warmth of the tree. Thoughts raced through his head. How to find Arcuballis and get out of the forest. How to get away from Anaya. Where Mackeli was. Who the interlopers were—

"Don't think so loud," Anaya said irritatedly. "Go to sleep."

With a sigh, Kith-Kanan finally closed his eyes.

✿ 7 ✿

hIgh SummeR, yeAR of the hawk

Elves fRom all coRneRs of Silvanesti had come to Silvanost for Trial Days, that period every year when the Speaker of the Stars sat in judgment of disputes, heard the counsel of his nobles and clerics, and generally tried to resolve whatever problems faced his people.

A platform had been built on the steps of the Temple of E'li. Upon it, Sithel sat on a high, padded throne, under a shimmering white canopy. He could survey the entire square. Sithas stood behind him, watching and listening. Warriors of the royal guard kept the lines orderly as people made their way slowly up the line to their ruler. Trial Days were sometimes amusing, often irritating, and always, always lengthy.

Sithel was hearing a case where two fishers had disputed a

large carp, which hit both of their hooks at the same time. Both elves claimed the fish, which had been caught weeks before and allowed to rot while they debated its ownership.

Sithel announced his judgment. "I declare the fish to be worth two silver pieces. As you own it jointly, you will each pay the other one silver piece for permitting it to spoil."

The gaping fishers would have complained but Sithel forestalled them. "It is so ordered. Let it be done!" The trial scribe struck a bell, signaling the end of the case. The fishers bowed and withdrew.

Sithel stood up. The royal guards snapped to attention. "I will take a short rest," he announced. "In my absence, my son, Sithas, will render judgment."

The prince looked to his father in surprise. In a low voice he said, "Are you sure, Father?"

"Why not? It will give you a taste of the role."

The speaker went to the rear of the platform. He watched Sithas slowly seat himself in the chair of judgment. "Next case," declared his son ringingly.

Sithel ducked through a flap in the cloth wall. There he saw his wife, waiting at a small table laden with food and drink. Snowy white linen walled off this end of the platform on three sides. The rear was open to the temple. The formidable facade loomed over them, fluted columns and walls banded with deep blue, bright rose, and grassy green stone. The heat of midday was upon the city, but a breeze wafted through the canopied enclosure.

Nirakina stood and dismissed a serving boy who had been posted at the table. She poured her husband a tall goblet of nectar. Sithel picked a few grapes from a golden bowl and accepted the goblet.

"How is he doing?" Nirakina asked, gesturing to the front of the platform.

"Well enough. He must get used to rendering decisions." Sithel sipped the amber liquid. "Weren't you and Hermathya attending the debut of Elidan's epic song today?"

"Hermathya pleaded illness and the performance was postponed until tomorrow."

"What's wrong with her?" The speaker settled back in his chair.

Nirakina's face clouded. "She would rather visit the Market than remain in the palace. She is proud and willful, Sithel."

"She knows how to get attention, that's certain," her husband said, chuckling. "I hear the crowds follow her in the streets."

Nirakina nodded. "She throws coins and gems to them—just often enough for them to cheer her madly." She leaned forward and put her hand over his where it rested on the goblet. "Sithel, did we make the right choice? So much unhappiness has come about because of this girl. Do you think all will be well?"

Sithel released his grip on the cup and took his wife's hand. "I don't think any harm will come of Hermathya's follies, Kina. She's drunk with acclaim right now, but she will tire of it when she realizes how empty and fleeting the adulation of the mob is. She and Sithas should have children. That would slow her down, give her something else on which to concentrate."

Nirakina tried to smile, though she couldn't help but notice how the speaker had avoided mention of Kith-Kanan at all. Her husband had a strong will. His anger and disappointment were not easily overcome.

The sound of raised voices swelled over the square. Sithel ate a last handful of grapes. "Let's see what disturbs the people," he said.

He stepped around the curtain and walked to the front edge of the platform. The crowd, in its orderly lines, had parted down the center of the square. There, between two lines of soldiers, were twenty to thirty newcomers. They were injured. Some were being carried on litters, others wore blood-stained bandages. The injured elves, male and female, approached the foot of the speaker's platform slowly and painfully. Guards moved forward to keep them away, but Sithel ordered that they be allowed to come.

"Who are you?" he asked.

"Great speaker," said a tall elf at the head of the group. His face was sun-browned and his body muscled from outdoor work. His corn-colored hair was ragged and sooty, and a dirty bandage covered most of his right arm. "Great speaker, we are all that is left of the village of Trokali. We have come almost two hundred miles to tell you of our plight."

"What happened?"

"We were a peaceful village, great speaker. We tended our

72

trees and fields and traded with all who came to the market in the town square. But on the night of the last quarter of Lunitari, a band of brigands appeared in Trokali. They set fire to the houses, broke the limbs off our fruit trees, carried off our women and children—" Here the elf's voice broke. He paused a moment to master his emotions, then continued. "We are not fighters, great speaker, but the fathers and mothers of Trokali tried to defend what was ours. We had sticks and hoes against swords and arrows. These here," he waved a hand in the direction of the battered group behind him, "are all that live out of a village of two hundred."

Sithas left the platform and went down the temple steps until he was on the level with the tall elf from Trokali.

"What is your name?" Sithas demanded.

"Tamanier Ambrodel."

"Who were these brigands, Tamanier?"

The elf shook his head sadly. "I do not know, sir."

"They were humans!" cried an elf woman with a badly burned face. She pushed her way through the crowd. "I saw them!" she hissed. "They were humans. I saw the hair on their faces!"

"They weren't all human," Tamanier said sharply. He raised his wounded arm. "The one who cut me was Kagonesti."

"Kagonesti and humans in the same band?" Sithas said in consternation. Murmurs surged through the crowd. He turned to look up at his father.

Sithel held up his hands. The scribe had to strike his bell four times before the crowd was quiet. "This matter requires further attention!" he proclaimed. "My son will remain here for the trials, while I will conduct the people of Trokali to the Palace of Quinari, where each shall give testimony."

Sithas bowed deeply to his father as an escort of twelve warriors formed in the square to convey the survivors of Trokali to the palace. The lame and sick made it a slow and difficult procession, but Tamanier Ambrodel led his people with great dignity.

Sithel descended the steps of the Temple of E'li, with Nirakina by his side. Courtiers scrambled to keep pace with the speaker's quick stride. The murmuring in the square grew as the people of Trokali trailed after.

Nirakina glanced back over her shoulder at the crowd. "Do you think there will be trouble?" she asked.

"There is already trouble. Now we must see what can be done to remedy it," Sithel answered tersely.

In short order they entered the plaza before the palace. Guards at the doors, responding to the speaker's brief commands, summoned help. Servants flooded out of the palace to aid the injured elves. Nirakina directed them and saw to the distribution of food and water.

Out of deference to Tamanier's weakened condition, Sithel took him no farther than the south portico. He bade Tamanier sit, overlooking the protocol that required commoners to stand in the presence of the speaker. The tall elf eased himself into a finely carved stone chair. He exhaled loudly with relief.

"Tell me about the brigands," Sithel commanded.

"There were thirty or forty of them, Highness," Tamanier said, swallowing hard. "They came on horseback. Hardlooking, they were. The humans wore mail and carried long swords."

"And the Kagonesti?"

"They were poor-looking, ragged and dirty. They carried off our women and children . . ." Tamanier covered his face with his hands.

"I know it is difficult," Sithel said calmly. "But I must know. Go on."

"Yes, Highness." Tamanier dropped his hands, but they shook until he clenched them in his lap. A quaver had crept into his voice. "The humans set fire to the houses and chased off all our livestock. It was also the humans who threw ropes over our trees and tore off their branches. Our orchards are ruined, completely ruined."

"Are you sure about that? The humans despoiled the trees?"

"I am certain, great speaker."

Sithel walked down the cool, airy portico, hands clasped behind his back. Passing Tamanier, he noticed the thin gold band the elf wore around his neck.

"Is that real gold?" he asked abruptly.

Tamanier fingered the band. "It is, Highness. It was a gift from my wife's family."

"And the brigands didn't take it from you?"

Realization slowly came to Tamanier. "Why, no. They never touched it. Come to think of it, great speaker, no one was robbed. The bandits burned houses and broke down our trees, but they didn't plunder us at all!" He scratched his dirty cheek. "Why would they do that, Highness?"

Sithel tapped two fingers against his chin thoughtfully. "The only thing I can think of is they didn't care about your gold. They were after something more important." Tamanier watched him expectantly, but the speaker didn't elaborate. He rang for a servant. When one appeared he told him to take care of Tamanier. "We will talk again," he assured the tall elf. "In the meantime, do not speak of this with anyone, not even your wife."

Tamanier stood, leaning crookedly, favoring his wounded side. "My wife was killed," he said stiffly.

Sithel watched him go. An honorable fellow, he decided. He would do well to keep an eye on Tamanier Ambrodel. The Speaker of the Stars could always use such an honorable man at court.

He entered the palace through a side door. A steady stream of servants trooped by, carrying buckets and soiled towels. Healers, who were clerics of the goddess Quenesti Pah, had arrived to tend the injured. Sithel looked over the bustle of activity. Trokali was two hundred miles from Silvanost. No human raiders had ever penetrated so far. And in the company of Kagonesti elves. . . .

The Speaker of the Stars shook his head worriedly.

* * * * *

After finishing the day's trials, Sithas dismissed the court. Though he had listened to each case fairly, he could not keep his thoughts away from the attack on the village of Trokali. When he returned to his rooms in the palace, everyone, from his mother to the humblest servant, was talking about the raid and its portent.

Hermathya waited for him in their room. No sooner had he entered, than she jumped to her feet and exclaimed, "Did you hear about the raid?"

"I did," Sithas said with deliberate nonchalance, shrugging

off his dusty outer robe. He poured cool water into a basin and washed his hands and face.

"What's to be done?" she prodded.

"Done? I hardly think that's our concern. The speaker will deal with the problem."

"Why do you not do something yourself?" Hermathya demanded, crossing the room. Her scarlet gown showed off the milky paleness of her skin. Her eyes flashed as she spoke. "The entire nation would unite behind the one who would put down the insolent humans."

"The 'one'? Not the speaker?" asked Sithas blandly.

"The speaker is old," she said, waving a dismissive hand. "Old people are beset with fears."

Dropping the towel he'd used to dry his hands, Sithas caught Hermathya's wrist and pulled her close. Her eyes widened, but she didn't shrink back. Sithas's eyes bored into hers.

"What you say smacks of disloyalty," he rumbled icily.

"You want what is best for the nation, don't you?" she replied, leaning into him. "If these attacks continue, all the settlers to the west will flee back to the city, as did the elves of Trokali. The humans of Ergoth will settle our land with their own people. Is that good for Silvanesti?"

Sithas's face hardened at the thought of humans encroaching on their ancient land. "No," he said firmly.

Hermathya put her free hand on his arm. "How then is it disloyal to want to end these outrages?"

"I am not the Speaker of the Stars!"

Her eyes were the deep blue of the sky at dusk as Hermathya moved to kiss her husband. "Not yet," she whispered, and her breath was sweet and warm on his face. "Not yet."

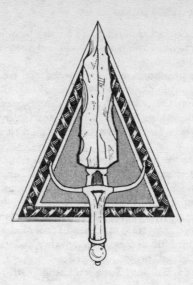

ᨓ 8 ᨓ

late Spring, In the forest

Mackeli had been gone three days when Anaya showed Kith-Kanan where she had secreted his sword and dagger. There could be no question now that something had happened to him and that they had to go to his rescue.

"There is your metal," she said. "Take it up. You may have need of it."

He brushed the dead leaves off the slim straight blade of his sword and wiped it with an oily cloth. It slid home in its scabbard with only a faint hiss. Anaya kept back when he held the weapons. She regarded the iron blades with loathing, as if they were the stinking carcasses of long dead animals.

"Mackeli's been gone so long, I hope we can pick up his trail," Kith-Kanan said. His eyes searched the huge trees.

"As long as Mackeli lives, I will always be able to find him," declared Anaya, "There is a bond between us. He is my brother."

With this pronouncement she turned and went back to the hollow tree. Kith-Kanan followed her. What did she mean—brother? Were the two siblings? He'd wondered at their relationship, but certainly hadn't noticed any family resemblance. Anaya was even less talkative on the subject than Mackeli had been.

He went to the door of the tree and looked in. Squatting before a piece of shiny mica, Anaya was painting her face. She had wiped her cheeks clean—relatively clean, anyway—with a wad of damp green leaves and now was applying paint made from berries and nut shells. Her brush was a new twig, the end of which she'd chewed to make it soft and pliable. Anaya went from one gourd full of pigment to another, painting zigzag lines on her face in red, brown, and yellow.

"What are you doing? Time is wasting." Kith-Kanan said impatiently.

Anaya drew three converging lines on her chin, like an arrowhead in red. Her dark hazel eyes were hard as she said, "Go outside and wait for me."

Kith-Kanan felt anger rising at her casual tone of command. She ordered him about like a servant, but there was nothing for him to do but stew. When Anaya finally emerged, they plunged into the deep shade of the woods. Kith-Kanan found his anger at her dissolving as he watched her move gracefully through the wood. She never disturbed a leaf or twig, moving, as Mackeli had said, like smoke.

They finally paused to rest, and Kith-Kanan sat on a log to catch his breath. He looked at Anaya as she stood poised, one foot atop the fallen log. She wasn't even breathing heavily. She was a muscular, brown-skinned, painted Kagonesti—quite savage by Silvanesti standards—but she was also practical and wise in the ways of the forest. Their worlds were so different as to be hostile to each other, but he felt at that moment a sense of security. He was not so alone as he had believed.

"Why do you look at me that way?" Anaya asked, frowning.

"I was just thinking how much better it would be for us to be friends, instead of enemies," said Kith-Kanan sincerely.

It was her turn to give him a strange look. He laughed and asked, "Now why are you looking at me like that?"

"I know the word, but I've never had a friend before," Anaya said.

*   *   *   *   *

Kith-Kanan would not have believed it, but the place Anaya led him through was even thicker with trees than any part of the forest he'd seen so far. They were not the giants of the old forest where she lived, but of a size he was more accustomed to seeing. They grew so close together, however, that it soon became impossible for him to walk at all.

Anaya grasped an oak tree trunk with her bare hands and feet and started up it like a squirrel. Kith-Kanan gaped at the ease with which she scaled the tree. The leaves closed around her.

"Are you coming?" she called down.

"I can't climb like that!" he protested.

"Wait then." He saw a flash of her red leg paint as she sprang from an oak branch to a nearby elm. The gap between branches was more than six feet, yet Anaya launched herself without a moment's hesitation. A few seconds later she was back, flitting from tree to tree with the ease of a bird. A twined strand of creeper, as thick as the prince's two thumbs, fell from the oak leaves and landed at his feet. This was more to his liking. Kith-Kanan spat on his palms and hauled himself up, hand over hand. He braced his feet against the tree trunk and soon found himself perched on an oak limb thirty feet from the forest floor.

"Whew!" he said, grinning. "A good climb!" Anaya was patently not impressed. After all, she had made the same climb with no vine at all. Kith-Kanan hauled up the creeper, coiling it carefully around his waist.

"It will be faster to stay in the treetops from now on," Anaya advised.

"How can you tell this is the way Mackeli went?"

She gathered herself to leap. "I smell him. This way."

Anaya sprang across to the elm. Kith-Kanan went more slowly, slipping a good deal on the round surface of the tree limb. Anaya waited for him to catch up, which he did by grasping an overhead branch and swinging over the gap. A dizzy glimpse of the ground flashed beneath his feet, and then Kith-Kanan's leg hooked around the elm. He let go of the oak branch, swung upside-down by one leg, and gradually worked his way onto the elm.

"This is going to take a long time," he admitted, panting for breath.

They continued on high in the treetops for most of the day. Though his hands were by no means soft, accustomed as they were to swordplay and his griffon's reins, Kith-Kanan's palms became scraped and sore from grasping and swinging on the rough-barked branches. His feet slipped so often that he finally removed his thick-strapped sandals and went barefoot like Anaya. His feet were soon as tender as his hands, but he didn't slip again.

Even at the slow pace Kith-Kanan set, they covered many miles on their lofty road. Well past noon, Anaya called for a rest. They wedged themselves high in a carpeen tree. She showed him how to find the elusive fruit of the carpeen, yellow and pearlike, hidden by a tightly growing roll of leaves. The soft white meat of the carpeen not only sated their hunger, it was thirst-quenching, too.

"Do you think Mackeli is all right?" Kith-Kanan asked, the worry clear in his voice.

Anaya finished her fruit and dropped the core to the ground. "He is alive," she stated flatly.

Kith-Kanan dropped his own fruit core and asked, "How can you be certain?"

Shifting around the prince with careless ease, Anaya slid from her perch and came down astride the limb where he sat. She took his scraped hand and held his fingertips to her throat.

"Do you feel the beat of my heart?" she asked him.

"Yes." It was strong and slow.

She pushed his hand away. "And now?"

"Of course not. I'm no longer touching you," he replied.

"Yet you see me and hear me, without touching me."

"That's different."

She raised her eyebrows. "Is it? If I tell you I can feel Mackeli's heart beating from far off, do you believe me?"

"I do," said Kith-Kanan. "I've seen that you have many wonderful talents."

"No!" Anaya swept a hand through the empty air. "I am nothing but what the forest has made me. As I am, so you could be!"

She took his hand again, holding his fingertips against the softly pulsing vein in her neck. Anaya looked directly in his eyes. "Show me the rhythm of my heart," she said.

Kith-Kanan tapped a finger of his other hand against his leg. "Yes," she coaxed. "You have it. Continue."

Her gaze held his. It was true—between them he felt a connection. Not a physical bond, like the grasp of a hand, but a more subtle connection—like the bond he knew stretched between himself and Sithas. Even when they were not touching and were many miles apart he could sense the life force of Sithas. And now, between Anaya's eyes and his, Kith-Kanan felt the steady surge of her pulse, beating, beating . . .

"Look at your hands," urged Anaya.

His left was still tapping out the rhythm on his leg. His right lay palm up on the tree limb. He wasn't touching her throat any longer.

"Do you still feel the pulse?" she asked.

He nodded. Even as he felt the surging of his own heart, he could feel hers, too. It was slower, steadier. Kith-Kanan looked with shock at his idle hand. "That's impossible!" he exclaimed. No sooner had he said this than the sensation of her heartbeat left his fingertips.

Anaya shook her head. "You don't want to learn," she said in disgust. She stood up and stepped from the carpeen tree to the neighboring oak. "It's time to move on. It will be dark before long, and you aren't skilled enough to treewalk by night."

This was certainly true, so Kith-Kanan did not protest. He watched the wiry Anaya wend her way through the web of branches, but the meaning of her lesson was still sinking in. What did it mean that he had been able to keep Anaya's pulse? He still felt the pain of his separation from Hermathya, a hard, cold lump in his chest, but when he closed his eyes and thought of Hermathya for a moment—a tall, flame-haired elf woman with eyes of deepest blue—he only frowned in concentration, for there was nothing, no bond, however slight, that connected him with his lost love. He could not know if she was alive or dead. Sadness touched Kith-Kanan's heart, but there was no time for self-pity now. He opened his eyes and moved quickly to where Anaya had stopped up ahead.

She was staring at a large crow perched on a limb near her head. When the crow spied Kith-Kanan, it abruptly flew away. Anaya's shoulders drooped.

"The corvae have not seen Mackeli since four days past," she explained. "But they have seen something else—humans."

"Humans? In the wildwood?"

Anaya nodded. She lowered herself to a spindly limb and furrowed her brow in thought. "I did not smell them sooner because the metal you carry stinks in my nose too much. The corvae say there's a small band of humans farther to the west. They're cutting down the trees, and they have some sort of flying beast, of a kind the corvae have never seen."

"Arcuballis! That's my griffon! The humans must have captured it," he said. In fact, he couldn't imagine how; as far as he could determine they were miles from the spot where he'd first landed, and it would have been very difficult for strangers, especially humans, to handle the spirited Arcuballis.

"How many humans are there?" Kith-Kanan inquired.

Anaya gave him a disdainful look. "Corvae can't count," she stated contemptuously.

They started off again as twilight was falling. For a brief time it actually brightened in the trees, as the sinking sun lanced in from the side. Anaya found a particularly tall maple and climbed up. The majestic tree rose well above its neighbors, and its thick limbs grew in an easy step pattern around the massive trunk. Kith-Kanan had no trouble keeping up with the Kagonesti in the vertical climb.

At the top of the tree Anaya stopped, one arm hooked around the gnarled peak of the maple. Kith-Kanan worked his way around beside her. The maple's pinnacle swayed under his additional weight, but the view was so breathtaking he didn't mind the motion.

As far as the eye could see, there was nothing but the green tops of trees. The horizon to the west was darkening from pink to flame red. Kith-Kanan was enchanted. Though he had often seen great vistas from the back of Arcuballis, his appreciation for such sights had been increased by the weeks he'd spent in this forest, where a glimpse of sky was a rare treat.

Anaya was not enraptured. She narrowed her sharp eyes and said, "There they are."

"Who?"

"The intruders. Do you not see the smoke?"

Kith-Kanan stared in the direction she pointed. To the north, a faint smudge of gray marred the sky's royal blue. Even as he stared at it, Kith-Kanan wasn't sure the smoke was really there. He blinked several times.

"They are burning the trees," Anaya said grimly. "Savages!"

The prince refrained from saying that to most of the civilized people of Krynn, it was she who was the savage. Instead he asked, "Which way to Mackeli?"

"Toward the smoke," she said. "The humans have taken him after all. I will see them bleed!"

Though Kith-Kanan was surprised at the depth of her feeling, he had no doubt she meant what she said.

They stayed in the treetops until the prince had begun to miss his handholds and then nearly fell forty feet to the ground. It was too dark to continue aloft, so Anaya and Kith-Kanan descended to the forest floor once more. They walked perhaps a mile in silence, Anaya gliding through the black tree trunks like a runaway shadow. Kith-Kanan felt the tension rising. He had never fought humans—he'd only met a few of them in Silvanost, and all of them were aristocrats. For that matter, he'd never fought anyone for real, in a fight where death was the likely outcome. He wondered if he could do it, actually thrust his sword through someone's body, or use the edge to cut them. . . . He reminded himself that these humans were holding Mackeli prisoner, and probably his royal griffon, too.

Anaya froze, silhouetted between two large trees. Her hand was out stiffly behind her, a signal for Kith-Kanan to halt. He did and heard what had stopped her. The tinny sound of a flute drifted through the forest, borne along by the smells of wood smoke and roasting meat.

When he looked toward Anaya she'd vanished. He waited. What was he supposed to do? Kith-Kanan shook himself mentally. You, a prince of House Royal, wanting directions from a Kagonesti savage! You are a warrior—do your duty!

He charged through the underbrush. At the first gleam of a campfire, Kith-Kanan drew his sword. Another twenty steps, and he burst into a clearing hewn from the primeval woodland. A large campfire, almost a bonfire, blazed in the center of the clearing. A dozen ruddy faces—thickly fleshed human faces, with their low foreheads, broad cheeks, and wide jaws—turned toward the elf prince. Some had hair growing on their faces. All stared at him in utter astonishment.

One of the humans, with pale brown hair on his face, stood up. "Terrible spirit, do not harm us!" he intoned. "Peace be with you!"

Kith-Kanan relaxed. These weren't desperate brigands. They were ordinary men and, by the looks of their equipment, woodcutters. He dropped his sword point and stepped into the firelight.

"It's one of them!" declared another human. "The Elder Folk!"

"Who are you?" demanded Kith-Kanan.

"Essric's company of woodmen. I am Essric," said the brown-haired human.

Kith-Kanan surveyed the clearing. Over thirty large trees had been felled in this one place, and he could see a path had been cut through the forest. The very biggest trees were trimmed of their branches and were being split into halves and quarters with wedges and mallets. Slightly smaller trees were being dragged away. Kith-Kanan saw a rough pen full of broad-backed oxen.

"This is Silvanesti land," he said. "By whose grant do you cut down trees that belong to the Speaker of the Stars?"

Essric looked to his men, who had nothing to tell him. He scratched his brown beard ruefully. "My lord, we were brought hither and landed on the south coast of this country by ships commanded by Lord Ragnarius of Ergoth. It is Lord Ragnarius's pleasure that we fell as many trees as his ships can carry home. We didn't know anyone owned these trees."

Just then, an eerie howl rippled across the fire-lit clearing. The humans all stood up, reaching for axes and staves. Kith-Kanan smiled to himself. Anaya was putting a scare into the men.

A clean-shaven man to Essric's left, who held a broadaxe in

his meaty hands, suddenly let out a cry and staggered backward, almost falling in the fire. Instead, he dropped into the arms of his comrades.

"Forest spirits are attacking!" Kith-Kanan shouted. His declaration was punctuated by a hair-raising screech from the black trees. He had to struggle to keep from laughing as the twelve humans were driven from their fire by a barrage of sooty stones. One connected with the back of one man's head, stretching him out flat. Panic-stricken, the others didn't stop to help him, but fled pell-mell past the ox pen. Without torches to light their way, they stumbled and fell over stumps and broken branches. Within minutes, no one was left in the clearing but Kith-Kanan and the prone woodcutter.

Anaya came striding into the circle of light. Kith-Kanan grinned at her and held up a hand in greeting. She stalked past him to where the human lay. The flint knife was in her hand.

She rolled the unconscious human over. He was fairly young and had a red mustache. A thick gold ring gleamed from one earlobe. That, and the cut of his pants, told Kith-Kanan that the man had been a sailor at one time.

Anaya put a knee on the man's chest. The human opened his eyes and saw a wildly painted creature, serrated flint knife in hand, kneeling on him. The creature's face stared down with a ferocious grimace twisting its painted designs. The man's eyes widened in terror, showing much white. He tried to raise an arm toward off Anaya, but Kith-Kanan was holding his wrists.

"Shall I cut out your eyes?" Anaya said coldly. "They would make fine decorations for my home."

"No! No! Spare me!" gibbered the man.

"Then tell us what we want to know," Kith-Kanan warned. "There was a white-haired elf boy here, yes?"

"Yes, wonderful lord!"

"And a griffon—a flying beast with an eagle's forepart and a lion's hindquarters?"

"Yes, yes!"

"What happened to them?"

"They were taken away by Voltorno," the man moaned.

"Who's Voltorno?" asked Kith-Kanan.

"A soldier. A terrible, cruel man. Lord Ragnarius sent him with us—"

"Why isn't he here now?" Anaya hissed, pushing the ragged edge of her knife against his throat.

"He—He decided to take the elf boy and the beast back to Lord Ragnarius's ship."

Anaya and Kith-Kanan exchanged looks. "How long ago did this Voltorno leave?" persisted Kith-Kanan.

"This morning," the unfortunate sailor gasped.

"And how many are there in his party?"

"Ten. S-Six men-at-arms and four archers."

Kith-Kanan stood up, releasing the man's hands. "Let him up."

"No," disagreed Anaya. "He must die."

"That is not the way! If you kill him, how will you be any different from the men who hold Mackeli captive? You cannot be the same as those you fight and have any honor. You must be better."

"Better?" she hissed, looking up at the prince. "Anything is better than tree-killing scum!"

"He is not responsible," Kith-Kanan insisted. "He was ordered—"

"Whose hand held the axe?" Anaya interrupted.

Taking advantage of their argument, the sailor shoved Anaya off and scrambled to his feet. He ran after his comrades, bleating for help.

"Now you see! You let him get away," Anaya said. She gathered herself to give chase, but Kith-Kanan told her, "Forget those humans! Mackeli is more important. We'll have to catch up with them before they reach the coast." Anaya sullenly did not reply. "Listen to me! We're going to need all your talents. Call the corvae, the Black Crawlers, everything. Have them find the humans and try to delay them long enough so that we can catch up."

She pushed him aside and stepped away. The big fire was dying, and the hacked out clearing was sinking into darkness. Now and then an ox grunted from the makeshift pen.

Anaya moved to the felled trees. She put a gentle hand on the trunk of one huge oak. "Why do they do it?" she asked mournfully. "Why do they cut down the trees? Can't they hear the fabric of the forest split open each time a tree falls?" Her eyes gleamed with unshed tears. "There are spirits in the wildwood,

spirits in the trees. They have murdered them with their metal."
Her haunted eyes looked up at the prince.

Kith-Kanan put a hand on her shoulder. "There's much to be
done. We must go." Anaya drew a shuddering breath. After
giving the tree a last gentle touch, she stooped to gather up her
throwing stones.

9

late Summer

Summer was fading. The harvests were coming in, and the markets of Silvanost were full of the fruits of the soil. Market week always brought a great influx of visitors to the city, not all of them Silvanesti. From the forests to the south and the plains to the west came the swarthy, painted Kagonesti. Up the Thon-Thalas came thick-walled boats from the dwarven kingdom, tall-masted deep-sea vessels from the human realms in the far West. All these ascended the river to Fallan Island where Silvanost lay. It was an exciting time, full of strange sights, sounds, and smells. Exciting, that is, for the travelers. For the Silvanesti, who regarded these races flooding their land with distaste and distrust, it was a trying time.

Sithel sat on his throne in the Tower of the Stars, weary but attentive as clerics and nobles filed up to him to voice their complaints. His duties did not allow him respite from the incessant arguing and pleading.

"Great Sithel, what is to be done?" asked Firincalos, high priest of E'li. "The barbarians come to us daily, asking to worship in our temple. We turn them away and they grow angry, and the next day a new batch of hairy-faced savages appears, asking the same privilege."

"The humans and dwarves are not the worst of it," countered Zertinfinas, of the Temple of Matheri. "The Kagonesti deem themselves our equals and cannot be put off from entering the sacred precincts with filthy hands and feet, and noxious sigils painted on their faces. Why, yesterday, some wild elves roughed up my assistant and spilled the sacred rosewater in the outer sanctum."

"What would you have me do?" Sithel asked. "Place soldiers around all the temples? There are not enough royal guardsmen in House Protector to do that—not to mention that most of them are sons or grandsons of Kagonesti themselves."

"Perhaps an edict, read in the Market, will convince the outsiders not to attempt to force their way into our holy places," Firincalos noted. A murmur of approval ran through the assembly.

"All very well for you," said Miritelisina, high priestess of Quenesti Pah. "How can we who serve the goddess of healing turn away eager supplicants? It is part of our trust to admit the sick and injured. Can we discriminate between Silvanesti and Kagonesti, human, dwarf, and kender?"

"Yes. You must," declared a voice silent until now.

All heads turned to the speaker's left, where Sithas had been standing. He had been listening to the different factions present their views. A long time he'd been listening, and now he felt he must speak. The prince stepped down to floor level, with the assembled clerics, and faced his father.

"It is vital that the purity of our temples and our city be preserved," he said with fervor. "We, the oldest and wisest race of Krynn, the longest lived, the most blessed, must keep ourselves above the hordes of lesser peoples who flood in, trying to partake of our grace and culture." He lifted his hands. "Where there is not purity, there can be no Silvanost and no Silvanesti."

Some of the clerics—not those of Quenesti Pah—bowed in appreciation of Sithas's declaration. Behind them, however, the guildmasters looked distinctly unhappy. Sithel, looking down on his son, was nodding slowly. He looked over the prince's head at the guildmasters and bade them come forward.

"Highness," said the master of the Jewelers Guild, "the outsiders bring many things we in Silvanesti do not have. The dwarves trade us the finest metal on Krynn for our foodstuffs and nectars. The humans bring expertly carved wood, the softest of leathers, wine, and oil. Even the kender contribute their share."

"Their share of larceny," muttered one of the clerics. Soft laughter rippled through the tower.

"Enough," Sithel commanded. His gaze rested once more on his son. "How do you propose we keep the foreigners out of our temples without losing their trade, which our nation does need?"

Sithas took a deep breath. "We can build an enclave here on Fallan Island, outside the city, and confine all trading to that point. No outsiders except valid ambassadors from other countries will be admitted within Silvanost's walls. If the humans and others wish to pay homage to the gods, let them put up their own shrines in this new enclave."

Sithel leaned back on his throne and stroked his chin. "An interesting notion. Why should the foreigners agree to it?"

"They do not want to lose the goods they get from us," Sithas reasoned. "If they don't agree, they will be turned away." The clerics looked at him with undisguised admiration.

"A perfect solution!" Zertinfinas exclaimed.

"Proof of the wisdom of the speaker's heir," added Firincalos unctuously.

Sithel looked past them to the guildmasters. "What say you, good sirs? Does this notion of my son's appeal to you?"

It did indeed. If the traders had to land at one specified point on Fallan, then the guilds could more easily impose landing fees on them. The various guildmasters voiced their approval loudly.

"Very well, let the plans be made," Sithel decided. "The forming of the docks and walls I leave to the guild of master builders. Once the plans are chosen, the forming of the stones can begin." As Sithel stood up, everyone bowed. "If that is all, then this audience is at an end." The speaker gave Sithas a thoughtful look, then turned and left the hall by the door behind the throne.

The clerics closed around Sithas, congratulating him. Miritelisina asked him if he had a name in mind for the new trading enclave.

Sithas smiled and shook his head. "I have not considered it in such detail yet."

"It should be named for you," Firincalos said exuberantly. "Perhaps 'Sithanost, the city of Sithas.' "

"No," the prince said firmly. "That is not proper. Let it be something the outsiders will understand. 'Thon-car, village on the Thon,' something simple like that. I do not want it named after me."

After freeing himself from the crowd, Sithas mounted the steps and went out the same door by which his father had left. His sedan chair awaited him outside. He climbed in and ordered, "To Quinari, at once." The slaves hoisted the carrying bars to their broad shoulders and set off at a trot.

Hermathya was waiting for him. The news had moved quickly through the palace, and she was brimming with delight at her husband's triumph.

"You've won them," she crowed, pouring Sithas a cup of cool water. "The clerics look upon you as their champion."

"I said only what I believed," Sithas noted quietly.

"True enough, but they will remember what you did, and they will support you in the future," she insisted.

Sithas dampened his fingers in the last drops of the water and touched his face with his fingertips. "Why should I need their support?"

Hermathya looked surprised. "Haven't you heard? Lady Nirakina has suggested to the speaker that you be appointed as co-ruler, to share the burden of power with your father."

Sithas was taken aback. "You've been listening from balconies again," he said with displeasure.

"I have only your interests in my heart," she said, a trifle coolly.

There was a long silence between them. Not much affection had grown between the firstborn and his beautiful wife since their marriage, and Sithas was growing more skeptical of her devotion with each passing day. Hermathya's ambition was as obvious as the Tower of the Stars and twice as big.

"I will go and speak with my father," Sithas said at last. Hermathya moved to join him. "Alone, Lady. I go alone."

Hermathya turned away from him, her face blazing crimson.

*   *   *   *   *

A servant announced the prince, and Sithel gave permission for him to enter. It was mid-afternoon, and the speaker was immersed in a steaming hot pool, his head resting on a folded towel. His eyes were closed.

"Father?"

Sithel opened one eye. "Get in, why don't you? The water is good and hot."

"No, thank you." Sithas took the direct approach. "Father, what is this I hear about mother wanting you to appoint me co-ruler?"

Sithel raised his head. "You do have your spies, don't you?"

"Only one, and I do not pay her. She works on her own account."

"Hermathya." Sithel smiled when the prince nodded. "She has spirit, that girl. I daresay if it were possible she'd want to be co-ruler, too."

"Yes, and bring the rest of Clan Oakleaf to rule with her. She already replaces palace servers with her own relatives. Soon we won't be able to walk the halls without tripping over some Oakleaf cousin or other," Sithas said.

"This is still House Royal," replied his father confidently.

At that, Sithel sat up, roiling the hot mineral water. He reached for a beaker sitting on the rim of the pool, then shook a handful of brown and white crystals into the water. The steam was immediately scented with a rare, spicy musk. "Do you know why your mother asked me to make you co-ruler?"

"No," Sithas replied.

"It was part of a compromise, actually. She wants me to call Kith-Kanan home—"

"Kith!" exclaimed Sithas, interrupting his father. "That is an excellent idea."

Sithel held up a hand. "It would cause great dissent among the clerics and nobles. Kith-Kanan broke some of our most ancient laws. He threatened the very foundations of the House Royal. My anger with him has faded, and I could bring him home—if he would properly apologize. There are many, though, who would oppose my lenience."

"But you are speaker," Sithas argued. "What difference do the grumblings of a few priests make to you?"

Sithel smiled. "I cannot tear apart the nation for love of my son. Your mother said that to assuage the clerics I should name you co-ruler. Then they would be assured Kith-Kanan would have no part of the throne after my death." Sithel gazed long into his eldest son's troubled eyes. "Do you still want me to dismiss Lady Nirakina's suggestion to make you my co-ruler?"

Sithas drew a long breath and let it out slowly. He knew that there was only one path to choose. He turned from the window. "If you seat me beside you on the throne, the people will say there is no Speaker of the Stars in Silvanost," he said quietly.

"Explain that!"

"They will say great Sithel is old, not strong enough to rule alone. And they will say Sithas is too young and has not the wisdom to be sole speaker. Two halves do not a speaker make." He looked down at his father's strong face. "You are the Speaker of the Stars. Do not relinquish one drop of your power or, as from a pinhole in a waterskin, it will all leak out and you will have nothing."

"Do you know what this decision means?" Sithel demanded.

The prince made a fist and pressed it against his mouth. There were other words he wanted to say; he wanted to have Kith home and let the consequences be damned. But Sithas knew he must not let these words out. The future of Silvanesti was at stake.

"Then I will be speaker, and will remain sole speaker, until the day the gods call me to a higher plane," Sithel said after a long silence.

"And . . . Kith-Kanan?"

"I will not call him," Sithel said grimly. "He must return on his own, as a supplicant begging for forgiveness."

"Will mother be angry with you?" Sithas asked softly.

The speaker sighed and scooped steaming water up in his hands, letting it trickle down over his closed eyes. "You know your mother," he said. "She will be hurt for a while, then she will find a cause to which she can devote herself, something to help her forget her pain."

"Hermathya will be angry." Of this, Sithas had no doubt.

"Don't let her bully you," counseled Sithel, wiping his face with his hands.

Sithas flushed. "I am your son. No one bullies me."

"I'm glad to hear it." After a pause, Sithel added, "I've just thought of another reason why you ought not want to be speaker just yet. I'm a husband, father, and monarch. So far, you're only a husband." A wry smile quirked his lips. "Have children. That will bring age and hasten wisdom."

ᛃ 10 ᛃ

four days on the trail

Kith-Kanan and Anaya paused in their pursuit of Voltorno's band. The half-human and his followers were headed almost due south, straight for the seacoast. Kith-Kanan was surprised when Anaya called a temporary halt. He was ready for anything, from a stealthy approach to a headlong, pitched battle. True, his feet ached and his hands were covered with cuts, but the knowledge that this Voltorno held not only Mackeli but his griffon steeled the prince to go on.

When he asked if she'd sensed Mackeli was near, Anaya said, "No. I smell animals nearby. It's time to hunt. You stay here and don't move around. I will return soon."

Kith-Kanan settled down with his back against a tree. In short order, he fell asleep. The next thing he knew, Anaya had tossed a brace of rabbits in his lap.

"You snore!" she said irritably. "I could have had us venison, but your roaring chased the deer away. All I could get were these rabbits." She frowned at the scrawny little animals. "These must have been deaf."

Quickly Anaya gutted and skinned the animals, then speared them over a twig fire. Kith-Kanan was impressed; her deftness was amazing. She dressed each rabbit in two strokes and started a fire with one nick of her flint against a blue field-stone. Kith-Kanan doubted he could strike a spark at all against such a common, frangible rock.

She bent to tend the fire. Kith-Kanan watched her back for a moment, then he put down the rabbit. Quietly he unbuckled his sword belt and let it down soundlessly to the ground. He added his dagger to the pile. Then, using the steps Mackeli had taught him, he crept up behind Anaya.

She straightened, still with her back to him. When he was two feet from her, she whirled, presenting the point of her knife to his face.

"You smell better without the metal, but you still breathe too loud," she said.

He pushed the flint knife aside and finished the step that brought them nose to nose. "Perhaps it's not my breathing you hear, but my heart. I can hear yours, too," he said teasingly.

Her brows knotted. "Liar."

Kith-Kanan put a finger to her cheek and began tapping lightly. "Is that the rhythm?" he said. It was, and the look of consternation on Anaya's face was delightful to him. She pushed him away.

"We've no time for games," she said. "Pick up your metal. We can walk and eat at the same time."

She moved on through the trees. Kith-Kanan watched her curiously as he buckled his swordbelt. Funny-looking Anaya, with painted face and most of her hair cropped shorter than his. He found himself taking pleasure in watching the easy way she wove through her forest home. There was a certain nobility about her.

The corvae circled ceaselessly, bringing Anaya news of the humans. Kith-Kanan and Anaya had followed them hotly all day, while the humans moved in a more leisurely manner. The prince felt ragged with fatigue, but he would not show weakness as long as Anaya remained bright and quick. Trouble was, she didn't show any signs of tiring.

It was well past midday, and for the fourth time she had held up her hand and bid Kith-Kanan be still while she scouted ahead. Sighing, he sat down on a lichen-spotted boulder. Anaya vanished into the pallid green saplings as Kith-Kanan took out his dagger and absently began cleaning his fingernails.

Seconds lengthened into minutes, and the prince began to think Anaya was taking too long. Her reconnaissance forays never took more than a minute or two, sometimes only a few seconds. He slipped his dagger into the top of his leggings and listened hard. Nothing.

A crow alighted at his feet. He stared down at the black bird, which regarded him silently, its beady eyes seeming quite intelligent. Kith-Kanan stood up, and the crow flapped into the air, circled around, and settled on his shoulder. He spared a nervous glance at the bird's sharp, pointed beak so close to his face. "You have something to show me?" he whispered. The crow cocked its head first left, then right. "Anaya? Mackeli?" The crow bobbed its head vigorously.

Kith-Kanan set out along the same path Anaya had gone down just a few minutes earlier. The crow actually directed him with pokes of its sharp beak. One hundred paces from a large boulder, Kith-Kanan heard the clinking of metal on metal. Ten steps more, and the faint whiff of smoke came to his nose. The crow plucked at his ear. Its beak stabbed painfully, and Kith-Kanan resisted the urge to swat the bird away. Then he saw what the crow was warning him about.

Ahead on the ground was a net, spread flat and covered with leaves. He knew the type; he'd often set such traps himself, for wild boar. Kith-Kanan squatted by the edge of the net and looked for trip lines or snare loops. He couldn't see any. Circling to his left, he followed the perimeter of the trap until the ground dropped away into a dry wash ravine. From there the smell of wood smoke was stronger. Kith-Kanan skidded a few feet down the bank and crept along, his head just below the level of the ground. Every now and then he would peek up and see where he was going. The third time he did this, Kith-Kanan got quite a shock. He put his head up and found himself staring into the eyes of a human—a dead human, lying on his back with his eyes wide and staring. The human's throat had been cut by a serrated knife.

The man wore rough woolen clothing, the seams of which were white with dried salt. Another sailor. There was a tattoo of a seahorse on the back of the dead man's hand.

Rough laughter filtered through the trees. As Kith-Kanan climbed out of the ravine and made for the sound, the crow spread its wings and flew away.

More ugly, cruel-sounding laughter. Kith-Kanan moved to his right, keeping a thick-trunked pine tree between him and the source of the sound. He dropped down to the ground and looked around the tree.

He saw six men standing in a glade. A smoky little fire burned on the right. On the left, wrapped in the folds of a heavy rope net, was Anaya. She looked defiant and unharmed.

"Are you sure it's female?" queried one of the men who held a crossbow.

"It 'pears to be. 'Ere, tell us what you are!" said another. He poked at Anaya with the tip of his saber. She shrank from the blade.

"What'll we do with her, Parch?" asked a third human.

"Sell 'er, like the other. She's too ugly to be anything but a slave!" noted the crossbowman. The men roared with coarse laughter.

Through the loops in the net, Anaya's eyes shone with hatred. She looked past her tormentors and saw, peeking around a tree, Kith-Kanan. He put a hand to his lips. Quiet, he willed her. Keep quiet.

"Smells a bit, don't she?" sneered the crossbowman called Parch, a lanky fellow with a drooping yellow mustache. He put down his weapon and picked up a heavy wooden bucket full of water. He flung the water on Anaya.

Kith-Kanan thought quickly. The leader, Voltorno, didn't seem to be present; these men acted callous and loud, like many soldiers did when their commander was absent. Retreating a few yards, the prince started around the glade. He hadn't gone more than a half-score steps when his foot snagged a trip line. Kith-Kanan dodged a spike-studded tree limb that was released, but the noise alerted the men. They bared their weapons and started into the woods, leaving one man to guard Anaya.

Standing with his back hard against a sticky pine, Kith-Kanan drew his sword. A human came crunching through the fallen leaves, appallingly noisy. The salty-fishy smell of his sailor's jersey preceded him. Kith-Kanan timed the man's steps and, when he was close, sprang out from behind the tree.

"By the dragon's beard!" exclaimed the man. He held out his saber warily. Without any preliminaries, Kith-Kanan attacked. Their blades clanged together, and the human shouted, "Over here, over here!" Other shouts echoed in the forest. In moments, Kith-Kanan would be hopelessly outnumbered.

The human's saber had little point for thrusting, so the elf prince jabbed his blade straight at the man, who gave ground clumsily. He was a seaman, not a warrior, and when he stumbled over a stone as he was backing away, Kith-Kanan ran him through. This was the first person he'd ever killed, but there was no time for reflection. As quietly as he could the prince ran to the glade. The other men were converging on their dead comrade, so that meant only one man stood between him and Anaya.

He hurtled into the glade, sword upraised. The guard—the one called Parch—gave a shrill cry of fright and reached for his weapon, a crossbow. Kith-Kanan was on him in a flash. He struck the crossbow from Parch's hands with a single sweep of his sword. The man staggered back, groping for the dagger he wore at his waist. Kith-Kanan advanced on him. Parch drew the dagger. Kith-Kanan easily beat aside the far shorter weapon and left poor Parch bleeding on the ground.

"Are you all right?" he shouted to Anaya as he hacked open the net. It spilled open, and Anaya nimbly leaped out.

"Filthy humans! I want to kill them!" she snarled.

"There's too many. Better to hide for now," Kith-Kanan cried.

She ignored him and went to the fire, where her flint knife lay on the ground. Before Kith-Kanan could protest, she drew the sharp stone across her arm, drawing scarlet blood. "They will die!" she declared. And with that, she dashed into the woods.

"Anaya, wait!" Kith-Kanan frantically followed her.

A hoarse scream sounded from his left. Feet churned through the leaves, running. A human, still holding his saber, ran towards the prince, his bearded face a mask of fear. Kith-Kanan stood in his way. The man traded cuts with him briefly, then threw his sword away and ran for his life. Confused, the Silvanesti trotted in the direction from which the bearded man had come, then stumbled upon the corpse of the man who had poked Anaya with his saber. No wonder the bearded human had been terrified. This other man's throat had been cut from ear to ear. Kith-Kanan clenched his teeth and moved on. He found another human, killed in the same manner.

The woods had fallen quiet, and the elf prince stepped carefully, suspecting an ambush. What he found instead nearly stopped his heart. Anaya had caught a third human and killed him, but not before the man had put a crossbow quarrel into her hip. She had dragged herself a few yards and had come to rest with both arms around an oak sapling.

Before Kith-Kanan knelt by her, he shoved his sword in its scabbard and gently pulled the blood-soaked deerskin away from her wound. The head of the quarrel had missed her hip bone, thank E'li, and was buried in the flesh between her hip and ribs. A nasty wound, but not a fatal one.

"I must take the arrow out," he explained. "But I can't pull it out the way it came in. I'll have to push it through."

"Do what must be done," she gasped, her eyelids squeezed shut.

His hands shook. Though he had seen hunters and soldiers injured before, never had Kith-Kanan had to deal with their wounds personally. He tore the leather fletching off the arrow and placed his hands on it. Steeling himself, he pushed on the nock end. Anaya stiffened and sucked air in sharply through her clenched teeth. He pushed until he could feel the iron arrow head in his other hand, beneath her body.

She didn't utter a sound, which made Kith-Kanan marvel at her courage. Once the quarrel was free, he threw it away. Then he unslung his waterskin and gently washed the wound clean. He needed something to bind it with. Under the green leather tunic Mackeli had fashioned for him, he still wore his shirt of linen. At last Kith-Kanan pulled off his tunic and tore the fine Silvanost linen into strips.

He tied the longest strips together to make a bandage, then began to wind it around Anaya's waist. Kith-Kanan split and tied the ends of the bandage, then gently hoisted Anaya in his arms. She was very light, and he carried her easily back to the glade. There he laid her in a patch of soft ferns, then dragged the dead men into the covering of the woods.

Anaya called for water. He put the skin to her lips, and she drank. After a few gulps she said weakly, "I heard them say Mackeli and your flying beast had been taken ahead to the ship. They knew we were following them. Their master, Voltorno, is half-human, and by means of magic he knew we were coming after them."

"Half human?" Kith-Kanan asked. He had heard whisperings of such crossbreeds, but had never seen one.

"Voltorno had his men stay behind to trap us." Kith-Kanan put the skin to her mouth again. When she had finished, she added, "You must leave me and go after Mackeli."

He knew she was right. "Are you sure you will be all right by yourself?"

"The forest won't hurt me. Only the intruders would do that, and they are ahead of us, carrying Mackeli. You must hurry."

With little delay the elf prince left the Kagonesti the waterskin and laid one of the men's abandoned cloaks over her. "I'll be back soon," he promised. "With Mackeli and Arcuballis."

The sun was sinking fast as Kith-Kanan plunged into the brush. He made great speed and covered a mile or more in minutes. There was a salty smell in the air. The sea was near.

Ahead, moonlight glinted off metal. As he ran Kith-Kanan spied the backs of two men, dragging a smaller person through the brush. Mackeli! He had a halter tied around his neck, and he stumbled along behind his much taller captors. The prince shouldered the crossbow and put a quarrel in the back of the human who was leading Mackeli. The second man saw his partner fall and, without pausing, he grabbed the halter rope and ran, jerking Mackeli forward.

Kith-Kanan followed. He leaped over the man he'd shot and let out the wailing cry elven hunters use when on the chase. The weird cry was too much for the man leading Mackeli. He flung the rope away and ran as hard as he could. Kith-Kanan loosed a quarrel after him, but the human passed between some trees and the shot missed.

He reached Mackeli, pausing long enough to cut the strangling rope from the boy's neck.

"Kith!" he cried. "Is Ny with you?"

"Yes, not far away," Kith-Kanan said. "Where's my griffon?"

"Voltorno has him. He put a spell on your beast to make him obey."

Kith-Kanan gave Mackeli the dagger. "Wait here. I'll come back for you."

"Let me go too! I can help!" the boy said.

"No!" Mackeli looked stubborn, so Kith-Kanan added, "I need you to stay here in case Voltorno gets past me and comes back this way." Mackeli's belligerence vanished, and he nodded. He positioned himself on guard with his dagger as Kith-Kanan ran on.

The boom of the surf rose above the sound of the wind. The forest ended abruptly atop a cliff, and Kith-Kanan had to dig in his heels to avoid plunging over the precipice. The night was bright. Solinari and Lunitari were up; moonlight and starlight silvered the scene below. With his keen vision, Kith-Kanan could see a three-masted ship wallowing in the offshore swells, its sails furled tightly against the yards.

A path led down the cliffside to the beach below. The first thing Kith-Kanan saw was Arcuballis, picking its way along the narrow path. The griffon's glow stood out strongly against the fainter ones of its captors. A red-caped figure—presumably the half-human Voltorno—led the griffon by its bridle. A human trailed restlessly behind the beast. Kith-Kanan stood up against the starry sky and loosed a quarrel at him. The man felt the quarrel pass through the sleeve of his tunic, and he screamed. Right away a swarm of men appeared on the beach. They moved out from the base of the cliff and showered arrows up at Kith-Kanan.

"Halloo," called a voice from below. Kith-Kanan cautiously raised his head. The figure in the red cape moved away from the captive griffon and stood out on the beach in plain sight. "Halloo up there! Can you hear me?"

"I hear you," Kith-Kanan shouted in reply. "Give me back my griffon!"

"I can't give him back. That beast is the only profit I'll realize on this voyage. You've got the boy back, leave the animal and go on your way."

"No! Surrender Arcuballis! I have you in my sight," Kith-Kanan warned.

"No doubt you do, but if you shoot me, my men will kill the griffon. Now, I don't want to die, and I'm certain you don't want a dead griffon either. What would you say to fighting for the beast in an honorable contest with swords?"

"How do I know you won't try some treachery?"

The half-human flung off his cape. "I doubt that will be necessary."

Kith-Kanan didn't trust him, but before the elf could say anything more, the half-human had taken a lantern from one of his men and was striding up the steep path to the top of the cliff, leading the griffon as he came. Arcuballis, usually so spirited, hung its head as it walked. The powerful wings had been pinioned by leather straps, and a muzzle made from chain mail covered the griffon's hooked beak.

"You have bewitched my animal," Kith-Kanan said furiously.

Voltorno tied the bridle to a tree and set the lantern on a waist-high boulder. "It is necessary." As the half-human faced Kith-Kanan, the elf studied him carefully. He was quite tall, and in the lantern's glow his hair was golden. A fine downy beard covered his cheeks and chin, revealing his human heritage, but Voltorno's ears were slightly pointed, denoting elven blood. His clothes and general bearing were far more refined than any of the humans with him.

"Are you sure you have enough light to see?" Kith-Kanan asked sarcastically, gesturing at the lantern.

Voltorno smiled brilliantly. "Oh, that isn't for me. It's for my men. They would hate to miss the show."

When Kith-Kanan presented his sword, Voltorno complimented him on the weapon. "The pattern is a bit old-fashioned, but very handsome. I shall enjoy using it after you're dead," he smirked.

The sailors lined the beach below to watch the duel. They cheered Voltorno and jeered Kith-Kanan as the two duelists circled each other warily. The half-human's blade flickered in, reaching for Kith-Kanan's heart. The elf parried, rolled the slim Ergothian rapier aside, and lunged with his stouter elven point.

Voltorno laughed and steered Kith-Kanan's thrust into the ground. He tried to stomp on the prince's blade, to snap the stiff iron, but Kith-Kanan drew back, avoiding the seafarer's heavy boots.

"You fight well," Voltorno offered. "Who are you? Despite the rags you wear, you are no wild elf."

"I am Silvanesti. That is all you need to know," Kith-Kanan said tightly.

Voltorno smiled, pleasantly enough. "So much pride. You think I am some renegade."

"It is easy to see which race you have chosen to serve," Kith-Kanan said.

"The humans, for all their crudity, have appreciation for talent. In your nation I would be an outcast, lowest of the low. Among the humans, I am a very useful fellow. I could find a place for you in my company. As I rise, so could you. We would go far, elf."

Voltorno spoke in an increasingly obvious lilt. His words rose and fell in a sort of sing-song intonation that Kith-Kanan found peculiar. The half-human was only a few feet from Kith-Kanan, and the elf prince saw that he was making small, slow gestures with his free hand.

"I owe my allegiance elsewhere," Kith-Kanan stated. His sword felt heavy in his hand.

"Pity." With renewed vigor, Voltorno attacked. Kith-Kanan fought him off clumsily, for the very air was beginning to seem thick, impeding his movements. As their blades tangled, Kith-Kanan lost his plan of defense and Voltorno's steel slipped by his hilt and pierced his upper arm. The half-human stepped back, still smiling like a beneficent cleric.

The weapon fell from Kith-Kanan's numb hand. He stared at it in dawning horror. His fingers had no more feeling than wood or wax. He tried to speak, but his tongue felt thick. A terrifying lethargy gripped him. Though in his mind he was yelling and fighting, his voice and limbs would not obey. Magic . . . it was magic. Voltorno had bewitched Arcuballis, now him.

Voltorno sheathed his own sword and picked up Kith-Kanan's. "How splendidly ironic it will be to kill you with your own sword," he noted. Then he raised the weapon—

And it flew from his hand! Voltorno looked down at his chest and the quarrel that had suddenly appeared there. His knees buckled, and he fell.

Mackeli stepped out of the dark ring of trees, a crossbow in his hands. Kith-Kanan staggered back away from the half-human. His strength was returning, in spite of the wound in his arm. Like a river freed from a dam, feeling rushed back into his body. He picked up his sword and heard shouts from the beach. The humans were coming to aid their fallen leader.

"So," said the half-human through bloody lips, "you triumph after all." He grimaced and touched his fingers to the quarrel in his chest. "Go ahead, end it."

Already the humans were running up the steep path toward them. "I've no time to waste on you," spat Kith-Kanan contemptuously. He wanted to sound strong, but his narrow escape had left him shaken.

He took Mackeli by the arm and hurried to Arcuballis. The boy hung back as Kith-Kanan removed the muzzle from the griffon's beak and cut the leather pinions from its wings. The fire was returning to the griffon's eyes. The creature clawed the ground with its talons.

Kith-Kanan touched his forehead to the beast's feathered head and said, "It's good to see you, old fellow." He heard the commotion as the humans came roaring up the cliffside. Mounting the griffon, Kith-Kanan slid forward in the saddle and said, "Climb on, Mackeli." The elf boy looked uncertain. "Hurry, the spell is broken but Voltorno's men are coming!"

After another second's hesitation, Mackeli grasped Kith-Kanan's hand and swung into the saddle behind him. Armed sailors appeared on top of the cliff, and they rushed to Voltorno. Behind them came a tall human with a full, red-brown beard. He pointed to the elves. "Stop them!" he cried in a booming voice.

"Hold on!" shouted Kith-Kanan. He slapped the reins across Arcuballis's neck, and the griffon bounded toward the men. They dropped and scattered like leaves in a whirlwind. Another leap and Arcuballis cleared the edge of the cliff. Mackeli gave a short, sharp cry of fear, but Kith-Kanan yelled with pure joy. Some of the humans got to their feet and loosed arrows at them, but the distance was too great. Kith-Kanan steered Arcuballis out over the foaming surf, turned, and gained height. As they swept past the site of the duel, he saw the red-bearded fellow raise Voltorno to his feet. That one wasn't going to die easily, the prince noted.

"It's good to see you!" Kith-Kanan shouted over his shoulder. "You saved my life, you know." There was no response from Mackeli and Kith-Kanan asked, "Are you well?"

"I was weller on the ground," Mackeli said, his voice high with anxiety. He tightened his fierce grip on Kith-Kanan's waist as he asked, "Where are we going?"

"To fetch Anaya. Hold tight!"

The griffon gave voice to its own triumphant cry. The trilling roar burst over the wildwood, announcing their return to the waiting Anaya.

✿ 11 ✿

Early Autumn, Year of the Hawk

The traditional way across the river to Silvanost was by ferry. Large, flat-bottomed barges were drawn back and forth across the Thon-Thalas by giant turtles. Some time in the distant past, priests of the Blue Phoenix, god of all animal life, had woven the spells that brought the first giant turtles into being. They had taken a pair of common river turtles, usually the size of a grown elf's palm, and worked their spells over them until they were as big as houses. Thereafter, the priests bred their own giants, creating quite a sizeable herd. The vast green domes of the turtles' shells had become a common sight as the placid beasts gave faithful service for many centuries.

Lady Nirakina stood on the riverbank, watching a barge of refugees, pulled by just such a turtle, arrive from the west bank. Beside her stood Tamanier Ambrodel, his arm still in a sling. A month had passed since the Trial Days, and during that time more and more settlers from the western plains and forests had retreated to Silvanost for protection.

"How many does that make?" asked Nirakina, shading her eyes to see the crowded barge.

Tamanier checked the tally he was keeping. "Four hundred and nineteen, my lady," he said. "And more coming all the time."

The settlers were mostly from the poorer families of Silvanesti who had gone west to work new land and make new lives for themselves. Though largely unharmed, they were footsore, exhausted, and demoralized. Their stories were all the same: bands of humans and Kagonesti elves had burned down their houses and orchards and ordered them to leave. The Silvanesti, unarmed and unorganized, had little choice but to pack their meager belongings and trek back to Silvanost.

Nirakina had received her husband's blessing to organize relief for the displaced settlers. A field along the southern end of the city was set aside for them, and a shanty town of tents and lean-tos had sprung up in the last few weeks. Nirakina had persuaded many of the city guilds and great temples to contribute food, blankets, and money for the care of the refugees.

Sithel was doing all he could for the refugees, too, but his job was made far more complicated by the demands of the state. The Tower of the Stars was filled daily with petitioners who entreated the speaker to call together the army and clear the plains of the raiders. Sithel quite rightly realized this was not a practical solution. A big, slow-moving army would never catch small, mobile raider bands.

"Our neighbors to the west, Thorbardin and Ergoth, would be very unhappy to see an elven army on their borders," Sithel told his more bellicose nobles. "It would be an invitation to war, and that is an invitation I will not countenance."

So the refugees continued to come, first in a trickle, then in a steady stream. As he was acquainted with them and knew first-hand the problems they faced, Tamanier Ambrodel was chosen by Lady Nirakina to be her chief assistant. He proved a tireless worker, but even with his efforts, the camp along the riverbank became dirty and rowdy as more and more frightened settlers swelled its ranks. A pall of smoke and fear hovered over the refugee camp. It did not take long for the residents of Silvanost to lose their sympathy and regard the refugees with disgust.

This day Nirakina had gone down to the water's edge to speak to the refugees as they came ashore. The weary, grimy travelers were amazed to see the speaker's wife waiting on the muddy bank, her richly made gown trailing in the mud, only Tamanier Ambrodel standing beside her.

"They are so sad, so tired," she murmured to him. He stood by her side making notations on a wax tablet.

"It's a sad thing to lose your home and those you love best, my lady." Tamanier filled a square of twenty and blocked it off. "That makes two hundred and twenty in one barge, including sixty-six humans and half-humans." He eyed her uncertainly. "The speaker will not be pleased that those not of our blood are entering the city."

"I know the speaker's heart," Nirakina said a little sharply. Her slight figure bristled with indignation. "It is the others at court who want to cause trouble for these poor folk."

An elf woman struggled ashore from a small boat, carrying a baby in her arms. She slipped and fell to her knees in the muddy water. Other exhausted refugees tramped past her. Nirakina, without hesitation, waded into the press of silent people and helped the elf woman to her feet. Their eyes met, and the raggedly dressed woman said, "Thank you, my lady."

With nothing else to say, she held her child to her shoulder and slogged ashore. Nirakina was standing, openly admiring the woman's dogged courage, when a hand touched her arm.

"You'd best be careful, Lady," Tamanier said.

Unheeding, Nirakina replied, "The priests and nobles will fume about this, about the mixed-blood people especially." Her serene expression darkened. "They should all be made to come here and see the poor innocents they would deny comfort and shelter!"

Tamanier gently tugged Lady Nirakina back to the riverbank.

*　*　*　*　*

On the other side of the city, the Tower of the Stars rang with denunciations of the refugees.

"When the gods created the world, they made our race first, to be the guardians of right and truth," declared Firincalos, high priest of E'li. "It is our sacred duty to preserve ourselves as the gods made us, a pure race, always recognizable as Silvanesti."

"Well said! Quite true!" The assembly of nobles and clerics called out in rising voices.

Sithas watched his father. The speaker listened placidly to all this, but he did not look pleased. It was not so much that his father disagreed with the learned Firincalos; Sithas had heard similar sentiments espoused before. But he knew the speaker hated to be lectured to by anyone, for any reason.

Since the Trial Days, Sithas had been at his father's side daily, taking a hand in the day-to-day administration of the country. He'd learned new respect for Sithel when he saw how his father managed to balance the pleas of the priests, the ideas of the nobles, and the needs of the guilds against his own philosophy of what was best for Silvanesti.

Sithas had learned respect—but not admiration. He believed his father was too flexible, gave in too often to the wrong people. It surprised him, for he had always thought of Sithel as a strong ruler. Why didn't he simply command obedience instead of constantly compromising?

Sithel waved for the assembled elves to be quiet. Miritelisina, high priestess of Quenesti Pah, was standing, seeking the speaker's grant to comment. The hall quieted, and Sithel bade Miritelisina begin.

"I must ask the pure and righteous Firincalos what he would do with the husbands, wives, and children now languishing in huts along the riverbank, those who are not pure in our blood yet who have the deepest ties to some member of our race?" Her rich voice filled the high tower. In her youth, Miritelisina had been a renowned singer, and she played upon her listeners with all her old skills. "Shall we throw them into the river? Shall we drive them from the island, back onto the swords and torches of the bandits who drove them east?"

A few harsh voices cried "Yes!" to her questions.

Sithas folded his arms and studied Miritelisina. She cut a regal figure in her sapphire headband and white robe with its trailing, sky-blue sash. Her waist-length, flaxen hair rippled down her back as she swept a pointing finger over the mostly male crowd of elves.

"Shame on you all!" she shouted. "Is there no mercy in Silvanost? The humans and half-humans are not here because they want to be! Evil has been done to them, evil that must be laid at someone's door. But to treat them like animals, to deny them simple shelter, is likewise evil. My holy brothers, is this the way of rightness and truth of which the honorable Firincalos speaks? It does not sound that way to me. I would more expect to hear such harsh sentiments from devotees of the Dragonqueen!"

Sithas stiffened. The willful priestess had gone too far! Firincalos and his colleagues thought so, too. They pushed to the front of the crowd, outraged at being compared to the minions of the Queen of Evil. The air thickened with denunciations, but Sithel, sitting back on his throne, did nothing to restrain the angry clerics.

Sithas turned to his father. "May I speak?" he asked calmly.

"I've been waiting for you to take a stand," Sithel said impatiently. "Go ahead. But remember, if you swim with snakes, you may get bitten."

Sithas bowed to his father. "This is a hard time for our people," he began loudly. The wrangling on the floor subsided, and the prince lowered his voice. "It is evident from events in the West that the humans, probably with the support of the emperor of Ergoth, are trying to take over our plains and woodland provinces, not by naked conquest, but by displacing our farmers and traders. Terror is their tool, and so far it is working far better than they could have dreamed. I tell you this first and ask you all to remember who is responsible for the situation in which we now find ourselves."

Sithel nodded with satisfaction. Sithas noted his father's reaction and went on.

"The refugees come to Silvanost seeking our protection, and we cannot fail to give it. It is our duty. We protect those not of our race because they have come on bended knee, as subjects must do before their lords. It is only right and proper that we shield them from harm, not only because the gods teach the virtue of mercy, but also because these are the people who grow our crops, sell our goods, who pay their taxes and their fealty."

A murmur passed through the assembly. Sithas's calm, rational tone, so long honed in debates with the priests of Matheri, dampened the anger that had reigned earlier. The clerics relaxed from their previous trembling outrage. Miritelisina smiled faintly.

Sithas dropped his hands to his hips and looked over the gathering with stern resolve. "But make no mistake! The preservation of our race is of the greatest importance. Not merely the purity of our blood, but the purity of our customs, traditions, and laws. For that reason, I ask the speaker to decree a new place of refuge for the settlers, on the western bank of the Thon-Thalas, for the sole purpose of housing all humans and half-humans. Further, I suggest that all non-Silvanesti be sent across to there from the current tent village."

There was a moment of silence as the assembly took in this idea, then the tower erupted with calls of "Well spoken! Well said!"

"What about the husbands and wives who are full-blooded Silvanesti?" demanded Miritelisina.

"They may go with their families, of course," replied Sithas evenly.

"They should be made to go," insisted Damroth, priest of Kiri Jolith. "They are an insult to our heritage."

Sithel rapped the arm of his throne with his massive signet ring. The sound echoed through the Tower of the Stars. Instant silence claimed the hall.

"My son does me honor," the speaker said. "Let all he has said be done." The priestess of Quenesti Pah opened her mouth to protest, but Sithel rapped on his throne again, as a warning. "Those Silvanesti who have taken humans as mates will go with their kin. They have chosen their path, now they must follow it. Let it be done." He stood, a clear signal that the audience was over. The assembly bowed deeply as one and filed out. In a few minutes, only Sithel and Sithas were left.

"That Miritelisina," said Sithel wryly. "She's a woman of extreme will."

"She's too sentimental," Sithas complained, coming to his father's side. "I didn't notice her offering to take the half-breeds into her temple."

"No, but she's spent a third of the temple treasury on tents and firewood, I hear." The speaker rubbed his brow with one hand and sighed gustily. "Do you think it will come to war? There's no real proof Ergoth is behind these attacks."

Sithas frowned. "These are not ordinary bandits. Ordinary bandits don't scorn gold in favor of wrecking fruit trees. I understand this new emperor, Ullves X, is an ambitious young schemer. Perhaps if we confront him directly, he would restrain the 'bandits' now at liberty in our western lands."

Sithel looked doubtful. "Humans are difficult to deal with. They have more guile than kender, and their rapaciousness can make a goblin pale. And yet, they know honor, loyalty, and courage. It would be easier if they were all cruel or all noble, but as it is, they are mostly . . . difficult." Rising from the throne, the speaker added, "Still, talk is cheaper than war. Prepare a letter to the emperor of Ergoth. Ask him to send an emissary for the purpose of ending the strife on the plains. Oh, you'd better send a similar note to the king of Thorbardin. They have a stake in this, too."

"I will begin at once," Sithas assented, bowing deeply.

*　*　*　*　*

Usually, diplomatic notes to foreign rulers would be composed by professional scribes, but Sithas sat down at the onyx table in his private room and began the letter himself. He dipped a fine stylus in a pot of black ink and wrote the salutation. "To His Most Excellent and Highborn Majesty, Ullves X, Emperor, Prince of Daltigoth, Grand Duke of Colem, etc., etc." The prince shook his head. Humans dearly loved titles; how they piled them after their names. "From Sithel, Speaker of the Stars, Son of Silvanos. Greetings, Royal Brother—"

Hermathya burst into the room, red-gold hair disheveled, mantle askew. Sithas was so startled he dropped a blot of ink on the page, spoiling the fine vellum.

"Sithas!" she exclaimed breathlessly, rushing toward him. "They are rioting!"

"Who's rioting?" he growled irritably.

"The farmers—the settlers lately come from the West. Word got out that the speaker was going to force them to leave

Silvanost, and they began to smash and burn things. A band of them attacked the Market! Parts of it are on fire!"

Sithas rushed to the balcony. He threw aside the heavy brocade curtain and stepped out. His rooms faced away from the Market district, but through the muggy autumn air he caught the distant sounds of screaming.

"Has the royal guard been turned out?" he asked, returning inside quickly.

Hermathya inhaled deeply, her pale skin flushed as she tried to get her breathing under control. "I think so. I saw warriors headed that way. My sedan chair was blocked by a column of guards, so I got out and ran to the palace."

"You shouldn't have done that," he said sternly. Sithas imagined Hermathya running down the street like some wild Kagonesti. What would the common folk think, seeing his wife dashing through town like a wild thing?

When she planted her hands on her hips, the prince noticed that Hermathya's mantle had slipped down, leaving one white shoulder bare. Her flame-bright hair had escaped its confining clasp and tendrils streamed around her reddened face. Her blush deepened at Sithas's words.

"I thought it important to bring you the news!"

"The news would have come soon enough," he stated tersely. He pulled a bell cord for a servant. An elf maid appeared with silent efficiency. "A bowl of water and a towel for Lady Hermathya," Sithas commanded. The maid bowed and departed.

Hermathya flung off her dusty mantle. "I don't need water!" she exclaimed angrily. "I want to know what you're going to do about the riot!"

"The warriors will quell it," the prince stated flatly as he returned to the table. When he saw that the parchment was ruined, Sithas frowned at the letter.

"Well, I hope no harm comes to Lady Nirakina!" she added.

Sithas ceased twirling the stylus in his fingers. "What do you mean?" he asked sharply.

"Your mother is out there, in the midst of the fighting!"

He seized Hermathya by the arms. His grip was so tight, a gasp was wrenched from his wife. "Don't lie to me, Hermathya! Why should Mother be in that part of the city?"

"Don't you know? She was at the river with that Ambrodel

fellow, helping the poor wretches."

Sithas released her quickly, and she staggered back a step. He thought fast. Then, turning to an elegant wardrobe made of flamewood, he pulled his street cloak off its peg and flipped it around his shoulders. On another peg was a sword belt holding a slender sword, the twin of his brother's. He buckled the belt around his waist. It settled lopsidedly around his narrow hips.

"I'm going to find my mother," he declared.

Hermathya grabbed her mantle. "I'll go with you!"

"You will not," he said firmly. "It isn't seemly for you to roam the streets. You will stay here."

"I will do as I please!"

Hermathya started for the door, but Sithas caught her wrist and pulled her back. Her eyes blazed furiously.

"If it weren't for me, you wouldn't even know about the danger!" she hissed.

Voice tight with control, Sithas replied, "Lady, if you wish to remain in my good graces, you will do as I say."

She stuck out her chin. "Oh? And if I don't, what will you do? Strike me?" Sithas felt impaled by her deep blue eyes and, in spite of his anxiety about his mother, he felt a surge of passion. The starjewel at Hermathya's throat flashed. There was color in her cheeks to match the heat in her eyes. Their life together had been so cold. So little fire, so little emotion. Her arms were smooth and warm in Sithas's hands as he leaned close. But in the instant before their lips met, Hermathya whispered, "I will do as I please!"

The prince pushed his wife back and turned away, breathing deeply to calm himself. She used her beauty like a weapon, not only on the commoners, but even on him. Sithas closed the collar of his cloak with a trembling hand.

"Find my father. Tell the speaker what has happened and what I intend to do."

"Where is the speaker?" she said sulkily.

He snapped, "I don't know. Why don't you look for him?" Without another word, Sithas hurried from the room.

On his way out, the prince passed the servant as she returned with a bowl of tepid water and a soft white towel. The elf maiden stood aside to let Sithas pass, then presented the bowl to Hermathya. She scowled at the girl, then, with one hand, knocked the basin from the servant's hands. The bronze bowl hit the marble floor with a clang, splashing Hermathya's feet with water.

🍃 12 🍃

Idyll at the End of Summer

ARCUBALLIS LOWERED ITS HEAD TO THE CLEAR WATER AND DRANK. Not far from the hollow tree, where Anaya and Mackeli lived, a spring welled up from deep underground, creating a large, still pool. The water spilled over the lip of one side of the pool, cascading down natural steps of granite and bluestone.

It was two days after Kith-Kanan had flown them all safely home. He had come to the pool daily since then to bathe his wounded arm. Though tender, it was a clean wound and showed every sign of healing well.

Despite her own injury, Anaya would not let Kith-Kanan carry her to the pool. Instead, she directed Mackeli to bring her certain roots and leaves, from which she made a poultice. As Kith-Kanan watched her chew the medicinal leaves her-

117

self, he listened for the fourth time to Mackeli's tale of capture and captivity.

"And then Voltorno told the woodcutters there were no evil spirits in the forest, and they believed him, until they came running back down the trail, screaming and falling on their hairy faces—"

"Do you suppose we could give him back?" Anaya interrupted with a bored expression.

"I think so," offered Kith-Kanan. "The ship may not have sailed yet."

Mackeli looked at the two of them open-mouthed. "Give me back!" he said, horrified. Slowly the boy smiled. "You're teasing me!"

"I'm not," said Anaya, wincing as she applied the chewed leaves and root paste to her wound. Mackeli's face fell until Kith-Kanan winked at him.

"Come with me to the spring," the prince said. It was better to leave Anaya alone. Her wound had made her testy.

Kith-Kanan led Arcuballis through the woods by its reins. Mackeli walked beside him.

"There is one thing I'm not clear about," Kith-Kanan said after a time. "Was it Voltorno who cast the spell on me that first night, the night he stole Arcuballis from me?"

"It must have been," Mackeli guessed. "His men were starved for meat, so Voltorno worked up a spell to enthrall any warm-blooded creatures in the area. The deer, rabbits, boar, and other animals had long since fled, warned of the humans by the corvae. All he got for his trouble was your griffon, which he knew was rare and valuable."

As Arcuballis drank its fill, the elf prince and the Kagonesti boy sat on a bluestone boulder and listened to the water cascading from the pool.

"I'm glad you and Ny are getting along," Mackeli noted. "She is not easy to live with."

"That I know."

The Kagonesti tossed a twig into the water and watched as it was drawn down the miniature falls.

"Mackeli, what do you remember about your parents? Your mother and father—what were they like?"

Mackeli's forehead wrinkled with deep thought. "I don't

know. I must have been a baby when they left."

"Left? Do you mean died?"

"No. Ny always said our parents left us and meant to come back some day," he said.

She and Mackeli looked so completely different, it was hard for Kith-Kanan to believe they were blood relatives.

"You know, Kith, I watched you fight with Voltorno. It was really something! The way you moved, swish, clang, swish!" Mackeli waved his hand in the air, holding an imaginary sword. "I wish I could fight like that."

"I could teach you," said Kith-Kanan. "If Anaya doesn't mind."

Mackeli wrinkled his nose, as if he smelled something bad. "I know what she'll say: 'Get out of this tree! You stink like metal!'"

"Maybe she wouldn't notice." The boy and the prince looked at each other and then shook their heads in unison. "She'd notice," Kith-Kanan said. "We'll just have to ask her."

They walked back to the clearing. Anaya had limped, no doubt painfully, out of the tree into the one sunny spot in the clearing. An ugly smear of greenish paste covered her wound.

"Ny, uh, Kith—has something to ask you," Mackeli said quickly.

She opened her eyes. "What is it?"

Kith-Kanan tied Arcuballis to a tree in the shaded end of the clearing. He came to where Anaya was reclining and squatted down beside her.

"Mackeli wants to learn the use of arms, and I'm willing to teach him. Is that agreeable to you?"

"You wish to take up metal?" she said sharply to the boy. Mackeli nodded as his sister sat up, moving stiffly. "A long time ago, I made a bargain with the spirits of the forest. In return for their allowing me to hear and speak with the animals and trees, I was to be their guardian against outsiders. All those who would despoil the forest are my enemies. And the forest told me that the worst of these intruders carried metal, which is soulless and dead, torn from the deep underground, burned in fire, and used only to kill and destroy. In time the very smell of metal came to offend my nose."

"You find it acceptable for me to carry a sword and dagger,"

119

noted Kith-Kanan.

"The Forestmaster chose you for a task, and I cannot fault her judgment. You drove the intruders out, saving my brother and the forest." She looked at Mackeli. "The choice is yours, but if you take up metal, the beasts will no longer speak to you. I may even have to send you away."

Mackeli's face showed shock. "Send me away?" he whispered. He looked around. The hollow oak, the shaded clearing, and Anaya were all he had ever known of home and family. "Is there no other way?"

"No," Anaya said flatly, and tears sprang up in Mackeli's eyes.

Kith-Kanan couldn't understand the elf woman's hardness. "Don't despair, Mackeli," he said consolingly. "I can teach swordsmanship using wooden staves in place of iron blades." He looked at Anaya and added a bit sarcastically, "Is that allowed?"

She waved one hand dismissively.

Kith-Kanan put a hand on Mackeli's shoulder. "What do you say, do you still want to learn?" he asked.

Mackeli blotted his eyes on his sleeve and sniffed, "Yes."

* * * * *

As summer lay down like a tired hound and autumn rose up to take its place, Kith-Kanan and Mackeli sparred with wooden swords in the clearing. It was not harmless fun, and many bruises and black eyes resulted from unguarded blows landed on unprotected flesh. But there was no anger in it, and the boy and the prince developed more than fighting skill on those sunny afternoons. They developed a friendship. Bereft of home and family, with no real plans for the future, Kith-Kanan was glad to have something to fill his days.

Early on, Anaya watched them dance and dodge, shouting and laughing as the wooden "blades" hit home. Her side healed quickly, more quickly than Kith-Kanan thought natural, and before long Anaya retreated to the woods. She came and went according to her own whims, often returning with a dressed out hart or a snare line of rabbits. Kith-Kanan believed she had finally come to accept his presence in her home, but she did not join in the easy camaraderie that grew between him and her brother.

One day, as the first leaves were changing from green to gold, Kith-Kanan went down to the spring. Mackeli was off collecting from a rich harvest of fall nuts, and Anaya had been gone for several days. He patted Arcuballis's flank in passing, then plunged into the cool shade along the path to the pool.

His newly sharpened senses caught the sound of splashing in the water halfway down the path. Curious, he slipped into the underbrush. Kith-Kanan crept along soundlessly—for his walking and breathing were much improved, also—until he came to the high ground overlooking the pool.

Treading water in the center of the pool was a dark-haired elf woman. Her raven-black tresses floated on the surface around her like a cloud of dense smoke. It took Kith-Kanan a moment to realize he was looking at Anaya. Her hair was free of its long braid, and all her skin paint was washed off; he nearly didn't recognize her clean-scrubbed features. Smiling, he sat down by the trunk of a lichen-encrusted oak to watch her swim.

For all her stealth on land, Anaya was not a graceful swimmer. She paddled back and forth, using a primitive stroke. The fishers of the Thon-Thalas could teach her a thing or two, Kith-Kanan decided.

When she climbed out of the water onto a ledge of granite, Kith-Kanan saw that she was naked. Accustomed though he was to the highly prized pallor of city-dwellers, he found her sun-browned body oddly beautiful. It was lithe and firmly muscled. Her legs were strong, and there was an unconscious, easy grace in her movements. She was like a forest spirit, wild and free. And as Anaya ran her hands through her hair and hummed to herself, Kith-Kanan felt the stirrings of emotions he had thought dead months ago, when he'd fled Silvanost.

Anaya lay down on the rock ledge, pillowing her head with one arm. Eyes closed, she appeared to sleep. Kith-Kanan stood up and meant to slip around the far side of the pool in order to surprise her. But the hill was steep, and the vines were green enough to be slippery when his sandals crushed them. That Kith-Kanan was watching Anaya, not his footing, made the going even more treacherous. He took two steps and fell, sliding feet-first down the hill into the pool.

He surfaced, choking and spitting. Anaya hadn't moved, but she said, "You go to a lot of trouble just to see me bathe."

"I—" the prince sneezed violently "—heard someone in the spring and came to investigate. I didn't know it was you." Despite the weight of his clothes and sword, he swam in long strokes to the ledge where she lay. Anaya made no move to cover herself, but merely moved over to give him room to sit on the rock.

"Are you all right?" she asked.

"Only my pride hurts." He stood up, averting his eyes from her. "I'm sorry I intruded. I'll go."

"Go or stay. It doesn't matter to me." When he hesitated, Anaya added, "I am not modest in the fashion of your city females."

"Yet you wear clothes," he felt obliged to say. Uncomfortable as he was with her nudity, he felt strangely unwilling to leave her.

"A deerskin tunic is good protection from thorns." Anaya watched Kith-Kanan with some amusement as his gaze flickered over her and away for a third time. "It bothers you. Give me your tunic." He protested, but she insisted, so he removed his wet tunic.

She pulled it over her head. The tunic covered her to her knees. "Is that better?"

He smiled sheepishly. "I can't get over how different you look," he said. "Without lines painted on your face, I mean." It was true. Her hazel eyes were large and darker than his twin's. She had a small, full-lipped mouth and a high forehead.

As if in response, Anaya stretched lazily, like a big cat. She put more into, and seemed to get more out of, a simple stretch than anyone Kith-Kanan had ever seen. "Don't the women of your race adorn themselves?" she inquired.

"Well, yes, but not to the point of disguising themselves," he said earnestly. "I like your face. Seems a pity to cover it."

Anaya sat up and looked at him curiously. "Why do you say that?"

"Because it's true," he said simply.

She shook herself. "Don't talk nonsense."

"I hope you're not angry with me any more for teaching Mackeli how to fight," he said, hoping to draw the conversation out a little longer. He was enjoying talking with her.

She shrugged. "My injury made me short-tempered. I wasn't angry with you." She gazed out at the clear water. After a moment, she said slowly, "I am glad Mackeli has a friend."

He smiled and reached a hand out to touch her arm. "You have a friend, too, you know."

Quickly Anaya rolled to her feet and pulled his tunic off. Dropping it, she dove into the pool. She stayed under so long that Kith-Kanan began to worry. He was about to dive in after her when Mackeli appeared on the other side of the pool, his bag bursting with chestnuts.

"Hello, Kith! Why are you all wet?"

"Anaya went in the water and hasn't come back up!"

Mackeli heaved the heavy sack to the ground. "Don't worry," he said. "She's gone to her cave." Kith-Kanan looked at him blankly. "There's a tunnel in the pool that connects to a cave. She goes down there when she's upset about something. Did you two have words?"

"Not exactly," Kith-Kanan said, staring at the water's surface. "I just told her I liked her face and that I was her friend."

Mackeli scratched his cheek skeptically. "Well, there's no use waiting there. She may not come up for days." He hoisted the sack onto his narrow shoulder and added, "The cave is Ny's secret place. We can't get in."

Kith-Kanan picked up his tunic and circled around the pool to where Mackeli stood. They walked up the path to the clearing. Every third step or so, Kith-Kanan looked back at the quiet spring. The forest woman was so difficult to understand. He kept hoping she would reappear, but she didn't.

* * * * *

The sun set, and Mackeli and Kith-Kanan roasted chestnuts in the fire. When they were full, they lay on their backs in the grass and watched a fall of stars in the sky. The stars trailed fiery red tails across the black night, and Kith-Kanan marveled at the beauty of the sight. Living indoors in Silvanost, Kith-Kanan had seen only a few such falls. As the elf prince stared into the sky, a gentle wind tickled the branches of the trees and ruffled his hair.

Kith-Kanan sat up to get another handful of chestnuts. He saw Anaya sitting cross-legged by the fire and almost jumped out of his skin.

"What are you playing at?" he asked, irritated at being so startled.

"I came to share your fire."

Mackeli sat up and poked a few roasted nuts from the ashes with a stick. Though they were hot, Anaya casually picked one up and peeled the red husk from the nut meat.

"Your task is long done, Kith," she said in a low voice. "Why haven't you returned to Silvanost?"

He chewed a chestnut. "I have no life there," he said truthfully.

Anaya's dark eyes looked out from her newly painted face. "Why not? Any disgrace you committed can be forgiven," she said.

"I committed no disgrace!" he said with heat.

"Then go home. You do not belong here." Anaya rose and backed away from the fire. Her eyes glowed in the firelight until she turned away.

Mackeli gaped. "Ny has never acted so strangely. Something is troubling her," he said as he jumped to his feet. "I'll ask—"

"No." The single word froze Mackeli in his tracks. "Leave her alone. When she finds the answer, she'll tell us."

Mackeli sat down again. They looked into the red coals in silence for a while, then Mackeli said, "Why *do* you stay, Kith?"

"Not you, too!"

"Your life in the City of Towers was full of wonderful things. Why did you leave? Why do you stay here?"

"There's nowhere else I want to go right now, and I've made friends here, or at least one friend." He smiled at Mackeli. "As for why I left—" Kith-Kanan rubbed his hands together as if they were cold. "Once I was in love with a beautiful maiden, in Silvanost. She had wit and spirit, and I believed she loved me. Then it came time for my brother, Sithas, to marry. His wife was chosen for him by our father, the Speaker of the Stars. Of all the suitable maidens in the city, my father chose the one I loved to be my brother's bride." He pulled his dagger and drove it to the hilt in the dirt. "And she married him willingly! She was glad to do it!"

"I don't understand," admitted Mackeli.

"Neither do I. Hermathya—" Kith-Kanan closed his eyes, seeing her in his mind and savoring the feel of her name on his lips "—seemed to love the idea of being the next speaker's wife more than being married to one who loved her. So, I left home. I do not expect to see Silvanost again."

The elf boy looked at Kith-Kanan, whose head hung down. The prince still gripped his dagger hilt tightly. Mackeli cleared his throat and said sincerely, "I hope you stay, Kith. Ny could never have taught me the things you have. She never told me the kind of stories you tell. She's never seen the great cities, or the warriors and nobles and priests."

Kith-Kanan had raised his head. "I try not to think beyond today, Keli. For now, the peace of this place suits me. Strange, after being used to all the comforts and extravagances of royal birth . . ." His voice trailed off.

"Perhaps we can make a new kingdom, here in the wild-wood."

Kith-Kanan smiled. "A kingdom?" he asked. "Just us three?"

With complete earnestness, Mackeli said, "Nations must begin somewhere, yes?"

🌿 13 🌿

Day of Madness

Sithas rode up the Street of Commerce at a canter, past the guild hall towers that lined both sides. He reined in his horse clumsily—for he wasn't used to riding—when he spied the guild elves standing in the street, watching smoke rise from the Market quarter.

"Has the royal guard come this way?" he called at them.

Wringing his hands, a senior master with the crest of the Gemcutters Guild on his breast replied, "Yes, Highness, some time ago. The chaos grows worse, I fear—"

"Have you seen my mother, Lady Nirakina?"

The master gemcutter picked at his long dark hair with slim fingers and shook his head in silent despair. Sithas snorted with frustration and twisted his horse's head away, toward the rising

pillar of smoke. "Go back inside your halls," he called contemptuously. "Bolt your doors and windows."

"Will the half-breeds come here?" asked another guild elf
tremulously.

"I don't know, but you'd better be prepared to defend your-
selves." Sithas thumped his horse's sides with his heels, then
mount and rider clattered down the street.

Beyond the guild halls, in the first crossing street of the commoners' district, he found the way littered with broken bar-
rows, overturned sedan chairs, and abandoned pushcarts.
Sithas picked his way through the debris with difficulty, for
there were many common folk standing in the street. Most
were mute in disbelief, though some wept at the unaccustomed
violence so near their homes. They raised a cheer when they
saw Sithas. He halted again and asked if anyone had seen Lady
Nirakina.

"No one has come through since the warriors passed this
way," said a trader. "No one at all."

He thanked them, then ordered them off the street. The elves
retreated to their houses. In minutes, the prince was alone.

The poorer people of Silvanost lived in tower houses just as
the rich did. However, their homes seldom rose more than four
or five stories. Each house had a tiny garden around its base,
miniature versions of the great landscape around the Tower of
the Stars. Trash and blown rubbish now tainted the lovingly
tended gardens. Smoke poisoned the air. Grimly Sithas continued toward the heart of this madness.

Two streets later, the prince saw his first rioters. A human
woman and a female Kagonesti were throwing pottery jugs onto
the pavement, smashing them. When they ran out of jugs, they
went to a derelict potter's cart and replenished their supply.

"Stop that!" Sithas commanded. The dark elf woman took
one look at the speaker's heir and fled with a shriek. Her human
companion, however, hurled a pot at Sithas. It shattered on the
street at his horse's feet, spraying the animal with shards. That
done, the impudent human woman dusted her hands and simply walked away.

The horse backed and pranced, so Sithas had his hands full
calming the mount. When the horse was once more under control, he rode ahead. The lane ended at a sharp turn to the right.

The sounds of fighting grew louder as Sithas rode on, drawing his sword.

The street ahead was full of struggling people—Silvanesti, Kagonesti, human, kender, and dwarves. A line of royal guards with pikes held flat in both hands were trying to keep the mass of fear-crazed folk back. Sithas rode up to an officer giving orders to the band of warriors, who numbered no more than twenty.

"Captain! Where is your commander?" shouted Sithas, above the roar of voices.

"Highness!" The warrior, himself of Kagonesti blood, saluted crisply. "Lord Kencathedrus is pursuing some of the criminals in the Market!"

Sithas, on horseback, could see far over the seething sea of people. "Are all these rioters?" he asked, incredulous.

"No, sire. Most are merchants and traders, trying to get away from the criminals who set fire to the shops," the captain replied.

"Why are you holding them back?"

"Lord Kencathedrus's orders, sire. He didn't want these foreigners to flood the rest of the city."

When the prince asked the captain if he'd seen his mother, the warrior shook his helmeted head. Sithas then asked if there was another way around, a way to the river.

"Keep them back!" barked the captain to his straining soldiers. "Push them! Use your pike shafts!" He stepped back, closer to Sithas, and said, "Yes, sire, you can circle this street and take White Rose Lane right to the water."

Sithas commended the captain and turned his horse around. A spatter of stones and chunks of pottery rained over them. The captain and his troops had little to fear; they were in armor. Neither Sithas nor his horse were, so they cantered quickly away.

White Rose Lane was narrow and lined on both sides by high stone walls. This was the poorest section of Silvanost, where the house-towers were the lowest. With only two or three floors, they resembled squat stone drums, a far cry from the tall, gleaming spires of the high city.

The lane was empty when Sithas entered it. Astride his horse, his knees nearly scraped the walls on each side. A thin trickle of scummy water ran down the gutter in the center of the lane. At the other end of the alley, small groups of rioters dashed past. These groups of three or four often had royal guards on their heels. Sithas emerged from White Rose Lane in time to confront four desperate-looking elves. They stared at him. Each was armed with a stone or stick.

Sithas pointed with his sword. "Put down those things. Go back to your homes!" he said sternly.

"We are free elves! We won't be ordered about! We've been driven from our homes once, and we'll not let it happen again!" cried one of the elves.

"You are mistaken," Sithas said, turning his horse so none of them could get behind him. "No one is driving you from here. The Speaker of the Stars has plans for a permanent town on the west bank of the Thon-Thalas—"

"That's not what the holy lady said," shouted a different elf.

"What holy lady?"

"The priestess of Quenesti Pah. She told us the truth!"

So, the riot could be laid at Miritelisina's door! Sithas burned with anger. He whipped his sword over his head. "Go home!" he shouted. "Go home, lest the warriors strike you down!"

Someone flung a stone at Sithas. He batted it away, the rock clanging off the tempered iron blade. One smoke-stained elf tried to grab the horse's bridle, but the prince hit him on the head with the flat of his blade. The elf collapsed, and the others hastily withdrew to find a more poorly armed target.

Sithas rode on through the mayhem, getting hit more than once by thrown sticks and shards. A bearded fellow he took for human swung a woodcutter's axe at him, so Sithas used the edge, not the flat, of his sword. The axe-wielder fell dead, cleaved from shoulder to heart. Only then did the prince notice the fellow's tapering ears and Silvanesti coloring. A half-human, the first he'd ever seen. Pity mixed with revulsion welled up inside the speaker's heir.

Feeling a bit dazed, Sithas rode to the water's edge. There were dead bodies floating in the normally calm river, a sight that only added to his disorientation. However, his dazed shock vanished instantly when he saw the body of an elf woman clad in a golden gown. His mother had a gown like that.

Sithas half-fell, half-jumped from horseback into the shallow water. He splashed, sword in hand, to the gowned body. It was Nirakina. His mother was dead! Tears spilling down his cheeks, the prince pulled the floating corpse to shallower water. When he turned the body over he saw to his immense relief that it was not his mother. This elf woman was a stranger to Sithas.

He released his hold on the body, and it was nudged gently away by the Thon-Thalas. Sithas stood coughing in the smoke, looking at the nightmare scene around him. Had the gods forsaken the Silvanesti this day?

"Sithas. . . . Sithas. . . ."

The prince whirled as he realized that someone was calling his name. He ran up the riverbank toward the sound. Once ashore, he was engulfed by the row of short towers that lined the riverbank. The tallest of these, a four-story house with conical roof and tall windows, was to his right. A white cloth waved from a top floor window.

"Sithas. . . ." With relief the prince noted that it was his mother's voice.

He mounted the horse and urged it into a gallop. Shouts and a loud crashing sound filled the air. On the other side of a low stone wall, a band of rioters was battering at the door of the four-story tower. Sithas raced the horse straight at the wall, and the animal jumped the barrier. As they landed on the other side, Sithas shouted a challenge and waved his sword in the air. Horse and rider thundered into their rioters' midst. The men dropped the bench they had been using as a battering ram and ran off.

Overhead, a window on the street side opened. Nirakina called down, "Sithas! Praise the gods you came!"

The door of the house, which was almost knocked to pieces, opened inward. A familiar-looking elf emerged warily, the broken end of a table leg clutched in his hand.

"I know you," said Sithas, dismounting quickly.

The elf lowered his weapon. "Tamanier Ambrodel, at your service, Highness," he said quietly. "Lady Nirakina is safe."

Nirakina came down the building's steps, and Sithas rushed to embrace her.

"We were besieged," Nirakina explained. Her honey-brown

hair was in complete disarray, and her gentle face was smeared with soot. "Tamanier saved my life. He fought them off and guarded the door."

"I thought you were dead," Sithas said, cupping his mother's face in his scratched, dirty hands. "I found a woman floating in the river. She was wearing your clothes."

Nirakina explained that she had been giving some old clothing to the refugees when the trouble started. In fact she and Tamanier had been at the focus of the riot. One reason they had escaped unharmed was that many of the refugees knew the speaker's wife and protected her.

"How did it start?" demanded Sithas. "I heard something about Miritelisina."

"I'm afraid it was her," Tamanier answered. "I saw her standing in the back of a cart, proclaiming that the speaker and high priests were planning to send all the settlers back across the river. The people grew frightened. They thought they were being driven from their last shelter by their own lords, sent to die in the wilderness. So they rose up, with the intention of forestalling a new exile."

Fists clenched, Sithas declared, "This is treason! Miritelisina must be brought to justice!"

"She did not tell them to riot," his mother said gently. "She cares about the poor, and it is they who have suffered most from this."

Sithas was in no mood to debate. Instead, he turned to Tamanier and held out his hand. Eyes wide, the elf grasped his prince's hand. "You shall be rewarded," said Sithas gratefully.

"Thank you, Highness." Tamanier looked up and down the street. "Perhaps we can take Lady Nirakina home now."

It was much quieter. Kencathedrus's warriors had herded the rioters into an ever-tightening circle. When the mob was finally subdued, the fire brigade was able to rush into the Market quarter. That occurred far too late, though; fully half of the marketplace had already been reduced to ruin.

*　*　*　*　*

The justice meted out by Sithel to his rebellious subjects was swift and severe. The rioters were tried as one and condemned.

Those of Silvanesti or Kagonesti blood were made slaves and set to rebuilding what they had destroyed. The humans and other non-elven rioters were driven from the city at pike point and forbidden ever to return, upon pain of death. All merchants who participated in the madness had their goods confiscated. They, too, were banished for life.

Miritelisina was brought before the speaker. Sithas, Nirakina, Tamanier Ambrodel, and all the high clerics of Silvanost were present. She made no speeches, offered no defense. Despite his respect for her, the speaker found the priestess guilty of petty treason. He could have made the charge high treason, for which the penalty was death, but Sithel could not bring himself to be that harsh.

The high priestess of Quenesti Pah was sent to the dungeon cells under the Palace of Quinari. Her cell was large and clean, but dark. Layers of inhibiting spells were placed around it, to prevent her from using her magical knowledge to escape or communicate with the outside world. Though many saw this as just, few found the sentencing a positive thing; not since the terrible, anarchical days of Silvanos and Balif had such a high-ranking person been sent to the dungeon.

"Is it right, do you think, to keep her there?" Nirakina asked her husband and son later, in private.

"You surprise me," said Sithel in a tired voice. "You, of all people, whose life was in the balance, should have no qualms about her sentence."

Nirakina's face was sad. "I am sure she meant no harm. Her only concern was for the welfare of the refugees."

"Perhaps she did not mean to start a riot," Sithas said empathetically, "but I'm not certain she meant no harm. Miritelisina sought to undermine the decree of the speaker by appealing to the common people. That, in itself, is treason."

"Those poor people," Nirakina murmured.

The speaker's wife retired to her bed. Sithel and his son remained in the sitting room.

"Your mother has a kind heart, Sith. All this suffering has undone her. She needs her rest." Sithas nodded glumly, and the speaker went on. "I am sending a troop of fifty warriors under Captain Coryamis to the west. They are to try to capture some of the brigands who've been terrorizing our settlers and to bring them back alive. Perhaps then we can find out who's truly behind these attacks." Sithel yawned and stretched. "Coryamis leaves tonight. Within a month, we should know something."

Father and son parted. Sithel watched the prince descend the far stairs, not the route to the quarters that he shared with Hermathya. "Where are you going, Sith?" he asked in confusion.

Sithas looked distinctly uncomfortable. "My old rooms, Father. Hermathya and I are—we are not sharing a bed these days," he said stiffly. Sithel raised one pale brow in surprise.

"You'll not win her over by sleeping apart," he advised.

"I need time to contemplate," Sithas replied. With a gruff good-night, he went on his way. Sithel waited until his son's footsteps had faded from the stone stairwell, then he sighed. Sithas and Hermathya estranged—for some reason that fact bothered him more than having to send Miritelisina to the dungeon. He knew his son, and he knew his daughter-in-law, too. They were both too proud, too unbending. Any rift between them was only likely to widen over time. Not good. The line of Silvanos required stability and offspring to insure its continuation. He would have to do something.

A prodigious yawn racked the speaker's body. For now, though, there was his own bed, his own wife, and sleep.

* * * * *

In the weeks following the rioting in the Market, a regular patrol of royal guards walked the streets. A squad of four warriors, moving through the city very late one night, spied a body lying on the steps of the Temple of Quenesti Pah. Two elves ran over and turned the body face-up. To their astonishment, they knew the dead elf well. He was Nortifinthas, and he was of their own company, sent with forty-nine other warriors to the western provinces. No word had been heard from the fifty warriors in over two weeks.

The night watch picked up their fallen comrade and hastened to the Palace of Quinari. Other patrols saw them and joined with them as they went. By the time the group reached the main door of the palace, it was over thirty strong.

Stankathan, the major-domo, arrived at the palace door in

response to the vigorous pounding of the guards. He stood in the open doorway, holding aloft a sputtering oil lamp.

"Who goes there?" Stankathan said in a voice husky with sleep. The officer who had found Nortifinthas explained the situation. Stankathan looked at the corpse, borne on the shoulders of his fellow warriors. His face paled.

"I will fetch Prince Sithas," he decided.

Stankathan went to Sithas's bachelor quarters. The door was open, and he saw the prince asleep at a table. The elder elf shook his head. Everyone knew that Prince Sithas and his wife were living apart, but still it saddened the old servant.

"Your Highness?" he said, touching Sithas lightly on the back. "Your Highness, wake up; there's been an . . . event."

Sithas raised his head suddenly. "What? What is it?"

"The night watch has found a dead warrior in the streets. Apparently he is one of the soldiers the speaker sent out weeks ago."

Sithas pushed back his chair and stood, disoriented by his sudden awakening. "How can that be?" he asked. He breathed deeply a few times to clear his head. Then, adjusting his sleep-twisted robe, the prince said, "I will see the warriors."

The major-domo led Sithas to the main door. There the prince heard the story of the finding of the body from the night watch officer.

"Show me," ordered Sithas.

The warriors laid the body gently down on the steps. Nortifinthas had numerous knife and club wounds, which had sufficed to drain his life away.

Sithas looked over the array of grim, concerned faces. "Take the body to the cellar and lay it out. Tomorrow perhaps the learned clerics can discover what happened," he said in a subdued voice.

Four guards hoisted Nortifinthas on their shoulders and went up the steps. Stankathan showed them the way to the palace cellar. After a time, when Stankathan returned with the bearers, Sithas dismissed the guards. To the major-domo he said, "When the speaker rises tomorrow, tell him at once what has occurred. And send for me."

"It shall be done, Highness."

* * * * *

The day dawned cool, and gray clouds piled up in the northern sky. Sithas and Sithel stood on opposite sides of the table where the body of Nortifinthas had been laid out. Everyone else had been banished from the cellar.

Sithel bent over and began to examine the dead elf's clothes with minute care. He fingered every seam, looked in every pocket, even felt in the corpse's hair. Finally Sithas could contain himself no longer.

"What are you doing, Father?"

"I know Captain Coryamis would not have sent this warrior back to us without some kind of message."

"How do you know he was sent? He could be a deserter."

Sithel stood up. "Not this fellow. He was a fine warrior. And if he had deserted, he wouldn't come back to Silvanost." Just then, Sithel froze. He reached for the shielded candle that was their only source of light, then held it close to the dead elf's waist.

"There!" The speaker hastily thrust the candle holder into Sithas's hand. Eagerly, Sithel unclasped the sword belt from the corpse. He held it up to Sithas. "Do you see?"

Sithas squinted hard at the inside of the belt. Sure enough, there were letters scratched in the dark leather, but they appeared random and meaningless. "I don't understand," he protested. "I see writing, but it's just gibberish."

Sithel removed the empty scabbard from the belt and gently laid it on the corpse's chest. Then he coiled the belt and tucked it inside his robe. "There are many things you have yet to learn, things that only come from experience. Come with me, and I'll show you how the dead can speak to the living without magic."

They left the cellar. An entire corps of courtiers and servants stood waiting for the two most important people in Silvanost to reappear. Sithel promptly ordered everyone to return to their tasks, and he and his son went alone to the Tower of the Stars.

"The palace is like an anthill," Sithel said, striding briskly across the Processional Road. "How can anything remain secret for very long?"

The prince was puzzled, but he covered his bewilderment

with the meditative mask he had learned from the priests of Matheri. It was not until they were alone, locked inside the audience hall of the tower, that his father spoke again.

"Coryamis sent the soldier back as a courier," confided Sithel. "Let us see what he brought us."

The emerald throne of the speaker was not simply made of that stone. The natural faceted gems were interspersed with hand-turned columns of rare and beautiful wood. These were of varying lengths and thicknesses, and some were even inlaid with gold and silver. Sithas looked on in mute wonder as his father detached piece after piece of wood from the ancient, sacred throne. Each time he removed a cylinder of wood, he would wind the dead soldier's belt around it, spiral fashion. The speaker would then stare at the writing on the belt for a second, remove the belt, and re-fit the wooden piece back into the throne. On the fifth attempt, Sithel gave a cry of triumph. He read up the length of the cylinder, turned it slightly, and read the next row of letters. When he was done, the Speaker of the Stars looked up, ashen faced.

"What is it, Father?" Sithas asked. The speaker handed him the rod and belt as a reply.

Now the prince understood. The message had been written on the belt while it was wound around a shaft of identical thickness to this one. When the belt was removed, the letters became a meaningless jumble. Now Sithas could read the last message sent by Coryamis.

There were many abbreviations in the writing. Sithas read the message out loud, just to be certain he had it right. " 'Great speaker,' " it said, " 'I write this knowing I may not be alive tomorrow, and this is the only chance I have to tell what has happened. Two days ago we were attacked by a body of humans, elves, and mixed-bloods. The horsemen trapped us between the foothills of the Khalkist Mountains and the falls of the Keraty River. There are only fifteen of us left. I will send this message with my best fighter, Nortifinthas. Great speaker, these men and elves are not bandits, they are formidable cavalry. They also knew where to ambush us and how many we were, so I feel, too, that we were betrayed. There is a traitor in Silvanost. Find him or all shall perish. Long live Silvanesti!' "

Sithas stared at his father in horrified silence for a long moment. Finally, he burst out, "This is monstrous!"

"Treachery in my own city. Who could it be?" Sithel asked.

"I don't know, but we can find out. The greater question is, who pays the traitor? It must be the emperor of Ergoth!" declared his son.

"Yes." Surely there was no one else with the money or reason to wage such an underhanded campaign against the elven nation. Sithel looked at the prince, who suddenly seemed much older than before. "I do not want war, Sithas. I do not want it. We have not yet received a reply from the emperor or from the king of Thorbardin regarding our request for a conference. If both nations agree to come and talk, it will give us a chance for peace."

"It may give the enemy the time they need, too," said Sithas.

The speaker took the belt and wooden cylinder from his son. He restored the cylinder to its place in the side of the throne. The belt he fastened around his own waist. Sithel had regained his calm, and the years fell away once more when resolve filled his face.

"Son, I charge you with the task of finding the traitor. Male or female, young or old, there can be no mercy."

"I shall find the traitor," Sithas vowed.

* * * * *

Dinner each night in the Quinari Palace was held in the Hall of Balif. It was as much a social occasion as a meal, for all the courtiers were required to attend and certain numbers of the priestly and noble classes, too. Speaker Sithel and Lady Nirakina sat in the center of the short locus of the vast oval table. Sithas and Hermathya sat on Nirakina's left, and all the guests sat to the left of them in order of seniority. Thus, the person to Sithel's right was always the most junior member of the court. That seat fell to Tamanier Ambrodel nowadays; for saving Lady Nirakina's life during the riot, he'd been granted a minor title.

The hall was full, though everyone was still standing when Tamanier and Hermathya arrived together. Sithel had not yet come, and no one could sit until the speaker did so himself. For his part, Sithas stood behind his chair, impassive. Hermathya hoped he might react jealously upon seeing her on the arm of the stalwart Tamanier, but the prince kept his pensive gaze focused on the golden plate set before him.

Sithel entered with his wife. Servants pulled the tall chairs for the speaker and Nirakina, and Sithel took his place. "May the gods grant you all health and long life," he said quietly. The vast hall had been constructed so that conversation at one end could be heard by parties at the other. The traditional greeting before meals carried easily to the entire oval table.

"Long life to you, Speaker of the Stars," the diners responded in unison. Sithel sat. With much shuffling and squeaking of chairs, the guests sat down, too.

A troop of servers appeared, bearing a large pot. The pot swung on a long pole supported on the shoulders of two elves. Behind these servants, two more servers carried a slotted bronze box, from which a dull glow radiated. The box was full of large hearthstones that had been banked against the kitchen fires all day. Two servants set the bronze box on a stone slab, and the pot carriers eased the great cauldron onto the box. Now the soup would stay hot all through dinner—which could last several hours.

Young elf maidens clad in shifts of opaque yellow gauze slipped in and out among the seated guests, filling their bowls with steaming turtle soup. For those not inclined to soup, there was fresh fruit, picked that morning in the vast orchards on the eastern shore. Elf boys staggered under the weight of tall amphorae, brimming with purple-red nectar. The goblets of the guests were kept full.

With the first course served, Stankathan signaled to the servants at the doors of the hall. They swung them open, and a trio of musicians entered. The players of flute, lyre, and sistrum arranged themselves in the far corner of the hall as conversation in the room began in earnest.

"I have heard," opened old Rengaldus, guildmaster of the gemcutters, "that there is to be a conclave with representatives of Ergoth."

"That's old news," said Zertinfinas, the priest. He hacked open a juicy melon and poured the seedy center pulp onto his plate. "The dwarves of Thorbardin are invited, too."

"I have never seen a human close up," remarked Hermathya. "Or talked to one."

"You haven't missed much, Lady," Rengaldus replied. "Their language is uncouth and their bodies thick with hair."

"Quite bestial," agreed Zertinfinas.

"Those are your opinions," Tamanier interjected. Many eyes turned to him. It was unusual for the junior noble to speak at all. "I knew humans out on the plains, and many of them were good people."

"Yes, but aren't they inherently treacherous?" asked the guildmaster of the sandalmakers. "Do humans ever keep their word?"

"Frequently." Tamanier looked to his patron, Sithas, for signs of displeasure. The speaker's son, as usual, ate sparingly, picking grapes one at a time from the cluster on his plate. He did not seem to have heard Tamanier's comments, so the favored young courtier continued. "Humans can be fiercely honorable, perhaps because they know so many of their fellows are not."

"They are unredeemably childish in their tempers," Zertinfinas asserted. "How can they not be? With only seventy or so years of life how can they accumulate any store of wisdom or patience?"

"But they are clever," noted Rengaldus. He slurped a mouthful of nectar and wiped his chin with a satin napkin. "A hundred years ago there wasn't a human alive who could cut a diamond or polish a sapphire. Now craftsmen in Daltigoth have learned to work gems, and they have undercut our market! My factors in Balifor say that human-cut gems are selling well there, mainly because they are far cheaper than ours. The buyers care less about quality than they do about the final price."

"Barbarians," muttered Zertinfinas into his cup.

The second course was brought out: a cold salad of river trout with a sweet herb dressing. Murmurs of approval circled the great table. Loaves of pyramid-shaped bread were also provided, smeared with honey, a confection greatly loved by elves.

"Perhaps one of the learned clerics can tell me," Hermathya said, cutting herself a chunk of warm bread, "why humans have such short lives?" Zertinfinas cleared his throat to speak, but from the opposite side of the table, a new voice answered the lady's question.

"It is generally considered that humans represent a middle race, farther removed from the gods and closer to the realm of the animals. Our own race—the first created, longer lived, and possessing a greater affinity for the powers of magic—is closest to the gods."

Hermathya tilted her head to get a better look at the soft-spoken cleric. "I do not know you, holy one. Who are you?"

"Forgive me, Lady, for not introducing myself. I am Kamin Oluvai, second priest of the Blue Phoenix. "The young elf stood and bowed to Hermathya. He was a striking-looking fellow, in his brilliant blue robe and golden headband, with its inlay of a blue phoenix. His golden hair was long even by elven standards. Sithas studied him circumspectly. This Kamin Oluvai had not been to many royal dinners.

"What about these humans?" complained Zertinfinas loudly, beginning to feel his nectar. "What is to be done about them?"

"I believe that is a matter best left to the speaker," Sithas replied. One hundred and fifty pairs of eyes looked to Sithel, who was listening with great care while eating his fish.

"The sovereignty of Silvanesti will be preserved," the speaker said calmly. "That is why the conclave has been called."

The prince nodded, then asked, "Is it true, Ambrodel, that there are more humans living in our western provinces than Silvanesti and Kagonesti?"

"More than the Silvanesti, Highness. But the true number of the Kagonesti is difficult to state. So many of them live in the remote parts of the forest, mountains, and plains—"

"Humans breed at any point past age fifteen," blurted Zertinfinas. "They regularly have five and six children in a family!" Whispers of surprise and concern circled the table. Elven parents seldom had more than two children in their entire, lengthy lifetimes.

"Is that true?" Nirakina queried Tamanier.

"At least in the wild country it is. I cannot say what families are like in the more settled areas of Ergoth. But many of the children do not survive into adulthood. Human knowledge of the healing arts is not nearly so advanced as ours."

The musicians completed their program of light tunes and

began to play "The Sea-Elf's Lament." The main course was served.

It came rolling in on a large cart, a huge sculpture of a dragon done in golden-brown pie crust. The "beast" reared up five feet high. His back was scaled with mint leaves, his eyes and talons made red with pomegranates. The head and spiky tail of the dragon were covered with glazed nut meats.

The diners applauded this culinary creation, and Sithel himself smiled. "You see, my friends, how the cook is master of us all," he proclaimed, rising to his feet. "For centuries the dragons preyed upon us, and now we have them to dinner."

Stankathan stood by the pastry dragon, a sword in his hand. He jerked his head, and servants positioned a golden tray under the dragon's chin. With a force that belied his age, the servant lopped off the dragon's head. A flight of live sparrows burst from the open neck of the creation, each bird having silver streamers tied to its legs. The assembly gave a collective gasp of admiration.

"I trust the rest of the insides are more thoroughly cooked," quipped Sithel.

The servants bore the head of the dragon to the speaker. With smaller knives, they carved it to pieces. Under the crusty pastry skin, the head was stuffed with delicate meat paste, whole baked apples, and sweet glazed onions.

Stankathan attacked the rest of the pastry like some culinary thespian portraying the mighty Huma slaying a real dragon. The body of the beast was filled with savory sausages, stuffed peppers, whole capons, and vegetable tarts. The room filled with noise as every diner commented on the elegance of this evening's feast.

Zertinfinas, rather loudly, called for more nectar. The serving boy had none left in his amphora, so he ran to the door to fetch more. Sithas called to the servant as he passed, and the elf boy dropped to one knee by the prince's chair.

"Yes, Highness?"

"The holy one has had too much to drink. Have the cellar master cut the nectar with water. Half for half," ordered Sithas in a confidential tone.

"As you command, sire."

"The cook really has outdone himself," Hermathya remarked. "This is a wonderful feast."

"Is it a special occasion?" asked Rengaldus.

"The calendar does not list a holiday," Kamin Oluvai noted. "Unless it is a special day for the speaker."

"It is, holy one. By this feast we do honor to a dead hero," Sithel explained.

Nirakina set down her goblet, puzzled. "What hero, my husband?"

"His name was Nortifinthas."

Head wobbling, Zertinfinas asked, "Was he a companion of Huma Dragonsbane?"

"No," Kamin Oluvai assisted. "He sat in the first great Synthal-Elish, did he not?"

"You are both mistaken," Sithel replied. "Nortifinthas was a simple soldier, a Kagonesti who died nobly in service to this house." Conversation around the table had died just as the flutist trilled the high solo from the lament.

"This morning," the speaker continued, "this soldier named Nortifinthas returned to the city from the western province. He was the only survivor of the fifty warriors I sent out to find the bandits who have troubled our people lately. All his comrades were slain. Even though he was fearfully wounded, the brave Nortifinthas returned with the last dispatch of his commander." Sithel looked around the table, meeting each guest eye to eye. The prince sat very still, his left hand clenched into a fist in his lap. "One of you here, one of you seated at my table eating my food, is a traitor."

The musicians heard this declaration and ceased playing. The speaker waved a hand to them to continue, and they did so awkwardly.

"You see, the force that wiped out my fifty warriors was not a band of hit-and-run bandits, but a disciplined troop of cavalry who knew where and when my soldiers would come. It was not a battle. It was a massacre."

"Do you know who the traitor is, Speaker?" Hermathya asked with great earnest.

"Not yet, but the person will be found. I spent most of my day compiling a list of those who could have known the route of my warriors. At this point, I suspect everyone."

The speaker looked around the large table. The gaiety was

gone from the dinner, and the diners looked at the delicacies on their plates without enthusiasm.

Sithel picked up his knife and fork. "Finish your food," he commanded. When no one else emulated him, he held up his hands expressively and said, "Why do you not eat? Do you want this fine meal to go to waste?"

Sithas was the first to take up his fork and resume eating. Hermathya and Nirakina did likewise. Soon, everyone was eating again, but with much less good humor than before.

"I will say this," Sithel added pointedly, cutting the glazed pomegranate eye from the pastry dragon's face. "The traitor's identity is suspected."

By now the elf boy had returned, his amphora full of diluted nectar. Into the absolute silence that followed his own last statement, the speaker said loudly, "Zertinfinas! Your nectar!"

The cleric, his head snapping up at the sound of his name, had to be pounded on the back several times to save him from choking on a piece of pastry.

Sithas watched his father as he ate. The speaker's every movement was graceful, his face serene with resolve.

✿ 14 ✿

While the Speaker Dined

The wildwood slowly regained its lively character. No longer was there that absence of animal life that Kith-Kanan had found so puzzling when he first arrived. Daily, deer came to graze in the clearing. Rabbits and squirrels cavorted in and around the trees. Birds other than the ubiquitous corvae appeared. Bears, boar, and panthers roared in the night. As Mackeli had said, they'd been warned of the humans. Now that the humans were gone, the animals had returned.

On this particular day, Mackeli wedged his tongue between his teeth and concentrated on lashing an arrowhead to a shaft. Kith-Kanan was teaching him the bow now. It was not something to which the boy took readily. As he tied off the end of the whipcord, the flint arrowhead sagged badly out of line.

"That's not tight enough," Kith-Kanan cautioned. He handed the boy his dagger. "Start again and make it *tight.*"

Neither of them had seen Anaya for over a week. It didn't bother Mackeli a whit, but Kith-Kanan found himself missing the strange forest woman. He wondered if he should go and look for her. Mackeli said, and Kith-Kanan did not doubt, that the prince would never find her unless she wanted to be found.

"What do you do if you need her in a hurry?" Kith-Kanan asked ingeniously. "I mean, suppose you got hurt or something. How would you call her?"

"If I really need Ny, she knows it and comes for me." Mackeli had almost finished his tying of the arrow.

"You mean, you just *will* her to come, and she does?"

The boy knotted the tough silk string. "Mostly." With a proud smile, he handed Kith-Kanan the newly lashed arrow. Kith shook it to see if the head would loosen. It didn't.

"Good," he said, handing the arrow back. "You only need twenty more to fill your quiver."

* * * * *

Late the next afternoon the wildwood rang with laughter and splashing as Kith-Kanan and Mackeli swam in the pool. Mackeli was progressing well under the prince's tutelage, so they had decided to finish their day with a swim in the crystal waters.

Mackeli was treading water and looking around the pool for Kith-Kanan. The boy was a better swimmer than his sister, but not so skilled as the elf prince.

"Where'd you go, Kith?" he said, eyeing the surface of the water uncertainly. Suddenly a hand closed on his left ankle and Mackeli gave a yelp. He found himself lifted up and launched skyward. Laughing and yelling all the way, he flew several feet and landed back in the pool with a loud splash. He and Kith-Kanan surfaced at the same time.

"It's not fair," Mackeli said, flinging his streaming hair from his eyes. "You're bigger than me!"

Kith-Kanan grinned. "You'll catch up someday, Keli," he said. Twisting gracefully in the water, the prince turned and swam toward the granite ledge on shore.

As Kith-Kanan hoisted himself up on the ledge, Mackeli called to him, "I want to learn to swim like you. You move like a fish!"

"Another result of my misspent youth." Kith-Kanan stretched out full-length on the warm ledge and closed his eyes.

Minutes later, something moved to block the sunlight. Without opening his eyes, Kith-Kanan said, "I know you're there, Keli. I heard you walk up. You'd better not—Hey!"

With a cry, the prince sat up. A very sharp spear point had been poked into his bare stomach. Squinting in the bright light, he looked up. Several pairs of moccasin-clad feet were gathered around Kith-Kanan, and their owners—four dark figures—loomed over him.

"Mackeli, my sword!" he called, leaping to his feet.

The boy, still in the pool, looked at his friend and laughed. "Calm down, Kith! It's only White-Lock."

Kith-Kanan stared. Shading his eyes, he realized that the four dark figures were Kagonesti males. They were brown-skinned, hard-muscled, and wore breechcloths of deerskin. Bows, quivers of arrows, and deerskin bags were slung over their muscled backs. Their exposed skin was covered by red, yellow, and blue loops and whorls of paint.

The tallest of the four—he topped Kith-Kanan by several inches—had a streak of white in his midnight-black hair. He and his comrades were looking at the Silvanesti nobleman with amused curiosity.

Naked and still damp from his swim, Kith-Kanan drew the tattered shreds of his dignity about himself. He pulled on his clothes as Mackeli came out of the pool and greeted the four strange elves.

"Blessings of Astarin upon you, White-Lock, you and yours," Mackeli said. He placed his hands over his heart and then held them in front of him, palms up.

The Kagonesti called White-Lock repeated the gesture. "And upon you, Mackeli," he said to the boy in a deep and solemn voice, though he continued to watch Kith-Kanan. "Do you now bring the Settled Ones to the sacred forests?"

Kith-Kanan knew that the term "Settled Ones" was meant as an insult. The Kagonesti were nomadic and never built permanent habitations. Before he could retort, Mackeli said, "Kith is my friend and my guest, White-Lock. Do the People no longer value courtesy to guests?"

A smile quirked White-Lock's lips and he said, "Blessings of Astarin upon you, guest of Mackeli."

"Would you and your hunting party honor me with a visit, White-Lock?" Mackeli asked. He pulled his clothes on.

White-Lock glanced at his companions. Kith-Kanan neither saw nor heard any exchange between them, but the tall Kagonesti said, "My companions and I do not wish to intrude upon the Keeper of the Forest."

"It is no intrusion," Mackeli replied politely.

Kith-Kanan was mildly surprised at the change that seemed to have come over the irrepressible boy. He spoke to the Kagonesti in a very composed and adult manner. They, in turn, treated him with great respect. Mackeli went on. "The keeper is away at present. Were she here, I know she would wish to make you welcome. Come, we can share stories. I have had a great adventure since we last met."

White-Lock looked once more to his three companions. After a moment's hesitation, he nodded and they all set out for the clearing.

As they walked, Kith-Kanan brought up the rear and studied these new acquaintances. In his travels around the western provinces of Silvanesti, he had met several Kagonesti. Those elves, however, had given up their nomadic and isolated ways to trade with the humans and Silvanesti who lived in the West. Many of them no longer painted their bodies, and they wore civilized clothing. These four were obviously not of that ilk.

As they made their way to the clearing, Mackeli introduced Kith-Kanan to the others in the group. There was Sharp-Eye, brown-haired and some inches shorter than White-Lock; Braveheart, who had sandy hair; and Otter. The latter was shorter than the rest, a head shorter than Kith-Kanan, and his pale yellow eyes twinkled with inner mirth. He was the only one who smiled outright at the elf prince. It was a merry smile, and Kith-Kanan returned it.

In the clearing, Mackeli bade them all be seated by the oak. He went inside and returned shortly with nuts, berries, and fruit. White-Lock took only a handful of red berries, though his comrades dug in with gusto.

"So, guest of Mackeli, how do you come to be in the wild-wood?" White-Lock asked, staring at the Silvanesti prince.

Kith-Kanan frowned. "I am a traveler, White-Lock. And my name is Kith. You would honor me by using it," he replied testily.

White-Lock nodded and looked pleased. Kith-Kanan remembered then that the more primitive Kagonesti didn't believe it was polite to use a person's name unless they'd been given leave to. He cudgeled his brain, trying to recall what else he knew about their race.

"White-Lock!" called a startled voice behind Kith-Kanan. "What in the name of the forest is this?"

They turned. The one called Otter was standing at the far end of the clearing, staring in awe at Arcuballis. The griffon was lying in the shade of a big tree. The beast opened one golden eye and regarded the amazed Kagonesti.

"That is Arcuballis," Kith-Kanan said proudly. With an inward smile, he uttered a sharp whistle. Arcuballis got quickly to its feet, and Otter nearly fell over backward as he stumbled away from the tall beast. Kith-Kanan gave another whistle, at first high-pitched, then sliding down the scale. The griffon unfolded its wings to their full extent and uttered a trilling call in imitation of Kith-Kanan's whistle. Otter jumped back again. At another whistle from the prince, Arcuballis folded its wings and made its way daintily across the clearing, coming to a stop several feet from the group.

Kith-Kanan was pleased to see that even White-Lock looked impressed. The Kagonesti leader told Otter to rejoin the group. "What is this beast, Kith?" White-Lock asked wonderingly.

"Arcuballis is a griffon. He's my mount and my friend." Kith-Kanan whistled once more and Arcuballis lay down where it was. In seconds, the beast closed its eyes in sleep again.

"He is beautiful, Kith!" Otter said enthusiastically. "He flies?"

"He does indeed."

"I should be honored if you would take me for a ride!"

"Otter," White-Lock said sharply.

Regret replaced the joy on Otter's face, and he subsided. Kith-Kanan smiled kindly at the yellow-eyed elf as the Kagonesti called Sharp-Eye spoke into the silence.

"Mackeli, you said you had a tale to share," he said. "Tell us of your great adventure."

All four Kagonesti settled down to listen. Even Otter tore his gaze from Arcuballis and gave his full attention to Mackeli. The Kagonesti were great ones for storytelling, Kith-Kanan knew. They rarely, if ever, wrote anything down. Their history, their news, all was passed orally from one generation to the next. If they liked Mackeli's story, it would be swapped between tribes until years hence, when it might be heard by every Kagonesti on Krynn.

Mackeli's green eyes widened. He looked at each of them in turn and began his story. "I was kidnapped by an evil wizard named Voltorno," he said softly.

Kith-Kanan shook his head bemusedly. Mackeli finally had a fresh audience for his tale. And the boy didn't let them down. None of the four Kagonesti moved so much as a finger during Mackeli's long recital of his kidnap, the pursuit by Kith-Kanan and Anaya, and the prince's duel with Voltorno. The silence was broken only by Otter's exclamation of triumph when Mackeli told how he and Kith-Kanan had flown away from Voltorno's men on Arcuballis.

When the story was finished, the Kagonesti looked at Kith-Kanan with new respect. The prince preened slightly, sitting up straighter.

"You fought well against the humans, Kith," Sharp-Eye concluded. The other Kagonesti nodded.

"We are sorry to have missed the Keeper of the Forest, Mackeli," White-Lock said. "To see the keeper is a great honor and pleasure. She walks with the gods and speaks with great wisdom."

A snort of laughter was surprised out of Kith-Kanan. "Anaya?" he exclaimed in disbelief. He was immediately sorry. The Kagonesti, including the fun-loving Otter, turned looks of stern reproach upon him.

"You are disrespectful of the keeper, Kith," White-Lock glowered.

"I'm sorry. I meant no disrespect," Kith-Kanan said apologetically. "White-Lock, I'm curious. I've met Kagonesti elves before but they weren't like you. They were more—uh—"

"Where did you meet these others?" White-Lock cut in.

"In the West," replied Kith-Kanan. "The western provinces

149

of Silvanesti."

"Settled Ones," Sharp-Eye said with much disgust. Brave-heart rubbed his hands together as if washing them, then flung them away from himself.

"Those you met have taken up the ways of the Settled Ones," said White-Lock, his voice hard. "They have turned their backs on the true ways."

Kith-Kanan was surprised by the loathing they all expressed. Deciding it did not behoove him to anger Mackeli's friends, he changed the subject. "Braveheart, how did you come by your name?"

Braveheart gestured to White-Lock. Kith-Kanan wondered if he'd committed another social breach by inquiring about the Kagonesti's name. White-Lock, though, didn't seem upset. He answered, "Braveheart was born mute, but his skill as a hunter and fighter earned him his adult name." Amusement danced in the hunter's eyes. "Are all your people so curious, Kith?"

Kith-Kanan looked chagrined. "No, White-Lock. My curiosity has gotten me in trouble before."

They all laughed, and the four Kagonesti hunters stood up. White-Lock brought his hands up to cover his heart and then held them out palms-up, first to Mackeli and then to Kith-Kanan. The boy and the prince returned the gesture.

"The blessings of Astarin upon you both," White-Lock said warmly. "Give our respects to the keeper."

"We shall, White-Lock. Blessings upon you all," Mackeli returned.

"Good-bye," Kith-Kanan called after them. With a last wave from Otter, the hunters disappeared into the forest.

Mackeli gathered up the uneaten food and stowed it back in the tree. Kith-Kanan remained standing, looking after the departed Kagonesti.

"They're a strange lot," Kith-Kanan mused aloud. "And they certainly don't care for their more 'settled' brothers. I thought the others I met were a lot less primitive." He chuckled. "And the way they talked about Anaya—as if she were a goddess!"

"They are good elves," Mackeli said when he returned. "They only want to live in peace with the forest, as they have for centuries. But most humans treat them like savages." The green eyes that looked up at Kith-Kanan were hard. "And

from what you've told me about your people, the Silvanesti
do no better."

*   *   *   *   *

Several more weeks went by. The episode of the Kagonesti
stayed with Kith-Kanan, and he continued to think on Mackeli's words. However, he was growing more and more worried
about Anaya. He questioned Mackeli, but the boy remained
unconcerned. Though Kith-Kanan knew she could take care of
herself, he still fretted. At night, he began to dream of her, deep
in the woods, calling to him, saying his name over and over. He
would then follow her voice through the black forest, but just
when he thought he'd found her, he would wake up. It was
frustrating.

After a time Anaya began to monopolize his waking
thoughts as well. The prince had told her he was her friend.
Was it more than that? What Kith-Kanan felt for the Kagonesti
woman was certainly different from what he felt for Mackeli.
Could he be in love with her? They had barely gotten to know
each other before she'd disappeared. But still the prince worried about her, and dreamed about her, and missed her.

Kith-Kanan and Mackeli were sleeping outside the tree one
pleasant night. The prince slept deeply and, for once,
dreamlessly—until something unseen tugged at his mind. He
opened his eyes and sat bolt upright, turning his head from side
to side. It was as if a sudden clap of thunder had wakened him.
Yet Mackeli slept on beside him. Night creatures chirped and
whirred softly in the forest, also undisturbed.

Kith-Kanan straightened his tunic—for he slept fully
clothed—and lay back down. He was completely awake when
the nameless something called to him once more. Drawn by
something he couldn't see, the prince got up and crossed the
clearing. The going was not easy, since the silver moon had set
and the red moon was almost down. It was an eerie crimson
orb just barely visible through the trees.

Kith-Kanan followed the path to the spring. Whatever was
pulling him brought him to that place, but when he arrived,
there seemed to be no one around. He dipped a hand in the cold
water and threw it on his face.

As the Silvanesti prince stared at his reflection in the pool, a second dark image appeared in the water next to it. Kith-Kanan leaped back and turned, his hand on his dagger hilt. It was Anaya, standing a few feet away.

"Anaya!" he uttered with relief. "You're all right. Where have you been?"

"You called me," she said evenly. Her eyes seemed to have a light of their own. "Your call was very strong. I couldn't stay away, no matter how I tried."

Kith-Kanan shook his head. "I don't understand," he said truthfully.

She stepped closer and looked up into his eyes. Her unpainted face was beautiful in the red moonlight. "Your heart spoke to mine, Kith, and I could not refuse to come. We were drawn together."

At that moment, Kith-Kanan thought he did understand. The idea that hearts could speak to each other was something he had heard about. His people were said to be able to perform a mysterious summons known as "the Call." It was said to work over great distances and was reputed to be irresistible. Yet Kith-Kanan had never known anyone who had actually done it.

He stepped closer and put a hand to her cheek. Anaya was trembling.

"Are you afraid?" he asked quietly.

"I have never felt like this before," she whispered.

"How do you feel?"

"I want to run!" she declared loudly. But she didn't move an inch.

"You called to me too, you know. I was asleep in the clearing just now and something woke me, something drew me down here to the spring. I couldn't resist it." Her cheek was warm, despite the coolness of the night. He cupped it in his hand. "Anaya, I have been so worried about you. When you didn't come back, I thought something might have happened to you."

"Something did," she replied softly. "All these weeks, I have been meditating and thinking of you. So many feelings were tumbling inside of me."

"I have been troubled also," the prince confessed. "I've lain awake at night trying to sort out my feelings." He smiled at her. "You've even intruded on my dreams, Anaya."

Her face twisted in pain. "It isn't right!"

"Why not? Am I so unappealing?"

"I am born of the forest! For ten times the length of your life I have lived in the wildwood, on my own and of my own. I did not take Mackeli until a short time ago—"

"Take Mackeli? Then, he is not your brother by blood, is he?"

Anaya looked at Kith-Kanan desperately. "No. I took him from a farmer's house. I was lonely. I needed someone to talk to . . ."

The emptiness in her eyes, the pain in her voice, touched Kith-Kanan's heart. He gripped Anaya's shoulders with both hands. In return, she put her arms around his waist and embraced him passionately.

After a moment, Anaya pulled back and said softly, "I want to show you something." She stepped into the pool.

"Where are we going?" he asked as he joined her in the cool spring.

"To my secret place." She took his hand and warned, "Don't let go."

They slid under the water's surface. It was as cold and as black as Takhisis's heart in the pool, but Anaya swam down, kicking with her feet. Something hard brushed Kith-Kanan's shoulder; he put a hand out and felt solid rock. They were in a tunnel. After a moment, Anaya planted her feet on the bottom and thrust upward. Kith-Kanan let himself be pulled along. Suddenly their heads broke the surface.

Treading water, Kith-Kanan looked around in wonder. A soft white light illuminated a vaulted ceiling that rose some fifteen feet above the pool's surface. The ceiling was smooth and pure white. All around the edge of the vault were painted the most beautiful murals Kith-Kanan had ever seen. They showed a variety of woodland scenes: misty glens, roaring waterfalls, and deep, dark forests.

"Come," Anaya said, drawing him along by the hand. He kicked forward until his toes bumped rock. It was not the sloping bottom of a natural pool. Kith-Kanan felt round-nosed steps cut into the rock as he and Anaya climbed out of the water.

The steps and floor of the cave were made of the same stone as the ceiling, a glassy white rock Kith-Kanan couldn't identify.

The cave itself was divided down the center by a row of graceful columns, deeply fluted and tapering to their tops. They appeared to be joined solidly into the floor and ceiling.

Anaya let go of his hand and let him wander forward on his own. He went to the source of the gentle white light, the third column in from the water's edge. A subtle glow and warmth emanated from the column. Hesitantly Kith-Kanan put out a hand to touch the translucent stone.

He turned to the Kagonesti, smiling. "It feels alive!"

"It is," she beamed.

The walls to the right of the colonnade were decorated with remarkable bas-reliefs, raised carvings that depicted elven women. There were four of them, life-sized, and between each relief was a carving of a different type of tree.

Anaya stood close beside the prince, and he put an arm around her waist. "What do these mean?" he said, gesturing at the reliefs.

"These were the Keepers of the Forest," she said proudly. "Those that came before me. They lived as I live now, guarding the wildwood from harm." Anaya went to the image farthest from the pool. "This was Camirene. She was Keeper of the Forest before me." Anaya moved to the right, to the next figure. "This was Ulyante." She slipped sideways to the third figure. "Here is Delarin. She died driving a dragon from the wildwood." Anaya touched the warm stone relief lightly with her fingertips. Kith-Kanan regarded the carved image with awe.

"And this," Anaya said, facing the figure nearest the pool, "is Ziatia, first guardian of the wildwood." She put her hands together and bowed to the image. Kith-Kanan looked from one relief to the next.

"It is a beautiful place," he said with awe.

"When I am troubled, I come here to rest and think," Anaya said, gesturing around her.

"Is this where you've been these past weeks?" he asked.

"Yes. Here, and in the wildwood. I—I watched you sleep many nights." She looked deep into his eyes.

Kith-Kanan could hardly take it all in. This beautiful cave, the many answers it provided and the mysteries it held. It was like the beautiful elf woman before him. She had provided him with answers this night, but in her deep eyes were even more mysteries and questions unanswered. For now, he gave himself up to the joy he felt, the joy at finding someone who cared for him, someone that he cared for. And he did care for her.

"I think I love you, Anaya," Kith-Kanan said tenderly, caressing her cheek.

She laid her head on his chest. "I begged the Forestmaster to send you away, but she would not. 'You must make the decision,' she said." She clasped Kith-Kanan with frightening strength.

He tilted her face up to his and bent down to kiss her. Anaya was no soft and timid elf maiden. The hard life of the wildwood had made her tough and strong, but as they kissed, Kith-Kanan could feel the tremors echoing through her body.

She broke the kiss. "I will not be a casual love," she vowed, and her eyes bored into his. "If we are to be together, you must swear to be mine always."

Kith-Kanan remembered how he had searched for her in his dreams, how frightened and alone he'd felt when he couldn't find her. "Yes, Anaya. Always. I wish I still had my starjewel, but Voltorno took it with my other belongings. I wish I could give it to you." She did not understand, and he explained the significance of the starjewel.

She nodded. "We have no jewels to give in the wildwood. We make our most sacred vows in blood." She took his hand and knelt by the pool, drawing him down beside her. Laying her palm against the sharp edge of the rock, she pressed down hard. When she pulled her hand back, it was bleeding. Kith-Kanan hesitated a moment, then he too cut his hand on the hard, glassy rock. They joined hands once more, pressing the wounds together. The blood of the Silvanesti House Royal flowed together with that of the forest-born Kagonesti.

Anaya plunged their joined hands into the water. "By blood and water, by soil and sky, by leaf and limb, I swear to love and keep you, Kith, for as long as I walk, for as long as I breathe."

"By Astarin and E'li, I swear to love and keep you, Anaya, for all my life." Kith-Kanan felt light-headed, as if a great weight had been taken from him. Perhaps it was the weight of his anger, laid across his shoulders when he'd left Silvanost in a rage.

Anaya drew their hands out of the water, and the cuts were healed. While he marveled at this, she said, "Come."

Together they moved to the rear of the cave, away from the pool. There, the glassy stone walls ended. In their place was a solid wall of tree roots, great twining masses of them. A sunken place in the floor, oval-shaped, was lined with soft furs.

Slowly, very slowly, she sank into the furs, looking up at him with eyes full of love. Kith-Kanan felt his heart beat faster as he sat beside his love and took her hands into his. Raising them to his lips, he whispered, "I didn't know."

"What?"

"I didn't know that this is what love truly feels like." He smiled and leaned closer to her. Her breath was warm in his face. "And," he added gently, "I didn't know that you were anything but a wild maiden, one who liked to live in the woods."

"That's exactly what I am," said Anaya.

*　*　*　*　*

She and Kith-Kanan talked of many things in the night and day they spent in the secret cave. He told her of Hermathya and of Sithas, and he felt his heart lighten as he confessed all. The anger and frustration were gone as if they'd never existed. The youthful passion he'd felt for Hermathya was completely unlike the deep love he now felt for Anaya. He knew there were those in Silvanost who would not understand his love for a Kagonesti. Even his own family would be shocked, he was sure. But he didn't dwell on that. He filled his mind with only good thoughts, happy thoughts.

One thing Kith-Kanan insisted upon, and to which Anaya eventually agreed, was that she tell Mackeli of his true origins. When they left the cave and returned to the oak tree, they found the boy sitting on a low branch, eating his evening meal.

When he saw the couple, he jumped from the branch and landed lightly in front of them. He took in their happy faces and the fact that they walked hand-in-hand, and demanded, "Are you two finally friends?"

Anaya and Kith-Kanan looked at each other, and a rare thing happened. Anaya smiled. "We are much more than friends," she said sweetly.

The three of them sat down with their backs to the broad oak's trunk. As Anaya told Mackeli the truth about his past, the sun dodged in and out of the clouds and red autumn leaves fell around them.

"I'm not your brother?" Mackeli asked when she had finished.

"You *are* my brother," Anaya replied firmly, "but we are not of the same blood."

"And if I was taken from my parents," he went on slowly, "who were you taken from, Ny?"

"I don't know, and I never shall. Camirene took me from my mother and father, just as I took you." She looked to the ground, embarrassed. "I needed a girl child to be the next Keeper of the Forest. I moved so hastily, I didn't take time to notice that you were a boy."

Kith-Kanan put an arm on Mackeli's shoulder. "You won't be too angry?"

Mackeli stood up and walked slowly away from them. His ever-present hood slipped down, revealing his white, Silvanesti hair. "It's all so strange," he said, confused. "I've never known any other life than the one I've had in the wildwood." He looked at Anaya. "I guess I'm not angry. I'm . . . stunned. I wonder what I would have been if I—if Anaya—"

"A farmer," said Anaya. "Your parents were farmers. They grew vegetables."

She went on to explain that once she realized she'd taken a boy-child instead of a girl, she tried to return the infant Mackeli to his parents, but their house was abandoned when she went back. So she had raised Mackeli as her brother.

Mackeli still seemed dazed by the tale of his abduction. Finally he asked, rather hesitantly, "Will you have to find a girl to raise to be keeper after you?"

Anaya looked beyond him to Kith-Kanan. "No. This time the Keeper of the Forest will give birth to her successor." Kith-Kanan held out a hand to her. When she took it, Mackeli quietly clasped his small hands around both of theirs.

15

three-Moons' day, year of the hawk

The ambassador from Thorbardin arrived in Silvanost on Three-Moons' Day, midway between the autumnal equinox and the winter solstice. The dwarf's name was Dunbarth, but he was called Ironthumb by most who knew him. In his youth he had been a champion wrestler. Now, in old age, he was esteemed as the most level-headed of all the counselors to the king of Thorbardin.

Dunbarth traveled with a small entourage: his secretary, four scribes, four dispatch riders, a crate of carrier pigeons, and sixteen warrior dwarves as his personal guard. The ambassador rode in a tall closed coach made entirely of metal. Even though the brass, iron, and bronze panels were hammered quite thin, with all the skill characteristic of the dwarven race, the coach was still enormously heavy. A team of eight horses drew the conveyance, which held not only Dunbarth, but his staff. The warrior escort rode sturdy, short-legged horses, not swift but blessed with phenomenal endurance. The dwarven party was met on the western bank of the Thon-Thalas by Sithas and an honor guard of twelve warriors.

"Good morrow to you, Lord Dunbarth!" Sithas said heartily. The ambassador stood on one of the steps hanging below the coach door. From there he was high enough to clasp arms with Sithas without the embarrassment of making the far taller elf bend over.

"Life and health to you, speaker's son," Dunbarth rumbled. His leggings and tunic were brown cloth and leather, but he sported a short purple cape and broad-brimmed light brown hat. A short feather plumed out from his hatband and matched in color the wide, bright blue belt at his waist. His attire offered a striking contrast to the elegant simplicity of Sithas's robe and sandals.

The prince smiled. "We have arranged ferries for your company." With a sweep of his hand he indicated the two large barges moored at the river's edge.

"Will you ride with me, son of Sithel?" asked Dunbarth importantly.

"I would be honored."

The dwarf climbed back into his coach, then Sithas grasped the handrail and stepped up into the metal wagon. The top was high enough for him to stand erect inside. Nevertheless, Dunbarth ordered his secretary, a swarthy young dwarf, to surrender his seat to Sithas. The elf prince sat. The escort filed in behind the coach, pennants whipping from the tips of their gilded pikes.

"A remarkable thing, this coach," Sithas said politely. "Is it made entirely of metal?"

"Indeed, noble prince. Not one speck of wood or cloth in the whole contraption!"

Sithas felt the silver curtains that hung in front of the side windows. The dwarves had woven them of metal so fine it felt like cloth.

"Why build it so?" he asked. "Wouldn't wood be lighter?"

Dunbarth folded his hands across his broad, round belly. "It would indeed, but this is an official coach for Thorbardin ambassadors traveling abroad, so it was made to show off the skills of my people in metal-working," he replied proudly.

With much shouting and cracking of whips, the ponderous coach rolled onto a barge. The team of horses was cut loose and brought alongside it. Finally, the coach and the warrior escorts were distributed on board.

Dunbarth leaned forward to the coach window. "I would like to see the elves who are going to row this ferry!"

"We have no need for such crude methods," Sithas said smoothly. "But watch, if it pleases your lordship."

Dunbarth leaned his elbow on the window edge and looked out over the starboard side of the barge. The ferry master, an elf long in years with yellow hair and mahogany skin, mounted the wooden bulwark and put a brass trumpet to his lips. A long, single note blurted out, sliding down the scale.

In the center of the river, a round green hump broke the surface for an instant, then disappeared again. Large ripples spread out from that point—large enough that when they reached the riverbank they all but swamped a string of canoes tied to the stone pier. The great barge rocked only slightly in the swells.

Again the green hump broke the surface, and this time it rose. The hump became a dome, green and glistening, made up of a hundred angular plates. In front of the dome, the brow of a massive green head appeared. A large orange eye with a vertical black pupil the size of a full-grown dwarf appraised the stationary barge. At the tip of the triangular head, two nostrils as big as barrels spewed mist into the air.

"It's a monster!" Dunbarth cried. "By Reorx!" His hand went to his waist, reaching for a sword he'd forgotten he did not wear.

"No, my lord," Sithas said soothingly. "A monster it may be, but a tame one. It is our tow to the far shore."

The dwarven warriors on the barge fingered their heavy axes and muttered to each other. The giant turtle, bred by the elves for just this job, swam to the blunt bow of the ferry and waited patiently as the ferry master and two helpers walked across its huge shell to attach lines to a stout brass chain that encircled the monster's shell. One of the turtle's hind legs bumped the barge, knocking the feet out from under the nervous warrior dwarves. The coach creaked backward an inch or two on its iron axles.

"What a brute!" Dunbarth exclaimed, fascinated. "Do such monsters roam freely in the river, Prince Sithas?"

"No, my lord. At the command of my grandfather, Speaker Silvanos, the priests of the Blue Phoenix used their magic to breed a race of giant turtles to serve as beasts of burden on the river. They are enormously strong, of course, and quite long-lived." Sithas sat back imperiously in his springy metal seat.

The ferry master blew his horn again, and the great reptile swung toward the shore of Fallan Island, a mile away. The slack went out of the tow line, and the barge lurched into motion. Sithas heard a loud clatter and knew that the warriors had been thrown off their feet again. He suppressed a smile.

"Have you ever been to Silvanost before, Lord Dunbarth?" he asked deferentially.

"No, I've not had the pleasure. My uncle, Dundevin Stonefoot, did come to the city once on behalf of our king."

"I remember," Sithas mused. "I was but a boy." It had been fifty years before.

The ferry pitched up and down as they crossed the midpoint of the river. A freshening wind blew the barge sideways, but the turtle paid no attention, paddling steadily on its familiar course. The barge, loaded with tons of coach, dwarves, Dunbarth, Sithas, and the prince's small honor guard, bobbed on its lines like a cork.

Gray clouds scudded before the scouring wind, hurrying off to the north. Sithas watched them warily, for winter was usually the time of storms in Silvanost. Vast cyclones, often lasting for days, sometimes boiled up out of the Courrain Ocean and lashed across Silvanesti. Wind and rain would drive everyone indoors and the sun would appear only once in two or three weeks. While the countryside suffered during these winter storms, the city was protected by spells woven by the clerics of E'li. Their spells deflected most of the natural fury away to the western mountains, but casting them for each new storm was a severe trial for the priests.

Dunbarth took the bumpy ride in good stride, as befits an ambassador, but his young secretary was not at all happy. He clutched his recording book to his chest and his face went from swarthy to pale to light green as the barge rocked.

"Drollo here hates water," Dunbarth explained with an amused glint in his eye. "He closes his eyes to take a bath!"

"My lord!" protested the secretary.

"Never fear, Master Drollo," Sithas said. "It would take far worse wind than this to upset a craft of this size."

The ferry master tooted another command on his horn, and the turtle swung the barge around. Lord Dunbarth's guard rattled from one bulwark to the other, and the horse team whinnied and shifted nervously as the deck moved beneath them. The mighty turtle butted his shell against the bow of the ferry and pushed it backward toward the dock. Elves on the dock guided the barge in with long poles. With a short, solid bump, the ferry was docked.

A ramp was lowered into the barge, and the dwarven guard mustered together to march ashore. They were much disheveled by the bumpy crossing. Plumes were broken off their helmets, capes were stained from the guards' falls into the scupper, armor was scuffed, but with commendable dignity, the sixteen dwarves shouldered their battle-axes and marched up the ramp to dry land. The horses were re-hitched to the coach and, as whips cracked, they hauled the coach up the ramp.

It began to rain as they rolled through the streets. Dunbarth peered through the curtains at the fabled capital of the elves. White towers gleamed, even under the lowering sky. The peaks of the tallest—the Tower of the Stars and the Quinari Palace—were clothed in murky clouds. Dunbarth, his face as open with wonder as a child's, admired the intricate spell-formed gardens, the graceful architecture, the almost musical harmony embodied by Silvanost's sights. Finally, he drew the curtains tight to keep out the gusting rain, then turned his attention to Sithas.

"I know you are heir to the Speaker of the Stars, but how is it you have the task of greeting me, noble Sithas?" he asked diplomatically. "Isn't it more usual for the younger son to receive foreign ambassadors?"

"There is no younger son in Silvanost," Sithas replied calmly.

Dunbarth smoothed his iron-gray beard. "Forgive me, Prince, but I was told the speaker had two sons."

Sithas adjusted the folds of his rain-spattered robes. "I have a twin brother, several minutes younger than I. His name is Kith-Kanan." Saying the name aloud was strange for Sithas. Though his twin was seldom far from his thoughts, it had been a very long time since the prince had had reason to speak his name. He said it silently to himself: *Kith-Kanan.*

"—twins are most uncommon among the elven race," Dunbarth was saying. With effort, Sithas focused on the conversation at hand. "Whereas, among humans, they are not at all uncommon." Dunbarth lowered his gaze. "Where is your brother, speaker's son?" he asked solemnly.

"He is in disgrace." Dunbarth's face registered only polite attention. Sithas inhaled deeply. "Do you know humans well?" he asked, eager to change the subject.

"I have made a number of journeys as emissary to the court of Ergoth. We've had many disputes with the humans over exchange rates of raw iron, copper, tin . . . but that's ancient history." Dunbarth leaned forward, close to Sithas. "It is a wise person who listens twice to everything a human says," he said softly. "Their duplicity knows no bounds."

"I shall keep that in mind," Sithas responded.

By the time the coach arrived at the palace, the storm had strengthened. There was no flashing lightning or crashing thunder, but a swirling, howling wind drove buckets of rain through the city. The coach pulled up close to the north portico of the palace, where there was some shelter from the wind and rain. There, an army of servants stood poised in the downpour, ready to assist the ambassador with his luggage. Lord Dunbarth stepped heavily down from his conveyance, his short purple cape lashing in the wind. He doffed his extravagant hat to the assembled servants.

"My lord, I think we should dispense with the amenities for now," Sithas shouted over the wind. "Our rainy season seems to have come early this year."

"As you wish, noble prince," Dunbarth bellowed.

Stankathan waited inside for the dwarven ambassador and Sithas. He bowed low to them and said, "Excellent lord, if you will follow me, I will show you to your quarters."

"Lead on!" said Dunbarth grandly. Behind him, the drenched Drollo let out a sneeze.

The ground floor of the north wing housed many of the

pieces of art that Lady Nirakina had collected. The delicate and lifelike statues of Morvintas, the vividly colored tapestries of the Women of E'li, the spell-molded plants of the priest Jin Falirus—all these lent the north wing an air of otherworldly beauty. As the dwarves passed through, servants discreetly mopped the marble floor behind them, blotting away all the mud and rainwater that had been tracked in.

Dunbarth and his entourage were lodged on the third floor of the north wing. The airy suite, with its curtains of gauze and mosaic tile floor in shades of gold and sea-green, was quite unlike any place in the dwarven realm of Thorbardin. The ambassador stopped to stare at a two-foot-long wooden model of a dove poised over his bed. When Drollo set Dunbarth's bags on the bed, the cloth-covered wings of the dove began to beat slowly, wafting a gentle breeze over the bed.

"By Reorx!" exclaimed the secretary. Dunbarth exploded with laughter.

"A minor spell," Stankathan explained hurriedly. "Activated when anything or anyone rests on the bed. If it bothers your lordship, I shall have it stopped."

"No, no. That's quite all right," Dunbarth said merrily.

"If you require anything, my lord, simply ring the bell," said Stankathan.

The elves withdrew. In the hallway beyond Dunbarth's closed door, Stankathan asked when the human delegation was expected.

"At any time," answered Sithas. "Keep the staff alert."

The major-domo bowed. "As you command, sire."

* * * * *

Lord Dunbarth dined that night with the Speaker of the Stars in a quiet, informal dinner that included only the closest confidantes of both sides. They talked for a long time about nothing of importance, taking the measure of each other. Lady Nirakina, in particular, seemed to find the elderly dwarf engaging.

"Are you married, my lord?" she asked at one point.

"No, Lady, never again!" Dunbarth boomed. He shrugged. "I am a widower."

"I am sorry."

"She was a good wife, my Brenthia, but a real terror at times." He drained a full cup of elven nectar. Smoothly, a servant stepped forward to refill his goblet.

"A terror, my lord?" asked Hermathya, intrigued.

"Quite so, Lady. I remember once she burst into the Council of Thanes and dressed me down for being late for supper five nights in a row. It took years for me to live that down, don't you know. The Daewar faction used to taunt me, when I was speaking in the council, by saying, 'Go home, Ironthumb, go home. Your dinner is ready.' " He laughed loudly, his deep bass voice echoing in the nearly empty Hall of Balif.

"Who are these Daewar?" asked Hermathya. "They sound rude."

"The Daewar are one of the great clans of the dwarven race," Sithel explained smoothly. He prided himself on his knowledge of dwarves and their politics. "You are yourself of the Hylar clan, are you not, Lord Dunbarth?"

The ambassador's blue eyes twinkled with happy cunning. "Your Highness is most knowledgeable. Yes, I am Hylar, and cousin to many kings of Thorbardin." He slapped a blunt hand on the back of his secretary, who was seated on his right. "Now, Drollo here, is half-Theiwar, which accounts for his dark looks and strange temperament." Drollo looked studiously at his plate and said nothing.

"Is it usual for dwarves to marry outside their class?" asked Sithas curiously.

"Not really. Speaking of such things," Dunbarth said languorously, "I hear tales that some elves have married humans."

A sharp silence fell in the hall. Sithel leaned back in his tall chair and put a finger to his lips. "It is unfortunately true," said the speaker tersely. "In the wilds of our western provinces, some of the Kagonesti have taken humans as mates. No doubt there is a shortage of suitable elven spouses. The practice is pernicious and forbidden by our law."

Dunbarth bowed his head, not in agreement, but in recognition of Sithel's admirable powers of restraint. The mixed-race issue was a very sensitive one, as the dwarf well knew. His own people were race-proud too, and no dwarf had ever been known to intermarry with another race.

"I met many half-humans among the refugees who lately

came to our city for shelter from bandits," Lady Nirakina said gently. "They were such sad folk, and many were quite presentable. It seems wrong to me to blame them for the follies of their parents."

"Their existence is not something we can encourage," Sithel countered with noticeable vigor. "As you say, they are known to be melancholy, and that makes them dangerous. They often figure in acts of violence and crime. They hate the Silvanesti because we are pure in blood, while they languish with human clumsiness and frailty. I suppose you in Thorbardin have heard of the riot we had in late summer?"

"There were mutterings of such an event," said Dunbarth casually.

"It was all due to the violent natures of some humans and half-humans we had unwisely allowed on the island. The riot was quelled, and the troublemakers driven away." Nirakina sighed noticeably. Sithel ignored his wife as he continued to make his point. "There can never be peace between Silvanesti and human, unless we keep to our own borders—and our own beds."

Dunbarth rubbed his red, bulbous nose. He had a heavy ring on each of his fingers, and they glittered in the candlelight. "Is that what you will tell the emissary from Ergoth?"

"It is," Sithel said vehemently.

"Your wisdom is great, Sithel Twice-Blest. My king has given me almost exactly the same words to speak. If we present a united front to the humans, they will have to accede to our demands."

The dinner ended quickly. Toasts were made to the health of the king of Thorbardin and to the hospitality of the Speaker of the Stars. That done, Lord Dunbarth and Drollo withdrew.

Sithas strode to the door after it closed behind the ambassador. "That old fox! He was trying to make an alliance with you before the humans even arrive! He wants to promote a conspiracy!"

Sithel dipped his hand in a silver bowl of rosewater, held by a servant. "My son, Dunbarth is a master of his craft. He was testing our eagerness to compromise. Had he behaved otherwise, I would have thought King Voldrin a fool to have sent him."

"This all seems very confusing to me," complained Lady Nirakina. "Why don't you all speak the truth and work from there?"

Sithel did a rare thing. He burst out laughing. "Diplomats tell the truth! My dear Kina, the stars would fall from heaven and the gods would faint with horror if diplomats started speaking the truth!"

* * * * *

Later that night came a knock on Sithas's door. A storm-drenched warrior strode in, bowed, and said in a ringing voice, "Forgive this intrusion, Highness, but I bring word of the emissary from Ergoth!"

"Yes?" said Sithas tensely. There was so much talk of treachery, he feared foul play had befallen the humans.

"Highness, the ambassador and his party are waiting on the bank of the river. The ambassador demands that he be met by a representative of the royal house."

"Who is this human?" Sithas asked.

"He gave his name as Ulwen, first praetor of the emperor of Ergoth," replied the soldier.

"First praetor, eh? Is the storm worse?" Sithas questioned.

"It is bad, Highness. My boat nearly sank crossing the Thon-Thalas."

"And yet this Ulwen insists on crossing immediately?"

The soldier said yes. "You will pardon me, sire, for saying so, but he is very arrogant, even for a human."

"I shall go," Sithas said simply. "It is my duty. Lord Dunbarth was met by me, and it is only just that I greet Praetor Ulwen likewise."

The prince left with the soldier, but not before sending word to the clerics of E'li, to ask them to begin working their spells to deflect the storm. It was unusual for so strong a storm to come before the winter season. The conference promised to be difficult enough without the added threat of wind and water.

167

‮ ‬16 ‮ ‬

While the Storm Raged

how wonderful this time is, kith-kanan thought. Not only did he have his growing love for Anaya, which was sweeter than anything he'd ever known, but his friendship with Mackeli, as well. They had become a family—Anaya, his wife, and Mackeli, like a son.

It was not an easy life, by any means. There was always work to be done, but there was time to laugh too, to swim in the pool, to take short flying excursions on Arcuballis, to tell stories around the fire at night. Kith-Kanan had begun to understand the Silvanesti who had left Silvanost to start new lives in the wilderness. The days ran their own course in the forest. There were no calendars and no clocks. There was no social hierarchy either; there were no rich and no poor. You hunted for yourself, provided for your own needs. And no one stood between an elf and the gods. As he looked over a forest glade, or knelt by a brook, Kith-Kanan felt closer to the gods than he ever had in the cold, marble precincts of Silvanost's temples.

No priests, no taxes, no protocol. For a long time, Kith-Kanan had believed that his life had ended the day he'd left Silvanost. Now he knew it had been a new beginning.

As the weeks went by, hunting grew poorer and poorer. Anaya went out, sometimes for two or three days at a time, and returned only with a brace of rabbits, squirrels, or other small game. At one point she had been reduced to catching pigeons, a poor return for her days in the woods. Nothing like this had ever happened before, according to Mackeli. Usually, Anaya went out and set a snare or trap and a likely prize would practically fall into it. Now, the animals were nowhere to be seen. In hopes of adding to the meager hunting, Kith-Kanan worked harder to develop his woodland skills. He hunted frequently, but had yet to bring anything back.

This day a lone hart moved slowly through the forest, its small hooves sinking deep into drifts of fallen leaves. Its black nose twitched as the wind brought smells from far away.

Kith-Kanan, wedged ten feet off the ground into the fork of a linden tree, was motionless. He willed the deer not to smell him, not to see him. Then, as slowly as possible, the prince drew his bow and swiftly let fly. His aim was true. The hart leaped away, but only for a few yards before it collapsed into the leaves.

Kith-Kanan let out a yell of triumph. Eight months in the wildwood, and this was his first hunting success. He skittered down the tree and ran to the fallen deer. Yes! The arrow had hit the beast right in the heart.

He dressed the carcass. As he slung it over his shoulder, Kith-Kanan realized that he couldn't stop grinning. Wouldn't Anaya be surprised?

The air was chill, and under his burden Kith-Kanan panted, sending little puffs of vapor from his nostrils and mouth. He walked quickly, making a lot of noise, but it didn't matter now. He had made a kill! He'd been walking for some time when the first flakes of snow began to fall. A sort of steady hiss pervaded the forest as the light flakes filtered down through the bare tree limbs. It wasn't a heavy fall, but as the prince's trek continued, the brown leaves on the forest floor gradually acquired a thin frosting of white.

He climbed the hill to the clearing, meeting Mackeli on the way.

"Look what I have!" Kith-Kanan exclaimed. "Fresh meat!"

"Congratulations, Kith. You've worked hard to get it," the boy said, but a frown creased his forehead.

"What's the matter?"

Mackeli looked at him and blinked. "It's snowing."

Kith-Kanan shifted the weight of the carcass to a more comfortable position. "What's wrong with that? It is winter, after all."

"You don't understand," said the boy. He took Kith-Kanan's quiver and bow, and together they proceeded up the hill. "It never snows in our clearing." They gained the crest of the hill. The clearing was already lightly dusted with snow.

With a stone axe, Kith-Kanan removed the rib section and gave it to Arcuballis. The griffon had been brought to the hollow oak, and a roof of hides had been stretched from the overhead limbs to keep the rains off the mount. The noble eagle head of Arcuballis protruded from the crude shelter. The beast repeatedly ruffled its neck feathers and shook its head, trying to shake off the snowflakes. Kith-Kanan dropped the meat at the griffon's feet.

"This is no weather for you, eh boy?" he said, scratching the animal's neck through its thick feathers. Arcuballis made hoarse grunting sounds and lowered its head to its meal.

Kith-Kanan left his dagger and sword in a covered basket inside Arcuballis's shelter. Brushing the snow off his shoulders, he ducked into the tree. It was snug and warm inside, but very close. A small fire burned on the hearth. As the prince sat cross-legged by the fire and warmed his hands, Mackeli scuttled about in the stores of nuts and dried fruit overhead.

After a short time, the bark-covered door swung open. Anaya stood in the doorway.

"Hello!" Kith-Kanan cried cheerfully. "Come in out of the cold. I had good hunting today!"

Anaya pulled the door closed behind her. When autumn arrived, she had changed from her green-dyed buckskins to natural brown ones. Now, coated with snow, she looked small and cold and unhappy. Kith-Kanan went to her and pushed back the hood from her head. "Are you all right?" he asked quietly, searching for an answer in her eyes.

"It's snowing in my clearing," she said flatly.

"Mackeli said that this is unusual. Still, remember that the weather follows its own laws, Anaya." Kith-Kanan tried to soothe the hopeless look on her face; after all, it was only a little snow. "We'll be fine. Did you see the deer I took?" He'd hung the quarters of meat outside to cool.

"I saw it," she said. Anaya's eyes were dull and lifeless. She pulled free of Kith-Kanan's arms and unlaced her rawhide jacket. Still standing by the door, she looked at him. "You did well. I didn't even see a deer, much less take one. Something is wrong. The animals no longer come as they used to. And now snow in the clearing. . . ."

The keeper threw her jacket on the floor and looked up at the chimney hole. Dry, cold flakes fell in, vanishing in the column of rising smoke before they reached the fire. "I must go to the cave and commune with the forest. The Forestmaster may know what has happened," she said, then sighed. "But I am so tired now. . . . Tomorrow. I will go tomorrow."

Kith-Kanan sat by the fire and pulled Anaya gently down beside him. When she put her head in his lap and closed her eyes, the prince leaned back against the side of the tree, intending to keep an eye on the fire. He continued to stroke Anaya's face. In spite of her distress over the snow, Kith-Kanan couldn't believe that anything was really wrong. He had seen snow in the streets of Silvanost after many years of none. As he'd said, the weather followed its own laws. Kith-Kanan's eyes closed, and he dozed. The fire shrank in its circle of stones, and the first flakes of snow reached the floor of the tree, collecting on Anaya's eyelashes.

Kith-Kanan awoke with the slow realization that he was cold. He tried to move and discovered he was buried under two bodies—Anaya on his left, and Mackeli on his right. Though asleep, the need for warmth had drawn them together. Furs were piled up around them, and as Kith-Kanan opened his eyes, he saw that more than half a foot of snow had collected in the tree. The snowfall had extinguished the coals of the fire and drifted around the sleeping trio.

"Wake up," he said thickly. When neither Anaya nor Mackeli moved, Kith-Kanan patted his wife's cheek. She exhaled sharply and turned over, putting her back to him. He tried to rouse Mackeli, but the boy only started to snore.

"By Astarin," he muttered. The cold had obviously numbed their senses. He must build a fire.

Kith-Kanan heaved himself up, pushing aside the inch of snow that had fallen across his lower legs. His breath made a long stream of fog. There was dry kindling in one of the wattle baskets, against the wall and out of the way of the falling snow. He dug the snow out of the hearth with his bare hands and laid a stand of twigs and bark shavings on the cold stones. With a flint and strike stone, he soon had a smoldering pile of tinder. Kith-Kanan fanned it with his breath, and soon a crackling fire was burning.

It had stopped snowing, but the bit of sky he could glimpse through the chimney hole was gray and threatening. Reluctantly the prince eased the door open, even against the resistance from the two feet of snow that had drifted against the tree.

The clearing had been transformed. Where formerly the forest had been wrought in green and brown, now it was gray and white. An unbroken carpet of snow stretched across the clearing. All the imperfections of the ground were lost under the blanket of white.

A snuffling sound caught his ear. Kith-Kanan walked around the broad tree trunk and saw Arcuballis huddled under its flimsy shelter, looking miserable.

"Not like your warm stall in Silvanost, is it, old friend?" Kith-Kanan said. He untied the griffon's halter and led it out a few yards from the tree.

"Fly, boy. Warm yourself and come back." Arcuballis made a few faltering steps forward. "Go on. It's all right."

The griffon spread its wings and took to the air. It circled the clearing three times, then vanished upward into the low gray clouds.

Kith-Kanan examined the venison haunches he'd hung up the day before. They were frozen solid. He untied one and braced it on his shoulder.

Back inside the tree, it was already much warmer, thanks to

the fire. Anaya and Mackeli were nestled together like spoons in a drawer. Kith-Kanan smiled at them and knelt to saw two cutlets from the venison haunch. It was hard going, but soon he had whittled the steaks out and had them roasting on a spit over the fire.

"Mmm." Anaya yawned. Eyes still closed, she asked, "Do I smell venison roasting?"

Kith-Kanan smiled again. "You certainly do, wife. I am making our dinner."

She stretched long and hard. "It smells wonderful." She yawned again. "I'm so tired."

"You just lie there and rest," he replied. "I'll provide for us this time." The prince gave his attention to the venison cutlets. He turned them carefully, making sure they were cooked all the way through. When they were done, he took one, still on its stick, and knelt by Anaya. "Dinner is served, my lady," he said and touched her shoulder.

Anaya smiled and her eyelids fluttered open. She raised her head and looked at him.

Kith-Kanan cried out in surprise and dropped the steak onto the wet ground.

Anaya's dark hazel eyes had changed color. They had become vividly green, like two shining emeralds.

✎ 17 ✎

Quartered With a Gentleman

Rain, driven sideways by the wind, tore at the elves who
stood on the stone pier at the river's edge. The far bank of the
Thon-Thalas could not be seen at all, and the river itself was
wild with storm-tossed waves. Through this chaos wallowed
the great barge, drawn as before by a giant turtle.

The more Sithas saw of the growing storm, the more he was
convinced it was not natural. His suspicion fell upon the waiting humans from Ergoth. Their emperor was known to have a
corps of powerful magicians in his service. Was this premature,
violent storm the result of some dire human magic?

"Surely, Highness, you should not risk this crossing!"
warned the commander of the escort standing with Sithas.

The prince held his sodden cloak closed at his throat. "The

ambassador from Ergoth is waiting, Captain," he replied. The turtle turned end-on to the storm waves, which crashed in green torrents over its high-domed shell. "It is important that we show these humans we are masters of our own fate," Sithas continued levelly. "Praetor Ulwen does not expect us to venture out in the storm to meet him. If we don't, when the storm ends he can rail long and loud about the timidity of elves." Sithas blotted water off his face with his wet cloak. "I will not cede that advantage to the humans, Captain."

The dark-haired Kagonesti did not look convinced.

The barge was close now. The thick wooden hull squeezed a swell of water between itself and the shore. This swell, some ten feet high, fell over Sithas and his escort, drenching them further. The guards cursed and muttered, shuffling about the pier. Sithas stood imperturbable, his pale hair running in rivulets down the back of his emerald cloak.

The ferry master shouted from the deck, "I can't moor in this swell, Highness!"

Sithas looked to the captain. "Follow me," he advised. Turning back the flaps of his cloak, Sithas gathered up the lower edge, so as not to entangle his legs. With a running start, he leaped the gap between the pier end and the heaving barge. The prince hit, rolled, and got to his feet again. The soldiers gaped in amazement.

"Come on! Are you fighters or farmers?" Sithas called.

The captain squared his shoulders. If the heir to the throne was going to kill himself, then he would die, too. Once the captain was across, he and Sithas stationed themselves to grab the hurtling warriors as they, too, landed on the barge.

The ferry's deck rose and fell like the chest of a breathing beast. When everyone was safely aboard, the ferry master blew his trumpet. The implacable mammoth turtle paddled away from shore.

Rain swirled and lashed at them. The scuppers ran full, and all sorts of loose debris sloshed back and forth on the ferry's deck. The ferocious pounding near the shore lessened as the raft gained the deeper water in the center of the river. Here the danger was from the churning current, as the wind drove the surface water against the natural flow of the river. The thick chains that secured the barge to the towing turtle snapped hard, first the port, then the starboard. The giant reptile rolled with these blows, which sometimes lifted one of its thick green flippers out of the water. As if resenting this challenge to its strength, the turtle put its head down and pulled even harder for the western bank.

The captain of the escort struggled forward to report to Sithas. "Sire, there's a lot of water coming into the boat. Waves are breaking over the sides." Unperturbed, the prince asked the ferry master what they should do.

"Bail," was all he had to say.

The soldiers got on their knees and scooped water in their helmets. A chain was formed, each elf passing a full helmet to the leeward side and handing an empty helmet back to the first fellow bailing.

"There's the shore!" sang out the ferry master. When Sithas squinted into the rain, he could make out a gray smudge ahead. Slowly the shoreline grew more distinct. On the slight hill overlooking the boat landing stood a large tent. A flag whipped from the center peak of the tent.

Sithas spat rainwater and again clutched his cloak tightly at his throat. In spite of their request to be met and conducted into the city, here the humans sat, encamped for the night. Already they were leading the speaker's son around by the nose. Such arrogance made Sithas's blood burn. Still, there was nothing to be gained by storming into the ambassador's tent in a blind rage.

He stared at the swimming turtle and then farther ahead at the gently sloping riverbank. With a firm nod to himself, Sithas teetered across the pitching deck to where the soldiers still knelt, bailing out water with their helmets. He told them to hold fast when the barge reached the shore and to be prepared for a surprise. When Sithas informed the ferry master of his idea, that tired, storm-lashed fellow grinned.

"We'll do it, sire!" he said and put his trumpet to his lips. On his first attempt, instead of a blaring call, water spurted out. Cursing, he rapped the trumpet's bell on the bulwark and tried again. The command note cut through the noise of the storm. The turtle swung right, pulling the barge to one side of the pier ahead. The trumpet sounded again, and the turtle raised its great green head. Its dull orange eyes blinked rapidly, to keep the rain out.

There were a half-dozen caped figures on the dock, waiting. Sithas assumed they were the Ergothian ambassador's unfortunate guards, ordered to wait in the rain should the elves deign to show up. When the barge turned aside, they filed off the dock and tried to get in front of the approaching ferry. The turtle's belly scraped in the mud, and its shell humped out of the water a full twenty feet high. The humans scattered before the awesome onslaught of the turtle. The elf warriors on deck let out a cheer.

The ferry master blew a long rattling passage on his horn, and the turtle dug its massive flippers into the riverside mud. The bank was wide and the angle shallow, so the great beast had no problem heaving itself out of the water. The driving rain rapidly cleansed it of clinging mud, and the turtle crawled up the slope.

The bow of the barge hit bottom, and everyone on board was thrown to the deck. The ferry master bounced to his feet and repeated the surging trumpet signal. All four of the turtle's flippers were out of the water now, and it continued up the hill. As Sithas got to his feet, he resisted an urge to laugh triumphantly. He looked down at the human guards, who were running from the sight of the turtle.

"Stand fast!" he shouted decisively. "I am Prince Sithas of the Silvanesti! I have come to greet your ambassador!" Some of the gray-caped figures halted. Others continued to run. One human, who wore an officer's plume on his tall, conical helmet, tentatively approached the beached barge.

"I am Endrac, commander of the ambassador's escort. The ambassador has retired for the night," he shouted up at Sithas.

"Then go and wake him! The storm may last another day, so this is your master's best chance to reach the city without suffering an avoidable, but major delay."

Endrac threw up his hands and proceeded up the hill. He was not much faster than the turtle, weighed down as he was by armor. The giant turtle ground its way up, inexorable, dragging the barge behind it. The warriors were plainly impressed by the feat, for the barge obviously weighed many tons.

Torches blossomed on the top of the hill, all around the elaborate tent of the Ergothian ambassador. Sithas was gratified to see all the frantic activity. He turned to the ferry master and told him to urge the beast along. The elf put the trumpet to his lips once more and sounded the call.

They were quite a sight, rumbling up the hill. The turtle's flippers, each larger than four elves, dug into the soft ground and threw back gouts of mud against the hull of the barge. The chains that shackled the beast to the boat rattled and clanked rhythmically. The giant grunted deep in its chest as the effort began to tell on it.

The ground flattened out, so the ferry master signaled for the turtle to slow down. The barge tilted forward on its flat bottom, jarring the elven warriors. They laughed and good-naturedly urged the ferry master to speed up again.

The ambassador's tent was only a few yards away now. A cordon of human soldiers formed around it, capes flapping in the wind. They stood at attention, spears against their shoulders. The turtle loomed over them. Endrac appeared.

"You there, Endrac!" Sithas shouted. "You'd best disperse your fighters. Our turtle hasn't eaten lately, and if you provoke him, he might eat your men."

Endrac complied, and his soldiers moved with grateful speed out of the turtle's way.

"There now, ferry master, you'd better rein him in," cried Sithas. A quick blast on the trumpet, and the turtle grunted to a stop.

A human in civilian dress appeared at the door of the tent. "What is the meaning of this?" he demanded.

"I am Sithas, son of Sithel, Speaker of the Stars. Your ambassador sent word he wished to be met. I have come. It will be a grave insult if the ambassador does not see me."

The human drew his cape around himself in a quick, angry motion. "A thousand pardons, noble prince," he said, vexed. "Wait but a moment. I will speak to the ambassador."

The human went inside the tent.

Sithas put one foot on the port set of chains that ran from the ferry to the halter encircling the turtle's shell. The links were as thick as the prince's wrist. No one but an elf could have walked the fifteen feet along the swaying length of chain in the rain, but Sithas did it easily. Once he reached the turtle's back, he was able to move briskly over the shell to the beast's head. The turtle, placid as all his kind were, paid no mind as the elf prince stepped gingerly on its head.

The human appeared again. This close, Sithas could see he was a mature man; his red-brown hair and full beard were sprinkled with gray. He was richly dressed in the vulgar Ergothian style—which meant he was clad in strong dark colors, wine-red and black, with a golden torc at his throat and a fur-lined cape.

"Well?" Sithas demanded from his lofty perch atop the turtle's head.

"The ambassador asks if you would care to come in out of the rain for a short time, while preparations are made to go," said the human more solicitously.

Using the deep creases in the skin of the creature's neck as hand and footholds, Sithas descended the twelve feet to the ground. Once down, he glanced up at the turtle; a huge eye regarded him benignly.

The bearded human was tall for his race. His gray eyes were hard as he bowed. "I am Ulvissen, seneschal to Ulwen, praetor of the empire," he said with dignity.

With a sweep of his arm, Ulvissen indicated Sithas should precede him. The prince strode into the tent.

It was the size of a largish house. The first room Sithas entered featured the imperial standard of Ergoth, a golden axe crossed with a hammer, on a field of dark crimson. The second room was larger and far more elaborate. Thick carpets covered the ground. In the center of the room, a fire burned on a portable black iron hearth. Smoke was carried out through a metal chimney, made of sections of bronze pipe jointed together. Couches and chairs covered with purple velvet were scattered around the room. A large chest full of rolled maps lay open to Sithas's left, and a table laden with decanters of drink stood on his right. Glass-globed oil lamps lit the room as bright as day. Wind howled outside, and rain drummed on the varnished silk roof.

A flap across the room was pulled back, and four thick-armed servants entered, carrying a chair supported by rods through its armrests. Seated in the chair was an ancient human, far older than Ulvissen. His bald head was hunched deep between his shoulders. His skin was the color of egg yolks, and his rheumy eyes seemed to have no distinct color. Sithas did not need to know much about human health to recognize that this was a sick man.

The prince was about to speak to this venerable man when another person entered, a female. She was altogether different from the frail figure in the chair. Tall, clad in a deep red velvet gown, she had dark brown hair that fell just past her shoulders. More voluptuous than any elven maiden, the human woman appeared less than half the age of the man in the chair.

When she spoke, it was with a velvety voice. "Greetings, Prince Sithas. On behalf of my husband, Praetor Ulwen, I greet you." She rested her hands on the back of the old man's chair. "My name is Teralind denCaer," she added.

Sithas bowed his head slightly. "In the name of my father, Speaker of the Stars, I greet you, Praetor Ulwen, and Lady Teralind," he said respectfully.

She came out from behind the chair and went to the table where the decanters were. Teralind poured a pale white liquid into a tall glass goblet. "We did not expect anyone to meet us. Not until the storm was over," she said, smiling slightly.

"I received the ambassador from Thorbardin this morning," Sithas replied. "It was only proper that I come and greet the emperor's envoy as well."

The old man in the chair still had said nothing, and he remained silent as Teralind drank. Then she passed in front of Sithas, gown rustling as she walked. By lamplight, her eyes were a foreign shade of brown, dark like her hair. Teralind sat, and bade Sithas sit down too.

"Excuse me, Lady, but is the praetor well?" he asked cautiously. The old human's eyes were closed.

"Ulwen is very old," she said with a tinge of sadness. "And it is very late."

"I can't help but wonder why the emperor did not chose a younger man for this task," Sithas ventured softly.

Teralind combed through her thick, wavy hair with the fingers of one hand. "My husband is the senior praetor of the empire. Also, he is the only member of the ruling council to have dealt with Silvanesti before."

"Oh? When was that?"

"Forty-six years ago. Before I was born, actually. I believe he worked on what was called the Treaty of Thelgaard," she said distractedly.

Sithas tried to remember the obscure treaty, and could only recall that it had something to do with the cloth trade. "I'm sorry I did not have the pleasure of meeting the praetor then," he said. "I must have been away." Teralind looked at the elf oddly for an instant. Humans never could adjust to elven life spans. "In deference to the age of the ambassador," Sithas added, "I would be willing to stay the night here and escort you all to the city tomorrow."

"That is acceptable. Ulvissen will find you a suitable place to rest," Teralind agreed. She rose suddenly to her feet. "Good night, Your Highness," she said courteously, then snapped her fingers. The servants hoisted Ulwen up, turned ponderously, and carried him out.

*   *   *   *   *

Sithas was given a bed in a private corner of the great tent. The bed itself was large enough to sleep four grown elves and far too soft for the prince's taste. It seemed strange to him that humans should prize comfort so excessively.

The rain struck the roof of the tent with a rhythmic beat, but that did not lull Sithas to sleep. Instead, his mind wandered to thoughts of Hermathya. He would have to work harder to reconcile their differences, he decided. But his wife's face did not remain long in Sithas's thoughts. Kith-Kanan soon pushed to the forefront. His twin would probably have enjoyed Sithas's little gesture of bringing turtle and barge to the ambassador's very door.

Kith was a long way off now, Sithas thought. So many miles and so much time lay between them. As the prince closed his eyes, he felt the faint but persistent tie that had always existed between him and Kith-Kanan, but now he concentrated on it. The rain grew louder in his ears. It was like a pulse, the beat of a living heart. Feelings began to come to him—the smell of the woodland, the sounds of night animals that no longer lived in the more settled parts of Silvanesti. He opened his mind further, and a flood of sensations came to him.

He saw, as in shadow, a dark elven woman. She was strong and deeply connected to the Power, even as the high clerics and the Speaker of the Stars were said to be. But the dark woman was part of an ancient group, different from the gods, but almost as great. Sithas had an impression of green leaves, of soaring trees, and pools of still, clear water. And there was a battle raging inside this woman. She was trying to leave the Power, and it did not want her to go. The reason she wished to leave was clear, too. She loved Kith, and he loved her. Sithas felt that very strongly.

A word came to him. A name.

"Anaya," he said aloud.

The link was broken when he spoke. Sithas sat up, his head swimming with strange, unexplained impressions. There was a struggle going on, a contest for possession of the dark elf woman. The struggle was between Kith-Kanan and the ancient powers of nature. The storm . . . not the work of human magicians, or any magicians. The storm was a manifestation of the struggle.

As Sithas lay back on the ridiculously large bed, a twinge of sadness entered his heart. The short connection had only emphasized how truly far from home his twin had journeyed.

And Sithas knew he dare tell no one what he'd learned.

✍ 18 ✍

In the Forest, Year of the Ram (2215 PC)

The changes in the keeper continued. Anaya's toes and fingers, then the points of her elbows, became light green. She felt no pain and suffered no loss of movement, though it did seem she was becoming less sensitive all the time. Her hearing, formerly so acute, became duller and duller. Her eyesight lost its uncanny focus. Her stealthy tread grew slow and clumsy. At first she was short-tempered with the changes, but her spirits gradually lightened. Things the Forestmaster had told her during her long sojourn away from Kith-Kanan were now making more sense, she said. These changes, Anaya believed, were the price of her life joined to Kith-Kanan's. While she might bemoan the loss of her preternatural agility and hunting skill, her new life did make her very happy.

The winter was long and, as the forest was no longer Anaya's to command, very hard. She and Kith-Kanan hunted almost every day that it wasn't actually snowing. They had some success; there were rabbits and pheasants and the occasional deer to be had. But they more often ate Mackeli's nuts and berries. As their bellies shrank and their belts tightened, conversation diminished, too. When the wind howled outside and the snow drifted so high the door became hard to open, the three sat within the hollow tree, each wrapped in his or her own thoughts. Days went by without any of them speaking a single word.

Mackeli, too, was changing, though his metamorphosis was more easily understood. He had reached the time in a young elf's life when the physical limitations of childhood give way to an adult physique. Compared to the great life span of an elf, these changes take place rather quickly. Even without an abundance of food, he grew taller, stronger, and restless—and often rude, as well. The boy's impatience was so high that Kith-Kanan forbade him to accompany them hunting; Mackeli's fidgeting scared off the already scarce game.

While his wife and friend changed in outward, tangible ways, Kith-Kanan grew, too, but inside. His values had changed since coming to the forest, certainly, and now his entire attitude toward life was undergoing fundamental change. All his life he had played at being prince. Since his brother Sithas was the heir, Kith-Kanan had no real responsibilities, no true duties. He took up warrior training and hunting as hobbies. He taught Arcuballis tricks and practiced aerial maneuvers. These activities had filled his days.

But it was different now. He could glide through the forest, silent as a wraith. He didn't have to rely on Mackeli's gathering skills or Anaya's hunting any longer. In fact, more and more, they relied on him. This was a good life, the prince decided, and he could now bless the day his father had taken Hermathya from him. Though he had cared for her, Hermathya was much better suited to his twin—both of them so correct, proper, and dutiful. And with his forgiveness of his father came a sense of loss. He found himself missing his family. Still, he knew that his life was in the forest, not the city.

Another, more natural, change had come to Anaya. She was

pregnant. She and her husband had been staring dreamily into
the fire one night when she had told him. At first Kith-Kanan
was stunned. His astonishment gave way to a great, heart-
filling joy. He embraced her so hard that she squealed in protest. The thought that a new life, one he had helped create, was
growing inside of her made Anaya that much more precious to
the prince. It made their life together that much richer. He
showered her with kisses and declarations of his love until
Mackeli grumbled for them both to shut up, since he was trying
to sleep.

The day came, not too long after, when the first icicles began
to melt off the oak's bare branches. The sun came out and
stayed for a week, and all the ice melted and ran off the tree.
The snow retreated to the deep shadows around the rim of the
clearing.

They emerged from the tree, blinking at the bright sunshine.
It was as if this was the first sunny day they'd ever experienced.
Anaya moved stiffly, rubbing her arms and thighs. Her hands
and feet were fully colored green by this time.

Kith-Kanan stood in the center of the clearing, eyes shut,
face turned to the sky. Mackeli, who was nearly as tall as Kith-
Kanan now, bounded around like a deer, though certainly not
as gracefully.

"We've never had such a winter," Anaya stated, gazing at the
snow still hiding at the base of the trees.

"If the weather holds, the hunting will be good," Kith-Kanan
noted confidently. "All the hibernating animals will be coming
out."

"Free! Ha, ha, free!" Mackeli rejoiced. He grabbed Anaya's
hands and tried to dance her around in a circle. She resisted and
pulled her hands away with a grimace.

"Are you all right?" asked Kith-Kanan worriedly.

"I am stiff and sore," she complained. She stopped rubbing
her arms and stood up straight. "I'll work the cold out of my
bones, don't worry."

The novelty, but not the pleasure, of the first spring day
wore off, and the trio returned to the tree to eat. In honor of the
fine day, Kith-Kanan cut down their last haunch of venison.
Kith-Kanan had been teaching Arcuballis to hunt for game and
bring back what it caught. The griffon could cover a much

wider range than they, and it grew more adept with each hunt. The last time the creature had brought back the very deer Kith-Kanan was carving.

Now, Kith-Kanan took Arcuballis from its hide tent and, with whistles and encouraging words, sent the beast off on another expedition. When the griffon was lost from sight, the elf prince built a fire outside, not an easy task with all the damp wood. He sliced off a sizeable roast from the hard, smoked haunch. While it cooked, Mackeli came out with his usual fare: arrow root, walnuts, dried blueberries, and wild rice. He looked at the brown assortment in his basket, then at the deer roast, sizzling and dripping fat into the fire. He squatted by Kith-Kanan, who was turning the meat on a rough spit.

"Could I have some?" asked Mackeli tentatively. Kith-Kanan gave him an astonished look. "It smells awfully good. Just a small piece?" the boy pleaded.

Kith-Kanan sliced off a thin strip of cooked meat, speared it with his dagger, and put it in Mackeli's basket. The elf boy eagerly picked it up with his fingers—and promptly dropped it again. It was quite hot. Kith-Kanan gave him a sharpened twig, and Mackeli snagged the piece of meat and raised it to his mouth.

A look of utter concentration came over his face as he chewed. Kith-Kanan inquired, "Do you like it?"

"Well, it's different." The slice was gone. "Could I have some more?" The elf prince laughed and cut a larger piece.

Anaya came out of the tree, dragging their furs and bedding into the sun. The red and yellow lines she had painted on her face enhanced the already startling green of her eyes. The elf woman glanced over at the two males, crouched by the fire, and saw Mackeli nibbling a slice of venison. She ran over and slapped the meat from his hand.

"It is forbidden for you to eat meat!" she said heatedly.

"Oh? And who forbids me? You?" demanded Mackeli defiantly.

"Yes!"

Kith-Kanan rose to pull them apart, but as one Mackeli and Anaya shoved him back. He sprawled on the wet turf, astonished.

"You did not kill the animal, Keli, so you have no right to eat it!" Anaya said fiercely.

"You didn't kill it either! Kith did!" he countered.

"That's different. Kith is a hunter, you're only a boy. Stick to your nuts and berries." The "boy" Anaya snarled at was now a head taller than she.

"Are those eyes of yours blind?" Mackeli argued. "Nothing is as it was. The spirits of the forest have turned their backs on you. You've lost your stealth, your keen senses, and your agility. You've turned *green!* I've gotten bigger and stronger. I can shoot a bow. You—" Mackeli was sputtering in his rage "—you don't belong in the forest any longer!"

Within the sharply painted lines, Anaya's eyes grew large. She made a fist and struck Mackeli smartly on the face. He fell on his back. Kith-Kanan realized things had gone too far.

"Stop it, both of you!" he barked. Anaya had advanced over Mackeli, ready to hit him again, but Kith-Kanan pushed her back. She stiffened, and for a moment he thought she would take a swing at him. After a moment, the anger left her and she stood aside.

The prince helped Mackeli to his feet. A smear of blood showed under the boy's nose.

"I know we've been cooped up together too long, but there's no reason for fighting," Kith-Kanan said severely. "Mackeli is reaching his adulthood, Ny, you can't hold him back." He turned to the boy, who was dabbing at his bleeding nose with his sleeve. "And you have no right saying things like that to her. Not even the Forestmaster herself has said Anaya doesn't belong in the wood any more. So guard your tongue, Keli. If you wish to be a warrior, you must learn self-control."

Suddenly they heard a pair of hands clapping behind them and a voice exclaiming, "Well said!"

Kith-Kanan, Anaya, and Mackeli turned abruptly. A score of men holding swords or crossbows flanked the hollow tree. Standing by the door, dressed in elegant but impractical crimson, was the half-human Voltorno—as strong and healthy as ever, from the look of it.

"You!" hissed Anaya.

"Stand very still," cooed Voltorno. "I would hate to perforate you after such a touching performance. It really was worthy of the finest playhouse in Daltigoth." He nodded, and the humans

187

fanned out carefully, surrounding the trio.

"So you survived your wound," Kith-Kanan said tersely. "What a pity."

"Yes," he said with calm assurance. "We had a first-rate healer on the ship. We returned to Ergoth, where I made known your interference in our operation. I was commissioned to return and deal with you."

Voltorno flipped back his hip-length cape, exposing a finely wrought sword hilt. He walked to Anaya, looking her up and down. "Bit of a savage, isn't she?" he said with a sneer to Kith-Kanan and turned to Mackeli. "Could this be our wild boy? Grown a bit, haven't you?" Mackeli kept his hands at his sides, but he was breathing hard. Voltorno shoved him lightly with one gloved hand. "You're the one who shot me," he said, still smiling pleasantly. "I owe you something for that." He pushed Mackeli again. Kith-Kanan gathered himself to spring on Voltorno. As if he were reading the prince's mind, Voltorno said to his men, "If either of them moves, kill them both."

The half-human grasped the gilded hilt of his sword and drew the slim blade from its scabbard. He held it by the blade; the pommel bobbed just inches from Mackeli's chest. The boy stared at the sword hilt as he backed away. Mackeli's heels crunched in some of the late snow until his back bumped a tree at the edge of the clearing.

"Where will you go now?" asked Voltorno, his gray eyes gleaming.

Kith-Kanan freed his dagger from his belt when the bowmen turned their attention to the half-human. The elf prince realized that only one of them was behind him, about eight feet away. He nudged Anaya lightly with his elbow. She didn't look at him, but nudged him back.

Kith-Kanan turned and hurled the dagger at the bowman. The good elven iron punched through the man's leather jerkin. Without a word, he fell back, dead. Kith-Kanan broke left, Anaya right. The humans started yelling and opened fire. Those on the left shot at Anaya. Those on the right shot at Kith-Kanan. The only thing they hit was each other.

About half of the group went down, shot by their own comrades. Kith-Kanan dived for the muddy ground and rolled to the man he'd killed with his dagger. The human's crossbow had discharged on impact with the ground. Kith-Kanan pulled a quarrel from the dead man's quiver and struggled to cock the bow.

Anaya also threw herself on the ground, drawing her flint knife as she fell. She was a good ten yards from Mackeli and the archers, who were reloading their weapons. Mackeli reacted to the confusion by trying to snatch Voltorno's sword, but the half-human was too quick for him. In no time Voltorno had reversed his grip and thrust his weapon at Mackeli. The boy ducked, and Voltorno's blade stuck in a tree.

"Get them! Kill them!" Voltorno shouted.

Mackeli ran in and out of the trees along the clearing's edge. Quarrels flicked by him.

Across the clearing, Anaya crawled away in the wet turf, using her toes and elbows. As the archers concentrated their fire on Mackeli, she rose and threw herself at the back of the nearest man. Her moves were not as graceful as they once were, but her flint knife was as deadly as ever. One of the men, wounded by a quarrel, managed to sit up and aim his crossbow at Anaya's back. Luckily, Kith-Kanan picked him off before he could shoot.

Mackeli had plunged into the woods. Several of the surviving humans ran after him, but Voltorno called them back.

Anaya also made it to cover in the woods. She ran only a dozen yards or so before dropping to the ground. In seconds, she was buried in the leaves. Two humans tramped right past her.

Kith-Kanan tried to cock the bow a second time. From a sitting position though, it wasn't easy; the bow was too stiff. Before he could get the string over the lock nut, Voltorno arrived and presented him with thirty inches of Ergothian iron.

"Put it down," Voltorno ordered. When Kith-Kanan hesitated, the half-human raked his sword tip over the prince's jaw. Kith-Kanan felt the blood flow as he dropped the crossbow.

"Your friends have reverted to type," said Voltorno with contempt. "They've run off and left you."

"Good," Kith-Kanan replied. "At least they will be safe."

"Perhaps. You, my friend, are anything but safe."

The eight surviving humans crowded around. Voltorno gave them a nod, and they dragged Kith-Kanan to his feet, punching and kicking him. They brought him to the far side of the clearing where they'd first come in and where they'd dropped their baggage. Voltorno produced a set of arm and leg shackles, then chained Kith-Kanan hand and foot.

* * * * *

Anaya burrowed away from the clearing, worming through the leaves like a snake. In times past, she could have done so without disturbing a single leaf on the surface. Now, to her ears, she sounded like a herd of humans. Fortunately Voltorno and his men were busy on the other side of the clearing.

When she was quite far away, she parted the leaves with her hands and crawled out. The ground was cold and wet, and Anaya shivered.

She wanted to return at once and free Kith-Kanan, but she knew she'd never trick the humans again. Not alone. She would have to wait until it was dark.

A twig snapped behind her, on her right. She kicked the leaves off her legs and faced the sound. Hugging a tree five yards away was Mackeli.

"You're noisy," she criticized.

"You're deaf. I stepped on four other twigs before that last one," he said coolly.

They met each other halfway. The hostility of the morning was gone, and they embraced.

"I've never seen you run like that!" she avowed.

"I surprised myself," admitted Mackeli. "Being more grown up does appear to have advantages." He looked down at his sister. "I'm sorry for what I said," he added earnestly.

"You only said what I've thought a thousand times," she confessed. "Now we have to think of Kith. We can go in after dark and take him—"

Mackeli took her by the shoulders and dropped to the ground, pulling her down beside him. "Shh! Not so loud! Ny, we've got to be smart about this. A year ago, we could have crept in and freed Kith, but now we're too slow and loud. We have to *think* better."

She scowled. "I don't have to *think* to know that I will kill that Voltorno," she insisted.

"I know, but he's dangerous. He used magic when he fought Kith before, and he's very clever and very cruel."

"All right then, what should we do?"

Mackeli glanced quickly around. "Here's what I think . . ."

* * * * *

When he'd finished ransacking the tree-home, Voltorno supervised his men in setting up traps around the clearing. Where the foot path had been worn in the grass, they strewed caltrops—small, spiky stars designed to stop charging horses. Against the hide leggings Anaya and Mackeli wore, they would be deadly.

In the grass around the tree, they set saw-toothed, spring loaded traps, such as humans sometimes used to catch wolves. String triggers were strung, a pull on which would send a crossbow quarrel whizzing. Even by the last of the afternoon light the traps were hard to see. Kith-Kanan shuddered as he watched these diabolical preparations and prayed fervently that Anaya's nose for metal had not deserted her completely.

Night fell, and the cold returned strongly enough to remind the raiders that summer wasn't around the next sunrise. Kith-Kanan shivered in the chill while he watched Voltorno's men wrap themselves in Anaya's warm furs.

Voltorno brought a tin plate of stew and sat on a log in front of the prince. "I was a bit surprised to find you still here," the half-human said. He drank beer from a tin cup. In spite of his thirst, Kith-Kanan's nose wrinkled in disgust; it was a drink no true elf would touch. "When I returned to Daltigoth, I made inquiries about you. A Silvanesti, living in the forest like a painted savage. I heard a very strange tale in the halls of the imperial palace."

"I don't believe it," said Kith-Kanan, staring at the fire built some distance in front of the hollow oak. "I don't believe the humans would allow you into the imperial palace. Even human royalty knows better than to let street garbage into their homes."

His face contorted in anger, Voltorno flipped a spoonful of hot stew into Kith-Kanan's already much-abused face. The elf prince gasped and, despite his bound hands, managed to rub the scalding liquid onto the shoulder of his tunic.

"Don't interrupt," said Voltorno nastily. "As I was saying, I heard a strange tale. It seems that a prince of the Silvanesti, the brother of the current heir to the throne, left the city under a cloud. He bared a weapon in the hallowed Tower of the Stars or some nonsense like that." Voltorno laughed. "It seems the prince's father married the son's sweetheart to his brother," he added.

"Sounds like a very sad story," Kith-Kanan said, betraying as little emotion as he could. His shoulders ached from being forced to sit hunched over. He shifted his feet a bit, making the chains clatter as he did.

"It has the quality of an epic about it," Voltorno agreed, stirring his stew. "And I thought to myself: what a prize that son would make. Imagine the ransom the elf prince's family would pay!"

Kith-Kanan shook his head. "You are gravely mistaken if you think you can pass me off as a prince," he said. "I am Silvanesti, yes—a warrior whose nagging wife drove him into the forest for peace and quiet."

Voltorno laughed heartily. "Oh, yes? It's no use, my royal friend," he said. "I've seen portraits of the royal house of Silvanesti. You are this errant son."

A shrill shriek pierced the night air. The humans reached for their arms, and Voltorno went quickly to steady his men. "Keep your eyes open," he cautioned them. "This could be a trick to divert us."

A flaming brand hurtled through the air, tumbling end over end and trailing sparks and embers. It hit the grass twenty feet from the tree. It tripped a trigger string, and a crossbow fired with a dull thud.

"Aahwoo!" came a wailing cry from the dark trees. The humans began to mutter among themselves.

A second flaming brand flew into the clearing, from the opposite side of the forest. Then a third, some yards from the second. And a fourth, some yards from that.

"They're all around us!" one man cried.

"Quiet!" said Voltorno.

Carefully avoiding the wicked caltrops, he strode out on the central path. The men clustered together near him in a tight circle facing outward from their campfire. From his staked position, Kith-Kanan smiled grimly.

A figure appeared at the end of the path, carrying a burning branch. Voltorno drew his sword. The figure stopped where the caltrops began, some four yards from the half-human. The torch Voltorno held lit Anaya's face. Her face and hands were painted black. A single red stripe ran vertically from her forehead, along her nose, over her chin, and to the base of her neck.

Voltorno turned to his men. "You see! It's just the girl," he crowed. He faced Anaya. "Where's the boy? Hiding?" he asked with a sneer.

"You have come into the wildwood once too often," Anaya intoned. "None of you will leave it alive."

"Someone shoot her," Voltorno said in a bored tone, but the humans were mesmerized. None of them moved. Taking a slow step toward her, the commander declared, "It's you who will die, girl."

"Then enter the forest and find me," she said. "You have bows and swords and iron blades. All I have is a knife of flint."

"Yes, yes, very boring. You'd like us to flounder around in the woods at night, wouldn't you?" remarked Voltorno, moving another step closer to her.

"It's too late," she warned. "One by one, you shall all die." With that, Anaya slipped away into the night.

"Such melodrama," grumbled the half-human, returning to the fire. "I guess one can't expect more from a pair of savages."

"Why didn't you use your great magic, Voltorno?" Kith-Kanan asked sarcastically.

Quite earnestly, one of the terrified humans began to explain. "Our master must be very close to the one he—" This helpful information was abruptly cut off as Voltorno backhanded the speaker. The human fell back, his face bleeding.

Now Kith-Kanan understood. Voltorno's repertoire of magic was probably quite limited. Perhaps he had only the spell of befuddlement he had used in his duel with Kith-Kanan. And he had to be very close to the one he wished to enchant, which was obviously why he had been sidling closer to Anaya.

The next morning Kith-Kanan awoke stiff and groggy. The chill had penetrated his bones, and his chains didn't allow him to rest comfortably. He was trying to stretch the ache from his legs when a shriek of pure horror rang through the clearing. Kith-Kanan jerked toward the sound.

One of the human guards was staring down at the bedroll of one of his comrades. His face was bone-white and his mouth slack. He would have given vent to another scream, but Voltorno arrived at his side and shoved him away.

Voltorno's face registered shock, too, as he looked down at the bedroll. The human who had screamed now babbled, "Master! They cut Gernian's throat! How?"

The half-human rounded on the frantic raider and commanded him to be silent. All the humans now ringed their dead companion. Each of them asked themselves the same questions: How had Anaya and Mackeli killed the man without being seen by the watch? How had they gotten through the traps? Voltorno was rattled, and the humans were close to panic.

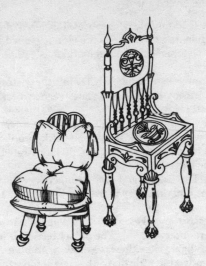

❧ 19 ❧

Sithas Returns

Morning, and the humans stirred half-heartedly through-
out the ambassador's large tent. Sithas heard them, their voices
hoarse from sleep, talking in the cloth-walled corridor outside
his room. He rose and shook the wrinkles from his clothes.

Ulvissen greeted the prince as he entered the tent's main sa-
lon. The seneschal offered him breakfast, but Sithas took only
a single apple from a bowl of fruit and forsook the rest. Humans had the habit of eating abysmally heavy meals, he knew,
which probably accounted for their thick physiques.

It had stopped raining during the night, though now the
wind blew steadily from the south, tearing the solid ceiling of
gray clouds into ragged, fluffy pieces. From their vantage point
on the hill overlooking the river, it seemed as if the broken

clouds were scudding along at eye level. Flashes of early morning sun illuminated the scene as the clouds passed before it.

"Strange weather," Ulvissen remarked as Sithas looked out
over the scene.

"We seldom get snow or ice here, but these storms blow in
from the southern ocean many times each winter," explained
the Silvanesti prince.

The river was alive with small craft taking advantage of the
lull. Ulvissen turned up the flaps of his thick, woolen cape as he
asked Sithas if river traffic was usually interrupted for the du-
ration of the storm.

"Oh, no. The fishers and barge runners are accustomed to
bad weather. Only the very worst winds will keep them tied to
the dock."

Sithas's escort and the ambassador's guards lined up as Ulwen and Teralind came out. The old ambassador looked even
worse by daylight. His skin was sallow, with blue veins boldly
visible. He moved so little that Sithas might have taken him for
a corpse, were it not that his eyes blinked now and then.

The gang of servants fell to and struck the tent. While the
windy air resounded with mallet strikes and the thud of falling
canvas, Sithas went to the barge. The giant turtle had drawn in
his head and legs during the night, and he was still asleep. Sithas rapped on the hull of the barge.

"Ferry master!" he called. "Are you there?"

The elderly elf's head popped out over the bulwark. "Indeed I
am, Highness!" He hopped up on the bulwark with a spryness
that belied his advanced age. A long pry bar rested on the boat-
man's shoulder, and he twirled it slightly as he went to where
the chains hooking the turtle to the barge were looped over
enormous iron hooks, spiked to the bow of the barge. Position-
ing the flat end of the pry bar under the chain links, he shouted,
"Clear away all!"

The soldiers of both races perked up. Sithas, who was walking back to stand with Ulvissen, halted and spun around. The
ferry master leaned on his bar, and the first chain slipped off its
hook. He shouted to clear the way again and popped the other
chain free. The elf prince saw that the humans were watching
with rapt interest. He hoped the ferry master knew what he was
doing.

The giant shackles fell against the shell of the turtle. This woke the beast, for the front hinge of its carapace, that part that closed in the giant animal's head, opened. The huge green head slowly emerged.

The ferry master raised his trumpet to his lips and sounded a single note. The turtle's legs came out, and he stood up. The rear of the turtle's shell bumped the barge, and the craft began to move.

"Look sharp!" sang out the ferry master.

With rapidly increasing speed, the fifty-foot barge slid down the muddy hill. It already had a natural groove to follow—the one it had made coming up the hill the night before. Churning a wave of mud before it, the barge accelerated down the slope. The ferry master played a cavalry charge on his horn.

"Madness!" exclaimed Teralind. "He'll smash himself to bits."

Sithas glanced over his shoulder and saw that the human woman had come forward, leaving her chair-bound husband with Ulvissen. As politeness dictated, he assuaged her fears as best he could. "It is a common thing. Do not fear, Lady, the craft is stoutly built." He prayed to Matheri that this was indeed so.

The flat stern of the barge hit the water, throwing up a tremendous wave. Then the barge slid completely off the bank into the river, leaving a cloud of mud in the water around it.

The turtle swung around ponderously. The humans who had been dismantling the tent scattered as the great beast swung toward them. With utmost placidity, the giant turned and walked down the hill. The incline and slippery mud bothered him not at all. As the ferry master commanded him with trumpet calls, the turtle slid quietly into the river and allowed the chains to be re-attached to the barge.

In another hour, the ambassador's party was ready to board. By the time they moved down a marble-paved path to the water's edge, the wind had slowed and died out completely.

The captain of the elven soldiers shook his head. "The lull's ending," he noted, resignation coloring his comment.

"More rain?" asked Ulvissen.

"And more wind," replied Sithas.

* * * * *

The ambassador's party made it to the island without incident. Waiting for them were three large sedan chairs and two horse-drawn wagons. Spray broke over the dock, soaking the poor porters who stood by the sedan chairs. With scant attention to protocol, the ambassador was bundled into one chair, Lady Teralind into another, and Sithas into the third. The wagons were for the baggage. Everyone else had to walk.

Sithas was surprised when he entered his private rooms in the palace. The window shutters were drawn against the rain, and waiting for him in the dim, unlit room was Hermathya.

"So you're home," she said with irritation. "Was it worth it?"

Her tone was arch, close to anger. Though he had no reason, Sithas felt his own emotions hardening, a fact that surprised him.

"It had to be done," he said smoothly. "As it is, things turned out rather well. We showed the humans of what stuff elves are made."

She trembled and strode past the prince to the shuttered window. Rain was seeping through the slats, pooling on the cool marble floor.

"And what are you made of?" she demanded, temper flaring.

"What do you mean? What's the matter?"

"You risked your life for etiquette! Did you give any thought to me? What would happen to me if you had been killed?"

Sithas sighed and sat in a chair made of intertwined maple saplings. "Is that what's bothering you? It's unworthy of you, Thya. After all, I was in no real danger."

"Don't be so damned logical! You've no idea what I mean!" Hermathya turned to the speaker's heir. Through clenched teeth, she said, "I've passed my first fertile time. It's gone, and we missed it!"

Sithas finally understood. Even though an elven couple might live as husband and wife a thousand years, they might only be fertile three or four times in their entire lives. These times were very irregular; even the healing clerics of Quenesti Pah couldn't predict a fertile time more than a day or two in advance.

"Why didn't you tell me sooner?" Sithas asked, his voice softening.

"You weren't here. You were sleeping by yourself."

"Am I so unapproachable?"

She fingered the edge of her embroidered collar. "Yes, you are."

"You have no problem getting what you want from others," Sithas went on heedlessly. "You collect gifts and compliments as a child picks flowers in a field. Why can't you speak to me? I am your husband."

"You are the elf I married," she corrected, "not the elf I loved."

Sithas stood quickly. "I've heard enough. In the future you—"

She moved toward him. "Will you listen to me for once? If you insist on risking your life on foolish errands, then you must give me a child. Our marriage can mean something then. An heir needs an heir. You want a son; I need a child."

The prince folded his arms, annoyed at her pleading tone. That emotion confused Sithas somewhat. Why did her pleading irritate him? "Perhaps it is the wisdom of the gods that this happened," he said. "It is not a good time to start a family."

"How can you say that?" she asked.

"It is Matheri's own truth. My life is not my own. I have to live for the nation. With all this trouble in the West, I may even have to take up arms for the speaker's cause."

Hermathya laughed bitterly. "You, a warrior? You have the wrong twin in mind. Kith-Kanan is the warrior. You are a priest."

Coldly Sithas told her, "Kith-Kanan is not here."

"I wish to Astarin he was! He would not have left me last night!" she said harshly.

"Enough!" Sithas went to the door. With exaggerated politeness, he said, "Lady, I am truly sorry to have missed the time, but it is done and no peace will come from dwelling on lost chances." He went out. Behind him, Hermathya dissolved in furious tears.

Sithas descended the steps, his face set hard as granite. Servants and courtiers parted for him as he went. All bowed, as was the custom, but none dared speak.

* * * * *

Two fine chairs were set up in the audience hall of the Tower of the Stars. One, short-legged and plush, was for Dunbarth, ambassador from Thorbardin. The second was a tall piece of furniture, its elegantly wrought curves gilded. Here sat Teralind. Her husband, the titular ambassador, sat in his special chair beside her. Praetor Ulwen did not speak and after a while it was easy to forget he was even present.

Sithel sat on his throne, of course, and Sithas stood by his left hand. The rest of the floor was taken up by courtiers and servants. Ulvissen, never far from Teralind and the ambassador, hovered behind the lady's golden chair, listening much and speaking little.

"The territory in question," Sithel was saying, "is bordered on the south by the bend of the Kharolis River, on the west by the city of Xak Tsaroth, on the east by the Khalkist Mountains, and on the north by the region where the Vingaard River is born on the great plain. In the time of my father, this region was divided into three areas. The northernmost was named Vingaardin, the central was called Kagonesti, and the southernmost was Tsarothelm."

Dunbarth waved a beringed hand. "Your Highness's knowledge of geography is considerable," he noted with exaggerated politeness, "but what is the point in your lecture?"

"As I was about to say, in the time of my father, Silvanos, these three provinces were unclaimed by any of our nations. They were ruled, and ruled poorly, by local lords who extorted taxes from the common folk and who warred constantly with each other."

"Such is not the case today," Teralind interjected.

"There is considerable violence in this area still," Sithel replied, "as evidenced by the massacre of fifty of my guard by a large force of mounted men."

Silence ensued. The elven scribes, who had been taking down every word spoken, held their styluses poised over their pages. Dunbarth looked at Teralind curiously.

"You do not object, Lady, to the speaker's description of the marauders as 'men?' " he asked pointedly, leaning forward on one elbow.

She shrugged her green velvet clad shoulders, and Ulvissen sidled closer to the back of her chair. "The emperor does not rule the entire race of men,"—she allowed. Sithas could almost hear the unspoken *yet* at the end of Teralind's statement—"any more than the king of Thorbardin rules all dwarves. I don't know who these bandits are, but if they are men, they are not men of Ergoth."

"Certainly not," Sithel continued smoothly. "You will not deny, though, that the emperor has done nothing to discourage the large number of human settlers who cross the plain and descend the rivers by boat and raft. They are displacing both the Kagonesti and those Silvanesti who have moved west to live. It must stop."

"There is not room enough in Ergoth for everyone to live and work, nor is there land enough to grow the food needed to feed them all," countered Teralind. "Why is it strange that human settlers should leave the boundaries of the empire and wander east into the region claimed by the Silvanesti, when that region is so sparsely settled?"

"None have tried to settle in Thorbardin," said Dunbarth unhelpfully.

Prince Sithas gestured to a scribe, who brought him a parchment scroll filled with tiny, precise writing. Two large wax seals were affixed to the bottom of the paper. "This is our copy of the agreement made between Speaker Sithel and Emperor Tion, dated four hundred years ago. It specifically forbids Ergoth from colonizing Vingaardin without the approval of the Speaker of the Stars."

"Emperor Tion was an old man. Many of the works done by him late in his life were faulty," Teralind commented tactlessly. Ulvissen, who'd been stroking his auburn beard in thought, leaned down and whispered in her ear. She nodded and continued, "No less than six of Tion's treaties have been repudiated over the years since his death. The treaty Prince Sithas holds is therefore of doubtful standing." At her side, the aged praetor stirred vaguely. Teralind paid no attention.

Dunbarth slid forward and dropped out of his chair. He tugged his tunic down smoothly over his barrel chest and said, "As I recall, it was Tion's plan to invade and conquer Sancrist, but he feared the elven nation would retaliate against his eastern border. For that reason he struck a deal with Speaker Sithel."

The prince had returned the parchment to the scribe. Curious, he asked, "And why did the invasion of Sancrist not take place?"

Dunbarth laughed merrily. "The Ergothian generals pointed out how difficult it would be to rule an island full of gnomes. The drain on the empire's treasury would have been enormous!" Some scattered laughter drifted through the hall. Sithel rapped on the floor with his five-foot-long regnal staff, and the snickering died.

"I believe what you say, Lady Teralind," Sithel noted blandly. "His Majesty Tion must have been distracted to imagine he could conquer and rule the gnomes, though he did not really seem so when I met him." Teralind flushed slightly at this reminder of the speaker's great life span. "But that doesn't change the fact that human settlers and human bandits have been taking life and land away from my subjects."

"If I may say something," Dunbarth interrupted, walking around the side of his chair. "Many people come to Thorbardin to buy our metals, and we have heard a great deal about the troubles on the plain. I think it is unfair to say, Your Highness, that it is simply a matter of humans pushing elves out. I understand that many of the bandits are elves themselves, of the Kagonesti race." He rubbed the broad toe of his left boot against the trousers of his right leg to remove a smudge on the brilliant shine. "And some of the bandits are half-elves."

Although this statement was of no surprise to Sithel or Sithas, it was a revelation that set the crowd of servants and retainers to buzzing. Sithas turned his back on the hall and spoke to his father in guarded tones. "What is the matter with that fellow? He acts as if he were the advocate for Ergoth!" Sithas muttered.

"Don't blame Dunbarth. He knows his country will gain the advantage if we and the humans cannot agree. He's thrown out this rubbish about half-humans to muddy the water. It means nothing," Sithel commented wisely.

The prince stood aside, and his father rapped for silence once more.

"Let us not confuse matters with talk of bandits and half-breeds," Sithel said genially. "There really is only one question: who rules these three provinces?"

"Who rules them in fact, or rules them by a signet pressed to a dollop of molten wax?" Teralind said testily.

"We must have law, Lady, or we shall be nothing but bandits ourselves," counseled Dunbarth. He smiled behind his curled silver beard. "Well-dressed, rich bandits, but bandits nevertheless." More laughter. This time Sithel let the laughter build, for it diffused the tension in the tower.

"There is no doubt the Speaker of the Stars bears an ancient claim to the land," Dunbarth continued, "or that Ergoth has certain rights where so many of its subjects are concerned."

Sithas lifted his eyebrows at this statement. "Subjects?" he asked quickly. "Are the humans living in the three provinces subjects, therefore, of the emperor of Ergoth?"

"Well, of course," conceded Teralind. Ulvissen leaned forward to speak to her, but she waved him away. The lady looked perplexed as she realized belatedly that she had contradicted her earlier statement that the bandits were not Ergothians. "What I mean to say is—"

Ulvissen tapped urgently on her shoulder. Teralind turned and snapped, "Stand back, sir! Do not interrupt me!" The seneschal instantly retreated a pace and stood rigidly at attention.

Sithas exchanged a glance with his father, and murmurs arose in the hall. Teralind's eyes darted around, for she knew she'd made a dangerous admission. She tried to salvage the situation by saying, "There is not a man, woman, or human child in the whole realm of Ansalon who does not owe allegiance to His Imperial Majesty."

Sithel did not try to speak until the murmuring had subsided. In precise, measured tones, he finally said, "Is it your intention to annex our lands?"

Teralind pushed herself back in her chair and frowned. Beside her, the frail form of Praetor Ulwen moved. He leaned forward slightly and began to shake. Tremors racked his frail body, and Ulvissen moved swiftly to his side. The seneschal snapped his fingers at the human contingent of servants loitering by the grand doors.

"Highness, noble ambassadors, I beg your pardon, but the praetor is seized with an attack," he announced in an anxious voice, "He must withdraw."

Dunbarth spread his hands graciously. Sithel stood. "You

have our leave to withdraw," the speaker said. "Shall I send one of our healers to the praetor's rooms?"

Teralind's head lifted regally. "We have a doctor of our own, thank you, noble speaker."

The porters took hold of the rails attached to Ulwen's chair and hoisted him up. The Ergothian delegation filed out behind him. When they were gone, Dunbarth bowed and led his dwarves out. Sithel dismissed his retainers and was finally alone with his son in the tower.

"Diplomacy is so tiring," the speaker said wearily. He stood and laid his silver scepter across the throne. "Give me your arm, Sith. I believe I need to rest for a while."

*   *   *   *   *

Tamanier Ambrodel walked beside Lady Nirakina through the palace. They had just come from the guild hall of the stone workers, where Lady Nirakina had viewed the plans for the new Market. It was an orderly, beautifully designed place, but its site and purpose depressed her. "It's simply wrong," she told Tamanier. "We are the firstborn race of the world and favored by the gods. As such, it is only right we share our grace with other people, not look upon them as lesser beings."

Tamanier nodded. "I heartily agree, Lady. When I lived in the wilderness, I saw many kinds of people—Silvanesti, Kagonesti, humans, dwarves, gnomes, kender—and no one lived better than his neighbor for any reason but his own hard work. The land doesn't care if it's plowed by human or elf. The rain falls the same on every farm."

They arrived at the door of Nirakina's private rooms. Before he left, Tamanier informed her, "I went to see Miritelisina, as you requested."

"Is she well?" she asked eagerly. "A priestess of such age and wisdom should not be held in a common dungeon."

"She is well," Tamanier said, "though unrepentant. She still does not admit to her crime."

"I do not believe she committed a crime," Nirakina said with fervor. "Miritelisina was moved by compassion. She only sought to warn the poor refugees of the plan to move them. I'm certain she had no idea they'd riot as they did."

Tamanier bowed. "I bear the holy lady no ill will. I tell you, though, that she will not repent—even to gain her freedom. Miritelisina believes that by remaining in prison, she will inspire others who want to help the refugees."

Nirakina gave the young courtier's arm a squeeze. "And what do you think, Tam? Whose cause do you favor?"

"Do you really have to ask? A short time ago, I was one of the poor wretches—homeless, penniless, despised. They deserve the speaker's protection."

"We'll have to see what we can do to win it," Nirakina replied warmly.

She went into her rooms, and Tamanier walked away, his step light. With the speaker's wife fighting for them, the homeless settlers would soon feel the grace of Sithel's favor. And who knew, perhaps Miritelisina would be freed to resume her good works for the poor.

He left the central tower of the palace and strolled the empty corridor balcony of the east wing.

Suddenly he heard voices. Foreign voices. He'd lived among humans long enough to know their speech.

"—play at this silly game?" complained a woman's voice, tight with emotion.

"As long as necessary. It's the emperor's will," a man's strong voice answered.

"The things I do for my father! I hope he appreciates it!"

"He's paying off your gambling debts, isn't he?" said the man drily.

Tamanier knew he shouldn't eavesdrop, but he was intrigued. He stood very still. Since the humans were in the corridor below him, their voices carried easily to him up the central atrium.

"I don't trust that Dunbarth," asserted the woman. "He switches sides like a click beetle."

"He has no side but his own. Right now Thorbardin isn't ready for war, so he hopes to play us off against the elves. He's clever, but I see what he's doing."

"He annoys me. So does Prince Sithas. How he stares! They say elves have second sight." The woman's voice rose. "You don't think he's reading my mind, do you?"

"Calm yourself," said the man. "I don't think he can. But if it troubles you, I'll speak to our friend about it."

Footsteps echoed on the balcony across the atrium from where Tamanier stood. He tensed, ready to be discovered. The voices below ceased their furtive talk.

Out of the afternoon shadows on the far side of the balcony Tamanier spied the young priest of the Blue Phoenix, Kamin Oluvai. Tamanier was surprised; why was the priest here? Kamin didn't see him, however, so Tamanier withdrew from the balcony rail. The humans he'd heard were certainly Lady Teralind and Ulvissen, but what did their strange conversation mean?

Court intrigue was foreign to him. Who was Teralind really? What was she concealing? Who was the "friend" Ulvissen referred to? Could it be the traitor of which Speaker Sithel had spoken that night at dinner?

Tamanier hurried away. He had to tell someone, and Sithas's room was nearby. The courtier was already feeling slightly relieved; certainly the prince would know what to do.

✎ 20 ✎

Day of Metamorphosis

The humans were breaking camp and getting ready to return to their ship. They worked with haste, and it was clear to Kith-Kanan that they wanted nothing more than to be away from such an accursed place. While they worked, Voltorno went to the elf prince. He had his men pry the stake out of the ground, then he grabbed Kith-Kanan's shackles and dragged him to the edge of the clearing.

"You out there! Woman and boy! I have your friend here! If any more of my men are so much as scratched, I'll make your royal friend suffer for it. I'll give him something more than a scar on his cheek. How do you think he'd look without an arm, a hand, or a leg? Do you hear me?"

The only answer was the soft sighing of wind in the still

bare branches.

"We're ready to go, master," said one of the humans.

"Then get moving, dolt." Voltorno was losing his air of confidence. Despite his aching limbs and the stinging sword cut on his cheek, Kith-Kanan was pleased. The angrier Voltorno got, the greater advantage Anaya and Mackeli would have.

The raiders marched down the path single file, with Kith-Kanan leading. Voltorno gave the prince over to one of his men and moved out ahead as the band left the path and entered the woods.

They snaked silently through the forest. In spite of their master's assurances, the men adopted a crouching walk, swinging their loaded bows slowly from side to side. Their fear was palpable, like a foul odor.

As they reached the old, deep forest, the trees got larger and farther apart. The raiders moved more quickly, using the trail they'd made on their way to the clearing. Occasionally Voltorno scanned the high tree branches, alert to any ambush from above. This added greatly to the alarm of his men. They started glancing up frequently, stumbling and bumping into each other.

Disgusted, Voltorno turned on them. "You make more noise than a pen of squealing pigs!" he hissed.

"And you don't breathe correctly either," Kith-Kanan put in.

Voltorno gave him a venomous glance and turned to resume the march. Just then, a loud cracking sound filled the air. The men stood, paralyzed, trying to find the source of the noise. A tree branch broke off a nearby oak and dropped to the ground ahead. The men started laughing with relief.

Behind them, a figure popped up out of the leaves and aimed a stolen crossbow at the back of the last man in line. The quarrel loosed, the dark figure slipped silently back into the bed of leaves. The wounded man made a gurgling sound, staggered forward a few steps, and collapsed.

"It's Favius! He's been shot!"

"Mind your front! Look for your target before you shoot!" Voltorno barked. The six men remaining formed a ring with Kith-Kanan in the center. Voltorno walked slowly around the ring, staring hard at the empty woods. There was nothing and no one to be seen.

He halted when he noticed one of his men holding an empty bow. "Meldren," he said glacially, "why is your bow not loaded?"

The man named Meldren looked at his weapon in surprise. "I must have triggered it off," he muttered.

"Yes, into Favius's back!"

"No, master! Favius was behind me!"

"Don't lie to me!" Fiercely Voltorno struck the man with the flat of his sword. Meldren dropped his crossbow and fell to the ground. None of the other men offered to help him or supported his story.

Voltorno picked up the man's crossbow and handed it to another of his company. "Meldren will walk in the rear," he ordered. "With any luck, the witch will kill him next."

The raiders relieved the dead man of his weapons and gear and moved on. The wretched Meldren, with only a short sword for defense, brought up the rear.

The trail they followed lead them down a draw, between a pair of giant oaks. Voltorno went down on one knee and held up his hand to halt the group. He studied the ground and then looked ahead.

"This has the look of a trap," he said with a wise air. "We'll not go through the draw. Four of you men go along the right edge. The rest follow me on the left."

The draw was a V-shaped ditch, twenty feet wide and eight feet deep at its lowest point. Four men crept along the right rim of the gully while Voltorno, Kith-Kanan, and two others walked along the left. As the half-human circled around, he clucked his tongue triumphantly.

"See?" he said. Leaning against an oak on the left was a thick log, poised to roll down into the draw if anyone disturbed the web of vines attached to it. This web extended down into the draw and covered the ground there. The men on the right came around their oak. Voltorno waved to them. The lead man waved back—and the ground beneath him gave way.

The "ground" they'd been standing on was nothing but a large log, covered loosely with dirt and leaves. Held in place by slender windfall limbs, the log collapsed under the men's weight. With shouts and cries for help, the four tumbled into the gully.

"No!" Voltorno shouted.

The men received only bruises and cuts from falling the eight feet into the ravine, but they rolled onto the mat of vines that was the trigger for the six-foot-thick log poised on the left bank. The vines snapped taut, the log rolled down, and the men were crushed beneath it. Voltorno, Kith-Kanan, and the remaining two raiders could only stand by and watch as this occurred.

Suddenly there was a whirring sound and a thump. One of the two humans dropped, a crossbow quarrel in his back. The last human gave a shriek. He flung down his weapon and ran off into the woods, screaming without letup. Voltorno shouted for him to come back, but the hysterical raider disappeared into the trees.

"It appears you're on your own, Voltorno," Kith-Kanan said triumphantly.

The half-human seized the prince and held him in front of his body like a shield. "I'll kill him, witch!" he screamed into the trees. He turned from side to side, searching madly for Anaya or Mackeli. "I swear I will kill him!"

"You won't live that long," a voice uttered behind him.

In shock, the half-human whirled. Anaya, still painted sooty black, stood nonchalantly before him, just out of sword's reach. Mackeli was behind her, his bow poised. Taking advantage of his captor's obvious shock at seeing these two foes so close by, Kith-Kanan wrenched himself from Voltorno's grasp and jumped away from him.

"Shoot her!" Voltorno cried dazedly. "Shoot her, men!"

Remembering belatedly that he had no one left to command, the half-human lunged at Anaya. Mackeli started to react, but the keeper shouted, "No, he's mine!"

Despite his wife's shouted claim, Kith-Kanan slogged forward under the burden of his chains. The prince was certain that Anaya didn't have a chance against a fine duelist like Voltorno. Her agility was drastically reduced, and the only weapon she carried was her flint knife.

The half-human thrust at her twice, then a third time. She dodged, adequately but without her old preternatural grace. He cut and slashed the air, and as Anaya scampered aside, the Ergothian blade bit into a tree. She ducked under Voltorno's reach and jabbed at his stomach. The half-human brought the sword's hilt down on her head. With a grunt of pain, Anaya sprawled on her face.

"Shoot!" Kith-Kanan cried. As Mackeli's finger closed on the trigger bar, Anaya rolled away from Voltorno's killing strike and repeated her warning to her friends.

"Only *I* may shed his blood!" she declared.

Voltorno laughed in response, but it was a laugh shrill with desperation.

Anaya got to her feet clumsily and stumbled in the thick leaves and fallen branches. As best she could, she jerked back, out of the way of Voltorno's sweeping slash, but she could not avoid the straight thrust that followed. Mackeli's green eyes widened in shock and he uttered a strangled cry as the blade pierced Anaya's brown deerskin tunic.

Though he saw what happened, Kith-Kanan was more shocked by what he heard—a roaring in his ears. For a moment, he didn't know what he was hearing, then he realized that the sound was Anaya's pulse. It hammered at the prince like thunder, and he felt as if he would collapse from the pain of it. Time seemed to slow for Kith-Kanan as he watched Anaya. His beloved's face showed no pain, only an unshakable determination.

Voltorno's lips widened in a smile. Though he would surely die himself, at least he'd killed the witch. That smile froze as Anaya grasped the sword that pierced her stomach and rammed it farther in. His fingers still locked around the handle, the half-human was jerked toward her. His puzzlement turned to horror as Anaya brought up her free hand and drove her flint knife into his heart.

Voltorno collapsed. So tightly did he grip the sword that, when he fell backward, he pulled it from Anaya's body. He was dead before he hit the ground.

Kith-Kanan struggled to Anaya's side and caught her as she collapsed. "Anaya," the prince said desperately. The front of her tunic was covered in blood. "Anaya, please . . ."

"Take me home," she said and fainted.

Mackeli found the key to Kith-Kanan's shackles in Voltorno's belt pouch. Freed of his bonds, the prince lifted Anaya in his arms. Mackeli offered to help.

"No, I have her," Kith-Kanan said brokenly. "She weighs nothing."

He strode away from the gully, past the places where Voltorno's men had died. Inside, Kith-Kanan concentrated on the sound and sensation of Anaya's heartbeat. It was there. Slow, labored, but it was there. He walked faster. At home there would be medicines. Mackeli knew things. He knew about roots and poultices. At the hollow tree there would be medicines.

"You have to live," he told Anaya, staring straight ahead. "By Astarin, you have to live! We've not had enough time together!"

The sun flickered through the leafless trees as they hurried toward the clearing. By now Kith-Kanan was almost running. Anaya was strong, he repeated over and over in his mind. Mackeli would be able to save her.

In the clearing, Arcuballis reared up on its hinds legs and spread its wings in greeting. The beast had returned from hunting to find everyone gone. Kith-Kanan paid it no heed as he rushed toward Anaya's home—*their* home.

The prince ran to the hollow tree and laid Anaya on a silver wolf pelt that Mackeli had dragged outside. Her eyes were closed and her skin was ice cold. Kith-Kanan felt for a pulse. There was none.

"Do something!" he screamed at Mackeli. The boy stared at Anaya, his mouth open. Kith-Kanan grabbed the front of his tunic. "Do something, I said!"

"I don't know anything!"

"You know about roots and herbs!" he begged.

"Ny is dead, Kith. I cannot call her back to life. I wish I could, but I can't!"

When the prince saw the tears in Mackeli's eyes, he knew that the boy spoke the truth. Kith-Kanan let go of Mackeli's tunic and rocked back on his heels, staring down at the still form of Anaya. Anaya.

Rage and anguish boiled up inside the prince. His sword lay on the ground by the tree, where Voltorno had found and discarded it. Kith-Kanan picked up the blade and stared at it. The half-human had murdered his wife, and he had done nothing. He'd let Voltorno murder his wife and child-to-be.

Kith-Kanan screamed—a horrible, deep, wrenching cry—
then slammed the flat of the blade against the oak tree. The
cold iron snapped five inches above the hilt. In anger he threw
the sword hilt as far as he could.

*   *   *   *   *

Night. Mackeli and Kith-Kanan sat inside the tree, not moving, not talking. They had covered Anaya with her favorite
blanket, one made from the pelts of a dozen rabbits. Now they
sat in darkness. The broken blade of his sword lay across Kith-
Kanan's lap.

He was cursed. He felt it in his heart. Love always eluded
him. First Hermathya had been taken away. So be it. He had
found a better life and a better wife than Hermathya would
ever have been. His life had just begun again. And now it had
ended. Anaya was dead. Their unborn child was dead. He was
cursed.

A gust of wind blew in the open door, sweeping leaves and
dust in tiny whirlwinds around Mackeli's ankles. He sat with
his head on his knees, staring blankly at the floor. The shriv-
eled brown oak leaves were lifted from the ground and spun
around. He followed their dancing path toward the doorway,
and his eyes widened.

The green glow that filled the open entrance to the hollow
tree transfixed Mackeli. It washed his face and silver hair.

"Kith," he murmured. "Look."

"What is it?" the prince asked tiredly. He looked toward the
doorway, and a frown creased his forehead. Then, throwing
the mantle off his shoulders, he got up. With a hand on the
door edge, Kith-Kanan looked outside. The soft mound that
was Anaya beneath her blanket was the source of the strange
green light. The Silvanesti prince stepped outside. Mackeli
followed.

The light was cool as Kith-Kanan knelt by Anaya's body and
slowly pulled the rabbit-fur blanket back. It was Anaya herself
that was glowing.

Her emerald eyes sprang open.

With a strangled cry, Kith-Kanan fell back. Anaya sat up.
The strong light diminished, leaving only a mild verdant aura

213

surrounding the elf woman. She was green from hair to toes.

"Y-You're alive!" he stuttered.

"No," Anaya said sadly. She stood, and he did likewise. "This is part of the change. This was meant to happen. All the animal life has left me, and now, Kith, I am becoming one with the forest."

"I don't understand." To speak with his wife when he'd all but resigned himself to never seeing her again brought Kith-Kanan great joy. But her manner, the tone of her words, frightened him more than her death. He couldn't comprehend what was happening.

The green Anaya put a hand to his cheek. It was cool and gentle. She smiled at him, and a lump grew in his throat. "This happened to the other keepers. When their time was done, they became one with the forest, too. I am dead, dear Kith, but I will be here for thousands of years. I am joining the wildwood."

Kith-Kanan took her in his arms. "What about *us*? Is this what you want?" he asked, and fear made his voice harsh.

"I love you, Kith," Anaya said passionately, "but I am content now. This *is* my destiny. I am glad I was able to explain it to you." She pulled free of his embrace and walked off a few yards.

"I have always liked this spot in the clearing. It is a good place," she said with satisfaction.

"Good-bye, Ny!" Mackeli called tearfully. "You were a good sister!"

"Good-bye, Keli. Live well."

Kith-Kanan rushed to her. He couldn't accept this. It was all too strange. It was happening too quickly! He tried to take Anaya in his arms once more, but her feet were fixed to the ground.

Her eyes rebuked him gently as she said consolingly, "Don't fight it, Kith." Her voice becoming faint, the keeper added, "It is right."

"What of our child?" he asked desperately.

Anaya placed a hand on her belly. "He is there still. He was not part of the plan. A long, long time from now he will be born. . . ." The light slowly dwindled in her eyes. "Farewell, my love."

Kith-Kanan held Anaya's face between his hands and kissed

her. For a moment only, her lips had the yielding quality of flesh. Then a firmness crept in. The elf prince pulled back and, even as he touched her face for the last time, Anaya's features slowly vanished. What had been skin roughened into bark. By the time Kith-Kanan spoke her name once more, Anaya had found her destiny. At the clearing's edge, the prince of the Silvanesti was embracing a fine young oak tree.

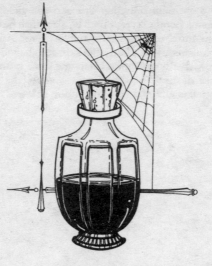

21

Silvanost, Year of the Ram

For a month the ambassadors met with the Speaker of the Stars, yet nothing was accomplished. Nothing, except that Speaker Sithel fell ill. His health had been deteriorating over the preceding weeks, and the strain of the conference had sapped his strength to the point that by the morning of the twenty-ninth day, he could not even rise from his bed. Sickness was so rare for the speaker that a mild panic gripped the palace. Servants dashed about, conversing in whispers. Nirakina summoned Sithas and Hermathya to the speaker's bedside. So grave was her tone, Sithas half-expected to find his father on the verge of death.

Standing now at the foot of his father's bed, the prince could see that Sithel was wan and dispirited. Nirakina sat beside her

---

216

ailing husband, holding a damp cloth to his head. Hermathya hovered in the background, obviously uncomfortable in the presence of illness.

"Let me call a healer," Nirakina insisted.

"It's not necessary," Sithel said testily. "I just need some rest."

"You have a fever!"

"I do not! Well, if I do, do you think I want it known that the Speaker of the Stars is so feeble he needs a healer to get well? What sort of message do you suppose that sends to our people? Or to the foreign emissaries?" This short speech left him winded, and he breathed heavily, his face pale against the cream-colored pillows.

"Regarding the ambassadors, what shall I tell them?" Sithas asked. "If you cannot attend the conference today—"

"Tell them to soak their heads," Sithel muttered. "That devious dwarf and that contentious human female." His words subsided.

"Now, husband, that's no way to talk," Nirakina said agreeably. "There's no stigma to being ill, you know. You'd get well a lot sooner if a healer treated you."

"I'll heal myself, thank you."

"You may lie here for weeks, fevered, ill-tempered—"

"I am not ill-tempered!" Sithel shouted.

Nirakina rose from the bed purposefully. To Sithas she directed her questions. "Who can we get? Who is the best healer in Silvanost?"

From the far wall, Hermathya uttered one word: "Miritelisina."

"Impossible," the prince said quickly, looking at his wife with reproach. "She is in prison, as you well know, Lady."

"Oh, tosh," responded his mother. "If the speaker wants the best healer, he can order her release." Neither father nor son spoke or showed any sign of heeding Nirakina's counsel. "Miritelisina is high priestess of Quenesti Pah. No one else in Silvanost can come near her expertise in the healing art." She appealed to Sithas. "She's been in prison more than six months. Surely that's punishment enough for a moment's indiscretion?"

Sithel coughed, a loud, racking paroxysm that nearly doubled him over in bed. "It's the old delta fever," he gasped. "It's known to recur."

"Delta fever?" asked Sithas.

"A legacy of misspent youth," the speaker said weakly. When he sat up in bed, Nirakina gave him a cup of cool water to sip. "I used to hunt in the marshes at the mouth of the Thon-Thalas when I was young. I caught delta fever then."

Nirakina looked up at Sithas. "That was more than two hundred years before you were born," she said reassuringly. "He's had other, milder attacks."

"Father, send for the priestess," Sithas decided gravely. The speaker raised his brows questioningly. "The negotiations with the dwarves and humans must go ahead, and only a strong, healthy speaker can see that justice is done."

"Sithas is right," Nirakina agreed. She pressed her small hand to Sithel's burning cheek. "Send for Miritelisina."

The speaker sighed, the dry, rattling sound rising from his fevered throat. "Very well," he said softly. "Let it be done."

* * * * *

Later that morning came a knock at the door. Nirakina called for the person to enter. Tamanier came in, looking downcast.

"Great speaker, I spoke with Miritelisina," he said abjectly.

"Where is she?" asked Sithas sharply.

"She—she refuses to come, my prince."

"What?" said Sithas.

"What?" echoed Nirakina.

"She will not come to Your Highness, nor will she accept pardon from prison," Tamanier announced, shaking his head.

"Has she gone mad?" demanded Sithas.

"No, sire. Miritelisina believes her suffering in prison will bring the plight of the homeless ones to the attention of all."

In spite of his weakness, the speaker began to laugh softly. "What a character!" he said. The laughter threatened to turn into coughing, so he checked himself.

"It's extortion," Sithas said angrily. "She means to dictate her own terms!"

"Never mind, son. Tamanier, have the door of Miritelisina's cell left open. Tell the warders to bring her neither food nor water. When she gets hungry enough, she'll leave."

"What will you do if she doesn't come?" Nirakina asked, bewildered.

"I shall survive," he replied. "Now, all of you go. I wish to rest."

Tamanier went on his errand. Sithas and Nirakina drifted out, looking back frequently at the speaker. Sithas marveled at how small and weak his father looked in the great bed.

Alone, Sithel sat up slowly. His head pounded, but after a moment it cleared. He put his feet on the floor, and the cool marble soothed him. He stood and moved carefully to a window. The whole of Silvanost spread out below him. How he loved it! Not the city, which was just a collection of buildings, but the people, the daily rhythm of life that made Silvanost a living place.

A rainstorm had ended the day before, leaving the air crystal clean with a bite of cold. High, lacy clouds stretched from the horizon to mid-sky, like delicate fingers reaching up to the abode of the gods.

All of a sudden Sithel gave a shudder. The white clouds and shining towers reeled before him. He clutched the curtains for support, but strength faded from his hands and he lost his grip. Knees buckling, he slid to the floor. No one was around to see him fall. Sithel lay still on the marble floor, warmed by a patch of sunshine.

*　*　*　*　*

Sithas walked the palace halls, looking for Hermathya. He saw that she had not stayed with the speaker, so fearful was she of catching his illness. Some sort of intuition drew him up the tower stairs to the floor where his old bachelor room was. To his surprise, the prince found his devotional candle lit and a fresh red rose, sacred to Matheri, lying on the table by his bachelor bed. He had no idea who had left it. Hermathya had no reason to come here.

The sight of the rose and candle soothed his worried mind somewhat. He knelt by the table and began to meditate. At last he prayed to Matheri for his father's recovery and for more understanding in dealing with Hermathya.

Time passed. How much, he didn't know. A tapping sound

filled the small chamber. Sithas ignored it. It grew louder. He raised his head and looked around for the source of the intrusive noise. He saw his seldom-worn sword, the twin of Kith-Kanan's weapon, hanging in its scabbard from a peg on the wall. The sword was vibrating inside its brass-bound sheath, causing the tapping noise.

Sithas rose and went to the weapon. He looked on in amazement as the length of iron shook itself like a trembling dog. He put out his hand, grasping the sword's hilt to try and still the vibrations. The shivering climbed Sithas's arm, penetrating his body and sending tingles up his arm. He took the sword hilt in both hands—

In a flash the speaker's heir had a sudden, clear impression of his twin brother. Great rage, great anguish, heartache, a mortal blow—

A loud *crack* smote his ears, and the sword ceased vibrating. Slightly dazed, Sithas drew the blade out. It was broken cleanly, about five inches above the hilt.

Fear seized him. Fear for Kith-Kanan. He had no idea how he knew, but as he held the stump of the sword, Sithas knew without a doubt that Kith was in grave danger, perhaps even near death. He had to tell someone—his father, his mother. Sithas rushed to the dark oaken door of his old room and flung it open. He was startled to find someone standing just outside, shadowed by the massive overhang of the stone arch over the door.

"Who are you?" Sithas demanded, presenting the foreshortened sword. The figure seemed ominous somehow.

"Your sword is broken," said the stranger soothingly. "Be at peace, noble prince. I mean you no harm."

The stranger stepped forward into the pale light emanating from Sithas's candle, still burning on the table. He wore a nondescript gray robe. A hood covered his head. The air around him throbbed with an aura of power. Sithas felt it, like heat on his face from a nearby fire.

"Who are you?" the prince repeated with great deliberation. The oddly menacing figure reached up with slim pink fingers to throw back the hood. Beneath the soft gray material, his face was round and good-natured. He was nearly bald; only a fringe of mouse-brown hair covered the sides of his head. His ears were small and tapered.

"Do I know you?" Sithas asked. He relaxed a bit, for the stranger looked like nothing more than a beggarly cleric.

"At a royal dinner some time ago, you met an elf with long blond hair who introduced himself as Kamin Oluvai, second priest of the Blue Phoenix. That was me." The strange elf seemed pleased with Sithas's evident surprise.

"You're Kamin Oluvai? You look nothing like him," said the puzzled prince.

"A simple disguise." He shrugged. "But in truth, Kamin Oluvai is another of my masks. My real name is Vedvedsica, and I am at Your Highness's service." He bowed low.

It was a northern name, such as Silvanesti used in regions near Istar. Such elves were reputed to be deeply involved in sorcery. Sithas watched Kamin Oluvai—or was it Vedvedsica?—warily.

"I'm very busy," the prince said abruptly. "What do you want?"

"I came in answer to a call, great prince. For some years I have been of use to your noble father, helping him in certain discreet matters. The speaker is ill, is he not?"

"A seasonal chill," said Sithas stiffly. "Speak plainly and tell me what you want, or else get out of my way."

"The speaker requires a healer to dispel his delta fever." Sithas could not hide his surprise at the fact that Vedvedsica knew the nature of his father's illness. "I have treated the speaker before, banishing the fever. I can do so again."

"You are not a priest of Quenesti Pah. Who do you serve?"

Vedvedsica smiled and stepped farther into the small room. Sithas automatically backed away, maintaining the distance between them. "Your Highness is an elf of great erudition and education. You know the unfairness of Silvanesti law, which only allows the worship of—"

"Who do you serve?" Sithas repeated sharply.

The gray-robed elf dropped his reticence. "My master is Gilean, the Gray Voyager."

Sithas tossed the broken end of his sword on the table. His concern was eased. Gilean was a god of Neutrality, not Evil. His worship was not officially recognized in Silvanost, but it wasn't actively suppressed either.

"My father has consulted with you?" he asked skeptically.

"Frequently." Vedvedsica's face took on a crafty expression, as if he were privy to things even the speaker's heir did not know.

"If you can cure my father, why did you come to me?" wondered Sithas.

"The speaker is an old, noble prince. Today he is ill. Someday, when he is gone, you will be speaker. I wish to continue my relationship with House Royal," he said, picking his words carefully.

Anger colored Sithas's face. He snatched up the broken sword and held the squared-off edge to the sorcerer's throat. His relationship with House Royal indeed! Vedvedsica held his ground, though he tilted his round head away from the blade.

"You speak treason," Sithas said coldly. "You insult me and my family. I will see you in chains in the lowest reaches of the palace dungeons, gray cleric!"

Vedvedsica's pale gray eyes bored into Sithas's furious face. "You wish to have your twin brother home, do you not?" the cleric asked insinuatingly.

The broken sword remained at Vedvedsica's throat, but Sithas's interest was piqued. He frowned.

The sorcerer sensed his hesitation. "I can find him, great prince," stated Vedvedsica firmly. "I can help you."

Sithas remembered the terrible feelings that had swept over him when he'd first grasped the vibrating sword. So much pain and rage. Wherever Kith was, he was in definite trouble.

"How would you do it?" asked the prince, almost too faintly to be heard.

"A simple act," noted the cleric. His gaze flickered down to the blade.

"I'll not break the law. No invocations to Gilean," said the prince harshly.

"Of course not, Highness. You yourself will do all that needs to be done."

Sithas bade him explain, but Vedvedsica's eyes traveled once more to the blade at his throat. "If you please, Highness—?" Sithas swung the weapon away. The sorcerer swallowed audibly, then continued. "There is in all of us who share the blood of

Astarin the ability to reach out to the ones we love, across great distances, and summon them to us."

"I know of what you speak," said Sithas. "But the Call has been forbidden to Kith-Kanan. I cannot break the speaker's edict."

"Ah," said the sorcerer with a wry smile. "But the speaker has need of my services to heal his fever. Perhaps I can strike a bargain."

Sithas was growing weary of this fellow's impudence. Striking bargains with the speaker indeed! But if there was the slightest hope of getting Kith back—and healing his father—

Vedvedsica remained silent, sensing his best hope lay in letting Sithas come to a decision of his own accord.

"What must I do to call Kith-Kanan home?" Sithas asked finally.

"If you have some object that is strongly identified with your brother, that will help your concentration. It can be a focus for your thoughts."

After a long, tense silence, Sithas spoke. "I will take you to my father," he said. He brought the broken sword up once more to the cleric's throat. "But if anything you have told me is false, I shall turn you over to the Clerical Court Council for trial as a charlatan. You know what they do to illicit sorcerers?" Vedvedsica waved a hand casually. "Very well. Come."

As Sithas opened the door, Vedvedsica caught his arm. The prince stared furiously at the cleric's hand until Vedvedsica deigned to remove it. "I cannot walk the halls of the palace in plain sight, great prince," the cleric said mysteriously. "Discretion is necessary for someone like myself." He took a small bottle from his sash and pulled the cork. An acrid smell flooded the small room. "If you will allow me to use this unguent. When warmed by the skin, it creates a fog of uncertainty around those who wear it. No one we pass will be certain they see or hear us."

Sithas felt he had no choice. Vedvedsica applied the reddish oil to his fingers and traced a magic sigil on Sithas's forehead. He did the same to himself. The unguent left a burning sensation on Sithas's skin. He had an intense desire to wipe the poisonous-smelling stuff off, but as the gray-clad cleric displayed no discomfort, the prince mastered the impulse.

"Follow me," advised Vedvedsica. At least that's what Sithas thought he said. The words came to his ear distantly, waveringly, as if the cleric spoke from the bottom of a well.

They ascended the steps, passing a trio of handmaids on the way. The elf girls' forms were indistinct to Sithas, though the background of stair and wall was solid and clear. The maids' eyes flickered over the prince and his companion, but no recognition showed on their faces. They continued on down the stair. The "fog of uncertainty" was working just as the cleric had claimed.

On the penultimate floor of the tower, they paused before the doors to the speaker's private rooms. Servants stood outside, idle. They paid no heed to the prince or the cleric.

"Strange," mused Sithas, words falling from his lips like drops of cold water. His own voice sounded muffled. "Why are they not inside with the speaker?"

He opened the door and hurried in. "Father?" he called. Sithas passed through the antechamber, with Vedvedsica close behind. After a glance around the room, he saw his father's crumpled form lying on the stone floor by the window. He shouted for assistance.

"They cannot hear you," Vedvedsica said, wafting into Sithas's line of sight. Desperately the prince knelt and lifted his father. How light he felt, the great elf who ruled the elven nation! As Sithas placed his father on the bed, Sithel's eyes fluttered open. His face was dazed.

"Kith? Is that you?" he asked in a strange, faraway voice.

"No, Father, it's Sithas," said the elf prince, stricken with anguish.

"You're a good boy, Kith . . . but a willful fool. Why did you bare a weapon in the tower? You know it's a sacred place."

Sithas turned to the waiting Vedvedsica. "Take the spell off us!" he demanded fiercely. The cleric bowed and dampened a cloth at a wash basin, then wiped the prince's forehead clean. Immediately, it seemed, the fog vanished from his senses. Just seconds later the cleric materialized, seemingly out of nowhere.

Swiftly Vedvedsica took some dried herbs from his shoulder pouch and crushed them into a pewter goblet that stood on a table near the speaker's bed. Concerned, Sithas watched him work. The cleric next soaked the crushed dry leaves in crimson nectar, swirled the goblet to mix the ingredients, and held out the goblet to the prince.

"Let him drink this," he said with confidence. "It will clear his head."

Sithas held the goblet to his father's lips. No sooner had the first red drops passed Sithel's mouth, than his eyes lost their rheumy haze. Tightly he gripped Sithas's wrist.

"Son, what is this?" He looked beyond Sithas and espied the sorcerer. Sharply he said, "Why are you here? I did not send for you!"

"But you did, great speaker." Vedvedsica bowed deeply from the waist. "Your fevered mind called to me for help some hours ago. I came."

"Do you know him, Father?" Sithas asked.

"All too well." Sithel sank back on his pillows, so the prince set the goblet aside. "I'm sorry you had to meet him under such circumstances, son. I might have warned you."

Sithas looked at Vedvedsica, his face mixed with gratitude and distrust. "Is he cured?"

"Not yet, my prince. There are other potions I must prepare. They will cure the speaker."

"Get on with it, then," Sithas commanded.

Vedvedsica flinched. "There is the matter of our bargain."

Sithel coughed. "What bargain have you made with this old spider?" the speaker demanded.

"He will cure your fever if you allow me to call Kith-Kanan home," Sithas said honestly. Sithel arched his white brows in surprise, and the prince averted his eyes from his father's intense gaze.

"Call Kith?" he asked skeptically. "Vedvedsica, you're no altruist. What do you want for yourself out of this?"

The cleric bowed again. "I ask only that the speaker's heir pay me such an amount as he thinks appropriate."

Sithel shook his head. "I don't see why Kith-Kanan should interest you, but I don't object," he said with a heavy sigh, then turned to his heir. "What will you pay him, Sithas?"

The prince thought once more of the broken sword and the terrible feeling of suffering he'd felt from his twin. "Fifty gold pieces," he said decisively.

Vedvedsica's eyes widened. "A most handsome amount,

great prince."

Father and son watched in silence as the cleric compounded his healing potion. When at last it was done, he filled a tall silver beaker with the muddy green fluid. To Sithas's surprise, Vedvedsica took a healthy swig of the mixture himself first and seemed satisfied. Then he held it out to the prostrate speaker.

"You must drink it all," he insisted. Sithas handed the beaker to his father. Sithel raised himself on his elbows and downed the brew in three swallows. He looked expectantly at his son. In turn, Sithas turned to Vedvedsica.

"Well?"

"The effect is a subtle one, great prince, but rest assured, the speaker will shortly be cured of his fever."

Indeed, Sithel's forehead had become cooler to the touch. The speaker exhaled gustily, and sat up straighter. A tinge of color was returning to his pale cheeks. Vedvedsica nodded grandly.

"Leave us, sorcerer," Sithel said tersely. "You may collect your payment later."

Another deep bow. "As the speaker commands." Vedvedsica produced the small bottle of unguent and began to apply it as before.

Holding up a hand, the prince said acidly, "Out the door first, cleric."

Vedvedsica's smile was wide as he departed.

*　*　*　*　*

Sithas left his father looking more fit than he had in a month, then proceded to make his way through the palace to spread word of his recovery. Vedvedsica wasn't mentioned. The speaker's recovery was reported as natural, a sign of the gods' favor.

Finally, Sithas went down the tower steps to Kith-Kanan's old room. No one was around. Dust lay thickly over everything for nothing had disturbed it since his brother had left in disgrace. How long ago had it been? Two years?

The room held all sorts of Kith's personal items. His silver comb. His second favorite bow, now warped and cracked from the room's dry air. All his courtly clothes hung in the wardrobe. Sithas touched each item of clothing, trying to concentrate his thoughts on his lost brother. All he felt were old memories. Some pleasant, many sad.

A strange sensation came over the prince. He felt as if he were moving up and away, though his body hadn't stirred an inch. Smoke from a campfire teased his nose. The sound of wind in a forest filled his ears. Sithas looked down at his hands. They were browned by the sun and hardened by work and combat. These were not his hands; they were Kith-Kanan's. The prince knew then that he must try to communicate with his twin, but when he opened his mouth to speak, his throat was tight. It was hard to form words. He concentrated instead on forming them in his mind.

Come home, he willed. *Come home, Kith. Come home.*

Sithas forced his lips to work. "Kith!" he cried.

Speaking his twin's name ended the experience abruptly. Sithas staggered backward, disoriented, and sat down on his twin's old bed. Dust rose around him. Streaks of sunlight, which had reached across the room when he came in, now had retreated to just under the window sill. Several hours had passed.

Sithas shook the queer disorientation out of his head and went to the door. He had definitely made contact with Kith, but whether he had made the fabled Call, he didn't know. It was late now, and he needed to see how his father was doing.

Sithas left the room so hastily he didn't pull the door completely closed behind him. And as he mounted the steps to the upper floor of the palace tower, the prince didn't notice the door to Kith-Kanan's room slowly swing open and remain that way.

🍃 22 🍃

Spring, Year of the Ram

The days seemed empty. Each morning Kith-Kanan went to sit by the young oak. It was slender and tall, its twining branches reaching heavenward. Leaf buds appeared on it, as they did on all the trees in the forest. But these buds seemed a symbol, a notice that the wildwood was once again furiously and joyously alive. Even the clearing erupted in wildflowers and vibrant green growth. The path to the pool covered over in a day with new grass and nodding thistles.

"There's never been a spring like this," Mackeli exclaimed. "Things are growing while you watch!" His spirits had recovered more quickly than Kith-Kanan's. Mackeli easily accepted that Anaya's change had been fated to happen, and he'd been trying to draw his friend out of his misery.

This beautiful day he and Kith-Kanan sat on a lower limb of the oak tree. Mackeli's gangling legs swung back and forth as he chewed a sweet grass stem and looked over the clearing. "It's like we're besieged," he added. Grass had grown to waist height in little more than a week. The bare ground around the tree, scuffed down to dirt by their daily walking on it, was gradually shrinking as the plants in the clearing grew.

"The hunting ought to be good," Mackeli enthused. His new-found appetite for meat was enormous. He ate twice as much as Kith-Kanan and grew stronger all the time. And since the griffon had grown more skilled in bringing back game for them, they were well fed.

With the explosion of flowering trees and plants had come the onslaught of the insects. Not the Black Crawlers of Anaya's acquaintance, but bees and flies and butterflies. The air was always thick with them now. Kith-Kanan and Mackeli had to keep a fire burning in the hearth at all times to discourage the bees from building a hive in the tree with them.

With Arcuballis bringing in a whole boar or deer once a day, there was little for the two elves to do. Still hoping to divert Kith-Kanan from his grief, Mackeli once more began to ask questions of Silvanost. They talked about the people, their clothing, eating habits, work routines, and more. Slowly, Kith-Kanan was persuaded to share his memories. To his surprise, he found himself feeling homesick.

"And what about—" Mackeli chewed his lower lip. "What about girls?"

Kith-Kanan smiled slightly. "Yes, there are girls."

"What are they like?"

"The maids of Silvanost are well known for their grace and beauty," he said, without much exaggeration. "Most of them are kindly and gentle and very intelligent, and a few have been known to take up horse and sword. Those are rare, though. They are red-haired, blond, sandy-haired, and I've seen some with hair as black as the nighttime sky."

Mackeli drew in his legs, crouching on the balls of his feet. "I would like to meet them! All of them!"

"No doubt you would, Keli," Kith-Kanan said solemnly. "But I cannot take you there."

Mackeli knew the story of Kith-Kanan's flight from

Silvanost. "Whenever Ny would get mad at me, I would wait a few days, then go and say I was sorry," he suggested. "Can't you tell your father you're sorry?"

"It's not that easy," Kith-Kanan replied defensively.

"Why?"

The prince opened his mouth to reply, but no words came out. Why, indeed? Surely in the time that had gone by his father's anger would have cooled. The gods knew his own anger at losing Hermathya had withered and died as if it had never been. Even now, as he spoke her name in his mind, no remembered passion stirred inside him. His heart would always belong to Anaya. Now that she was gone, why should he not return home?

In the end, though, Kith-Kanan always decided that he could not. "My father is Speaker of the Stars. He is bound by traditions he cannot flout. If he were only my father and angry with me, perhaps I could return and beg his forgiveness. But there are many others around him who wouldn't want me back."

Mackeli nodded knowingly. "Enemies."

"Not personal enemies, just those priests and guildmasters who have a vested interest in keeping things as they've always been. My father needs their support, which is why he married Hermathya to Sithas in the first place. I'm sure my return would cause much unrest in the city."

Mackeli dropped out of his crouch. He swung his legs back and forth in the air. "Seems complicated," he said. "I think the forest is better."

Even with the ache of Anaya's loss in his heart, Kith-Kanan had to agree as he looked over the sunny clearing carpeted with flowers.

* * * * *

The Call struck him like a blow.

It was evening, four days after the prince's discussion of Silvanost with Mackeli, and they were skinning a mountain elk. Neither Kith-Kanan nor the boy could explain why the griffon had flown two hundred miles to the Khalkist Mountains to catch the elk, but that was the nearest source of such animals. They were nearly finished with the skinning when the Call came.

Kith-Kanan dropped his flint skinning knife in the dirt. He jumped to his feet, hands outstretched as if he'd been stricken blind.

"Kith! Kith, what's wrong?" Mackeli cried.

Kith-Kanan could no longer see the forest. Instead, he saw vague impressions of walls, floor, and ceiling made of white marble. It was as if he'd been lifted up out of his body and set down in Silvanost. He held a hand to his face and, in place of his leather tunic and callused palm, he saw a smooth hand and a white silk robe. The ring on his finger he recognized as belonging to Sithas.

A jumble of sensations assaulted his mind: worry, sadness, loneliness. Sithas was calling his name. There was trouble in the city. Arguments and fighting. Humans at court. Kith-Kanan reeled as it came at him in a rush.

"Sithas!" he cried. When he spoke, the Call ended abruptly. Mackeli was shaking him by his tunic. Kith-Kanan broke the boy's grip and shoved him back.

"What is it?" Mackeli asked, frightened.

"My brother. It was my brother, back in Silvanost . . ."

"You saw him? Did he speak?"

"Not in words. The nation is in peril—" Kith-Kanan pressed his hands to his face. His heart was pounding. "I must go back. I must go to Silvanost." He turned and walked into the hollow tree.

"Wait! Do you have to go *now?*"

"I have to go. I have to leave now," Kith-Kanan insisted tensely.

"Then take me with you!"

Kith-Kanan appeared in the doorway. "What did you say?"

"Take me with you," Mackeli repeated in a hopeful tone. "I'll be your servant. I'll do anything. Clean your boots, cook your food—anything. I don't want to stay here alone, Kith. I want to see the city of my people!"

Kith-Kanan went to where Mackeli stood, still holding his skinning knife. With the muddle of feelings clearing from his brain, he realized he was glad Mackeli wanted to go with him. He felt closer to him than he had to anyone except Anaya—and

Sithas. If he was going back to face who knows what in Silvanost, he didn't want to lose that friendship and support now.

Clapping a hand to the boy's shoulder, Kith-Kanan declared, "You shall go with me, but never as my servant. You can be my squire and train to be a warrior. How does that sound?"

Mackeli was too overcome to speak. He threw his arms around Kith-Kanan and hugged him fiercely.

"When shall we leave?" the boy asked.

Kith-Kanan felt the powerful tug of the Call. Now, now, now. It coursed through his body like a second heartbeat. He steeled himself against the insatiable pull. It was late and there were preparations which must be made before they departed.

"Tomorrow morning," he decided.

*   *   *   *   *

Day came like the cracking of an egg. First all was smooth, unbroken night, then just a chip of sunlight showed to the east. It was enough to rouse the eager Mackeli, who splashed water on his face and announced himself ready to go.

"Is there nothing you want to take with you?" Kith-Kanan wondered.

Mackeli surveyed the inside of the tree. The flint tools, gourd bottles, clay-daubed baskets, none of them were worth taking, he said. Still, they needed food and water, so they loaded a pair of wicker baskets with meat, nuts, berries, and water, balancing the weight so Arcuballis could carry it all. Alone of the three of them, the griffon was still heavily asleep. When Kith-Kanan whistled through his teeth, Arcuballis raised its aquiline head out from under one wing and stood on its mismatched feet. Kith-Kanan gave the beast some water while Mackeli tied the food baskets to the back of the saddle.

A sense of urgency spurred them on. Mackeli chattered incessantly about the things he wanted to do and see. He scrubbed the residue of paint from his face, announcing that he didn't want the city-dwellers to think he was a savage. Kith-Kanan tested the harness fittings under the griffon's neck and chest, and Mackeli climbed onto the pillion. At last, though, Kith-Kanan hesitated.

"What is it?" the boy asked.

"There is one thing I must do." He cut across the flower-choked clearing to the slender oak that had been Anaya. He stopped two yards away and looked up at the limbs reaching toward the sky. He still found it hard to accept that the woman he loved was here now, in any form. "Part of my heart stays with you here, my love. I have to go back now; I hope you understand." Tears welled in his eyes as he took out his dagger. "Forgive me," he whispered, then reached up and quickly sliced off a four-inch green shoot, well laden with bright green buds. Kith-Kanan cut a small slit in the tough deerhide of his tunic, directly over his heart, and put the shoot there.

The elf prince gazed up at the young tree, then looked around at the clearing where they had been so happy. "I love you, Anaya," he said. "Farewell." Turning, he walked quickly back to the griffon.

Kith-Kanan swung onto Arcuballis's back and settled himself into the saddle. He whistled and touched the griffon with his heels, signaling the creature to be off. As the griffon bounded across the clearing, its strong legs tearing through the new growth, great torrents of petals and pollen flew into the air. At last the mount opened its wings and, in a stupendous bound, leaped into the air. Mackeli yelped with delight.

They circled the clearing, gaining height with each circuit. Kith-Kanan looked down for a few seconds, then he lifted his face and studied the clouds. He turned Arcuballis's head northeast. They leveled out at a thousand feet. The air was warm, and a steady wind buoyed Arcuballis, enabling him to glide for long stretches with hardly a wingbeat.

Mackeli leaned forward and shouted in Kith-Kanan's ear, "How long will it take us to get there?"

"One day, perhaps two."

They passed over a world rapidly greening. Life seemed to be bursting from the ground even as they flew by. The lower air was full of birds, from tiny swallows to large flocks of wild geese. Farther below, the forest thinned, then gave way to plain. As the sun reached its zenith, Kith-Kanan and Mackeli saw the first signs of civilization since leaving the wildwood. There was a village below, laid out in a circle, with a sod wall surrounding it for protection. A pall of smoke hung over the village.

"Is that a city?" asked Mackeli excitedly.

"No, that's barely a village. It looks like they've been attacked." Worry and the edge of fear set Kith-Kanan's heart to pounding as he hauled back on the reins. Arcuballis tipped over in a shallow dive. They flew through the smoke. Coughing, the elf prince steered the griffon in a slow circle around the despoiled village. Nothing moved. He could see the bodies of the fallen lying atop the wall and in between the huts.

"It's terrible," Kith-Kanan said grimly. "I'm going to land and take a look. Be on guard, Keli."

Arcuballis touched down lightly outside the wall, near one of the rents that had been torn in it. Kith-Kanan and Mackeli dismounted. Mackeli had a crossbow, salvaged from Voltorno's band, and Kith-Kanan had his compound bow. His scabbard hung empty by his side.

"You see what they did?" Kith-Kanan said, pointing to the gap in the sod wall. "The attackers used grappling hooks to pull down the wall."

They stepped over the rubble of dried sod and entered the village. It was eerily quiet. Smoke eddied and swirled in the shifting wind. Where once people had talked and argued and laughed, there was now nothing but empty streets. Broken crockery and torn clothing were strewn here and there. Kith-Kanan turned over the first body he came to—a Kagonesti male, slain by sword. He could tell the elf had died not very long before, a day or two at most. Turning the fellow face-down once more, Kith-Kanan paused and shook his head. Horrible. During the Call he had sensed from Sithas that there was trouble in the land, but this? This was murder and rapine.

As they continued through the silent village, all the other dead they found were Kagonesti or Silvanesti males. No females, no children. All the farm animals were gone, as was practically everything else of value.

"Who could have done this?" Mackeli asked solemnly.

"I don't know. Whoever it was, they didn't want their identity known. Do you notice, they took their own dead with them?"

"How can you tell?"

Kith-Kanan pointed at the scattering of dead villagers. "These fellows didn't just lay down and die. They died fighting, which means they must've taken a few of their enemies with them."

On the west side of the village, they found a mass of footprints—horses, cattle, and people. The raiders had taken their elven and animal captives and driven them out onto the great plain. Mackeli asked what lay in that direction.

"The city of Xak Tsaroth. No doubt the raiders will try to sell their prizes in the markets there," said Kith-Kanan grimly. He gazed at the flat horizon as if he might catch a glimpse of the bandits who had committed this outrage. "Beyond Xak Tsaroth is the homeland of the Kagonesti. It's forest, much like the wildwood we just left."

"Does your father rule all this land?" Mackeli said curiously.

"He rules it by law, but out here the real ruler is the hand that wields the sword." Kith-Kanan kicked the dry plains soil, sending up a gout of dust. "Come, Keli. Let's go."

They trudged back to the griffon, following the outside curve of the village wall. Mackeli dragged his feet and hung his head. Kith-Kanan asked what was troubling him.

"This world beyond the forest is a dark place," he said. "These folk died because someone wanted to rob them."

"I never said the outside world was all marble cities and pretty girls," Kith-Kanan replied, draping an arm across the boy's shoulders. "Don't be too discouraged, though. This sort of thing doesn't happen every day. Once I tell my father about it, he will put an end to this brigandage."

"What can he do? He lives in a far away city."

"Don't underestimate the power of the Speaker of the Stars."

* * * * *

It was twilight of the second day when the white tops of the city towers first appeared. Arcuballis sensed the end of their journey was near; without Kith-Kanan's urging, the beast quickened its wingbeat. The land raced by. The broad Thon-Thalas, mirroring the deep aquamarine of the evening sky, appeared, approached, and then flashed beneath the griffon's tucked-in feet.

"Hello! Hello down there!" Mackeli called to the boaters and fishers on the river. Kith-Kanan shushed him.

"I may not be coming back to the warmest of welcomes," he cautioned. "There's no need to announce our return, all right?" The boy reluctantly fell silent.

Kith-Kanan found himself experiencing great doubt and no small amount of trepidation. How would he be received? Could his father forgive his outrage? One thing he knew, he was certainly not the same elf he had been when he left here. So much had happened to him, and he found himself looking forward to the time when he could share it with his twin.

Kith-Kanan had noticed the beginning of a settlement on the western bank of the river. From the grid layout, it looked like a town was being built on the river, opposite the piers and docks of Silvanost. Then, as they approached the city from the south, he saw that a large section of the Market was a blackened ruin. This alarmed him, for if the city had been attacked, it might not be his father and twin who would be waiting for him when he landed. The prince was only a little relieved when he saw that the rest of the city appeared normal.

For his part, Mackeli leaned far to the side, staring with unabashed amazement at the wonders below. The city glittered in the sunlight. Marble buildings, green gardens, and sparkling pools filled his eyes. A thousand towers, each a marvel to the forest-raised boy, jutted above the artfully manicured treetops. Rising higher than all the rest was the Tower of the Stars. Kith-Kanan circled the great pinnacle and recalled with a pang the day he'd done it last. The number of days was small compared to an elf's entire life, but the gulf it represented seemed as great as one thousand years.

Arcuballis was ready for home. The beast banked away from the tower with only a minimum of direction from Kith-Kanan and headed for the rooftop of the Quinari Palace. A line of torches burned along the flat roof, the flames whipped by a steady wind. The rosy palace tower was tinted a much deeper shade of red by the last rays of the setting sun.

Mackeli held tightly to Kith-Kanan's waist as the angle of descent steepened. A single white-robed figure stood beside the line of torches.

The griffon raised its head and wafted its wings rapidly. The mount's forward speed diminished, and its clawed forelegs touched down on the roof. When its hind legs found purchase, Arcuballis folded its wings.

The figure in white, a dozen yards away, lifted a torch from its holder and walked toward the grounded griffon. Mackeli held his breath.

"Brother," Kith-Kanan said simply as he dismounted.

Sithas held up the torch. "I knew you would come back. I've waited here every night since I called you," said his twin warmly.

"I am glad to see you!" The brothers embraced. Seeing this, Mackeli threw a leg over and slid down the griffon's rump to the roof. Sithas and Kith-Kanan drew apart and clapped each other on the shoulders.

"You look like a ragged bandit!" Sithas exclaimed. "Where did you get those clothes?"

"It's a very long story," Kith-Kanan replied. He was grinning so widely his face ached; Sithas's expression mirrored his. "And you, when did you stop being a priest and become a prince?" he exclaimed, thumping Sithas's back.

Sithas kept smiling. "Well, a lot's happened since you left. I—" He stopped, seeing Mackeli come up behind Kith-Kanan.

"This is my good friend and companion Mackeli," Kith-Kanan explained. "Keli, this is my brother, Sithas."

"Hello," said Mackeli casually.

"No," Kith-Kanan chided. "Bow, like I told you."

Mackeli bent awkwardly at the waist, bending nearly double. "Sorry, Kith! I meant, hello, Prince Sithas," he said ingenuously.

Sithas smiled at the boy. "You've plenty of time to learn court manners," he said. "Right now, I'll wager you'd both like a hot bath and some dinner."

"Ah! With that, I could die happy," Kith-Kanan said, placing a hand over his heart. Laughing, he and Sithas started toward the stairwell, with Mackeli following a pace behind. Kith-Kanan suddenly halted.

"What about father?" he asked apprehensively. "Does he know you called me?"

"Yes," said Sithas. "He was ill for a few days, and I asked him for permission to use the Call. He consented. A healer

237

brought him through, and he's well now. We've been dealing with ambassadors from Ergoth and Thorbardin, too, so things have been quite busy. We'll go to him and mother as soon as you're presentable."

"Ambassadors? Why are they here?" Kith-Kanan asked. "And, Sith, what happened to the Market? It looks as though it was sacked!"

"I'll tell you all about it."

As the twins reached the steps, Kith-Kanan looked back. Stars were coming out in the darkening sky. The weary Arcuballis had dropped into a sleeping crouch. Kith-Kanan looked from the star-salted sky to the nearby bulk of the Tower of the Stars. Without really thinking about it, his hand went to the sprig of oak he'd snipped from Anaya's tree and drew it out. It had changed. Where there had been tight buds, now the shoot was furnished with perfect green leaves. Even though it had been cut from the tree two days past, the sprig was green and growing.

"What is that?" asked Sithas curiously.

Kith-Kanan drew a deep breath and shared a knowing glance with Mackeli. "This is the best part of my story, Brother." Tenderly he returned the oak shoot to its place over his heart.

🌿 23 🌿

Night of Reunion

freshly bathed, clothed, and fed, Kith-kanan and Mackeli followed Sithas to the Hall of Balif. There the speaker, Lady Nirakina, and Lady Hermathya were having a late, private dinner.

"Wait here," Sithas said, stopping his twin and Mackeli just outside the hall door. "Let me prepare them."

Most of Mackeli's attention was focused on his surroundings. Since entering the palace, he'd touched the stone walls and floor, felt bronze and iron fittings, and goggled at the courtiers and servants that passed by. He was dressed in one of Kith-Kanan's old outfits. The sleeves were too short for him, and even though his ragged hair was combed as neatly as possible, he still looked like a well-costumed scarecrow.

Servants who recognized Kith-Kanan gaped in astonishment. He smiled at the elves, but admonished them in a low voice to go about their business as he stepped close to the hall door and listened. Hearing his father's voice, even so indistinctly, brought a lump to his throat. Kith-Kanan peered around the door, but Sithas held a hand out to him. Straight as an arrow, he walked proudly into the now-silent hall. Then there was a gasp, and a silver spoon rang on the marble floor. Hermathya bent to retrieve the lost utensil.

Sithas stopped Mackeli so that Kith-Kanan could approach the table alone. The wayward prince of the Silvanesti stood across the oval table from his parents and former lover.

Nirakina rose halfway to her feet, but Sithel commanded her tersely to sit back down. The lady sank back into her chair, tears glistening on her cheeks. Kith-Kanan bowed deeply.

"Great speaker," he began. Then: "Father. Thank you for letting Sithas call me home." Both elf women snapped around to stare at Sithel, for they had not known of the speaker's leniency.

"I have been angry with you a long time," Sithel replied sternly. "No one in House Royal ever shamed us as you did. What have you to say?"

Kith-Kanan dropped to one knee. "I am the greatest fool who ever lived," he said, looking down at the floor. "I know I shamed you and myself. I have made peace with myself and the gods, and now I want to make peace with my family."

Sithel pushed back his chair and stood. His white hair seemed golden in the candlelight. He'd regained some of the weight he'd lost while ill, and the old fire in his eyes was renewed. He strode with firm, even steps around the table to where his younger son knelt.

"Stand up," he said, still in his commanding speaker's voice.

As Kith-Kanan got up, Sithel's stern countenance softened. "Son," he said when they were face to face.

They clasped hands about each others forearms in soldierly fashion. But it wasn't enough for Kith-Kanan. He embraced his father with fervor, a fervor returned by Sithel. Over the speaker's shoulder, Kith-Kanan saw his mother, still weeping, but now the tears tracked down on each side of a radiant smile.

Hermathya tried to maintain her aloofness, but her pale face and trembling fingers betrayed her. She dropped her hands to her lap and looked away, at the wall, at the ceiling, at anything but Kith-Kanan.

Sithel held the prince at arm's length and studied his sun-browned features. "I cannot deny you," he said, his voice breaking with emotion. "You are my son, and I am glad to have you back!"

Nirakina came and kissed him. Kith-Kanan brushed away her tears and let her walk him back around the table to where their places were set. They came to Hermathya, still seated.

"You are looking well, Lady," Kith-Kanan said awkwardly.

She looked up at him, blinking rapidly. "I am well," she replied uncertainly. "Thank you for noticing." Seeing Kith-Kanan at a loss for words, Sithas moved to intervene. He ushered Mackeli forward and introduced him. Sithel and Nirakina found the boy's rustic manners both charming and amusing.

Now that the news was out, servants were roused from their work, even from bed, and whole troops of them filed into the hall to pay their respects to the returned prince. Kith-Kanan had always been popular with the members of House Servitor for his lively manner and kind heart.

"Quiet, all of you! Quiet!" Sithel shouted, and the throng became still. The speaker called for amphorae of fine nectar, and there was a pause as cups of the sweet beverage were passed through the crowd. When everyone had a share, the speaker raised his goblet and saluted his newly restored son.

"To Prince Kith-Kanan," he exclaimed. "Home at last!"

"Kith-Kanan!" answered the great assembly. They all drank.

All but one. Hermathya held her cup tightly until her knuckles were as white as her face.

*   *   *   *   *

The servants finally dispersed, but the family remained. They surrounded Kith-Kanan and talked for hours, telling him what had happened during his absence. He, in turn, regaled them with his adventures in the wildwood.

"You see me now, a widower," Kith-Kanan said sorrowfully, gazing at the dregs of nectar in his cup. "Anaya was claimed by the forest she had served so long."

"Was this Anaya nobly born?" Nirakina delicately asked.

"Her birth was a mystery, even to her. I suspect she was stolen from her family by the guardian before her, just as she took Mackeli from his parents."

"I'm not sorry she did so," Mackeli said staunchly. "Anaya was good to me."

Kith-Kanan allowed his family to assume Anaya was Silvanesti, like Mackeli. He also kept from them the news of his unborn child. The loss was too recent, and he wanted to keep some memories for himself.

Sithas broke the quiet interlude by commenting on the half-human Voltorno. "It fits with what we already suspect," he ventured. "The emperor of Ergoth is behind the terror in our western provinces. He not only wants our land, but our timber, too." Everyone knew that Ergoth had a sizable navy and needed wood for ships. Their own land was relatively poor in trees. Also, unlike elves, humans tended to build houses out of wood.

"At any rate," the speaker noted, "the emissaries have been here nearly five weeks and nothing's been accomplished. I was ill for a few days, but since my recovery we've made no progress at all."

"I'd be glad to speak to the ambassadors of the things I saw and heard in the forest," Kith-Kanan offered. "Men from Ergoth have been landing on our southern coast to plunder the forest. They would have taken Mackeli to Daltigoth as a slave. That's a fact."

"That's probably what the raiders have done with the other captives," Sithas said darkly. "The wives and children of the Silvanesti settlers."

Kith-Kanan told of the sacked village he and Mackeli had seen on their way home. Sithel was disturbed to hear that a settlement so close to the capital had been attacked.

"You will come to the tower tomorrow," the speaker declared. "I want the Ergothians to hear what you have seen!"

Sithel rose. "It is very late," he said. "The session begins early, so we'd all better take our rest." Mackeli was already snoring. Hermathya, likewise, was dozing where she sat, curled up in her chair.

Kith-Kanan roused Mackeli with a shake, and the boy sat up.

"Funny dream, Kith. I went to a great city, and people lived inside stone mountains—"

"Not so funny," Kith-Kanan said, smiling. "Come on, Keli, I can put you in Sithas's old room. Is that well with you, Brother?" Sithas waved his agreement.

Kith-Kanan kissed his mother's cheek and said good night. Her face shone with contentment, which made her look decades younger.

"Good night, son," she said devotedly.

A servant with a candelabrum arrived to conduct Mackeli to his bed. Sithel and Nirakina went out. At last, the brothers stood by the door.

"I'll leave you to your wife," Kith-Kanan said, nodding toward the sleeping Hermathya. Rather awkwardly, he added, "I'm sorry I missed the wedding, Sith. I hope you two are happy."

Sithas stared at his wife's sleeping form for a few seconds, then said, "It has been no bargain being married to her, Kith." Kith-Kanan could not conceal his surprise. He asked in a whisper what was wrong.

"Well, you know how willful she is. She takes every opportunity to make herself known to the people. She throws trinkets from the windows of her sedan chair when she goes out. People follow after her, calling her name." Sithas's mouth hardened to a thin line. "Do you know what the city wits call us? 'The Shadow and the Flower.' I don't suppose I need to explain who is who, do I?"

Kith-Kanan suppressed a wry smile. "Thya always was chaos in motion."

"There's more to it than that. I think—" Sithas cut himself off as a servant came down the corridor toward the open door. The yellow glow of his candles flowed ahead of him like a stolen sunrise.

"Good night, Kith," Sithas said suddenly. He summoned the servant and told him to guide the prince up the dark stairs to his room. Kith-Kanan regarded his twin curiously.

"I shall see you in the morning," he said. Sithas nodded and held the hall door. As soon as Kith-Kanan went out, Sithas shut the door firmly.

Inside the hall, Sithas spoke sharply to Hermathya. "It's very childish, this pretense of sleep."

She sat up and yawned. "Quite a compliment from the master of pretense."

"Lady, have you no respect for us or our position?"

Hermathya pushed her heavy chair away from the table. "Respect is all I do have," she replied calmly. "Heavy, thick, rigid respect."

*   *   *   *   *

The Palace of Quinari was sleeping, nearly everyone within it walls exhausted by the homecoming of Kith-Kanan. But in the gallery leading away from the central tower, two figures met in the dark and broke the silence with their whispers.

"He's come back," said the female voice.

"So I have heard," answered the male. "It's not a problem."

"But Prince Kith-Kanan is a factor we hadn't considered!" In her distress the female spoke louder than was necessary—or prudent.

"*I* considered him," said the male voice calmly. "If anything, his return will be to our advantage."

"How?"

"Kith-Kanan enjoys a certain popularity with all those who find his brother cold and uninspiring—elves such as the royal guard, for example. Moreover, my evaluation of the errant prince tells me he is more open and trusting than either his father or brother. And a trusting person is always more useful than a doubter."

"You are clever. My father chose well when he picked you." The female voice was once more calm and soft. There was the sound of heavy cloth being crushed and a kiss. "I wish we didn't have to meet in shadows like this."

"Don't you think it's romantic?" murmured the male voice.

"Yes . . . but it annoys me that so many think you are harmless."

"My best weapon. Would you take it away from me?"

"Oh, never. . . ."

There was silence for a while, then the female voice said, "How long till sun-up?"

"An hour or so."

"I'm worried."

"What about?" he asked.

"The whole affair is getting too complicated. Sometimes when I'm sitting in the audience hall I want to scream, the tension is so great."

"I know," the male voice said soothingly, "but our task is quite simple. We have only to delay and dissemble and keep the elves talking. Daily, our numbers swell. Time is our ally, my darling. Given enough time, the mighty elven nation will fall."

Their slippered feet made only the slightest whisper on the cool marble floor as the conspirators stole down the gallery to the steps. They had to get back to their rooms before the palace stirred. No one must see them together, not even the members of their own delegation.

❧ 24 ❧

the day following

The entrance of Kith-Kanan into the Tower of the Stars the next day created a stir. Gone were Kith-Kanan's tattered green buckskins. Now he wore smooth white robes and a silver circlet on his head. With great ceremony he was introduced to Lord Dunbarth. The dwarf doffed his floppy hat and said, "It is a great honor to meet you, Prince. I've heard much about you."

"Perhaps we shall be friends anyway," was the wry reply.

Meeting the human delegation was more forced. Praetor Ulwen sat in his portable chair like a wax image. Only the slight rise and fall of the blanket over his chest testified he was alive. Lady Teralind accepted Kith-Kanan's hand, holding it for a long minute as she assessed this newest addition to the conference. He noted the dark circles under her eyes. The lady hadn't slept very well the night before.

Ulvissen saluted, human fashion. Kith-Kanan imitated his gesture.

"Have we met before?" the elf prince asked, looking carefully at the bearded human.

"I don't think so, noble prince," Ulvissen replied coolly. "I served most of my military career on ships. Perhaps Your Highness met another human who looked like me. I understand it is hard for elves to distinguish one bearded man from another."

"There is much in what you say." Kith-Kanan walked away, but the idea that he'd seen Ulvissen before troubled him still. He paused before his father, bowed, and took his old seat on the speaker's right. A human with a full, red-brown beard— where had he seen him?

"The fifteenth session of the Conference of Three Nations will now begin," said Sithas, acting as his father's herald. "Seated for Silvanesti is Prince Kith-Kanan." The scribes at their tables wrote busily.

Dunbarth stood up—which had the effect of making him shorter, as his chair's legs were longer than his own. "Great speaker, noble princes, Lord Praetor, Lady Teralind," he began. "We have been here many days, and the principal obstacle in the way of peace is this question: Who rules the western plains and the forest? The noble speaker and his heir present as proof of their claim ancient treaties and documents. Lady Teralind, on behalf of the emperor of Ergoth, makes her claim from the point of view of the majority, claiming that most of the people who live in the disputed territory are Ergothians." Dunbarth took a deep breath. "I summarize these positions as I have presented them to my king. I have this day received his reply."

Murmurs of interest rose. Dunbarth unfolded a heavy piece of parchment. The golden wax seal of the king of Thorbardin was visible.

"Ahem," said the dwarf. The muttering subsided. " 'To my right trusty and well-loved cousin, Dunbarth of Dunbarth, greetings: I hope the elves are feeding you well, cousin; you know how meager their eating habits are . . .' " The emissary peered over the parchment at the speaker and winked. Kith-Kanan covered his mouth with one hand to hide his smile.

Dunbarth continued: " 'I charge you, Dunbarth of Dunbarth, to deliver to the Speaker of the Stars and the praetor of Ergoth this proposal: that the territory lying on each side of the Kharolis Mountains, seventy-five miles east and west, be entrusted to the Kingdom of Thorbardin, to be governed and administered by us as a buffer zone between the empires of Ergoth and Silvanesti.' "

There was a moment of crystalline silence as everyone in the tower took in the message.

"Absolutely preposterous!" Teralind exploded.

"Not an acceptable proposal," said Sithas, albeit more calmly.

"It's only a preliminary idea," Dunbarth protested. "His Majesty offers concessions, here—"

"Totally unacceptable!" Teralind was on her feet. "I ask the speaker, what do you think of this outlandish notion?"

All eyes turned to Sithel. He leaned back against his throne, his mask of composed command perfect. "The idea has some merit," he said slowly. "Let us discuss it." Dunbarth beamed. Teralind's face got very white, and Ulvissen was suddenly at her elbow, warning her to stay calm.

At that moment Kith-Kanan felt a flash of recognition; he remembered where he'd seen Ulvissen before. It had been the day he'd rescued Mackeli from Voltorno. When the half-human had fallen after their duel, a crowd of humans from his ship had raced up the hillside. The tallest human there had had a full, red-brown beard like Ulvissen's. And since the human had already admitted that he'd spent most of his career aboard ships. . . . The prince started as his twin's voice interrupted his thoughts.

Sithas was asking the speaker what merit he had found in the dwarves' suggestion.

Sithel paused a moment before replying, considering his words carefully. "It is not King Voldrin's offer to rule the troublesome region that I favor," he said. "It is the idea of a buffer zone, independent of not just our rule and the emperor's, but of Thorbardin's as well."

"Are you proposing we create a new country?" Teralind said curiously.

"Not a sovereign state, a buffer state," replied the speaker.

Ulvissen tugged on his mistress's sleeve urgently. Feeling harassed, Teralind turned her back to Sithel for a moment to speak with the seneschal. She then asked the company for a brief adjournment. Dunbarth sat down, carefully tucking the crinkly parchment letter from his king into his brocade vest. Despite the opposition to his king's proposal, he was quite pleased with himself.

Kith-Kanan watched all this with barely contained agitation. He could hardly denounce Ulvissen during a diplomatic meeting—not when such an accusation would violate the law of good behavior in the Tower of the Stars on his first day back in Silvanost! Moreover, could he be certain Ulvissen was the man he'd seen with Voltorno? Bearded humans did tend to look alike. In any event, the elaborate manners and elliptical conversations of the ambassadors struck him as silly and wasteful of time.

"My king suggests a division of rights among the three nations," Dunbarth resumed when Teralind signaled herself ready. "Ergoth to have grazing rights, Silvanesti to have growing rights, and Thorbardin to have the mineral rights—"

"Any proposal that puts the territory under any one nation's control is unacceptable," Teralind said shrilly. A strand of dark brown hair had come loose from its confining clasp. She absently looped it behind one ear. "Unless Ergothian rights are guaranteed," she added curtly.

The delegations, mingled as they were behind the chairs of their respective leaders, began to debate among themselves the merits of a joint administration of the disputed land. Their voices got louder and louder. After a moment, Kith-Kanan couldn't stand it any longer. He jumped to his feet.

Sithel raised a hand for quiet. "My son Kith-Kanan would speak," he said. The faintest trace of a smile crossed his lips.

"As you know, I have only just returned to Silvanost," the prince said, speaking quickly and nervously. "For some time I have been living in the wildwood, far to the south, where I came to know all sorts of people. Some, like my friend Mackeli, called the forest home. Others saw it as a place to be plundered. Ships from Ergoth have been lying off the coast while their crews steal inland to cut timber—"

"This is outrageous!" Teralind exploded. "What has this to do

249

with the current question? Worse, these charges have no proof behind them!"

For once Sithel cast aside his assumed air of impartiality. "What my son tells you is true," he said icily. "Believe it." The force in his words stifled Teralind's reply, and the speaker bade Kith-Kanan continue.

"The heart of the matter is that while kings and emperors wrestle over problems of national pride and prestige, people— innocent elves and humans—are dying. The gods alone know where the true blame lies, but now we have a chance to put an end to the suffering."

"Tell us how!" said Teralind sarcastically.

"First, by admitting that peace is what we all want. I don't have to be a soothsayer to know there are many in Daltigoth and Silvanost who think war is inevitable. So I ask you, is war the answer?" He turned to Lord Dunbarth. "You, my lord. Is war the answer?"

"That's not a proper diplomatic question," countered the dwarf uncomfortably.

Kith-Kanan would not be put off. "Yes or no?" he insisted.

The entire company was looking at Dunbarth. He shifted in his chair. "War is never the answer, where people of good will—"

"Just answer the question!" snapped Teralind. Dunbarth arched one bushy eyebrow.

"No," he said firmly. "War is not the answer."

Kith-Kanan turned to the silent, crippled praetor and his wife. "Does Ergoth think war is the answer?"

The praetor's head jerked slightly. As usual, his wife answered for him. "No," Teralind replied. "Not when peace is cheaper."

He turned at last to his father. "What do you say, great speaker?"

"You're being impudent," Sithas warned.

"No," his father said simply, "it's only right he ask us all. I don't want war. I never have."

Kith-Kanan nodded and looked around at the entire group. "Then, can't some way be found to rule the land jointly, elves, humans, and dwarves?"

"I don't see what the dwarves have to do with this," said Teralind sulkily. "Hardly any of them live in the disputed land."

"Yes, but we're speaking of our entire land border," Dunbarth reminded her. "Naturally, we are concerned with who is on the other side of it."

Sunlight filtered into the hall through the hundreds of window slits up the walls of the tower; a mild breeze flowed in through the doorway. The day beckoned them out of the stuffy debate. Sithel rubbed his hands together and announced, "This is a good time to pause, not only for reflection on the question of peace, but also to take bread and meat, and stroll in the sunshine."

"As ever, Your Highness is the wisest of us all," said Dunbarth with a tired smile.

Teralind started to object, but the speaker declared the meeting adjourned for lunch. The hall rapidly emptied, leaving Teralind, Praetor Ulwen, and Ulvissen by themselves. Wordlessly, Ulvissen gathered the frail praetor in his strong arms and carried him out. Teralind worked to master her anger, tearing one of her lace handkerchiefs to bits.

* * * * *

It was a fine day, and the delegations spilled out the huge front doors into the garden that surrounded the mighty tower. Servants from the palace arrived bearing tables on their shoulders. In short order the processional walkway at the tower's main entrance was filled with tables. Snow-white linen was spread on the tables, and a pleasant array of fruit and meats was set out for the speaker's guests. A cask of blush nectar was rolled to the site, its staves making booming noises like summer thunder as the barrel rolled.

The ambassadors and their delegations crowded around the tables. Dunbarth took a brimming cup of nectar. He tasted the vintage, found it good, and wandered over to inspect the food. From there he spied Kith-Kanan standing at the edge of the garden by himself. Food in hand, the dwarf strolled over to him.

"May I join you, noble prince?" he asked.

"As a guest you may stand where you want," Kith-Kanan replied genially.

"An interesting session this morning, don't you think?" Dunbarth pulled apart a capon and gnawed at a leg. "This is the most progress we've made since we first convened."

Kith-Kanan took a large bite from an apple and regarded the dwarf with some surprise. "Progress? All I heard was a lot of contentious talk."

The dwarf flipped up the brim of his hat in order to hoist his golden goblet high. He drained the nectar and wiped the sticky liquid from his mustache. "Reorx bless me, Highness! Diplomacy is not like a hunt. We don't track down our quarry, pot him, and cart him home to be eaten. No, noble prince, diplomacy is like an old dwarf combing his hair—every hair that comes out in his comb is a defeat, and every one that stays in his head is a victory!"

Kith-Kanan chuckled and looked around the garden. He missed the weight of a sword at his hip. And even more, he missed the sights and smells of the forest. The city seemed too bright, the air tinged with too much smoke. Odd, he'd never noticed those things before.

"What are you thinking, Highness?" asked Dunbarth.

What was he thinking? He returned his gaze to the dwarf. "The praetor's wife is rather short-tempered, and the praetor himself never speaks. You'd think the emperor would have more able representatives," Kith-Kanan commented. "I don't think Lady Teralind does their cause much good."

Dunbarth looked for a place to throw the capon leg bone, now that he had cleaned it of meat. A servant appeared as if summoned and collected the refuse. "Yes, well, smooth and subtle she's not, but a lot can be accomplished by sheer stubbornness, too. Prince Sithas—" Dunbarth quickly recalled to whom he spoke and thought the better of what he had been about to say.

"Yes?" Kith-Kanan prompted him.

"It's nothing, Highness."

"Speak, my lord. Truth is not to be feared."

"I wish I had Your Highness's optimism!" A passing servitor refilled Dunbarth's cup. "I was going to say that Prince Sithas, your noble brother, is a match for Lady Teralind in stubbornness."

Kith-Kanan nodded. "It is only too true. They are much alike. Both believe they have right always on their side."

He and Dunbarth exchanged some further pleasantries, then the dwarf said an abrupt good-bye. He wanted to mingle with the others a bit, he said, and wandered off aimlessly. But Kith-Kanan could read the purpose in his stride. He shook his head. Dwarves were supposedly bluff and hearty, but Dunbarth was more subtle than a Balifor merchant.

The prince strolled off on his own, among the head-high hedges of flowering vines and the artfully molded sculptures of boxwood and cedar. The vigorous spring seemed to have followed him from the wildwood to Silvanost. The garden was a riot of bloom.

He thought of the clearing where he and his little family had lived. Had the bees built their hives in the hollow oak yet? Were the flowering trees dropping their blossoms into the pool that was the entrance to Anaya's secret cave? In the midst of all the splendor and majesty that was Silvanost, Kith-Kanan remembered wistfully the simple life he had shared with Anaya.

His reverie was broken when he rounded a corner in the hedges and found Hermathya seated alone on a stone bench.

Kith-Kanan briefly considered turning and avoiding his former lover, but he decided that he couldn't hide from her forever. Instead of leaving, he went up to her and said hello.

Hermathya did not look up at him, but gazed off into the blossoms and greenery. "I woke up this morning thinking I had dreamed you returned. Then I asked my maidservant, and she said it was true." Her voice was low, controlled, and her hair shone in the sunlight. She wore it pulled back in a jeweled clasp, as befitted a high-born, married elf woman. Her pale arms were bare, her skin smooth and unblemished. He thought she was even more beautiful than when he'd left Silvanost.

She asked him to sit. He declined.

"Are you afraid to sit next to me?" she said, meeting his eyes for the first time. "It was once your favorite place to be."

"Let's not bring up the past," Kith-Kanan said, keeping his distance. "That's over and done with."

"Is it?" Her eyes, as always, caught and held him.

He was intensely aware of her, as near as he was, and she stirred him. What elf could be so close to her flame-bright loveliness and not be moved? However, Kith-Kanan no longer loved Hermathya; he was certain of that.

"I've been married," he said pointedly.

"Yes, I heard that last night. Your wife is dead, isn't she?"

No, only changed, he thought. But he replied, "Yes, she is."

"I thought about you a great deal, Kith," Hermathya said softly. "The longer you were away, the more I missed you."

"You forget, Thya, I asked you to flee with me and you refused."

She seized his hand. "I was a fool! I don't love Sithas. You must know that," she exclaimed.

Hermathya's hand was smooth and warm, but Kith-Kanan still pulled his hand free of hers. "He is your husband and my brother," he said.

She didn't hear the warning in his statement. She leaned her head against him. "He's a pale shadow of you, as a prince . . . and a lover," she said bitterly.

Kith-Kanan moved away from the bench. "I have no intention of betraying him, Thya. And you must accept the fact that I do not love you."

"But I love you!" A tear trickled down her cheek.

"If that's true, then I pity you. I have passed into another life since we loved each other, years ago. I'm not the head-strong young fool I once was."

"Don't you care for me at all?" she asked, her face anguished.

"No," he said truthfully, "I don't care for you at all."

One of Dunbarth's dwarven servants came running through the maze of hedges. "Great prince!" he said breathlessly. "The speaker is recalling the assembly."

Kith-Kanan walked away and did not look back at Hermathya, though he could hear her crying until he reached the entrance to the Tower of the Stars.

When he was out of earshot, Hermathya clenched her eyes shut, squeezing the tears from them. "So be it," she hissed to herself. "So be it!" She picked up the golden goblet Kith-Kanan had left nearby and bashed the soft metal against the marble bench. The goblet was soon a twisted, misshapen lump.

* * * * *

The afternoon session dragged on as the three sides tried to decide who would govern the proposed buffer state. It was a tricky question, and every suggestion that came up was debated and discounted. Clerics and guildmasters from the city grew tired of the endless discussion and drifted away, thinning the crowd in the audience hall. After a time, Praetor Ulwen's head nodded forward. His wife looked like she wanted a long nap herself.

"I can't agree to give away mineral rights or crop-growing rights," Teralind said testily, for the third time. "How do you expect our people to live? They can't all herd cattle."

"Well, your idea to have enclaves belonging to different nations is no solution," Sithas said, tapping the arm of his chair to emphasize each word. "Instead of one large disputed territory, we'll have scores of tiny ones!"

"Separate communities might be the answer," mused Dunbarth, "if they are able to trade with each other—"

"They would fight over the choicest land," the speaker said. He rubbed a hand against his left temple. "This is getting nowhere. Surely one of us can come up with a fair and adequate solution."

No one said anything. Kith-Kanan shifted nervously in his seat. He had said virtually nothing during this session. Something Anaya had mentioned to him once was nagging at him. "I don't meddle with the forest. I just protect it." Perhaps that was the answer . . .

The prince stood quickly. The sudden movement startled everyone; they'd practically forgotten he was there. Sithel looked at his son questioningly, and Kith-Kanan self-consciously straightened the folds of his white robe.

"It seems to me," he said with dignity, "that the entire problem with the western provinces comes from the fact that new settlers are pushing the old ones out. No one here, I think, would defend such activity." Sithas and Dunbarth glanced at Teralind. She put her nose in the air and shrugged.

Kith-Kanan moved to the center of the floor. Sithas shifted restlessly as all eyes fixed on his brother. "If everyone is agreed upon the principle that all persons, regardless of race, have a right to settle on empty land, then the problem becomes a simple one: how to protect the legitimate settlers from those who seek to drive them off their land."

"I sent soldiers once," said the speaker flatly. "They were betrayed and slaughtered."

"Forgive me, Father," Kith-Kanan said, "but from what I have heard of the incident, they were too few and not the right kind of soldiers. If we are going to share the bounty of these lands, then the burden of protecting them must be shared. Soldiers from the city have no stake in the area; they simply obey the orders of the speaker." The prince looked around at the company. "Do you not see? What's needed is a local force, a militia, in which the farmer has his own shield and spear with which to protect his land and that of his neighbor."

"Militia?" said Teralind with interest. Ulvissen was suddenly at her elbow trying to tell her something.

"Arm the farmers?" asked Dunbarth. The brim of his hat had lost its snap and drooped down over his eyes. He brushed it back.

"Peasants with spears would never stand up to mounted bandits," asserted Sithas.

"They would if they were trained and led by experienced soldiers," Kith-Kanan countered. He was thinking on his feet now. "One sergeant for each company of twenty; one captain for each band of two hundred."

"Are you speaking of all settlers in the disputed lands being armed?" asked Dunbarth. "Even those not of elven blood?"

"Definitely. If we arm one group and not another, it's just an invitation for war. A mixed militia will bind the people together, serving shoulder to shoulder with men of other races."

"I still say farmers and cow herders will never catch a fast-moving party of raiders," Sithas said stiffly.

Kith-Kanan's enthusiasm brought him right up to his brother's chair. "Don't you see, Sith? They don't have to *catch* the bandits. They only have to be able to fend them off. Why, the ruined village Mackeli and I saw had a sod wall eight feet high all around it. If the villagers had had a few spears and had known how to fight, they all might have been saved."

"I think it is an excellent idea," Sithel remarked.

"I like it, too."

Kith-Kanan swiveled around to see if what he'd just heard was true. Teralind was sitting proudly, hands folded on the lap of her burgundy gown. "I like it," she repeated firmly. "It puts the responsibility on the people living there." Behind her Ulvissen was livid with ill-suppressed anger. "No army need be sent in, yours or ours. The emperor will save much money."

"I have some doubts about the efficacy of such a militia," Dunbarth put in, "but never let it be said that Dunbarth of Dunbarth wasn't willing to give it a try!" The dwarf whipped off his bothersome hat. "I smell peace!" he declared, throwing the hat to the shiny marble floor.

"Don't be hasty," Sithas warned. His cool voice dampened the growing elation in the hall. "My brother's plan has its merits, but it doesn't address the problem of sovereignty. I say, let there be a militia, but only elves may bear arms in it."

Kith-Kanan looked stricken, and Teralind rapidly lost her serene expression. She said, "No! That's impossible. Ergoth will not allow humans to live as hostages among an army of elves!"

"Quite right," said Dunbarth, picking up his hat and dusting it off against his leg.

"We cannot abandon our ancestral right to this land!" Sithas insisted.

"Be still," the speaker said, frowning. Now it was Sithas's turn to look aggrieved. "This is a practical business we're in. If Ergoth and Thorbardin like Kith-Kanan's proposal, I cannot in good conscience throw away the best chance we have for peace."

Sithas opened his mouth to speak, but Sithel stifled him with a glance. The prince turned away, his lips pressed together in a thin line.

After a short while, when more specific details were worked out, a basic agreement was reached. Each of the three nations was to provide a corps of experienced warriors to serve as organizers of the new militia. Armories would be set up, where the warrior officers would reside. And in times of trouble all able-bodied settlers within twenty miles would present themselves at the armory to receive weapons and leadership. No single nation would command the militia.

"You expect professional warriors to live in the wilderness, shepherding a motley rabble of farmers?" Sithas asked with ill-concealed irritation. "What will keep them in their place?"

Kith-Kanan folded his arms. "Land," he declared. "Give them

a stake in the peace of the country."

"Give them enough to be worth working," said Dunbarth, catching the gist of Kith-Kanan's idea.

"Exactly! Five acres for every sergeant. Twenty acres for every captain. A whole new class of gentry will arise, loyal to the land and to their neighbors," Kith-Kanan predicted.

The speaker ordered the scribes to prepare a draft of the decree. Then, as it was nearly dusk, he adjourned the session. Everyone stood while Sithel went out, looking tired but very pleased. Teralind's shoulders sagged, and she was supported on the arm of Ulvissen, who did not look at all happy with events. Neither did Sithas as he left. Kith-Kanan was about to start after him when Dunbarth called to him.

"My prince," he enthused, "Congratulations on your masterful stroke!"

Kith-Kanan watched his twin disappear out the private exit to the palace. "Yes, thank you," he said distantly.

"I praise the gods for bringing you back," continued the dwarf, folding his hands across his round belly. "That's what this problem needed, a fresh perspective." Dunbarth cleared his throat.

"Oh, your pardon, my lord. I'm being rude," said Kith-Kanan, turning his attention to the ambassador from Thorbardin.

"Do not trouble about it." Dunbarth glanced at the rear exit and commented, "Your brother is proud, and he hasn't yet learned the benefit of flexibility. Your father is wise. He understands."

The elf prince's brow furrowed with thought. "I suppose," he replied uncertainly.

Guards opened the vast double doors of the tower. Beyond the entryway, the red rays of the setting sun painted the world scarlet. Only Dunbarth's small retinue, two scribes and his secretary, Drollo, remained, waiting patiently for their master.

Dunbarth's eyes shone as he plopped his hat on his head. "Noble prince, would you dine with me? I have an urge to try some inn in your city tonight—not that the dining is poor in the palace. Far from it! It's just that I crave some hearty, simple fare."

Kith-Kanan smiled. "I know a place, right on the river. Fried catfish, cabbage rolls, a suet pudding . . ."

"Beer?" said the dwarf hopefully. Elves didn't drink beer, so the ambassador hadn't had any since coming to Silvanost.

"I think the innkeeper ought to be able to scratch some up," Kith-Kanan assured him.

The elf prince and the dwarven ambassador walked out the high doors and into the crimson evening.

*   *   *   *   *

After leaving the Tower of the Stars, Sithas walked through the starlit streets. He wanted to be alone, to think. Anger propelled his steps, and habit steered him to the Temple of Matheri, where so much of his early life had been spent. The crystal dome of the sanctum of the god rose above the sculpted trees like a rising moon, lit a golden yellow from within. Sithas took the steps two at a time. At the door, he dipped his hands in the bowl of rose petals set on a tripod and scattered them on the paving before him.

In quick, barely audible tones, he said, "Wise Matheri, grant me entrance that I may commune with you." The buffed wooden doors parted silently, with no hand to stir them. Sithas went inside.

In the center of the floor, directly under the great dome, the ever-burning lamp of Matheri stood. The silent, smokeless flame cast harsh shadows around the circular room. Along the outer edge of the temple were the meditation chambers of the monks. Sithas knew them well. This was where he had lived for thirty years of his life.

He went to his old cubicle. It was empty, so he entered. Sitting on the hard floor, he crossed his legs. The prince tried to meditate, to find the reason for his resentment of Kith-Kanan's success. As the priests had taught him, he imagined a dialogue with himself.

"You are angry, why?" he asked aloud.

In his mind, he formed a reply. *Kith's suggestion is dangerous to the nation.*

"Is it? Why?"

It allows the humans to remain on land that rightfully

belongs to us.

"They have been there for years. Is their presence intrinsically bad?"

The land belongs to the elven nation. No one else.

"An inflexible attitude. Is this the reason you're angry?"

Sithas paused and considered. He closed his eyes and examined closely the feelings that crowded inside his heart.

No. I've been working at father's side for weeks, discussing, planning, thinking, and re-thinking, yet nothing was accomplished. I should have thought of the militia plan. I have failed.

"You are jealous of Kith-Kanan."

I have no reason to be jealous. I am the speaker's heir. Yet a short time ago I found myself wishing I hadn't called him back.

"Why did you?"

He's my brother. I missed him. I thought father might die—

Before he could ponder his feelings further, the carved rosewood door of the cell swung open. Sithas looked up, ready to lash out at whomever would intrude. It was Hermathya.

"What are you doing here?" he demanded harshly.

She stepped into the little room. Covered from head to toe in a midnight-black cape, she dropped the hood from her head. Diamonds gleamed faintly from her earlobes.

"I knew you would be here," she said in a low voice. "You always come here when you're upset."

Sithas felt an icy mask of resolve fall into place, covering his painful emotions. "I am not upset," he said coldly.

"Tosh, I heard you raving to yourself as soon as I came in."

He stood and brushed the dust from his knees. "What is it you want?" he demanded again.

"I heard what happened at the tower today. It doesn't look good for you, does it? All these days of negotiating for nothing, then Kith solves everything in one day."

She was only reinforcing what his bitter heart had been saying. Sithas moved until he was only inches from her. He could smell the rosewater she'd bathed in. "Are you trying to provoke me?" he asked, staring into her eyes.

"Yes." He felt her breath on his face when she said it. "I'm trying to provoke you into being a prince and not some sort of high-born monk!"

He drew away. "You are as tactful as ever, Lady. Leave me to recover my temper. Your advice is not needed or welcome."

Hermathya made no move to go. "You need me," she insisted. "You've always needed me, but you're too stubborn to know it."

Sithas swept a hand over the single candle that lit the cubicle. Darkness, save for a stray shaft of light that slipped in around the closed door, claimed the room. He could see the heat outline of Hermathya, her back to the door, and she could hear his quick breathing.

"When I was a child, I was sent to this temple to learn patience and wisdom. The first three days I was here, I wept all my waking hours because I'd been separated from Kith. I could live without my mother and father, but cut off from Kith . . . I felt like I'd been cut open and part of me had been torn out."

Hermathya said nothing. The diamonds in her ears sparkled like stars in the scant light.

"Later, when we were older, I was allowed to go home to the palace and visit a few days each month. Kith was always doing something interesting—learning to ride, fence, shoot a bow. He was always better than me," Sithas said. Resignation was creeping into his voice.

"There is one thing you have that he hasn't," Hermathya said soothingly, reaching out in the dark for Sithas's hand.

"What?"

"Me."

Sithas uttered a short, sardonic laugh. "I daresay he could have you if he wanted you!"

She snatched her hand from his and slapped Sithas hard across the cheek. Her blow stung his face. Forgetting his training, the prince seized his wife roughly and brought their faces together until they were only a finger's width apart. Even in the dim cubicle, he could see her pale features clearly, and she his.

She said desperately, "I am your wife!"

"Do you still love Kith-Kanan?" Despite the coldness of their marriage, Sithas braced himself for her answer.

"No," she whispered fiercely. "I hate him. Anything that angers you, I hate."

"Your concern for me is touching. And quite new," he said skeptically.

261

"I admit that I thought I might still love him," she whispered, "but since seeing him, I know it's not true." Tremors shivered through her. "You are my husband," Hermathya declared passionately. "I wish Kith-Kanan were gone again, so he couldn't ever make you feel small!"

"He's never tried to make me feel small," Sithas retorted.

"And what if he wins your father's favor completely?" she parried. "The speaker could declare Kith-Kanan his heir if he felt he would do a better job of ruling than you."

"Father would never do that!"

Her lips were by his ear. She pressed her cheek against his and felt his tight grip relax. Quickly she said, "The militia must have an overall commander. Who better than Kith-Kanan? He has the skills and experience for it. With all those square miles to patrol, he could be gone for decades."

Sithas turned his head away, and she knew he was thinking about it. A small, triumphant smile played about her lips. "By then," she murmured, "we will have a son of our own, and Kith could never come between you and the throne."

The prince said nothing, but Hermathya was patient. Instead of prompting him further, she laid her head on his chest. His heartbeat was strong in her ear. After a time, Sithas slowly brought his hand up and stroked her copper-gold hair.

25

By Next Dawn

When it came to the spread of important news, the great
city of Silvanost was just like a tiny village.

By the next morning, word of the tentative agreement between the speaker and the representatives of Ergoth and
Thorbardin had penetrated every corner of the capital. The
city, and the elven nation itself, seemed to let out a long-held
breath. Fear of war had been uppermost in the minds of all the
people, followed closely by fear that large numbers of refugees would once more be driven back into the city by the bandit raids.

When the new day dawned, rimmed by low clouds and
chilly with the threat of rain, the people of Silvanost behaved
as if it was a bright, sun-filled day. The nobility, priests, and

guildmasters heard cheering as their sedan chairs were carried through the streets.

Kith-Kanan went into the city that morning on horseback with Lord Dunbarth. It was the prince's first chance to see Silvanost since his return. His appetite had been whetted when he and the dwarf had dined at the Inn of the Golden Acorn. There, with good food and drink, stirred by the strains of a bardic lyre, Kith-Kanan had rediscovered his love for the city, dormant for all his months in the wildwood.

He and Dunbarth rode through the crowded streets of the family quarter, where most of Silvanost's population lived. Here the houses were less grand than the guildmasters' halls or the priestly enclaves, but they mimicked the styles of the great homes. Beautifully sculpted towers rose, but only for three or four stories. Tiny green plots of land in front of each home were molded by elven magic to support dazzling gardens of red, yellow, and violet flowers; shrubs formed into wave patterns like the river; and trees that bowed and twined together like the braids in an elf maiden's hair. Nearly every house, no matter how small, was built in imitation of the homes of the great, around a central atrium that held the family's private garden.

"I didn't realize how much I missed it," Kith-Kanan said, steering his horse around a pushcart full of spring melons.

"Miss what, noble prince?" asked Dunbarth.

"The city. Though the forest became my home, a part of me still lives here. It's like I'm seeing Silvanost for the first time!"

Both elf and dwarf were dressed plainly, without the fine embroidery, golden jewelry, or other outward signs of rank. Even their horses were trapped in the simplest possible style. Kith-Kanan wore a wide-brimmed hat, like a fisher, so that his royal features would be less obvious. They wanted to see the city, not be surrounded by crowds.

Together the duo turned off Phoenix Street and rode down a narrow alley. Kith-Kanan could smell the river even more strongly here. When he emerged in the old Market quarter, ruined by the great riot and now under repair, Kith-Kanan reined up and surveyed the scene. The entire marketplace, from where his horse stood down to the banks of the Thon-Thalas, had been razed. Gangs of Kagonesti elves swarmed around the site,

sawing lumber, hauling stones, mixing mortar. Here and there
a robed priest of E'li stood, directing the work.

For a large project, like a high tower, magic would be used to
shape and raise the stones of the walls and meld the blocks together without need for mortar. In the mundane buildings of
the marketplace, more ordinary techniques would be used.

"Where do all the workers come from?" Kith-Kanan wondered aloud.

"As I understand it, they're slaves from estates to the north
and west, owned by the priests of E'li," said Dunbarth without
inflection.

"Slaves? But the speaker put severe limits on the number of
slaves anyone could own!"

Dunbarth stroked his curly beard. "I know it may shock
Your Highness, but outside of Silvanost the speaker's laws
aren't always followed. They are bent to suit the needs of the
rich and powerful."

"I'm certain my father doesn't know about this," Kith-Kanan
said firmly.

"Forgive me, Highness, but I believe he does." Dunbarth remarked confidentially, "Your mother, the Lady Nirakina, has
many times pleaded with the speaker to free the slaves of
Silvanesti to no avail."

"How do you know these things? Aren't they private matters
of the palace?"

The dwarf smiled benignly. "It is a diplomat's purpose to listen as well as talk. Five weeks in the Quinari Palace exposes one
to all sorts of gossip and idle talk. I know the love lives of your
servants and who among the nobility drinks too much—not to
mention the sad plight of slaves in your own capital city." With
that, Dunbarth's smile vanished.

"It's intolerable!" Kith-Kanan's horse sensed his rider's agitation and pranced around in a half-circle. "I'll put a stop to this
right now!"

He tightened the reins and turned his mount's head. Before
he could ride over to confront the supervising priests, Dunbarth caught his reins and held him back.

"Don't be hasty, my prince. The priesthoods are very powerful. They have friends at court who will speak against you."

Kith-Kanan was indignant. "Who do you mean?"

Dunbarth's gaze was level. "I mean your brother, the noble Sithas."

Kith-Kanan squinted from under the brim of his hat. "My twin is not a slave driver. Why do you say this to me, my lord?"

"I only say what is true, Highness. You know the court; you know how alliances are made. Prince Sithas has become the defender of the temples. In turn, the priests support him."

"Against whom?"

"Anyone who opposes him. The priestess Miritelisina, of the Temple of Quenesti Pah, for one. She tried to defend those who fled from the slaughter on the plains. You know of the riot?" Kith-Kanan knew Sithas's version of the story. He indicated Dunbarth should continue. "The riot began because Prince Sithas and the priests, along with the guildmasters, wanted to expel the poor farmers from the city. Miritelisina warned them. They misunderstood her and, believing they were to be sent back to the plains, rioted. For that the priestess was put in prison. The speaker has let her go free, but she continues her work for the poor and homeless."

Kith-Kanan said nothing, but watched as three Kagonesti passed by with a ten-inch-thick log braced on their shoulders. In each one he saw Anaya—the same dark eyes and hair, the same passion for freedom.

"I must speak out against this," he said at last. "It is wrong for one of the firstborn race to own another."

"They will not hear you, Highness," Dunbarth said sadly.

Kith-Kanan put his horse's head toward the palace. "They will hear me. If they don't listen, I'll shout at them till they do."

They rode back at a brisk canter, avoiding the clogged streets in the center of the city and keeping to the riverside roads. By the time they reached the plaza in front of the palace, a light rain had started to fall. Mackeli was standing in the courtyard in his new squire's livery, a studded leather jerkin and helmet. When Kith-Kanan rode up, Mackeli hurried over and held the prince's horse while he dismounted.

"You look splendid," Kith-Kanan said, sizing up Mackeli's new outfit.

"Are you sure this is what squires wear?" asked the boy. He hooked a finger in the tight collar and tugged at the stiff leather. "I feel like I've been swallowed by a steer."

Kith-Kanan laughed and clapped him on the shoulder. "Wait until you put on your first real armor," he said exuberantly. "Then you'll feel like one of our giant turtles has swallowed you!"

The three left the horses for the servants to stable and entered the palace. Maids appeared with dry towels. Kith-Kanan and Dunbarth made perfunctory swipes at their faces, then handed the cloths back. Mackeli dried himself carefully, all the while eyeing the handmaids with frank interest. The girls, both of whom were about the boy's age, blushed under his studied gaze.

"Come along," Kith Kanan scolded, dragging at Mackeli's sleeve. Dunbarth plucked the towel from his hand and returned it to the servants.

"I wasn't finished," Mackeli protested.

"If you'd dried yourself any longer, you'd have taken hide and hair off, too," observed the dwarf.

"I was looking at the girls," Mackeli said bluntly.

"Yes, like a wolf looks at his dinner," noted Kith-Kanan. "If you want to impress the fair sex, you'd best learn to be a little more discreet."

"What do you mean?"

"He means, don't stare," advised Dunbarth. "Smile at them and say something pleasant."

Mackeli was puzzled. "What should I say?"

Kith-Kanan put a hand to his chin and considered. "Pay them a compliment. Say, 'What pretty eyes you have!' or ask them their name and say, 'What a pretty name!' "

"Can I touch them?" asked Mackeli innocently.

"No!" exclaimed the two in unison.

They spotted Ulvissen in the corridor, accompanied by one of the human soldiers. The Ergothian seneschal was handing the soldier a large brass tube, which the man furtively tucked into a leather bag hung from his shoulder. Ulvissen stood up straight when he saw Kith-Kanan. The soldier with the tube saluted and went on his way.

"How goes it, Master Ulvissen?" the prince asked blandly.

"Very well, Your Highness. I have dispatched a copy of the preliminary agreement we've made to His Imperial Majesty."

"Just now?"

Ulvissen nodded. Behind his beard and graying hair, he looked haggard. Kith-Kanan guessed Lady Teralind had kept him up very late, preparing the dispatch.

"Would you know where my father and Prince Sithas might be?"

"I last saw them in the reception hall, where seals were being put to the copies of the agreement," said Ulvissen courteously. He bowed.

"Thank you." Kith-Kanan and Dunbarth walked on. Mackeli too drifted past the tall, elder human, looking at him with curiosity.

"How old are you?" asked Mackeli impetuously.

Ulvissen was surprised. "Forty and nine years," he replied.

"I am sixty-one," said the boy. "Why is it you look so much older than I?"

Kith-Kanan swung around and took Mackeli by the elbows. "Forgive him, Excellency," said the prince. "The boy has lived all his life in the forest and knows little about manners."

"It is nothing," said Ulvissen. Yet he continued to watch with an intense expression as the prince and the dwarf ambassador hustled Mackeli away.

*   *   *   *   *

The reception hall of the palace was on the ground floor of the central tower, one floor below the Hall of Balif. Dunbarth took his leave of Kith-Kanan in the corridor outside. "My old bones need a nap," he apologized.

Mackeli started to follow the prince, who told him to remain behind. The boy objected, but Kith-Kanan said sharply, "Find some other way to be useful. I'll be back soon."

When Kith-Kanan entered, the vast round room was full of tables and stools, at which scribes were furiously writing. The entire transcript of the conference was being written out in full and copied as quickly as the master scribe could finish a page.

Sithel and Sithas stood in the center of this organized chaos, approving sheets of parchment covered with spidery handwriting. Boys darted among the tables, filling inkpots, sharpening styluses, and piling up fresh stacks of unmarked vellum. When

Sithel espied him, he shoved the parchment aside and gestured for the assistant to leave.

"Father, I need to speak with you. And you, Brother," Kith-Kanan said, gesturing to a quieter side of the hall. When they had moved, the prince asked bluntly, "Do you know that gangs of slaves are working in the city, working to rebuild the Market?"

"That's common knowledge," said Sithas quickly. He was especially elegant today, having forsworn his usual robe in favor of a divided kilt and a thigh-length tunic of quilted cloth of gold. His headband, too, was golden.

"What about the law?" asked Kith-Kanan, his voice rising. "No household is supposed to have more than two slaves at a time, yet I saw two hundred or more working away, watched over by clerics from the Temple of E'li."

"The law only applies to those who live in Silvanost," Sithas said, preempting his father again. Sithel kept quiet and let his sons argue. He was curious to see which would prevail. "The slaves you saw come from temple estates on the Em-Bali River, north of the city," added the speaker's firstborn.

"That's an evasion," Kith-Kanan said heatedly. "I never heard of a law that applied only in Silvanost and not to the entire nation!"

"Why all this concern about slaves?" Sithas demanded.

"It isn't right." Kith-Kanan clenched his hands into fists. "They are elves, the same as us. It is not right that elves should own one another."

"They are not like us," Sithas snapped. "They are Kagonesti."

"Does that automatically condemn them?"

Sithel decided it was time to intervene. "The workers you saw were sold into slavery because they were convicted of crimes against the Silvanesti people," he said gently. "That they are Kagonesti is of no significance. Your concern for them is misplaced, Kith."

"I don't think so, Father," his son argued earnestly. "We're all proud of our Silvanesti blood, and that's good. But pride should not lead us to exploit our subjects."

"You have been in the woods too long," said Sithas coolly. "You have forgotten how the world works."

"Hold your tongue," Sithel intervened sharply. "And you

too, Kith." The Speaker of the Stars looked rueful. "I am glad to know both my sons feel so passionately about right and wrong. The blood of Silvanos has not run thin, I can see. But this debate serves no purpose. If the slaves in the Market are well treated and do their allotted work, I see no reason to tamper with the situation."

"But, Father—"

"Listen to me, Kith. You've only been back four days. I know you grew used to much freedom in the forest, but a city and a nation cannot operate like a camp in the wildwood. Someone must command, and others must obey. That's how a speaker can protect the weak and rule with justice."

"Yes, Father." When Sithel explained it like that, it almost made sense. Still, Kith-Kanan knew that no amount of logic and lawful argument would ever convince him that slavery was anything but wrong.

Sithas listened to Sithel's words with his arms folded in satisfaction. Kith was not as infallible as he seemed, thought the firstborn. Facing down Kith's sentimental ramblings made him feel every inch the next Speaker of the Stars.

"Now I have a command for you, son," Sithel said to Kith-Kanan. "I want you to lead the new militia."

Utter silence. Kith-Kanan tried to digest this. He was just back home, and now he was being sent away. He looked at Sithas—who glanced away—then back at the speaker. "Me, Father?" he asked, dazed.

"With your experience as a warrior and ranger, who better? I have already spoken with Lady Teralind and Lord Dunbarth, and they agree. A speaker's son, ranger, and a friend of the Kagonesti, you are the best choice."

Kith-Kanan looked to Sithas. "This was your idea, Sith?"

His brother shrugged. "Clear reasoning pointed to you and no one else."

Kith-Kanan ran a hand through his tousled hair. The crafty old Dunbarth knew all through their ride this morning and hadn't said a word. In fact, had he led the way to the Market to show Kith-Kanan the slaves at work there? To prepare him for this?

"You can refuse," noted the speaker, "if you wish." He plainly expected no such reaction from his stalwart son.

A rush of images and thoughts flooded Kith-Kanan's mind. In quick succession he saw the ruined village he and Mackeli had found; Voltorno, roving and plundering at will through Silvanesti; Anaya, mortally stricken, fighting bows and swords with a flint knife; Kagonesti slaves, stripped of their lives.

The prince also heard his own words: "If the people had possessed a few spears, and had known how to fight, they might all have been saved".

Kith-Kanan's gaze remained on his twin for a long moment, then he looked at the speaker.

"I accept," he said quietly.

* * * * *

With Mackeli at his side, Kith-Kanan spent the next few days interviewing members of the royal guard who had volunteered for the militia. As he had predicted, the lure of free land was a powerful inducement to soldiers who seldom owned anything more than the clothes on their backs. Kith-Kanan could select the very best of them as his sergeants.

A great public celebration had been declared, both to honor the new agreement with Ergoth and Thorbardin and to honor Kith-Kanan's ascent to command of the new militia of House Protector. The force was already being called the Wildrunners, after the old name given to the armed bands of Kagonesti who had fought for Silvanos during the wars of elven unification.

* * * * *

"I still don't understand why we don't just fly out there," Mackeli said, struggling under the weight of real armor and a pot-shaped iron helmet.

"Griffons are reserved as mounts of House Royal," Kith-Kanan said. "Besides, there aren't enough of them for this whole company." He cinched a rope tight around the last bundle of his personal gear. His chestnut charger, Kijo, bore the weight of bedroll and armor well. Kith-Kanan had been pleased to discover that his old mount was still as spirited as ever.

Mackeli regarded the horses skeptically. "Are you sure these beasts are tame?"

Kith-Kanan smiled. "You rode Arcuballis one thousand feet up in the air, and now you're worried about riding on horseback?"

"I know Arcuballis," the boy said apprehensively. "I don't know these animals."

"It will be all right." Kith-Kanan went down the line of horses and warriors. The last knots were made, and the good-byes were being said.

The Processional Road was full of elves and horses. Two hundred and fifty warriors and an equal number of mounts milled about. Unlike Sithel's earlier, ill-fated expedition, Kith-Kanan's band was to be entirely mounted and self-sufficient. This was the largest force to leave Silvanost since the days of the founding wars.

It was a splendid spectacle, and the sides of the street were lined with townsfolk. The warriors had discarded their fancy parade armor in favor of more practical equipment. Each elf wore a hammered iron breastplate and a simple, open-faced helmet. Bronze shields, shaped like hourglasses, hung from each saddlehorn. Every warrior carried a bow, twenty arrows, a sword, a knife, and a heavy javelin that could be used for thrusting or throwing. The horses wore only minimal trapping, as mobility was more important than protection.

Kith-Kanan tucked his gauntlets under his arm as he mounted the steps to the processional entrance of the Tower of the Stars. There stood his father and mother, Sithas and Hermathya, Lady Teralind, Praetor Ulwen in his chair, and Ulvissen. Lord Dunbarth had begged off attending the departure ceremony. He was afflicted with a colic, according to his faithful secretary, Drollo. Kith-Kanan knew that the old rascal had been living it up in the inns and taverns along the riverfront since the treaty had been approved by the emperor of Ergoth and the king of Thorbardin.

The prince ascended the steps in measured tread, keeping his eyes fixed on his father. Sithel was wearing the formal Crown of Stars, a magnificent golden circlet that featured as its central stone the famed Eye of Astarin, the largest emerald in all of Krynn. The gem caught the rays of the midmorning sun and sent flashes of verdant light across the street and gardens.

Beside Sithel stood Lady Nirakina. She was dressed in a gown of palest blue and wore a filigree silver torc around her throat. Her honey-colored hair was held in a silver cloth scarf. There was something sad and remote about her expression—no doubt it was the realization that she was losing her younger son again, after he'd been home less than a month.

Kith-Kanan reached the step just below the landing where the royal family was gathered. He removed his helmet and bowed to his father.

"Noble father, gracious mother," he said with dignity.

"Stand with me," said Sithel warmly. Kith-Kanan made the final step and stood beside his father.

"Your mother and I have something to give you," the speaker said in a private tone. "Open it when you are alone." Nirakina handed her husband a red silk kerchief, the corners of which were tied together. Sithel pressed this into Kith-Kanan's hand.

"Now for the public words," the speaker said with the faintest trace of a smile. Sithel looked out over the crowd. He raised his hand and declaimed, "People of Silvanost! I present you my son, Kith-Kanan, in whose trust I place the peace and safety of the realm." To Kith-Kanan he asked loudly, "Will you faithfully and honorably discharge the duties of lord constable in all parts of our realm and any other provinces you may enter?"

Loudly and clearly Kith-Kanan replied, "By E'li, I swear I will." The crowd roared in approval.

Standing apart on the speaker's left were Sithas and Hermathya. The lady, who was radiantly beautiful in cream white and gold, had a serene expression on her fine-boned face. But Kith-Kanan's twin smiled on him as he approached for a blessing.

"Good hunting, Kith," said Sithas warmly. "Show the humans what elven mettle is like!"

"That I'll do, Sith." Without warning, Kith-Kanan embraced his brother. Sithas returned Kith-Kanan's embrace with fervor.

"Keep yourself safe, Brother," Sithas said softly, then broke away.

Kith-Kanan turned to Hermathya. "Farewell, Lady.".

"Good-bye," she replied coldly.

Kith-Kanan descended the steps. Mackeli was holding Kijo's

reins. "What did the lady say?" he asked, gazing up at Hermathya with rapt admiration.

"You noticed her, did you?"

"Well, yes! She's like a sunflower in a hedge of thistles—"

Kith-Kanan swung into the saddle. "By Astarin! You're starting to sound like a bard! It's a good thing we're getting you out of the city. Anaya wouldn't know you, talking like that!"

The warriors followed Kith-Kanan and Mackeli in ranks of five, wheeling with precision as the prince led them down the curving Processional Road. The assembled Silvanesti let out a roar of approbation, which quickly turned into a steady chant:

"*Kith-Ka-nan, Kith-Ka-nan, Kith-Ka-nan . . .*"

The chanting continued as the slow procession wound its way to the riverside. Two ferry barges were waiting for the warriors. Kith-Kanan and the Wildrunners boarded the ferries, and the huge turtles towed them away. The people of Silvanost lined the shore and called out Kith-Kanan's name until long after the barges were lost against the dark strip of the western riverbank.

26

Early Summer, Year of the Ram

Lord Dunbarth's party loaded all their possessions onto wagons and formed up to depart. Sithas and his honor guard were there to see the dwarven ambassador off.

"Much better weather than when I arrived," Dunbarth remarked. He was sweating under his woolen coat and vest. Summer was upon Silvanost, and a warm, humid wind blew in from the river.

"It is indeed," Sithas said pleasantly. In spite of Dunbarth's professional caginess, Sithas liked the old dwarf. There was a basic goodness about him.

"You'll find a case of amber nectar in your carriage," said the prince. "With the compliments of Lady Nirakina and myself."

"Ah!" The dwarf looked genuinely touched. "Many thanks,

275

noble prince. I shall be sure to share it with my king. He esteems elven nectar almost as much as Thorbardin ale."

The ambassador's escort, augmented by an honor guard of twenty elven warriors, paraded past the wagons. Dunbarth and his secretary, Drollo, climbed into their closed metal coach. As the ambassador pushed back the fine mesh curtains, he extended a ring-heavy hand to Sithas.

"In Thorbardin we wish friends a long life when parting, but I know you'll outlive me by centuries," Dunbarth said, a twinkle in his eye. "What do elves say when they part?"

"We say, 'Blessings of Astarin' and 'May your way be green and golden,'" Sithas replied. He clasped the ambassador's thick, wrinkled hand.

"May your way be green and golden, then, Prince Sithas. Oh, and some news for you, too: our Lady Teralind is not what she pretends to be."

Sithas raised a brow. "Oh?"

"She is Emperor Ullves's eldest daughter."

Sithas feigned mild interest. "Really? That's interesting. Why do you tell me this now, my lord?"

Dunbarth tried to hide his smile. "The dealing is done, so there's no advantage to my keeping her identity secret. I've seen her before, you see. In Daltigoth. Hmm, I thought your noble father might like to know so that he could—um—ah, give her a royal send-off."

"My lord, you are wise for one so young," Sithas said, grinning.

"Would that I *were* young! Farewell, Prince!" Dunbarth rapped on the side of the coach. "Drive on!"

*   *   *   *   *

When he returned to the palace, Sithas was summoned to the Ergothian's quarters. There he was awaited by his father, his mother, and her courtier, Tamanier Ambrodel. The prince quickly informed them of the dwarven lord's revelation.

At one end of the room, Teralind was giving final orders to her servants in a cross, high-pitched voice. Dresses of heavy velvet and delicate lace were being squeezed into crates, which were then nailed shut. Toiletries rattled into rattan hampers.

The strongbox containing Teralind's jewelry was locked with a stout padlock and given to a soldier to guard personally.

Sithel approached this hectic scene. He halted in the center of the room and clasped his hands behind his back. Lady Teralind had no choice but to leave off her packing and attend the speaker. She combed a strand of hair back from her face and curtsied to Sithel.

"To what do I owe this honor?" she asked in a hurried tone that made it plain she regarded it as no honor at all.

"It's just come to my attention that I have been remiss in my duty," Sithel noted with heavy irony. "I greeted you and your husband as befitted an ambassador, when I should have done you more honor. It is not often I have an imperial princess under my roof."

A twitch passed over Teralind's face. "What?" she murmured.

"Surely you don't deny your father? He is the emperor, after all."

The tension left the woman's shoulders. Her back straightened slightly, and she immediately took on a more relaxed and regal attitude. "It doesn't matter now. You are quite right, Highness. I am Xanille Teralind, first daughter of His Majesty, Ullves X." She looped the stray strand of hair back again. "How did you find out?"

"Lord Dunbarth recognized you. But why did you hide your identity?" asked Sithel curiously.

"To protect myself," she averred. "My husband is a helpless invalid. We traveled a long way from Daltigoth, through regions where my father is not loved. Can you imagine the danger we would have faced if every bandit chief and warlord knew I was an imperial princess? We should have needed a hundred times the escort we came with. And how would Your Highness have felt if we had shown up before Silvanost at the head of a thousand warriors?"

"You are right. I would have thought you were trying to intimidate me," Sithel said genially. He glanced at Tamanier Ambrodel. At the signal, the courtier handed the speaker a small rolled slip of vellum. Although Sithel made a fist around the scroll, he didn't yet open it.

The prince studied his father, mother, and Tamanier. What

were they up to? No one had told him what was going to happen—and yet, something was about to happen, that was plain.

"Where, my lady, is your seneschal?" Sithel asked nonchalantly.

"Ulvissen? Seeing to the loading of my baggage. Why?" The question seemed to put Teralind on the defensive.

"Would you summon him? I wish to speak with the man."

In short order Ulvissen himself entered from the courtyard where the Ergothians' wagons were being loaded. He was sweating heavily in his thick wool and leather outfit. In turn he bowed grandly to Teralind and Sithel.

"You wished to speak to me, Highness?" he asked the speaker awkwardly.

"Yes. Since this is a day of revelations, I see no reason why you shouldn't be part of them." Sithel opened his hand, displaying the slip of vellum. "I have here a report prepared by Prince Kith-Kanan before his departure to the West. In it, he describes a half-human bandit he met in the wilderness, Voltorno by name. Many months ago, he encountered this Voltorno in the company of a band of humans. He states that you were one of these men."

Ulvissen looked from the small scroll to the speaker's face, but betrayed no guilt. "No offense intended, great speaker, but your son is mistaken. I have never been to Silvanesti prior to coming as my lady's seneschal," he said evenly.

"Mistakes are possible, even by Kith-Kanan," Sithel said, closing his fingers around the parchment again. "Which is why I had my scribes search the archives of the Temple of Kiri Jolith. There are kept accounts of all wars and battles fought since the dawn of time. And whose name should be found as high admiral of the Ergothian fleet, but one Guldur Ul Vissen? A name strangely similar to your own, wouldn't you agree? Since your princess saw fit to come here in disguise, it does not tax belief to think you may have also." The speaker clasped his hands behind his back. "What have you to say, Master Ulvissen?"

Ulvissen regarded the Speaker of the Stars with utter coolness. "Your Highness is mistaken," he said firmly. "A similarity of names proves nothing. Vissen is a common name in Ergoth."

"Do you agree, Lady?"

Teralind flinched. "Yes. What is the point? I've told you why I pretended to be someone else. But my seneschal is who he claims to be."

Sithel tucked the parchment into his sash. "As an imperial princess, please go with my best wishes and every hope of safety, but do not bring your 'seneschal' to Silvanost again. Do you understand?" The harsh tone was unusual for the speaker. "Those who despoil my country and kill my subjects are not welcome in my city or my house. Please let this be known when you arrive in Daltigoth, Lady."

With that, the speaker turned on his heel and walked away. Nirakina followed. Tamanier bowed and did likewise. Sithas, wide-eyed, went last.

In the rotunda outside the humans' quarters, Sithel turned to his wife with a broad smile on his face. He shook a fist at the ceiling.

"At last!" he said fiercely. "I've given that contentious woman her own back!" He turned to Tamanier. "You have been of great service to me. You shall be rewarded."

Tamanier blinked and bowed. "I seek only to serve Your Highness and Lady Nirakina," he said.

"So you shall." Sithel pondered for a moment, stroking his pointed chin. "I wish to appoint you chamberlain of the court. The management of daily court life shall fall to you. You will be known as Lord Ambrodel, and your clan shall have the right to inherit the title." The speaker folded his arms and asked, "What say you to that, Lord Ambrodel?"

Tamanier gaped like a startled child. At last he collected himself and dropped to one knee. "I thank you, Highness," he said humbly. "I will serve you to the end of my days!"

"I think my days will end before yours," Sithel said wryly. "But you can serve my son after."

Laughing, the royal family and their new chamberlain left the rotunda. Sithas put a hand on Tamanier Ambrodel's arm.

"A word, my new lord," Sithas said in a confidential whisper, pulling him aside.

"Yes?" said Tamanier discreetly.

"Let us go to a more private location."

They left the palace. Outside, the air was sweet with flowers and the marble walks were covered with blossoms fallen from the trees. Sithas said nothing until they were some distance from any observers.

"You know someone in the palace has been giving information to the Ergothians," Sithas said conspiratorially, looking eastward to the fine houses of the nobility. "I would appreciate it if you would help me find out who the traitor is."

"I'll do what I can, noble prince," said Tamanier earnestly.

"Good. As chamberlain, you'll have access to every part of the palace. I want you to use your authority to root out the spy and reveal him to me." Sithas paused and looked straight at Tamanier. "But be wise. I don't want the wrong person accused. And I don't want the culprit alerted."

"Do you have any suspects?" asked Tamanier.

"Officially, no. Personally, yes," Sithas said grimly. "I suspect my own wife, Lady Hermathya."

"Your wife!" Tamanier was so shocked he could hardly believe what he had heard.

"Surely, noble prince, your wife loves you. She would not betray you to the humans!"

Sithas rubbed his hands slowly together. "I only have suspicions. All I can say about Hermathya's motives is that she so loves attention and the cheers of the people, that she spends huge amounts of money to keep their favor. I do not give her coins to scatter in the streets, yet she never seems to lack for money."

Shocked, yet pitying the prince at the same time, Tamanier asked, "Do you suspect anyone else?"

"Yes, and perhaps he is the stronger candidate. His name is Vedvedsica. He is a sorcerer and a priest, he claims, of Gilean the Gray Voyager. My father sometimes uses his clairvoyant skills, but Vedvedsica is a greedy conniver who would do anything for gold or power."

"The emperor of Ergoth has plenty of gold," Tamanier said sagely.

They talked for several minutes more. Tamanier vowed to detect the traitor, and Sithas listened approvingly, nodded, then walked away. The newly created chamberlain was left in the east garden, surrounded by fallen petals and singing birds.

*   *   *   *   *

The farmers were apprehensive when they first saw the column of armed warriors ride by, but when they realized who the Wildrunners were, they came to greet these newcomers. Along the way, Kith-Kanan sent troopers to help one farmer to fell a tree, another to free an ox from a boggy ditch, and a third to mend a fence. Word of these kindnesses spread ahead of the Wildrunners' march and increased the number of enthusiastic elves—Silvanesti and Kagonesti—who came out to greet Kith-Kanan and his troops.

For the next few days, the way of the march was lined with grateful farmers and their families, bearing gifts of new nectar, smoked meat, and fruit. Wreaths of flowers were hung around the Wildrunners' necks. Kith-Kanan's mount Kijo was draped with a garland of white roses. At one point, the prince ordered his pipers to play a lively tune, and the Wildrunners passed through the countryside in a swirl of music, flowers, and smiling settlers. It was more like a festival than a military expedition. Some of the more veteran warriors were astonished.

Now, ten days from Silvanost, sitting around the blazing campfire, warriors asked Kith-Kanan why he was making such a show of helping the farmers and herders they met.

"Well," he explained, stirring his soup with a wooden spoon, "if this militia idea is to succeed, the people must see us as their friends and not just their protectors. You see, our ranks will be filled by the same farmers, woodcutters, and herders we help along the way. They will be the troops, and all of you will be their leaders."

"Is it true we're to take in humans and dwarves in the ranks?" asked a captain with some distaste.

"It is," said Kith-Kanan.

"Can we rely on such fighters? I mean, we all know humans can fight, and the dwarves are stout fellows, but will they obey orders to attack and slay fellow humans or dwarves if those orders come from an elf?" asked one of the older sergeants.

"They will, or they'll be expelled from the militia and lose its protection," Kith-Kanan responded. "You ask if humans will serve us by fighting humans. Some will, some won't. We'll be fighting elves, too, I expect. I've heard tales of robber bands made up of humans, Kagonesti, and even mixed-bloods. If they rob, if they kill, then we will bring them to justice. We make no distinctions out here."

Sleep followed dinner, and guards were posted. The horses were corralled in the center of the camp, and one by one the lamps went out in the Wildrunners' tents.

Mackeli usually slept at Kith-Kanan's side, and that night was no exception. Though the boy often slept soundly, the months he'd spent out of the old forest hadn't completely dulled his senses; he was the first one to sense something amiss. He sat up in the dark tent and rubbed his eyes, unsure of what had roused him. He heard nothing, but he saw something very odd.

Pink shadows wavered inside the tent. Mackeli saw his own hand, washed pink by an unknown light. He slowly raised his head and saw that a red circle of light showed through the tent's canvas roof. A glare of heat on his face, Mackeli had no idea what the red glow portended, but he was sure it wasn't friendly. He shook Kith-Kanan awake.

"Wha-What is it?" mumbled the prince.

"Look!" hissed Mackeli.

Kith-Kanan blinked at the red glow. He brushed the long hair from his eyes and threw back his blanket. In lieu of the sword he'd broken in the wildwood, he'd brought along a fine new weapon. Mackeli drew his own sword from its scabbard as, warily, Kith-Kanan lifted the flap on the tent with the tip of his blade.

Hovering over the camp, about twenty feet in the air, was a ball of red fire the size of a cart wheel. The crackling red light covered the camp. Kith-Kanan immediately felt a prickling sensation on his skin when the red glow touched him.

"What is it?" asked Mackeli wonderingly.

"I don't know . . ."

The elf prince looked across the camp. The sentries were frozen, one foot raised in midstep, mouths open in the act of giving the alarm. Their eyes stared ahead, unblinking. Even the horses were rooted in place, some with hooves raised and necks arched in odd angles.

"They're all paralyzed somehow," Kith-Kanan said in awe. "This is evil magic!"

"Why aren't *we* paralyzed?" Mackeli asked, but Kith-Kanan had no answer to that.

Through the line of tents shadowy figures moved. Blood-colored light sparkled on naked sword blades. Kith-Kanan and Mackeli ducked down behind a tent. The shadow figures came on. There were five of them. By their clothing, features, and coloring, Kith-Kanan saw they were raffish Kagonesti. He held a finger to his lips, warning Mackeli to remain silent.

The Kagonesti approached the tent Kith-Kanan and Mackeli had been sleeping in minutes before. "Is this the tent?" hissed one of them.

"Yeah," replied the leading elf. His face was heavily scarred, and instead of a left hand, he had a cruel-looking metal hook.

"Let's be done with it an' get outta here," said a third Kagonesti. Hook-Hand made a snarling sound in his throat.

"Don't be so hasty," he advised. "There's plenty of time for the kill and to fill our pockets besides."

With sign language, Kith-Kanan indicated to Mackeli that he should circle around behind the band of magic-wielding killers. The boy vanished like a ghost, barefoot and wearing only his trousers. Kith-Kanan rose to his feet.

Hook-Hand had just ordered his men to surround the prince's tent. The killers slashed the ropes holding the tent up. As the canvas cone collapsed, the five killers waded in, hacking and stabbing through the tent cloth.

Suddenly, with a shout, Mackeli burst from concealment and bravely attacked the gang. He ran the first one through, even as that elf was turning to face him. Kith-Kanan gritted his teeth. Mackeli had attacked too rashly, so the prince had to rush his own attack. With a shout, Kith-Kanan entered the fray; he felled a mace-wielding killer with his first stroke. Hook-Hand kicked through the slashed canvas of the fallen tent to get clear. "That's him, boys!" he shouted as he retreated. "Finish 'em!"

From five, the villains were now down to three. Two of the Kagonesti went for Mackeli, leaving Hook-Hand and Kith-Kanan to duel. The scar-faced elf cut and thrust with deadly efficiency. Snatching up a cut length of rope with his hook, he lashed at Kith-Kanan. The knotted end stung hard against the prince's cheek.

Mackeli was not doing well against the other two. Already they had cut him on his left knee and right arm. Sweat sheened his body in the weird crimson glow. When the killer on his left thrust straight at him, Mackeli beat his blade and counterthrust into his opponent's chest. This moment of triumph was short-lived. The other attacker stabbed Mackeli before the boy could free his blade. Cold iron touched his heart, and he fell to the ground.

"I got 'im!" shouted the victorious killer.

"Ya fool, that ain't the prince—this is! Help me get 'im!" Hook-Hand shouted back, out of breath.

But Mackeli managed to heave himself up with great effort and stab his foe in the leg. With a scream, the Kagonesti went down. He fell against Hook-Hand's back, throwing his chief off balance. That was all Kith-Kanan needed. Ignoring the flailing rope, he closed in and rammed his blade through the assassin. Hook-Hand let out a slow, rattling gasp and died as he fell.

Mackeli lay face-down in the dirt. His right arm was out-stretched, still clutching his sword. Kith-Kanan threw himself down by the boy. He gently turned him over and then felt his own heart constrict. Mackeli's bare chest was covered with blood.

"Say something, Keli!" he begged. "Don't die!"

Mackeli's eyes were open. He looked at Kith-Kanan, and a frown tugged one corner of his mouth.

"This time . . . I can't obey, Kith," he said weakly. The life left his body with a shuddering sigh. Sightlessly his green eyes continued to gaze up at his friend.

An anguished sob wracked Kith-Kanan. He clutched Mackeli to him and wept. What curse was he under? How had he offended the gods? Now all of his family from the wildwood was gone. All gone. His tears mingled with Mackeli's blood.

A sound penetrated Kith-Kanan's grief; the brute that Mackeli had stabbed in the leg groaned. Kith-Kanan lowered the boy's body to the ground and gently closed his eyes. Then, with a growl, he grabbed the wounded mercenary by the tunic and dragged him to his feet.

"Who sent you?" he snarled. "Who sent you to kill me?"

"I don't know," gasped the elf. He trembled on his injured leg. "Mercy, great lord! I'm just a hireling!"

Kith-Kanan shook him by the shirt front, his face twisted into a hideous mask of rage. "You want mercy? Here's mercy:

tell me who hired you, and I'll cut your throat. Don't tell me, and it will take far longer for you to die!"

"I'll tell, I'll tell!" babbled the terrified elf. Kith-Kanan threw him to the ground. The light from the fireball suddenly grew more intense. The elf let out a scream and threw an arm over his face. Kith-Kanan turned in time to see the fiery globe come hurtling at them. As he leaped aside, the fireball hit the wounded elf. There was a thunderclap, and the globe exploded.

Slowly, sight and hearing returned to Kith-Kanan, and darkness reclaimed the camp. The prince raised his head and found that his right arm and leg were scorched from the fireball's impact. The wounded elf was gone, vaporized.

* * * * *

Mackeli was buried in a simple grave on the banks of the Khalkist River. The Wildrunners laid his sword across his chest, as was the custom with elven warriors. At the head of his grave, in lieu of a marker, Kith-Kanan planted the sprig of oak he'd snipped from Anaya's tree. All this time it had remained green. The prince was certain the sprig would grow into a fine tree, and that Mackeli and Anaya would be united somehow in renewed life once more.

As the camp was breaking up, Kith-Kanan fingered the small ring he now wore on his left little finger. This was the ring Silvanos had given to his great general Balif during the Dragon War. Sithel had passed the ring on to his son as a parting gift; it had been wrapped in the red silk handkerchief the speaker had passed to his son. Kith-Kanan had donned the ring with pride, but now he wondered if it was an unintentional portent of tragedy. After all, Balif had been murdered by his rivals, certain high-ranking elves who resented the kender's influence with Silvanos. Now similar treachery had struck at Kith-Kanan and had taken his young friend.

With somber diligence the Wildrunners struck their tents. When they were done, the senior captain, a Kagonesti named Piradon, came to Kith-Kanan.

"Highness, all is ready," he announced.

Kith-Kanan studied the captain's face. Like all the Kagonesti who served in the royal guard, Piradon did not wear skin paint. It made his face seem naked.

"Very well," he said flatly. "The usual columns of four, and I want outriders ahead, behind, and on both flanks. No one's going to surprise us again."

Kith-Kanan put a foot in his stirrup and swung a leg over his horse. He slapped the reins against his horse's rump and cantered down to the road. The golden ring of Balif felt tight on his finger, making his pulse throb in his fingertip. The prince decided then that the feeling would stand as a constant reminder of Mackeli's death and of his own vulnerability.

✤ 27 ✤

high Summer, Year of the Ram

Deprived of Anaya and bereft of Mackeli, kith-kanan threw
himself into his duty with a will that would have astonished
those who had known him as a callow, self-centered youth. He
drove his warriors as hard as he drove himself, and in weeks
molded them into a quick-thinking, quick-acting force.

Two months passed. High summer came to the plain, and the
days grew very hot. Daily thunderstorms soaked the steaming
plains and green forest, quenching the thirsty land so bursting
with life. Grass grew on the plain as tall as a grown elf's shoulder, so tall, in fact, that the herders had to cut swaths through it
with scythes twice weekly. Vines and bracken choked the paths
in the forest, making travel difficult, but the Wildrunners were
too busy to complain. Tall mountains of clouds, like castles of

white smoke, passed serenely overhead as the Wildrunners set up camp in order to construct a new armory, one Kith-Kanan had already dubbed Sithelbec.

Militia outposts like the one under construction had been established all across the plain in the past eight weeks, and settlers of every race flocked to their standards. Humans, elves, kender, dwarves—they were all tired of being victims, subject to the whims of the roving robbers. The captains and sergeants of the Wildrunners drilled them with pikes and shields, and showed them how to stand up to the mounted brigands. Everywhere Kith-Kanan's force stopped, an armory was founded. Stout stone houses were built by the Wildrunners, and there all the militia's weapons were stored. At the sounding of a gong, all able-bodied people in the locale would rush to the arsenal and arm themselves. In an attack, the Wildrunner officers stationed close at hand would lead them out to repel the raiders.

By a few weeks before midsummer, the south and central plains had been pacified. In most cases, the brigands hadn't even stayed around to fight the new militia. They'd simply vanished. Parnigar, eldest of the sergeants, had pronounced himself dissatisfied with the results of the campaign, however.

"What fault can you find?" Kith-Kanan had asked his trusted aide, the closest person to him since Mackeli's death. "I'd say we were succeeding far better than we could have hoped."

"Aye, that's the problem, sir. The brigands have given up too easily. They've scarcely tried to test us," Parnigar countered.

"Just shows that thieves have no stomach for honest combat." The old soldier nodded politely, but it was plain he hadn't been convinced.

The construction of Sithelbec began with a stockade of logs around the inner blockhouse of stone. Here, at the edge of the western forest, Kith-Kanan planned to extend law and order.

Inside the forest, however, was a different proposition. There were many elves of the Kagonesti race living in the woods, but they were hardy and independent and did not take kindly to armed soldiers on their land. These woods elves got along much better with their human neighbors than they did with the Kagonesti under Kith-Kanan's command. Worse, the western woods elves scorned the prince's offers of protection.

"Who do we need protection from?" they had asked scornfully when confronted. "The only invaders we see are you."

The woods elves spat on Kith-Kanan's representatives or threw stones at them, then melted into the trees.

The Wildrunners were all for going into the forest and converting the stubborn woods elves at the point of a sword, but Kith Kanan would not allow it. Their success was built upon the trust the common people had in them; if they turned tyrannical, everything they'd accomplished would be for nought. It would take time, but the prince believed that he could even win over the wild Kagonesti.

As work on Sithelbec continued, Kith-Kanan received a dispatch from his father. The Speaker of the Stars had accepted the prince's invitation to the outpost. Sithel was coming, accompanied by Sithas and a caravan of guards and courtiers.

Kith-Kanan studied the dispatch, penned by his twin. The speaker's retinue was large and slow-moving; it would be at least two weeks before they reached Sithelbec. Even with that grace period, the fortress would not be finished in time. Kith-Kanan exhorted his warriors to do their best, but to save their strength for fighting—even though bandits were becoming as rare as cool breezes in the hot and steamy summer nights.

*   *   *   *   *

The work was still unfinished when the banners of the speaker's party appeared on the horizon. Kith-Kanan called in all his patrols and formed his warriors before the gates of Sithelbec.

The Wildrunners looked on in awe as the speaker's party came into view. First came forty guards on horseback, armed with long lances. Pennants fluttered from their lance tips. Behind them came an honor guard of nobles, sixty-two of them, bearing the banners of Silvanos's clan, the city of Silvanost, the great temples, the major guilds, and the lesser towns of Silvanesti. The nobles formed a square behind the line of lancers. Next came Sithas and his entourage, all clad in scarlet and white. Finally, the Speaker of the Stars rode up, flanked by one hundred courtiers wearing the speaker's colors. The tail of the procession consisted of the rest of the guards and all the baggage wagons.

"By Astarin," muttered Kith-Kanan. "Is there anyone left in Silvanost?"

The nobles parted ranks, the lancers moved to one side, and Sithas rode forward. "Greetings, Brother. Is everything in order?" asked the heir to the throne.

Kith-Kanan grinned. "Not everything," he said, looking up at Sithas. "But we're doing well enough."

The leader of the Wildrunners strode through the blocks of mounted elves toward his father. Soldiers, nobles, and courtiers parted for him with mechanical precision. There was Sithel, astride a splendid white charger, his golden mantle draped across the animal's rump. The crown of Silvanos sparkled on his brow.

Kith-Kanan bowed from the waist. "Hail, great speaker!"

"Hail to you, my son." Sithel waved the emerald and ivory scepter of Silvanos, and Kith-Kanan straightened. "How have you been?"

"Mostly well, Father. The militia has been a great success. Incidents of marauding have ceased and, until recently, everyone we met was with us."

Sithel laid the scepter in the crook of his arm. "Until recently?" he asked with a frown.

"Yes. The inhabitants of the woods are not eager for our help. I believe we can eventually win them to our side, though."

The speaker's charger shook its head and did a slow half-circle. A groom ran forward to hold the animal's bridle as Sithel patted his horse's snowy neck.

"I would hear more about this," he said solemnly. Kith-Kanan took the bridle from the groom and led his father's mount toward the unfinished fortress.

*   *   *   *   *

The vast formation of soldiers and courtiers dispersed, and a regular tent city grew up on the plain in and around the stockade of Sithelbec. The speaker moved into the incomplete keep, as did Sithas. There, on a rough table of green oak planks, Kith-Kanan served them dinner and told them about the problems they'd been having winning the confidence of the woods elves.

"The impudence of it," Sithas complained vehemently. "I think you should go in and drag the wretches out."

Kith-Kanan couldn't believe his ears. "And make them blood enemies forever, Sith? I know the Kagonesti. They prize freedom above all things and won't submit even with a sword at their throat. Unless we're willing to burn down the whole forest, we'll never flush them out. It's their element; they know every inch of it. Most of all, it's their home."

There was a moment of silence, then Sithel broke it.

"How is the hunting?" he asked pleasantly.

"Outstanding," Kith-Kanan said, glad of the change in subject. "The woods are fairly bursting with game, Father."

They gossiped a bit about life back in the city. Lady Nirakina and Tamanier Ambrodel were continuing their efforts on behalf of the homeless. The new Market was almost finished. Given the huge abundance of the coming harvest, even the new, expanded Market would be taxed to handle the volume.

"How is Hermathya?" Kith-Kanan asked politely.

Sithas shrugged. "As well as always. She spends too much and still craves the adoration of the common folk."

They made plans for a boar hunt that would take place on the morrow. Only a small party would go—the speaker, Sithas, Kith-Kanan, Kencathedrus, another royal guard, Parnigar, and half a dozen favored courtiers. They would assemble at dawn and ride into the forest armed with lances. No beaters or hounds would be used. The speaker viewed such measures as unsporting.

*　*　*　*　*

Though the sun had not yet shown itself, there was an early heat in the air, a promise of the stifling day to come. Kith-Kanan stood by a small campfire with Parnigar, eating some bread and porridge. Sithas and Sithel emerged from the half-built keep, dressed in drab brown hunting clothes.

"Good morning," Kith-Kanan said energetically.

"Going to be hot, I think," appraised Sithel. A servant appeared silently at his elbow with a cup of cool apple cider. A second servant offered Sithas similar refreshment.

The courtiers appeared, looking ill at ease in their borrowed hunting clothes. Kencathedrus and Parnigar were more lethal looking. The commander leaned on his lance with an easy grace, seeming fully awake, the benefit of many years rising before the sun. The hunting party ate in relative silence, chewing bread and cheese, spooning porridge quickly, and washing everything down with cider.

Sithel finished first. He thrust his empty cup and plate at a servant and took a lance from the pyramid of weapons stacked outside the keep.

"To horse," he announced. "The prey awaits!"

The speaker mounted with ease and swung the long ash lance in a broad circle around his head. Kith-Kanan couldn't help but smile at his father, who, despite his age and dignity, was more expert with horse and lance than any of them, except perhaps Kencathedrus and Parnigar.

Sithas was a fair horseman, but fumbled with the long lance and reins. The courtiers, more used to loose robes and tight protocol, wobbled aboard their animals. The nervous animals were made more so by the lances bobbing and dancing just behind their heads.

Forming a triangle, with Sithel in the lead, the party rode toward the forest, half a mile away. Dew was thick on the tall grass, and crickets sang until the horses drew near. The silver rim of Solinari could been seen on the western horizon.

Sithas rode on the speaker's left. Kith-Kanan rode on his father's right, resting the butt of his lance in his stirrup cup. They rode at an easy pace, not wanting to tire the horses too early. If they flushed a boar, they'd need all the speed they could muster from their chargers.

"I haven't been hunting in sixty years," Sithel said, breathing deeply of the morning air. "When I was your age, all the young bucks had to have a boar's head on their clan hall wall to show everyone how virile they were." Sithel smiled. "I still remember how I got my first boar. Shenbarrus, Hermathya's father, and I used to go to the marshes at the mouth of the Thon-Thalas. Marsh boar were reputed to be the fiercest of the fierce, and we thought we'd be the most famous hunters in Silvanost if we came back with a trophy. Shenbarrus was a lot thinner and more active in those days. He and I went down river by boat. We landed on Fairgo Island and immediately started tracking a large beast."

"You were on foot?" asked Kith-Kanan, incredulous.

"Couldn't get a horse on the island, son. It was too marshy. So Shenbarrus and I went in the spikerod thickets, armed with spears and brass bucklers. We got separated and the next thing I knew, I was alone in the marsh, with ominous rustlings in the bushes around me. I called out: 'Shenbarrus! Is that you?' There was no answer. I called again; still no answer. By then I was certain the noise I'd heard was a boar. I raised my spear high and thrust it through the thick brush. There was a scream such as mortal elf never heard, and Shenbarrus came pounding through the spikerod into the open. I'd jabbed him in, hmm, the seat of his robe."

Kith-Kanan laughed. Sithas laughed and asked, "So you never got your marsh boar?"

"Oh, I did!" Sithel said. "Shenbarrus's yells flushed a monster of a pig out of the brush. He ran right at us. Despite his painful wound, Shenbarrus stabbed first. The pig thrashed and tore up the clearing. I got my spear back and finished the beast off."

"Who got the head?" asked Sithas.

"Shenbarrus. He drew first blood, so it was only right," said his father warmly.

Kith-Kanan had been in Hermathya's father's house many times and had seen the fierce boar's head in the dining hall over the fireplace. He thought of old Shenbarrus getting poked in the "seat of his robe" and he burst out laughing all over again.

The sky had lightened to pink by the time they reached the dark wall of trees. The party spread out, far enough apart for easy movement, but near enough to stay in sight of one another. All idle talk ceased.

The sun rose behind them, throwing long shadows through the trees. Kith-Kanan sweated in his cotton tunic and mopped his face with his sleeve. His father was ahead to his left, Parnigar slightly behind to his right.

Being in the forest again brought Anaya irresistibly to mind. Kith-Kanan saw her again, lithe and lively, flitting through the trees as silent as a ghost. He remembered her brusque manners, her gentle repose, and the way she felt in his arms. That he remembered best of all.

The heavy rains of summer had washed the sandy soil of the

forest away, leaving chuckholes and protruding roots. Kith-Kanan let his horse pick its way along, but the animal misjudged its footing and hit a hole. The horse stumbled and recovered, but Kith-Kanan lost his seat and tumbled to the ground. The stump of a broken sapling gouged him in the back, and he lay there for a moment, stunned.

His vision cleared and he saw Parnigar leaning over him. "Are you all right, sir?" the old sergeant asked concernedly.

"Yes, just dazed. How's my horse?"

The animal stood a few yards away, cropping moss. His right foreleg was held painfully off the ground.

Parnigar helped Kith-Kanan stand as the last of the hunting party passed by. Kencathedrus, in the rear, asked if they needed any help.

"No," Kith-Kanan said quickly. "Go on. I'll see to my horse."

The horse's lower leg was bruised but, with care, it wouldn't be a crippling injury. Parnigar offered Kith-Kanan his horse, so he could catch up to the rest.

"No, thank you, Sergeant. They're too far ahead. If I go galloping after them, I'll scare off any game in the area." He put a hand to his aching back.

Parnigar asked, "Shall I stay with you, sir?"

"I think you'd better. I may have to walk back to Sithelbec from here." His back stabbed at him again, and he winced.

The news that Kith-Kanan had dropped out was passed ahead. The speaker expressed regret that his son would miss the hunt. But this was a rare day, and the expedition should continue. Sithel's course through the trees meandered here and there, taking the path best suited to his horse. At more than one place he paused to examine tracks in the moss or mud. Wild pig, definitely.

It was hot, but the elves welcomed such heat—for it was a good change from the ever-present coolness of the Quinari Palace and the Tower of the Stars. While Silvanost was constantly bathed in fresh breezes, the heat of the plains made the speaker's limbs feel looser and more supple, his head clearer. He reveled in the sense of freedom he felt out here and urged his horse on.

In the far distance, Sithel heard the call of a hunting horn. Such horns meant humans, and that meant dogs. Sure enough, the sound of barking came very faintly to his ears. Elves never used dogs, but humans rarely went into the woods without them. Human eyesight and hearing being so poor, Sithel reckoned they needed the animals to find any game at all.

The horns and dogs would likely frighten off any boar in the area. In fact, the dogs would flush everything—boar, deer, rabbits, foxes—out of hiding. Sithel shifted his lance back to his stirrup cup and sniffed. Humans were so unsporting.

There was a noise in the sumac behind and to his right. Sithel turned his horse around, lowered the tip of his lance, and poked through the bushes. A wild pheasant erupted from the green leaves, bleating shrilly. Laughing, the speaker calmed his prancing horse.

Sithas and a courtier named Timonas were close enough to see each other when the hunting horn sounded. The prince also realized that it meant humans in the woods. The idea filled him with alarm. He tightened his reins and spun his horse in a tight circle, looking for other members of the party. The only one he could spot was Timonas.

"Can you see anyone?" Sithas called. The courtier shouted back that he could not.

Sithas's alarm increased. It was inexplicable, but he felt a dangerous presentiment. In the heat of the summer morning, the prince shivered.

"Father!" he called. "Speaker, where are you?"

Ahead, the speaker had decided to turn back. Any boar worth bagging had long since left these woods, driven off by the humans. He retraced his path and heard Sithas's call from not too far away.

"Oh, don't shout," he muttered irritably. "I'm coming."

Catching up to him, Sithas pushed through a tangle of vines and elm saplings. As the prince spurred his mount toward the speaker, the feeling of danger was still with him. Out of the corner of his eye, he saw the glint of metal in a stand of cedar.

Then he saw the arrow in flight.

Before Sithas could utter the cry that rose to his lips, the arrow had struck Sithel in the left side, below his ribs. The Speaker of the Stars dropped his lance and pitched forward, but he did not fall from the saddle. A scarlet stain spread out from the arrow, running down the leg of Sithel's trousers.

Timonas rode up on Sithas's left. "See to the speaker!" Sithas cried. He slapped his horse's flank with the reins and bore down on the cedar trees. Lance lowered, he burst through the dark green curtain. A quick glimpse of a white face, and he brought the handguard of his lance down on the archer's head. The archer pitched forward on his face.

The royal guardsman accompanying the party appeared. "Come here! Watch this fellow!" Sithas shouted at him and then rode hard to where Timonas supported Sithel on his horse.

"Father," Sithas said breathlessly. "Father . . ."

The speaker stared in wordless shock. He could say nothing as he reached a bloody hand to his son.

Gently Sithas and Timonas lowered the speaker to the ground. The rest of the hunting party quickly collected around them. The courtiers argued whether to remove the arrow, but Sithas silenced them all as Kencathedrus studied the wound. The look he gave the prince was telling. Sithas understood.

"Father," Sithas said desperately, "Can you speak?"

Sithel's lips parted, but no sound came. His hazel eyes seemed full of puzzlement. At last, his hand touched his son's face, and he breathed his last. The hand fell to the ground.

The elves stood around their fallen monarch in abject disbelief. The one who had ruled them for three hundred and twenty-three years lay dead at their feet.

Kencathedrus had retrieved the fallen archer from the guardsman who watched him. The commander dragged the unconscious fellow by the back of his collar to where Sithel lay. "Sire, look at this," he said. He rolled the inert figure over.

The archer was human. His carrot-colored hair was short and spiky, leaving his queerly rounded ears plainly visible. There was a stubble of orange beard on his chin.

"Murder," muttered one of the courtiers. "The humans have killed our speaker!"

"Be silent!" Sithas said angrily. "Show some respect for the dead." To Kencathedrus he declared, "When he wakes we will find out who he is and why he did this."

"Perhaps it was an accident," cautioned Kencathedrus, inspecting the man. "His bow is a hunting weapon, not a war bow."

"He took aim! I saw him," Sithas said hotly. "My father was mounted on a white horse! Who could mistake him?"

The human groaned. Courtiers surrounded him and dragged him to his feet. They were not very gentle about it. By the time they finished shaking and pummeling him, it was a wonder he opened his eyes at all.

"You have killed the Speaker of the Stars!" Sithas demanded furiously. "Why?"

"No—" gasped the man.

He was forced to his knees. "I saw you!" Sithas insisted. "How can you deny it? Why did you do it?"

"I swear, Lord—"

Sithas could barely think or feel. His senses reeled with the fact that his beloved father was dead.

"Get him ready to travel," the prince ordered numbly. "We will take him back to the fortress and question him properly there."

"Yes, Speaker," said Timonas.

Sithas froze. It was true. Even as his father's blood ran into the ground, he was the rightful speaker. He could feel the burden of rulership settle about him like a length of chain laid across his shoulders. He had to be strong now, strong and wise, like his father.

"What about your father?" Kencathedrus asked gently.

"I will carry him." Sithas put his arms under his father's lifeless body and picked it up.

They walked out of the grove, the human with his arms wrenched behind him, the courtiers leading their horses, and Sithas carrying his dead father. As they came, the sound of hunting horns grew louder and the barking of dogs sounded behind them. Before the party had gone another quarter-mile, a band of mounted humans, armed with bows, appeared. There were at least thirty of them, and as they spread out around the party of elves, the Silvanesti slowed and stopped.

One human picked his way to Sithas. He wore a visored helmet, no doubt to protect his face from intruding branches. The man flipped the visor up, and Sithas started in surprise. He knew that face. It was Ulvissen, the human who had acted as seneschal to Princess Teralind.

"What has happened here?" Ulvissen asked grimly, taking in

the scene.

"The Speaker of the Stars has been murdered," Sithas replied archly. "By that man."

Ulvissen looked beyond Sithas and saw the archer with his arms pinioned. "You must be mistaken. That man is my forester, Dremic," he said firmly. "He is no murderer. This was obviously an accident."

"Accident? That's not an acceptable answer. I am speaker now, and I say that this *assassin* will face Silvanesti justice."

Ulvissen leaned forward in his saddle. "I do not think so, Highness. Dremic is my man. If he is to be punished, I will see to it," he said strongly.

"No," disagreed Sithas.

The elves drew together. Some still carried their lances, others had courtly short swords at their waists. Kencathedrus held his sword to the neck of the human archer, Dremic. The standoff was tense.

Before anyone could act, though, a shrill two-tone whistle cut the air. Sithas felt relief well up inside him. Sure enough, through the trees came Kith-Kanan at the head of a company of the militia's pikemen. The prince rode forward to where Sithas stood, holding their father in his arms.

Kith-Kanan's face twisted. "I—I am too late!" he cried in anguish.

"Too late for one tragedy, but not too late to prevent another," Sithas said. Quickly he told his twin what had happened and what was about to happen.

"I heard the hunting horns at Sithelbec," Kith-Kanan said. "I thought there might be a clash, so I mustered the First Company . . . but this; if only I had stayed, kept up with Father—"

"We must have our man back, Highness," Ulvissen insisted. His hunting party nocked arrows.

Sithas shook his head. Before he'd even finished the gesture, some of the humans loosed arrows. Kith-Kanan shouted an order, and his pikemen charged. The humans, with no time to reload, bolted. In seconds, not one human could be seen, though the sound of their horses galloping away could be heard clearly.

Kith-Kanan halted the militia and called the Wildrunners back to order. Kencathedrus had been hit in the thigh. The unfortunate Dremic had been shot by his own people and now lay dead on the grass.

"We must get back to Silvanost, quickly," Sithas advised. "Not only to bury our father but to tell the people of war!"

Before the confused Kith-Kanan could question or protest, he was shocked to hear his own Wildrunners cheer Sithas's inflammatory words. The humans' cowardly flight had aroused their blood. Some were even ready to hunt down the humans in the forest, but Kith-Kanan reminded them that their duty was to their dead speaker and their comrades back at the fort.

They marched out of the woods, a solemn parade, bearing the bodies of the fallen on their horses. The dead human, Dremic, was left where he lay. A shocked and silent garrison greeted them at Sithelbec. Sithel was dead. Sithas was speaker. Everyone wondered if the cause of peace had died with the great and ancient leader.

Kith-Kanan readied his warriors in defensive positions in case of attack. Watch was kept throughout the night, but it proved to be a peaceful one. After midnight, when he'd finished his work for the day, Kith-Kanan went to the shell of the unfinished keep, where Sithas knelt by the body of their slain father.

"The Wildrunners are prepared should an attack come," he said softly.

Sithas did not raise his head. "Thank you."

Kith-Kanan looked down at his father's still face. "Did he suffer?"

"No."

"Did he say anything?"

"He could not speak."

Hands clenched into fists, Kith-Kanan wept. "This is my fault! His safety was my duty! I urged him to come here. I encouraged him to go hunting."

"And you weren't present when he was ambushed," said Sithas calmly.

Kith-Kanan reacted blindly. He seized his twin by the back of his robe and hauled him to his feet. Spinning him around, he snarled, "You were there, and what good did it do him?"

Sithas gripped Kith-Kanan's fists and pulled them loose from his shirt. With angry precision, he said, "I am speaker. I *am*. I am the leader of the elven nation, so you serve *me* now,

Brother. You can no longer fly off to the forest. And do not trouble me about the rights of Kagonesti or half-human trash."

Kith-Kanan let out a breath, long and slow. The twin he loved was swamped by hatred and grief, he told himself as he looked into Sithas's stormy eyes. With equal precision he answered, "You *are* my speaker. You are my liege lord, and I shall obey you even unto death." It was the ancient oath of fealty. Word for word, the twins had said it to their father when they'd reached maturity. Now Kith-Kanan said it to his twin, his elder by just three minutes.

28

BURDENED BY COMMAND

Sithel's body was borne back to his capital with haste. Sithas felt dignity was less important than speed; he wanted to present the nation with the terrible news as quickly as possible. The Ergothians might move at any time, and the elven nation was not ready to meet them.

The dire news flashed ahead of the caravan. By the time Sithel's body was ferried across the Thon-Thalas, the city was already in mourning. The river was so thick with boats, it could be walked across. From the humblest fisher to the mightiest priest, all elves turned out to view the speaker for the last time. By the thousands they lined the street to the Tower of the Stars, bare-headed out of respect. Waiting for the cortege at the tower was Lady Nirakina. She was so stricken that she had to be carried in a sedan chair from the palace to the tower.

There were no hails or cheers as Speaker Sithas walked through the streets, leading the funeral cortege. His father lay in state in the Temple of E'li as thousands of his subjects came to pay him a last farewell. Then, with a minimum of ceremony, Sithel was put to rest beside his own father in the magnificent mausoleum known as the Crystal Tomb.

The very next day, Sithas composed an ultimatum to the emperor of Ergoth. "We consider the death of our father Sithel to be nothing less than deliberate murder," Sithas wrote. "The Elven Nation demands retribution for its speaker's death. If Your Imperial Highness wishes to avoid war, we will accept an indemnity of one million gold pieces, the expulsion of all Ergothian subjects from our western territories, and the surrender of all the men present at the murder of our father, including Ulvissen."

Kith-Kanan had had to delay his departure from Sithelbec. He arrived in Silvanost two days after his father's funeral, incensed that Sithas had acted so precipitously with the last rites and his ultimatum to the emperor of Ergoth.

"Why did you not wait?" he complained to his twin in the Tower of the Stars. "I should have been here to see father's last rites!" Kith-Kanan had just come from a long visit with his mother; her grief and his own weighed heavily upon him.

"There is no time for empty ceremony," Sithas said. "War may be near, and we must act. I have ordered prayers and offerings to our father be made in every temple every night for thirty days, but for now I must rally the people."

"Will the humans attack?" asked Hermathya anxiously from her place at Sithas's side.

"I don't know," the speaker replied grimly. "They outnumber us ten-to-one."

Kith-Kanan looked at the two of them. It was so unnatural to see them where Sithel and Nirakina had been so often seated. Hermathya looked beautiful, perfectly groomed and dressed in a gown of gold, silver, and white. Yet she was cold. Whereas Nirakina could inspire respect and love with a smile and a nod, all Hermathya seemed capable of doing was looking statuesque. Of course she did not meet Kith-Kanan's eyes.

On the emerald throne, Sithas looked strained and tired. He was trying to make fast and hard decisions, as he felt befitted a monarch in time of trouble. The burden showed on his face and in his posture. He looked far older than his twin at this moment.

The tower was empty except for the three of them. All morning Sithas had been meeting with priests, nobles, and masters of the guilds, telling them what he expected from them in case of war. There had been some patriotic words, mostly from the priests, but in all the tone of the audience had been very subdued. Now only Kith-Kanan remained. Sithas had special orders for him.

"I want you to form the Wildrunners into a single army," he commanded.

"With what purpose?" his twin asked.

"Resist the Ergothian army, should it cross the border into the forest."

Kith-Kanan rubbed his forehead. "You know, Sith, that the whole militia numbers only twenty thousand, most of whom are farmers armed with pikes."

"I know, but there's nothing else to stop the humans between their border and the banks of the Thon-Thalas. We need time, Kith, time for Kencathedrus to raise an army with which to defend Silvanost."

"Then why in Astarin's name are you so eager to start a war with Ergoth? They have two hundred thousand men under arms! You said it yourself!"

Sithas's hands clenched the arms of his throne, and he leaned forward. "What else can I do? Forgive the humans for murdering our father? You know it was murder. They laid a trap for him and killed him! Is it such a coincidence that Ulvissen was in the area and that one of his supposed foresters perpetrated the crime?"

"It is suspicious," Kith-Kanan conceded, with less heat than before. He pulled his helmet on, threading the chin strap into its buckle. "I will do what I can, Sith," he said finally, "but there may be those who aren't as willing to fight and die for Silvanesti."

"Anyone who refuses the speaker's call is a traitor," Hermathya interjected.

"It is easy to make such distinctions here in the city, but on the plains and in the woods, neighbors mean more than far-off monarchs," Kith-Kanan said pointedly.

"Are you saying the Kagonesti will not fight for us?" asked Sithas angrily.

"Some will. Some may not."

Sithas leaned back and sighed deeply. "I see. Do what you can, Kith. Go back to Sithelbec as quickly as you can." He hesitated. "I know you will do your best."

A brief glance passed between the twins. "I'll take Arcuballis," said Kith-Kanan and went quickly.

When the prince had departed, Hermathya fumed, "Why do you allow him to be so familiar? You're the speaker. He should bow and call you Highness."

Sithas turned to his wife. His face was impassive. "I have no doubts about Kith's loyalty," he said heavily. "Unlike yours, Lady, in spite of your correct language and empty flattery."

"What do you mean?" she said stiffly.

"I know you hired Kagonesti thugs to murder Kith-Kanan because he would not dishonor me by becoming your lover. I know *all*, Lady."

Hermathya's normally pale face grew waxen. "It's not true," she said, her voice wavering. "It's a foul lie—Kith-Kanan told you, didn't he?"

"No, Lady. Kith doesn't know you hired the elves who murdered his friend. When you employed a certain gray-robed sorcerer to contact a band of killers, you didn't know that the same sorcerer also works for me. For gold, he will do anything—including tell me everything about your treachery."

Hermathya's entire body shivered violently. She rose unsteadily from her throne and backed across the platform, away from Sithas. The silver and gold hem of her heavy robe dragged across the marble floor.

"What will you do?" she gasped.

He stared at her for a long minute. "To you? Nothing. This is hardly the time for the speaker to put his wife in prison. Your plot failed, fortunately for your life, so I will let you keep your freedom for now. But I tell you this, Hermathya—" he rose and stood tall and straight before her "—if you so much as frown at my brother, or if you ever have contact with Vedvedsica again,

I will shut you away someplace where you'll never see the sun again."

Sithas turned and strode with resolve from the tower. Hermathya remained standing for a moment, swaying to and fro. Finally, her legs gave way. She collapsed in the center of the platform and wept. The rich silver and gold of her robes gleamed in the light from the window slits.

* * * * *

The griffon's wings beat in quick rhythm as Kith-Kanan and Arcuballis flew to the west. An array of armor and arms weighed Arcuballis down, but the powerful beast never faltered in flight. As they passed over the vast southern forest, Kith-Kanan couldn't help but look down at the green canopy and wonder. If Anaya hadn't changed, would he still be down there somewhere, living the free life of a wild elf? Would Mackeli still be alive? These thoughts gnawed at him. His happiest days had been the time spent with Anaya and Mackeli, roaming the wildwood, doing whatever the moment called for. No duty. No onerous protocol. Life had been an eternal, joyous spring.

And just as quickly, Kith-Kanan found himself dismissing these thoughts from his mind. It can't always be spring, and one can't always be young and carefree. He wasn't an ordinary elf after all, but a prince of the blood. His life had held many pleasures and very little had ever been asked of him. Now it was time for him to earn what he had enjoyed. Kith-Kanan fixed his gaze on the distant blue horizon and steeled himself for war.

DragonLance® Saga

Elven Nations Trilogy

The Kinslayer Wars
Douglas Niles

Kith-Kanan commits the ultimate heresy for an elven prince and falls in love with a human. Soon after, his twin brother, the first-born ruler of all Silvanesti elves, Sithas, declares war on the humans of Ergoth, and Kith-Kanan finds himself caught between two mighty forces.
On Sale August 1991.

The Qualinesti
Paul B. Thompson and Tonya R. Carter

One of the most fabled of all of Krynn's legends—untold before now—is the founding of Qualinost and the creation of the magnificent society of the renegade elves, the Qualinesti. Kith-Kanan becomes the first Speaker of the Suns, but he is haunted by his failures: the unfaithfulness of his wife, and the mysterious behavior of his son and successor.
On Sale November 1991.

DragonLance® Saga

Meetings Sextet

Kindred Spirits
Mark Anthony and Ellen Porath

The reluctant paternal dwarven hero, Flint Fireforge, is invited to the elven kingdom of Qualinesti, where he meets a young, unhappy half-elf named Tanis. But when Laurana, the beauteous daughter of the elves' ruler, declares her love for Tanis, a deadly rival for her affections concocts a scenario fraught with risk and scandal for both the half-elf and his dwarven ally. On Sale April 1991.

Wanderlust
Mary Kirchoff and Steve Winter

Tasslehoff Burrfoot accidentally pockets one of Flint's copper bracelets and Tanis good-naturedly defends the top-knotted newcomer to Solace—triggering a thoroughly unpredictable tale, which includes a sinister stranger who has evil on his mind for the three new friends. On Sale September 1991.

Dark Heart
Tina Daniell

At long last, the story of the beautiful, dark-hearted Kitiara Uth Matar, from the birth of her twin brothers, the frail mage Raistlin and the warrior Caramon. Kitiara's increasing fascination with evil throws her into the company of a roguish stranger and an eerie mage whose fates are intermingled with her own. On Sale January 1992.

1992 DRAGONLANCE® CALENDAR

THE BEST ARTWORK OF THE POPULAR
DRAGONLANCE® WORLD IS SHOW-
CASED IN FOURTEEN POSTER-QUALITY RE-
PRODUCTIONS. THE 1992 CALENDAR
FEATURES THE YEAR'S BEST ARTWORK FROM
THE ENTIRE DRAGONLANCE PRODUCT
LINE—WHICH INCLUDES BEST-SELLING
GAMES AND BOOKS—WITH PAINTINGS BY
AWARD-WINNING PROFESSIONALS GERALD
BROM, CLYDE CALDWELL, JEFF EASLEY,
AND FRED FIELDS. ON SALE JUNE 1991.

FORGOTTEN REALMS
FANTASY ADVENTURE ®

Song of the Saurials
The Finder's Stone Trilogy, Book Three

Kate Novak
and Jeff Grubb

When the Harpers judged the Nameless Bard responsible for the death of his apprentices, they sentenced him to exile. Now the Harpers are reconsidering their decision, but with the arrival of the monster Grypht, Nameless's new trial dissolves in a string of disappearances and murder. It is up to Alias the swordswoman, Akabar the mage, Dragonbait the paladin, and Ruskettle the thief to prove one enemy is behind all the chaos—the ancient, evil god Moander the Darkbringer. On Sale March 1991.

Feathered Dragon
The Maztica Trilogy, Book Three

Douglas Niles

The greatest city in Maztica lies in ruins; a plague of hideous monsters descends across the land. From the ashes of destruction, a tenuous alliance forms. The only hope of victory requires aid from beyond the Forgotten Realms. On Sale April 1991.

Sojourn
The Dark Elf Trilogy, Book Three

R. A. Salvatore

Drizzt Do'Urden fights to survive the elements of Toril's harsh surface. The drow begins a sojourn through a world entirely unlike his own. He struggles to understand his new home and its inhabitants, but acceptance among the surface-dwellers doesn't come easily. On Sale May 1991.

NOW ON YOUR HOME COMPUTER: THE
DRAGONLANCE™ GAME WORLD COMES ALIVE!

Available for: ATARI ST, IBM, AMIGA, C-64/128.
Visit your retailer or call 1-800-245-4525 for VISA /MC
orders. To receive SSI's complete catalog, send $1.00 to:

STRATEGIC SIMULATIONS, INC.
1046 North Rengstorff Avenue
Mountain View, CA 94043

THE ALL NEW

ALL NEW FORMAT, FEATURES, AND FICTION!

AMAZING®
STORIES

Robert Silverberg
John Brunner
Kristine Kathryn Rusch
Arthur C. Clarke

The world's oldest science
fiction magazine ...

BEGINS IN MAY 1991